LADY IN WAITING

MELODY TYDEN

SILATRIA
CAVE
LASSARIA

CHAPTER ONE

The arrow hit the target in front of me with a satisfying *thwack*. Straight down the middle, another bullseye, it joined the four arrows already lodged there.

If I were a knight at a tournament, crowds would be cheering, but in the secluded woodland glade, my audience consisted of only my lady-in-waiting, Elodie. She turned to me impatiently, her disapproval clear on her face. "Alright, you've proven yourself, but just for the record, I never said you couldn't do it."

Removing the quiver from my back, I went to retrieve the arrows from the target while giving her an incredulous look. "Yes, you did. I said I could make five in a row, and you said no one would believe me."

She groaned as a gust of wind blew her skirt across the forest floor. "You never listen to me, Dee. I said that no one would believe any princess would *want* to do it."

I shrugged, the distinction making no difference to me. "Either way; I can do it, and I want to, so you're still wrong."

"If I agree that I'm wrong, can we please head back to the castle?" she begged. "Your mother will have my head if you're late for the feast tonight."

Since she had a point, I gave in. My mother figured out a long time ago that she could rant and rave at me all she wanted without it bothering me at all, but when she shouted at Elodie, my dear friend's gentle nature could hardly bear it. Her eyes would well with tears and her hands would tremble, and I couldn't stand to see her upset. That made it far more effective, in terms of my mother getting what she wanted, for her to threaten Elodie instead of me.

As we walked back through the woodlands surrounding my family's castle, just the thought of tonight's feast made me shudder. The impending meal had been the whole reason I came out with my arrows in the first place. I needed to take my frustration out on something, and the painted target at the end of the field seemed a harmless enough candidate. I could pretend that the target represented the man being celebrated with tonight's feast.

The man I would soon be forced to marry.

It didn't matter that we had never met each other before. It didn't matter that we might have nothing in common or might not find each other appealing in the slightest. All that mattered was that my father wanted land and his father wanted money, and they had signed an agreement to exchange the two things as part of our wedding agreement.

Just like that, they expected me to go play happy wife to some random prince who probably believed, like my mother did, that princesses were only meant to run the royal household and have babies.

My opinion on the subject made no difference.

Unfortunately, the world we lived in dictated my future, and I knew that, short of running away and throwing myself entirely on the mercy of fate, I had no choice in the matter. As my parents' only daughter, they had spent a long time negotiating the most advantageous match for me. The most advantageous match for *them*, anyway. As far as I could see, it held no advantage for me.

It felt like I had spent my whole life waiting for and dreading this moment in equal measure. Elodie used to tease me that although she served as my lady-in-waiting, the real lady in waiting was me, stuck in limbo until I found out who I would be bound to and what kind of life awaited me on the other side of my wedding vows.

"Since when are we letting beggars come to the feast?" my brother, Arthur, teased as he caught sight of me entering the castle courtyard. The open space within the stone walls bustled with activity and last-minute preparations for tonight's gathering, the fires in the kitchens roaring as the smell of roasting meat drifted out to us. Servants hurried to and fro, carrying our most impressive dinnerware into the main hall in the castle's keep, while Arthur reached over and rubbed my head, making my hair even messier than it had been. "The prince is going to run away screaming when he gets a look at you."

"I should be so lucky," I muttered, pushing his hands away and fixing him with a dirty look. Although I had been born first, my three younger brothers towered over me, but that didn't seem to inspire any protective instincts in them. They still treated me like one of the boys. We had grown up doing everything together as I learned to hunt and ride and fight alongside them, and I felt most at home in that world.

However, once my body started to look more like a woman's, my mother had ordered me indoors, telling me the time had come to learn all about running a royal household. I did it because I had no choice, but I still took the opportunity to sneak out whenever possible, just as I had this afternoon.

My brothers were the ones with all the freedom and all the opportunities. Arthur, who still behaved like a boy sometimes, had actually become a strong and capable prince, and would take over as king when our father died. Though our kingdom couldn't compete in terms of size, it had been blessed with natural resources and a long coastline which made us a valuable ally for our surrounding neighbours. Many of them had hoped my father would marry me off to their offspring, but he wanted only the best for his daughter. He'd had his eye on the bigger and stronger kingdom to our north for quite some time.

Meanwhile, my youngest brothers, Edward and Henry, would be given titles and lands of their own and the chance to make their own way in the world. That made me the only one who had to leave our kingdom, leaving the only home I'd ever known to go live with a man I would only meet once before our wedding.

That meeting would take place in less than an hour, and Elodie groaned once again as she realized just how long we'd been gone.

"Please hurry, Your Highness."

She always used my title within the public areas of the castle, but when we were in private, I became Dee and she was Lodee, the same as we had been since we were children. She had been my shadow for as long as either of us could remember. We were nothing alike, but we complemented each other very well, like two sides of the same coin.

"We have so much work to do," she told me, practically pushing me up the stairs to the room she and I had shared for years.

Did I really look that bad? A quick glance in the mirror as we arrived told me that her concerns were only slightly exaggerated. My mother normally kept tight control over the household budget, but a mirror and dresses were luxuries she would allow since they were a means to what she saw as my ultimate end goal.

Looking into the glass now, I could see a few twigs had snagged in my blonde hair, a scratch marred my cheek from an arrow that I'd held a little too closely earlier, making one of my blue eyes appear bruised, and dirt had stained the bottom of my dress, not to mention the small tear on one of the sleeves. Maybe if I turned up at the feast like this, the prince would be so horrified, he'd turn tail and run.

Unfortunately, I seemed to be the only one hoping for that outcome, so with a sigh, I let Elodie get to work.

~Cassian~

"Cass, if we don't keep moving, we're going to be late."

Bran brought his horse up alongside the river where I had stopped to let my own horse have a long drink of water. I'd given my closest friend the excuse of my horse's thirst as a reason for our stop, but I simply didn't want to go any further and Bran knew that. I'd have to try harder if I wanted to fool him.

"You've got to turn up eventually, so wouldn't it be better to show up on time and avoid upsetting everyone before you even meet them?"

He had a point, of course. He always had a point. Bran's advice was consistently reliable and accurate. I ignored it at my peril, but I decided to do it anyway as I let the horse continue to drink.

"We could always claim we were attacked by bandits," I suggested. "We could say they stole our clothes, and we could hardly turn up at King Alfred's feast naked, could we?"

Bran raised his eyes to the heavens in a clear sign of frustration. "Just because that worked when you were fifteen doesn't mean it will work for you now."

I couldn't help smiling at the memory. My father had been entertaining a visiting royal party, another king with another daughter he hoped to saddle me with. Desperate to get out of attending, I came up with the story about bandits to explain my absence. My father had bought it until my younger brother, Eric, exposed my lie. He never liked me getting away with anything unless he took part too.

Bran sighed beside me as I still showed no sign of getting ready to move. "Listen, Cass, I know you're not keen on this marriage, but you've got to marry someone, right? Maybe she won't be as bad as you think. Eric said he found her pretty."

That hardly filled me with confidence. Eric had vastly different taste in women than I did. He'd jump into bed with pretty much anything in a skirt. There didn't even need to be a bed. I'd walked in on him in a variety of positions and locations over the years. Neither privacy nor propriety seemed to be a concern to him at all.

Eric had spied my intended fiancée, Alfred's daughter, at a fair nearly a year ago. He wasn't supposed to be there. Travelling incognito at the time, no one knew his true identity, so he couldn't go up and speak to her, but even from a distance, she made quite an impression on him. He had made it clear enough, once the marriage negotiations had started, that if I didn't want her, he'd be more than happy to take her on.

That would have worked for me too, but unfortunately, my father disagreed with that plan. We only got her dowry if she married the crown prince, and that title fell to me.

I might not have met this particular princess before, but I'd met enough other princesses to have a very good idea of what she'd be like. The ones I had met were all much the same: spoiled, delicate women with no thoughts in their heads other than which clothes to wear or what they should embroider next.

I liked women well enough in the bedroom, but outside of that, I preferred to spend my time in the company of men. Hunting, fighting, and being outdoors were the things that interested me, which made my current system of having a kept mistress who I visited at night but hardly saw otherwise work perfectly well for me. The last thing I wanted was a wife who would throw off the perfectly comfortable balance I'd found in my life.

Unfortunately, I had no choice. As the prince, my feelings on the subject made no difference. I had to marry for the good of the kingdom, and that meant taking on this princess and the money that came with her.

"Alright," I said to Bran, giving in. "Let's head out and get this over..."

Before I could finish my sentence, an arrow flew by my head, narrowly missing my nose.

"Bandits!" Bran called out to alert the others.

For a moment, I almost laughed. Maybe they really *would* steal our clothes and I wouldn't have to lie. But as two more arrows flew past, I quickly realized the time for jokes had passed.

Bran immediately moved in front of me, facing the direction the arrow had come from, ready to protect me with his life if needed. Just another reason men were better to have around: every woman I'd ever met would be cowering behind me, not standing in front of me.

Giving my horse a kick, I took off along the river with Bran close behind. There had been four other men with us, but we were down by one when we came out of the trees. I'd never been this deep into Lassarian territory before, making the terrain here completely foreign to me. A grassy plain stretched out ahead of us, which would be good for speed but had nothing to provide us with cover. Our other option would be to go right and follow the river and try to stay in the trees.

"Right," I instructed, shouting the order into the air behind me and taking the turn. My men fell in behind me, their horses' hooves thundering against the ground as arrows continued to fly past us. The man behind Bran took a hit, tumbling off his horse as I winced. I hoped he would be okay, but I couldn't stop. If anyone recognized me, it could be disastrous. Someone of my standing would be a prize catch for bandits looking for ransom. Luckily, I wore my riding clothes and not the formal clothes I'd brought along for the engagement feast, so nothing about my appearance at the moment would give me away.

Just when I thought we'd lost them, more men appeared from the trees ahead of us.

"Left!" I yelled now, making as wide a turn through the trees as I could to avoid the riders coming up behind me. The trees were thicker here and the light dimmer, but I pressed ahead anyway. We needed to put some distance between us and our attackers.

The sound of running water from the river grew louder, letting me know it had started to swing back our way. Suddenly, the trees ended, and the ground ahead of us seemed to vanish.

"Waterfall!" I shouted, hoping my warning could be heard over the sound of the water as I pulled hard on the reins to stop my horse. We came to a halt at the cliff's edge, perilously close to the steep drop, as my heart pounded from the exertion of the chase and the rush of adrenaline from our close call.

"Cass, are you okay?" Bran's worry-filled voice asked from behind me.

"Fine," I yelled back. "Stay there, I'm coming back."

As I pulled on the reins to turn, my horse's back hooves caught on some loose gravel, and began to slip. "Come on," I encouraged, digging my heels into the charger's side as he grappled for purchase, but to no avail. "Bran!"

I managed to shout my friend's name, but I couldn't get anything else out. We were already going over the edge.

~Cordelia~

An hour after the feast should have begun, the prince still hadn't shown up and my parents were furious. Though they tried not to let it show, I could see it in the way my father's hand gripped the head of his sword as he spoke to his guests and in the way my mother's lips tightened every time she glanced towards the door. The great hall had been decorated with the best Lassaria had to offer, our finest tapestries hung on the walls, candles at every table with golden centrepieces and beer in every cup. If the guest of honour were here, everything would be perfect.

Eventually, they couldn't wait any longer. The guests needed to be fed, so my father made the announcement for everyone to take their seats. I found my place at the long table on the raised dais at the end of the hall next to my brother and the empty seat that had been reserved for my fiancé.

Personally, I couldn't be more thrilled. If he decided not to turn up at all, maybe my parents would be so offended that the whole thing would be called off. I could only hope.

No sooner had the thought crossed my mind than a trumpet blast sounded, signaling the arrival of an important guest, and my stomach sank. Apparently, he decided to come after all, he just couldn't be bothered to arrive on time. That seemed like a bad sign. If he couldn't even respect me enough to show up for this occasion, chances seemed slim that he would take my feelings into consideration in other things either.

Everyone in the hall turned to the door as a small group of men walked in led by a tall man in the red, gold and black colours of the Silatrian kingdom, his head held high.

That must be him.

He had long, dark hair, hanging down to his shoulders and a broad, muscled frame. At first glance, he could be considered attractive, but that impression quickly faded as he scanned the room in an arrogant, assured manner, his eyes stopping to rest on more than one of the ladies present before his gaze wandered over to the table where my family sat.

Our eyes met and a smile tugged at the corner of his mouth. Even from this distance, I could see desire on his face, but whether it burned for my money or my body, I couldn't tell. Either way, it had nothing to do with me as a person. He looked exactly like everything I had expected and everything I had feared come to life.

With long, confident strides, he walked over to us, the attention of everyone in the room focused on his every move, a wave of whispers following in his wake.

"Your Majesty," he greeted my father, giving him a low, flourished bow, and I had to refrain from rolling my eyes at the showy and insincere gesture.

"Prince Eric," my father replied, sounding more confused than anything. "We weren't expecting you this evening. Why are you here? Where's your brother?"

Eric?

Suddenly, I looked at the man in front of me with new eyes. So, this wasn't my intended fiancé, but his younger brother, Eric, a man whose reputation definitely preceded him. I might not have been overjoyed about my parents' choice of bridegroom for me, but at least if he had lovers, he had been discreet about it, unlike the man in front of us now. If rumours were to be believed, Eric had nearly run out of women in his hometown who hadn't shared his bed.

The prince looked around in mild surprise. "Cassian isn't here? I left a couple of days after him, I expected he would have been here days ago. I simply came to congratulate the lucky couple."

He looked over at me again with a smirk on his face that made me shudder. I rubbed my arms with my hands, trying to pretend the chill in the air had caused my reaction, but it looked like he knew the truth and it only served to amuse him.

"He hasn't arrived yet," my mother replied, biting the ends off each of her words. The prince's absence obviously made her angry, and having it pointed out only made matters worse, even though everyone gathered would have noticed it already.

"Well, I'm sure he's on his way." Eric's sincerity was impossible to judge. Every word out of his mouth seemed to have a double meaning. "In the meantime, I'd be delighted to keep Princess Cordelia company until he turns up."

It took every ounce of my self-control not to shudder again. "That's very kind, Your Highness, but I'm not sure it would be proper."

I hoped that my mother would hear the desperation in my voice and take the hint, but as usual, she turned a blind eye to my preferences.

"You may as well take your brother's place," she invited, gesturing to the seat beside me. "We are just about to eat."

With a smirk, Eric came around the table, his heavy boots clomping along the dais, and settled into Cassian's empty chair between me and my father. As demanded by propriety, he spoke to my father during the first course of our dinner, while I turned my attention to Arthur on the other side of me.

"Looks like your future brother-in-law would like to be more than friendly," Arthur laughed under his breath, clearly getting the same vibe from him that I had.

"Do you know him?" I asked, also speaking quietly so no one could overhear us. "Eric, I mean?"

"We've met once or twice when I went along on visits to Silatria with our father," Arthur told me. "Trust me, you're getting the better brother. Cassian's nothing like Eric."

That should have relieved me, but if my groom-to-be possessed such fine qualities, where on earth was he?

Soon, the servants brought out the next course, and I turned my attention to Eric. Following tradition, I waited for him to speak first. The male always got to take the lead, and Eric took his time, clearly enjoying the fact that I had no choice but to wait on him.

"Are you looking forward to your wedding, Princess?" he finally asked.

Although the question itself sounded innocent enough, his tone implied something else entirely. It couldn't be clearer that he meant the night following the wedding.

"I haven't given it much thought," I replied honestly enough, keeping my tone light. "And you may call me Princess Cordelia, but not simply Princess. I am more than my title, Prince Eric."

A spark of amusement flashed in his eyes. "I can see that. Although I'd like to see more."

His eyes moved across my body in an entirely too intimate way and I had to fight the urge to cover my chest. The dress Elodie had chosen for me tonight pressed tight across my bosom, drawing attention to it intentionally, meant to entice my fiancé. The way Eric looked at it simply made me uncomfortable.

"Your eyes would be better used to watch your back, Your Highness, if my father were to hear you speaking that way."

He laughed, clearly entertained by my indignation. "I heard you had some fire in you, Princess Cordelia." He used my name as I'd requested, but he drew it out, exaggerating it so much that it almost sounded like an insult. "And I do like a bit of fire."

He clearly wanted a reaction from me, but I refused to give him the satisfaction. "Well, that fire will need to keep you warm from a distance. You may recall that I'm meant to be marrying your brother."

My reply only seemed to amuse him further. "So it would seem, Princess. For now. Things can always change."

By the time the meal ended, I couldn't get away from the table fast enough. Prince Cassian still hadn't turned up and everyone seemed to have given up on the possibility of him putting in an appearance. Eric offered his apologies on behalf of his brother, but I couldn't help wondering what this would mean for my marriage. Could my parents forgive such an insult? I supposed it would depend on the excuse that the prince gave for not showing up, whenever he finally did arrive.

With Elodie at my side, I made my way around the room, fielding curious questions from all my parents' friends and the nobility of our kingdom, everyone wanting to know my fiancé's location. After half an hour of the same conversation over and over again, the repetition had exhausted me. I managed to catch my mother at a free moment and thankfully, she gave me her permission to leave.

If the prince did turn up tonight, he would just have to wait and see me in the morning.

With a sigh of relief, I headed up the stone steps, Elodie close behind me as always. We could hear giggling from the hallway ahead as we reached the top of the stairs, and we turned the corner just in time to see Prince Eric going into one of the chambers next to mine with one of my less discerning ladies, Arabella Eastam. She had never been one of my favourites, and after this, I liked her even less.

"What a vile man," Elodie gasped. I had already told her about the things he said to me over dinner, and her outrage on my behalf made me smile.

"He is," I agreed. "And he delights in it, which is all the more frustrating."

"Well, hopefully we won't see too much of him when we move to our new home." We moved into my chamber and she drew the heavy beam across the door behind us, locking the world out.

The thought of living under the same roof as that rake hardly appealed to me. Would my husband protect me? How could I be sure of that when he couldn't even be bothered to show up for our own engagement feast? I hadn't wanted him to come, but now that the night had ended, I was almost equally offended that he hadn't.

"Let's just get ready for bed," I said to Elodie. "Hopefully, the morning will bring better news. Maybe we'll never have to see either of the Silatrian princes ever again."

~Cassian~

A groan echoed in my throat as I tried to open my eyes. My whole body hurt and I felt... wet. Why was I wet? The sound of rushing water pushed through the fog of my thoughts, and vague memories began to come back to me. I could recall a chase, and a river, and a waterfall, and...

I forced my eyes open. Above me, I could only see darkness at first, but gradually, things began to take shape, and it sunk in that the darkness above me was the night sky. As I looked around, I realized I lay in the mud at the side of a river. I had vague memories of falling over the cliff, landing in the river and managing to pull myself out before collapsing. My head hurt then, and it still hurt now. My horse had vanished into thin air.

I also couldn't see the waterfall anymore, which must mean the river had carried me downstream for a while before I got out. I couldn't begin to guess how far I had gone.

None of this pleased me. Although, on the plus side, I had gotten out of going to the engagement feast.

I chuckled at my own train of thought, and immediately regretted it as pain shot through my ribs. They must have been injured in the fall which would make riding more difficult for a while, but at the moment I had nothing to ride anyway. I needed to get somewhere dry and warm and safe, and I would have to get there on foot. I hoped my men had escaped the bandits and were on their way to look for me, but I couldn't just sit around and wait for them. For the time being, I would have to fend for myself.

Hauling myself to my feet turned out to be easier said than done, each part of my body sore or tender, but eventually, I stood upright and began walking, putting one foot in front of the other, focusing on one step at a time. Assuming there would eventually be a settlement along the river, I followed the course of it, and before too long, my theory proved true. A small collection of buildings appeared in front of me, all of them dark, their inhabitants likely asleep.

I picked a small house at the edge of the village and knocked gently on the door, not wanting to alarm anyone. Perhaps it needed to be louder, though, as nobody came to the door, so I tried again. This time, a shuffling noise came from within and the door opened, revealing a middle-aged man holding a candle.

"Who are you?" he asked me suspiciously. "What do you want?"

"I need somewhere to sleep for the night," I explained, avoiding the first question. "And some dry clothes. I can pay."

Luckily, I always travelled with a few coins sewn into my clothing, for situations just like this. Not that I had ever anticipated this exact predicament, going over a cliff into a river, but I was prepared for it all the same.

The mention of money seemed to ease the man's suspicions, and he opened the door wider. "There isn't much here, but you can find a dry spot. Fell into the river, did you?"

He said it like it happened all the time. "Yes," I agreed, telling a half-truth. "My horse got spooked and threw me off. I don't suppose you've seen a lone horse running around?"

It would have surprised me if he said yes, and he didn't. "No horses today. Come on in and take off those wet rags."

I had to hide my smile. The 'rags' I wore could pay for this man's house ten times over, but I handed them over anyway, stripping down to nothing before putting on the loose nightshirt he offered me.

"You can sleep there, on the floor." He pointed to an open space near the hearth. "I'll get a blanket."

He did, and I accepted it gratefully. It might not be the height of comfort, but I regularly travelled rough. At least I found myself indoors and dry now.

In the morning, the man gave me some new clothes and a small satchel into which I packed my muddied clothes from the day before. He made me breakfast and directed me to the nearest town where I might be able to buy myself a new horse. "Just follow the river," he said. Grateful to have stumbled across someone so friendly, I paid him handsomely for his help before setting out.

As I walked, my thoughts drifted to the feast I had missed last night. I couldn't imagine the king and queen were very pleased that I hadn't shown up. Maybe they would call off the whole arrangement. I wouldn't be upset about that, except that it just meant my father would choose someone else for me to marry instead and he wouldn't be at all pleased with me for losing the Lassarian dowry.

But really, I could hardly be blamed for this, as my broken ribs would attest.

A couple of hours passed before the next town came into view, by which time my hunger and thirst were nearly overwhelming. Luckily, a small inn sat at the edge of town, so I made my way inside before doing anything else. Someone there should be able to tell me where I could find a horse.

"Beer and a pie," I requested when the owner welcomed me to the dining room. He nodded and directed me to a long communal table where a few other men were already eating. Taking a seat next to them,

I gave them a friendly nod. They returned the greeting without breaking their own conversation.

"The reward is ten crowns," the man sitting closest to me told the other two. "It's worth a try."

"But the body could be anywhere," one of the others argued. "The river goes on for miles."

"I bet it's not that far," the third one replied. "There are enough rocks and bends for it to get caught on. I'd wager it's closer to the waterfall than you think it is."

The word 'waterfall' got my attention as the innkeeper set my beer and a room temperature pie down in front of me. I placed two coins on the table which he promptly placed in his small pouch. When he had walked away, the men resumed their conversation.

"How many others know about this?" the second man asked. He seemed the least keen to go on whatever adventure they were planning.

"Hardly any," the first one told him impatiently. "That's why we need to do it. Just imagine: ten crowns for a day's work. Less than a day if we find him quickly."

My curiosity got the better of me and I couldn't help asking, "Who or what are you looking for?" They all turned to me as if surprised that I had heard them, even though they were sitting right next to me, so I offered an explanation for my interruption. "I've been walking along the river all morning. Maybe I could help."

"You're not from around here, are you?" the man next to me asked, giving me a somewhat suspicious look.

"No, and I've got no interest in your reward if you get one. I just like a good story. Let me buy you a drink."

The men all seemed to relax as I said I didn't want any share of the money, and their mood turned even more friendly when I offered to get the next round. Once the innkeeper had refilled everyone's glass, the man next to me leaned closer.

"I had to go to the fletcher's early this morning and some men came in looking for new arrows; foreigners with fancy clothes. They said they'd lost someone in their party last night, a nobleman who went over the falls at Clifford Heights. They figured he wouldn't have survived, but they were offering a reward to anyone who could locate his body."

"Ten crowns, I presume?" I asked wryly, as if they hadn't mentioned the amount several times already.

"Right," the man agreed, missing the sarcasm in my voice. "Or one crown if he's alive and we can point them to him."

My brow furrowed at that revelation. When he started his story, I assumed my own men were looking for me and had already begun planning on making my way further into town to find them, but this last detail made no sense. Why would they be offering more for me dead than alive?

"Did you see a tall man with ginger hair among the foreigners?" I asked. Bran stood out in a crowd, and if he had been there, it had to be my men, no matter what they had said.

But the man in front of me shook his head. "No, no one like that."

"How many were there?" I asked next. If all of my men had survived the attack, there would have been five of them; less if they hadn't all made it.

"Seven or eight," the man guessed, and my suspicions were confirmed.

These weren't my men, but based on what he'd said, it had to be me they were looking for. How many other men went over the waterfall last night? I couldn't imagine it happened all that often. And if these men were after my body and willing to pay such a high price for it, they must know my identity, which meant they would have known it when they attacked us, and they weren't random bandits at all.

They must have attacked us on purpose, hoping to kill me.

But hardly anyone knew where I would be. My father had kept the details of the marriage arrangement quiet until the final agreement could be settled, so whoever set this up knew exactly where I'd be travelling, which meant they had to be someone close to me.

Someone close to me who wanted me dead.

I took another mouthful of beer, swilling it around my mouth as I tried to work things out in my head. If I went out now and bought a horse and went on to King Alfred's castle, as I'd been intending to do when I got up this morning, whoever had made the attempt would know they'd failed and they might well try again. Clearly, my life was still in danger.

I needed to be smart about this. For the time being, they believed me dead and that gave me an advantage. I could conceal myself to see who benefitted the most from my death, which would help me figure out exactly who had masterminded this attack and why.

Despite the danger, a thrill of excitement ran through me. Nothing this interesting had happened to me in quite some time, and it definitely interested me far more than the reason I had come to this kingdom in the first place.

New plans and ideas took shape in my head as I finished the rest of my meal and headed out into the town. I'd need to find a place to hide out for a few days until the immediate danger had passed, and a way of making some more money. The coins I had with me would only last so long.

A small twinge of guilt tugged at me as the princess who'd been waiting for me crossed my mind, but I quickly pushed the regret aside. I had more important things to worry about. My proposed marriage would just have to wait.

CHAPTER TWO

~Cordelia~

Three weeks later

"You can't be serious."

I stared at my mother in disbelief, hoping the words that had just come out of her mouth were a weak attempt at humour.

Unfortunately, she simply stared back at me, completely unsympathetic. "I am perfectly serious, Cordelia. The messenger from King Philip arrived this morning. As Prince Cassian is presumed dead, his title as crown prince has passed to Prince Eric, and that means your marriage contract does as well. The prince's men will be arriving in a few days to escort you to Silatria."

The room seemed to spin around me but I refused to give in to the sensation. I had never been the kind of woman who fainted, and I had no intention of starting now. I grabbed onto Elodie's hand instead and squeezed it until I regained my balance.

"He's sent a list of expectations," my mother continued, not appearing to notice my distress. "Nothing too surprising. He insists that you remain isolated on the journey, for the sake of propriety. You'll be allowed to have Elodie with you, and if you need to interact with your escorts for any reason, she can do it on your behalf."

Eric had concerns about propriety? That seemed rather hypocritical given his own extreme failings in that area.

"Please, Your Majesty," I said, addressing my mother formally and with all the politeness and humility I could fake thanks to her years of training. "There must be a way out of this. You met him when he came to the feast. He bedded half my ladies and apparently half the servants too during the three days he spent here. How can I marry a man like that?"

I had managed to avoid spending any time with Eric during his stay with us other than during meals. The morning after the failed engagement feast, two men arrived who said they had been travelling with Prince Cassian. They told my parents that they'd been attacked on the way and had become separated from the prince. They arrived hoping that he would have already made his way to us, but we had to break it to them that we hadn't seen him.

Two days later, those men left with Eric, and we hadn't heard a word more from any of them until this correspondence my mother had just read, advising us that Cassian had been declared lost and I would be marrying Eric instead.

Cassian's fate brought me no joy. Though I hadn't wanted to marry him, I didn't wish him dead either, and I couldn't help feeling guilty that he had met his end while on his way to meet me.

And even more foolishly, I thought, for just a brief moment as my mother read out the first part of the letter, that his death would mean the end of the marriage discussions with Silatria. I never anticipated that they would simply substitute one brother for the other.

"You were always contracted to marry the crown prince of Silatria," my mother pointed out. "That is now Prince Eric. The contract never specified Cassian. So long as they have a crown prince, the contract stands, and there is no way to break it without embarrassing your father and this kingdom."

Any last small hopes I had of avoiding this marriage faded with those words. My mother held my father's reputation sacred above all things. She had spent her whole life building and protecting it, and under no circumstances would she put my happiness above it. She never had, and she never would.

"How am I meant to live with him?" I asked, directing the question more at myself than at her, barely aware that I had said the words out loud.

For the briefest of moments, a look of sympathy crossed my mother's face. "You will find a way. You are going in with your eyes open, which might not sound like a blessing, but believe me, it is. You already know what he is, so you will not be surprised or disappointed by anything you find there."

It didn't sound like much of a blessing. At least with Cassian, there had been a glimmer of hope that my life would be bearable. With Eric, that hope ceased to exist.

As Elodie and I left the room, I couldn't say which of us leaned on the other more. If anyone could be more devastated by this turn of events than me, it would be Elodie. Since we were children, she had our whole lives planned out: I would marry a prince who would appreciate me for my own virtues and who would make me happy, and once we were settled in our new kingdom, we would find a husband for her. She had daydreamed and told me stories about this long before I had given any serious thought to marriage or husbands.

And now, if my happiness seemed lost, her whole dream of our future had gone with it. In some ways, she might even be more upset than I was.

"We'll survive this, Lodee," I told her once we were back in the privacy of my room. "I won't let him break us."

The words sounded brave coming out of my mouth, but the truth remained that I could do very little about it. If my husband chose to sleep with a different woman every night, he could. If he beat me or starved me or chained me up in the room, that fell within his rights. As soon as our signatures were on the marriage contract, I became his property and if he chose to, he could make my life completely miserable.

We were given three days to prepare for the trip. Among my staff, only Elodie would make the trip with me, and my new husband would provide me with all the other servants I needed when we arrived. That decision had been made partly out of deference to my parents, so they did not have to lose any of their own staff to send with me, but also partly out of practicality.

We didn't want to attract any attention while travelling, so the smaller the party size, the better. Bandits were becoming a real issue in the territories that we would be travelling through on the way from our kingdom to Silatria, and they were growing increasingly violent. The sad fate of Prince Cassian was only one example. Everyone involved had agreed that we should try our best to pose as mere nobility rather than royalty. Elodie and I were to dress modestly, all of our finer things tucked away in the chests we'd be transporting.

A small carriage would be provided for me and Elodie to ride in, the carriage driver, and four armed guards to escort us to the border of our kingdom. There, we would be handed off to the guards provided by the Silatrian prince who would take us the rest of the way, as if we were merely another cargo they had to deliver.

All too soon, the morning of our departure arrived and my parents and brothers gathered in the courtyard to see us off. Arthur looked genuinely saddened to see me go, while my mother provided a few last-minute instructions on being a dutiful wife and queen. Almost before I knew it, we were in the carriage and moving down the dirt trail that led away from my home, the castle growing smaller in the distance behind us with every passing minute.

"How should we pass the time, Dee?" Elodie asked, linking her arm through mine in an attempt to cheer me up. "Do you want me to tell you a story?"

No storyteller in the world could compare to Elodie for me, and I had always loved to listen to the adventures her mind could create. Today, however, the lack of adventure in my own future dampened my mood to the point of despair. For the next week, I would be stuck in this carriage, and then stuck next to a womanizing, arrogant, selfish man for the rest of my life thereafter.

"I can try to remember some of your old favourites," Elodie offered when I remained silent. "Like the one about the princess who saved the prince from the bandits? Or the one where she traded places with the washerwoman?"

Despite myself, the memories of Elodie's past stories made me smile. The heroine was always a princess who bore a strong resemblance to me both in looks and in temperament. The one with the washerwoman had always been one of my particular favourites. In it, the princess traded jobs with the humble woman for a day so she could see how the regular people lived, and as I thought back across the story, an idea popped into my head.

The prince's men who were meeting us had never met me before. They were expecting to escort a princess and a lady-in-waiting, but they likely wouldn't know which of us filled which role.

What if...

What if, just for the week of our journey, Elodie and I traded places? She could pretend to be the princess and stay safely tucked away in the carriage, as Eric expected his future bride to. And I... well, maybe I could talk my way into getting my own horse and actually seeing and enjoying some of the ride before I had to give up all my freedom for good.

The more I thought about it, the more I liked the idea. For the first time in a long time, real excitement took hold inside me and I turned to my friend with a genuine smile. "Lodee, I know how we can pass the time. Instead of just telling one of your stories, how about this time we actually act it out?"

~Cassian~

Travelling on horseback towards the meeting point, I couldn't help smiling at the way things had turned out. The last few weeks had definitely been some of the most unusual of my entire life. Things were clearer to me now than they had been on that morning in the inn three weeks ago, but there were still several things I needed to figure out, which would be my top priority now.

As soon as I realized my situation, I sent a letter to Bran. No matter who else may be trying to harm me, I never suspected Bran for a second. The truest friend I ever had, I knew he would be devastated that he couldn't find me. I wrote to him at King Alfred's castle, assuming he would go there in search of me, and using the code we had communicated in since we were children together. We were the only two people in the world who knew how to interpret it.

I told him in the letter that I was alive and well but laying low, and explained to him what I had overheard. I also let him know where to find me, having secured a temporary room at the inn where I'd eaten on my first day in town.

Just a couple of days after I sent the letter, I received a reply from him in the same coded language. He assured me he understood the situation entirely and informed me that everyone presumed me dead. He would be travelling back to Silatria with Eric, keeping his eyes and ears open the whole time for any details that might help me. He promised to be in touch as soon as he had more information.

I reread the letter three times, certain I had misunderstood. He mentioned travelling with Eric, but why would Eric have been at King Alfred's castle in the first place? Unfortunately, by the time I received the letter, they would already be on the road and I had missed the chance to send a reply asking for more details. I would just have to wait until I heard from him again.

Meanwhile, I got myself some work as a day labourer at one of the farms outside town. The pay hardly amounted to anything but they provided me with food and it made a nice change from my usual duties to be able to spend the days outdoors working in the field. The other men who worked there were surprisingly well informed about everything happening at King Alfred's court. It turned out we were less than half a day's ride from there, so several of the men had family or friends who worked in the castle. I managed to learn quite a lot from them.

They told me that, although King Alfred had a steady income from the resources of the land, poor management of some of those resources threatened to upset the balance of power within the kingdom. With three sons in line to each take at least part of the pie, factions were forming. That made the marriage agreement with my father very important to him. The land that we were gifting the Lassarians in exchange for Princess Cordelia's dowry would be given to the middle son straight out, in the hopes that he could then attract a wealthy bride of his own who would bring in an equal amount to what they were sending with Cordelia.

I recognized this balancing act very well. My father had to play the same game, trying to ensure a somewhat equitable distribution of fortune between Eric and myself, even though I would be inheriting the crown and the kingdom.

But as interesting as the information might be, it brought me no closer to figuring out who had tried to kill me, so I breathed a sigh of relief when I received another message from Bran a few days ago. This time, the contents were even more surprising to me than his first letter had been.

He would soon be returning to Lassaria with a small complement of men, in order to accompany Princess Cordelia and her lady-in-waiting back to Silatria. When she arrived there, she would be marrying the crown prince: Eric.

It hadn't taken much time at all for the princess to move on to my brother, I couldn't help noticing. Although I knew I shouldn't take it personally since she'd never even met me, it offended me anyway.

Now, I had to meet up with Bran. He had promised he would 'get rid' of one of the men accompanying him so that I could take his place. The other men with him had never met me before so they wouldn't know who I was, and neither would the princess. The week-long journey would give us plenty of time to compare notes and come up with the best strategy for determining how to expose the person or people who had tried to have me killed, and then I could reveal to my father's court that I had not, in fact, died, and retake my rightful place.

It seemed straightforward enough.

"Cass!" Bran's voice called out to me as I rounded a bend in the trail and I caught sight of him on foot, his horse tied to a nearby tree. His face broke into a relieved grin as we made eye contact.

As quickly as I could, I dismounted my own horse and walked over to him, both of us embracing the other warmly.

"I'm so glad you weren't seriously hurt," he told me, his eyes full of genuine pleasure at our reunion. "Though you're certainly looking a bit scruffier."

I deserved that description. I had stopped shaving and my hair had grown out over the last few weeks. With the full beard and slightly curly hair, I hoped that even those who might have glimpsed me before wouldn't immediately recognize me.

"Come and get changed, we don't have a lot of time," he instructed, handing me a uniform that matched his own in the black and red colours of my kingdom. I found some privacy behind the trees and changed my clothes before returning to Bran and the horses. Soon, we were back on the road, heading towards the border.

"So, what did you do to the man meant to be wearing this uniform?"

Bran grinned at me. "He'll be fine, don't worry. I just added a touch of lily-of-the-valley to his stew last night and he's been emptying his stomach all morning. I told him to stay put until he got better, and I told the others I would find a replacement, which I have."

I smiled back gratefully. He had always been clever when it came to things like this, and I appreciated that he was on my side.

"How do you want me to introduce you to the others?" he asked. "And to the princess?"

With everything else going on, I had almost forgotten I would be meeting the princess today, the woman I had been betrothed to and would still need to marry, assuming I survived and reclaimed my position. "I think I better use a different name. Obviously, I can't use Cassian, and even Cass might be suspicious."

Bran nodded in agreement. "What should I call you, then?"

I thought back to our childhood games and how we had always used the second half of our names as our alter-egos. His full name was Branigan, so I had called him Gan, and he had called me Sean, taken from Cassian.

"How about Sean?" I suggested, and Bran grinned again, immediately recognizing the reference.

"Fine, but you're still calling me Bran."

We laughed together, and soon, we were back with the other two men. I recognized neither of them, and from the looks of disdain they gave me, they obviously didn't recognize me either. They assumed Bran had simply picked me up as a last-minute replacement. Not long afterwards, a carriage appeared along the road, driven by one man and escorted by four others on horseback.

As de facto leader of our small party, Bran greeted the men, exchanging pleasantries on behalf of our sovereigns. As I sat as still as possible on my horse, a movement in the window of the carriage caught my eye, and I glanced over to see a pair of bright blue eyes peering out curiously from around the curtain. Did they belong to the princess? The eyes watched Bran curiously and then looked over each of the rest of us in turn.

When they got to me, they widened as she realized she had my attention, but to my surprise, she held my gaze steady. I hadn't expected her to be so bold.

Since she had no idea about my true identity, I could be less proper and prince-like too. Instead of looking away or bowing, I rolled my eyes and made a talking motion with my hand, showing my own impatience with how long this handover had dragged on. I could have sworn she looked amused for just a second before disappearing once again behind the curtain.

At last, the king's men surrendered the carriage to our care, the Lassarian men returned the way they had come, and we all headed north, out of the kingdom and towards Silatria.

I couldn't help glancing back at the carriage, the memory of the humour in those blue eyes making me more curious about the person they belonged to than I'd expected to be, but for now, the curtain remained firmly closed.

~Cordelia~

Settling back into the seat as the carriage began to move again, I tried to figure out what had caused the odd, fluttery feeling in my stomach. Although similar to the excitement I'd been feeling ever since Elodie had agreed to switch places with me, it felt different too. Anticipation rose inside me even stronger than before, as if something important had happened or might be about to happen.

And it had all started when I caught that man staring at me.

I had only wanted to get a glimpse of our new escorts as we were handed over to the Silatrian men, and to see exactly what they were doing for so long. My gaze fell first on the tall man with red hair speaking to the head of my father's guard. They attempted to out-do each other with civility and flowery speeches, and I quickly lost interest.

Three other men sat on their horses, dressed in the colours of the Silatrian kingdom: black tunics with white breeches and a red doublet. Their riding attire looked much simpler than the royal uniform, which fit in with what we had been told about trying not to draw too much attention to ourselves.

One had dirty blonde hair, so light it almost appeared white, cut short, with a similar-coloured moustache. The next had long, dark hair, pulled back at the base of his neck. And the last one... I only had a moment to take in his appearance before I registered him staring straight back at me.

From what I had seen in that brief moment, he had dark hair, not long but not short either, naturally curly, with a trimmed beard. His eyes were also dark, though I couldn't tell from this distance exactly what shade they were. Before I could figure it out, he suddenly rolled his eyes at me and motioned towards his colleague, indicating clearly that he also felt this whole process could be completed much faster.

My face broke into a smile at the playful gesture, but I quickly pulled back from the window before he could see it, tugging the curtain tightly closed. It really hadn't been proper for him to engage with me that way, even as the lady-in-waiting I intended to imitate. And yet, the whole encounter left me feeling hopeful. If he wouldn't insist on standing on ceremony, perhaps I would be able to enlist his help in getting me a little more freedom for the rest of the journey.

Elodie soon fell asleep beside me as the carriage rolled along, only waking with a start once we came to a standstill again.

"What's going on?" she mumbled, still half-asleep. "Why did we stop?"

"I think we're stopping for food," I guessed. I certainly hoped so. My stomach had been complaining for the last half hour and the situation with my bladder had also begun to border on desperate. Pulling the carriage curtain back, I took a curious look at our surroundings for myself.

We had left the trail, stopping at a small clearing within the forest we'd been travelling through most of the day. The prince's men were all busy. One of them tied up their horses, another appeared to be relieving himself against a tree while the red-haired man and the one who had made eye contact with me earlier were setting out some supplies around some logs. No one seemed to be concerned about us at all, to my frustration.

Well, I had no intention of sitting there and waiting for them to remember our existence. I pulled open the carriage door myself and, turning back to face the inside of the carriage, began to step down the small ladder to the ground.

"Dee, where are you going?" Elodie gasped.

"I need to go into the woods before I burst," I told her. "You can come with me, Your Highness."

I winked as I called her by my title, and she pursed her lips at me in disapproval. "We can't just wander off on our own."

"We can if they give us no choice," I argued.

My feet hit the solid ground and I turned around in triumph, only to find myself staring straight into a broad set of shoulders.

"I was just about to come and see if you needed anything," a deep voice said, and I looked up to the face connected to those shoulders, the same face that had been appearing, unbidden, in my thoughts for the past hour.

His eyes were a chestnut shade of brown, I could see now that they were closer to me. A few shades lighter than his hair, they stood out beneath his dark eyebrows and held a hint of amusement, as if he thought it funny that I had climbed out of the carriage on my own.

"Were you?" I challenged. "Because it looked to me like you were all taking care of yourselves before you considered what Her Highness might need."

His eyes widened in surprise at the reprimand, but only for a second. Soon enough, his face softened into a friendly smile. "So, you are not the princess, then?"

"My name is Elodie Auclair," I introduced myself, giving Elodie's name. "Lady-in-waiting to Her Highness, Princess Cordelia. For the sake of convenience while we're travelling, you may call me Dee." I had decided to adopt my own nickname so that I wouldn't get caught out if I forgot to respond to Elodie's name.

A teasing spark lit up the man's eyes. "Well, if I may, then I suppose I will. It's a pleasure to meet you, Dee."

He offered me his hand, palm up, almost as a dare, waiting to see what I would do. I had no idea what his station might be and if it allowed him to be this familiar with me, but I had never been one to back down from a challenge. Giving him what I hoped was a cool and confident look, I placed my hand on his.

His fingers were rough and warm, and when he bent to kiss the back of my hand, his lips felt even warmer. I could almost feel the imprint of them like a brand where they had touched my skin.

"And you are?" I asked, realizing he hadn't given me his name yet. To my embarrassment, my hand trembled as I pulled it back from him. I could only hope he hadn't noticed.

"Sean," he replied, his eyes still full of good humour even as his steady gaze unnerved me with its novelty. No one but a prince would dare to hold a princess' gaze this way, but as he had no idea I was a princess, he wouldn't know how impertinent his actions were.

And, I had to admit, I didn't entirely mind it.

I waited for him to say more, but that appeared to be all he intended to say. "Do you have a family name, Sean?" I prompted. "Or were you abandoned in the wilderness as a child, where no one taught you to introduce yourself properly or look after the people in your charge?"

His lips twitched as if they fought back a smile. "Sean Moran, but you can simply call me Sean, my lady. I am at your service, and Her Highness'. We're just preparing some lunch, but is there anything you need in the meantime?"

"A privy," I told him bluntly. "Or whatever passes for one out here."

He nodded, suddenly business-like in the face of my request. "Of course. My apologies, I should have realized. I can find you both a private place."

He looked up into the open carriage now, appearing to notice Elodie for the first time.

"Your Highness, if I may?"

He held out his hand for her and Elodie took it, gracing him with a small nod. I had told her to simply nod if she felt uncomfortable in her new role. No one expected a princess to talk to her inferiors so it wouldn't be seen as strange if she remained silent.

When he had helped her out of the carriage, he offered her his arm before leading us both into the woods until we were out of sight from the rest of the party.

"I'm afraid it's not much," he said, gesturing to our surroundings. "But it will have to do for now."

"Here?" Elodie squeaked, looking at me in dismay. "I can't."

"I'm afraid it's here or wait until the next town, Your Highness," Sean warned her smugly. "Which is several hours away still."

It sounded like the prospect of making her wait would be entertaining to him and I narrowed my eyes at him. "We'll be fine," I told him, then turned to Elodie, silently begging her not to give him the satisfaction of showing her discomfort. "I will help you, Your Highness. You can leave us now, Sean."

He nodded in acknowledgement. "I'll be just up there, still within earshot if you need me."

As he wandered off, Elodie looked around once more, miserably. "Is the whole week going to be like this?"

I had almost forgotten that while I had a great deal of experience riding and hunting with my brothers, Elodie most certainly hadn't. She much preferred the comforts of the castle. "It's fine Lodee, don't worry. I'll hold your skirts so they don't get wet."

She groaned in disgust, but eventually we both managed to do what we needed and headed back towards the carriage, finding Sean waiting for us halfway.

"Better?" he asked, directing the question at me with just a hint of a smirk.

"When will the food be ready?" I asked, ignoring the inappropriateness of his question. Our bodily functions were hardly any of his concern. "Her Highness is hungry."

On cue, my stomach let out a loud growl, and this time Sean laughed out loud, making my cheeks flush. Whether embarrassment or the deep, soothing sound of his laugh caused that reaction, I couldn't entirely say.

"It appears she's not the only one," he teased me. "Come along, I'll introduce you to the others and we'll get you both fed in no time."

~Cassian~

I'd only had two minutes' worth of interaction with the princess, but so far, she met every expectation I had of her. Aloof and proper, she neither looked directly at me nor spoke a word to me. As we walked through the woods, she held her skirts off the ground with her free hand, as if the dirt on the ground might contaminate her.

This trip, or any kind of life outside the castle walls, would be a challenge for her. I had no trouble picturing her sitting in her chamber with her ladies gathered around her, sewing and gossiping, just like every other princess I had ever met.

As we walked side-by-side with her arm in mine, I tried to imagine her as my wife. She was pretty, as Eric had said. Her long, brown hair hung down her back in elaborate plaits, and her fashionably pale skin showed just how little time she spent outdoors. Her figure, highlighted by her expensive dress, certainly looked shapely.

And yet, despite all that, the idea of her in my bed held no appeal for me. Based on the limpness of her arm in mine, I could only guess that she would be the type of woman who simply laid back and waited for the act to be over. I had been with women like that as a younger man, and I could do without repeating the experience.

Dee, on the other hand... well, I hadn't expected anything like her.

After we stopped to rest, Bran and I had been arguing with each other as we unpacked the supplies for lunch, debating who should be in charge of handling the princess. Bran thought it should be me since I obviously had the most experience in dealing with royalty. As my intended bride, it would give me a good chance to get to know her. Meanwhile, spending this rare week of freedom babysitting a pampered, helpless woman couldn't appeal to me less.

Just as I made that argument, I glanced over at the carriage in time to see the door open and a truly stunning woman appear. I only got a glimpse of her for a second, just a brief peek of her honey-gold hair and heart-shaped face, before she turned around and began climbing down from the carriage on her own.

"You know what? You're right, I can look after them," I offered abruptly, walking away from Bran before he could question my sudden change of heart.

I arrived just as the woman reached the ground, and as soon as Dee turned around, I couldn't look away. Her blue eyes were the ones I had seen from the carriage earlier, blue eyes full of life and the promise of something I couldn't quite put my finger on. It felt like some secret lurked just beneath the surface, some mystery that I could solve if I could only look into those eyes long enough.

Her hair hung loose, with a gentle curl, and her skin had a slightly tanned tone with a few freckles around her nose that told me she had spent her share of time in the sun.

That all happened before she even spoke to me, and when she did, she stunned me even more. No woman had ever spoken to me like that before. She didn't know I was a prince, which partly explained it. Right now, to her, I appeared not much more than a servant. But I couldn't help thinking that even if she did know, it wouldn't stop her from telling me exactly what she thought on any given subject.

I couldn't imagine her being intimidated by very much at all.

As we returned back to the rest stop, Dee and Princess Cordelia headed back towards their carriage. "Your Highness?" I asked in confusion. "I thought you were hungry. Don't you want to come and eat?"

Both women looked towards the spot where the other men were already seated. "Prince Eric's instructions were for the princess to remain separate from the escort," Dee reminded me.

Bran had told me that, but I'd forgotten.

"I will bring some food to the carriage for her," Dee continued. "If you wouldn't mind helping her back up?"

Once again, I could hear the reprimand in her tone. She clearly thought I left a lot to be desired when it came to my job and I couldn't really argue with her. After all, I had never done this before, and she had distracted me.

After helping the princess back into the carriage, I offered my arm to Dee next, who raised her eyebrows at me. "I walked to the woods and back on my own just fine. I think I can make it a few more feet."

I laughed almost without meaning to. I had never met a noblewoman like her and I couldn't help wondering exactly where the princess had found her. They seemed an unlikely pair, but then, I supposed Bran and I did too. Sometimes the most valuable trait in a friend, particularly when you were in a position of power, was the ability and willingness to tell you the truth about anything, and I suspected that Dee gave Cordelia that in spades.

"My lady, allow me to introduce the rest of your escort," I said to her, speaking more formally in front of the others as we approached the rest of the group. "This is Bran, John and Thomas."

I gestured to each of them in turn and they each bowed politely.

"This is Lady Elodie, lady-in-waiting to Princess Cordelia," I said to the men, completing the introductions.

"It's a pleasure to meet you all," Dee greeted them, also adjusting her tone. Although it sounded a bit more restrained and polite, it still held the same authority and conviction. "As we'll be seeing a lot of each other over the next week, please, just call me Dee. Anything you need to ask the princess or share with her can go through me."

"Of course," Bran replied politely. "And if there is anything the princess needs from us, just let me know and we will do our very best to provide it."

Dee nodded in acknowledgement. "Thank you. For now, just some lunch that I could take to her in her carriage is all that's required."

Bran and I quickly placed some bread and cheese onto a piece of cloth and I gathered the corners together. "If you can carry this, my lady, I will bring you both something to drink."

Dee took the cloth from me, and, to my surprise, quickly tied the ends into an expert knot to keep it secure. "Thank you, Sean."

She gave me a quick smile before turning and walking back towards the carriage.

"Wait, I'll help you..." I started to protest, to no avail. Bran hadn't finished pouring out some of the small beer into the cups, and Dee was already halfway back to the carriage. I watched as she hoisted herself back up inside on her own, enjoying the view of her rather perfect backside as she bent over to avoid hitting her head on the top of the door.

"Careful, Sean." Bran's voice beside me carried a hint of amusement but also a warning. "Remember which woman you're meant to be marrying."

"I didn't say a damn thing," I protested, and he raised his eyebrows at me.

"I know you better than that," he pointed out. "I don't need you to tell me that you're interested. I haven't seen you look at a woman that way in a very long time."

As usual, he had it exactly right. I hadn't been this intrigued by a woman in .... well, ever, really.

"She's just taken me by surprise," I said, determined not to give him the satisfaction of knowing exactly how well he had me pegged. "Now that I know what to expect, it will be fine."

He handed me the cups and gave me a firm clap on the back. "We'll see about that, my friend."

His smug tone seemed unnecessary, but I shrugged it off as I headed back towards the carriage, my heart beating just a little faster in anticipation of the woman waiting for me there.

CHAPTER THREE

Elodie waited for me in the carriage, her lips puckered in disapproval as I pulled myself back up the steps. Pretending not to notice her expression, I closed the door behind me and untied the makeshift bag that contained the food for our lunch, setting it down on the seat next to her.

After grabbing one of the large pieces of bread, I sat on the bench across from her and took a bite. "What?" I finally asked when she kept staring at me.

Elodie sighed in exasperation. "I know we agreed to trade places, Dee, but you shouldn't get carried away. You need to try to behave as I would. I would never be as familiar with that man as you were."

I couldn't argue with that. Elodie always knew each person's position and the proper way that we should interact with them based on that. That had never been as much of a concern to me, though, and this week, I cared even less.

Besides, Sean didn't seem concerned about social position and formality either.

"We're out in the middle of nowhere," I pointed out, gesturing at the woods we could see through the carriage window. "No one is concerned with etiquette. We just need to get along with these men for the next week and then we'll probably never see them again."

"But what if we do?" she asked, her brow lined with worry. "What if they're Prince Eric's regular men? What will he think when he finds out you were pretending to be someone else? I don't know, Dee, I'm beginning to think this is all a bad..."

"Excuse me, Your Highness?"

Sean's voice interrupted Elodie's complaint, and my stomach fluttered at the deep rumble of it. I must be hungrier than I thought, I decided, taking another good-sized bite out of my bread.

Elodie stared at me pointedly, her eyes wide and lips tight, and belatedly, I remembered that I should answer for her.

"Yesh?" I called out, my mouth still full. Elodie squeezed her eyes closed in embarrassment.

"I brought your drinks," he replied, still with that same hint of humour in his voice as before. "May I join you?"

Join us? I looked around the small space of the carriage as Elodie shook her head at me vehemently.

"He can't, Dee!" Her whispered voice was full of outrage. "It's not proper, and I wouldn't know what to say."

"You don't need to say anything. I'll do all the talking," I assured her in a whisper of my own, swinging myself back onto the seat next to her to leave the one across from us free.

It definitely went against propriety, so Sean had been bold to ask, knowing that the prince wanted us kept separate. All of which only made me more curious about why he would disobey his own orders that way.

"Come in," I invited, and the carriage door opened, revealing Sean's face, his expression just as casual as before.

"I have your drinks," he said, holding out two cups. "Could I pass these to you, Dee?"

I reached over to grab them from him and settled back in my seat, giving one of the cups to Elodie as Sean easily pulled himself up into the carriage and took the seat across from us.

The small space inside the carriage suddenly seemed a whole lot smaller with his large, muscular frame filling it. He was in excellent shape, I couldn't help noticing. His riding boots and breeches did little to hide the firm muscles of his legs.

I had rarely been in such close quarters with any man other than my brothers, and I'd certainly never noticed *their* legs before.

"What exactly is your position in the prince's household?" I asked him once he had settled in.

Elodie may think I paid no attention to her warnings, but I knew she had a point. If Sean was a close confidant of my future husband, it could make my current deception tricky to explain. It would be best to figure out how likely he might be to share any details about this trip with the prince.

Thankfully, his answer quickly set my mind at ease. "Actually, I'm only serving him temporarily for this journey. I used to work under his brother, Prince Cassian, before his unfortunate passing. Once we arrive back in Silatria, I won't be in Prince Eric's employ any longer."

I had to bite my lip to hold back my smile. That could hardly be more perfect. Nothing that Sean saw or heard on this trip would make its way back to the prince, leaving us free to continue our charade.

Sean's eyes dipped to my mouth, his eyes appearing to darken as he watched me free my lip from my teeth. The fluttering in my stomach got even worse than it had been before. Maybe I had started to come down with something?

"What can you tell Her Highness about Prince Eric?" I asked, looking over at Elodie in an attempt to distract myself from my body's strange reaction. "She only met him briefly. It would be nice for her to know about his interests and inclinations."

Sean's gaze moved to Elodie too, making me realize he hadn't looked at her before now.

"I'm afraid I don't know him all that well," Sean said, addressing his reply to the both of us, but his voice held a hint of restraint which differed from his usual laid-back tone. It suggested he might be holding something back. "As I said, I served his brother. My information is second-hand at best."

"Second-hand information is better than none at all," I pointed out. "Would you still like to hear it, Your Highness?"

I met Elodie's eyes, hoping she would recognize how much I wanted to hear what Sean had to say, and of course she understood me perfectly. She gave Sean a small, tight smile and nodded her head.

Sean took a deep breath, his nostrils flaring as he debated what to say. "If you insist. I would say, from my observations, that Prince Eric is a determined man, and not someone who is easily satisfied. He works hard, and his wife will certainly be well provided for, but I don't know that he finds much joy in his work or his success. He is the type of man who, if you gave him half the world, would want to know who had received the other half."

I appreciated his candour more than I could say, even though my heart sank as I listened to him. I heard the words between the lines perfectly clearly. As someone not easily satisfied, the prince wouldn't be satisfied with just one woman in his bed. The fact that he found no joy in his work made it clear that he wouldn't do things unless they had some kind of benefit for him.

These observations neither surprised nor shocked me. Yet, even through my disappointment, I couldn't help but be intrigued at Sean's insights. These hardly sounded like the descriptions of someone who barely knew the man. Unless, perhaps, he had heard these things from Eric's brother directly?

"Were you close to Prince Cassian?" I asked.

Sean's eyes widened in surprise, but only for a moment before he resumed his usual friendly half-smile. "You could say that, yes."

"We were very sorry to hear what happened to him," I said, offering my condolences. Elodie nodded in agreement beside me before taking a delicate sip of her drink.

"What did you know about him?" Sean asked, a spark of curiosity in his eyes. "I imagine you must have been told some things when he and the princess were betrothed."

This conversation shouldn't really take place in front of Elodie, but as I had already told her, I saw no need to be overly formal with Sean given our current circumstances.

"We weren't told much," I answered for the both of us. "As I'm sure you can appreciate, the princess' father arranged the engagement, the same as the current arrangement."

"I can indeed appreciate that," Sean agreed, his eyes flitting to Elodie for just a moment before returning to me. "It's not the most enlightened way to decide who to spend the rest of your life with, is it?"

I could hardly have put it better myself, but Elodie obviously thought he went too far. She gasped beside me at the presumption of Sean's remark, causing her to inhale the piece of cheese she had in her mouth, and she began to cough violently.

"Are you alright, Your Highness?" Sean instantly leapt to his feet, bent at the waist to avoid hitting his head, and leaned towards both of us in the confined space. I could almost feel the heat from his body.

Elodie held out a hand to hold him back as she continued to cough, clearly not wanting him to touch her, so I quickly reached behind her and gave her a sharp jab between the shoulder blades. When she kept coughing, I repeated the gesture, harder, and this time it seemed to dislodge the offending piece of food and her coughs grew gentler.

Sean picked up her cup and offered it to her, helping her to take a drink.

Despite his obvious strength, it appeared he could also be quite gentle, I noticed, watching the delicate way he held the cup to her lips.

When Elodie's breathing had returned to normal, rather than retaking his seat, Sean opened the door. "I should go back now, Your Highness, my lady. We'll be heading out again soon."

He had already disappeared before I could get his name out. "Sean, wait."

In less than a second, he returned to the doorway. "Yes?"

Though I didn't know how he would respond to my request, I had to ask anyway. The only way to get what I wanted would be to ask for it.

"Could I ride alongside you this afternoon?"

~Cassian~

Had I heard Dee correctly? She already had a way of surprising me, never saying exactly what I expected her to, but even so, I hadn't anticipated her talking about riding.

What did she mean that she wanted to ride 'alongside' me? We only had enough horses for our escort. Surely, she would have seen that when we made the handover. And most noblewomen I'd come across didn't know much about riding anyway, and only ever did it as a last resort. They generally travelled by carriage, just as Dee and the princess were doing now.

But with no horse, and presuming she probably couldn't ride properly anyway, what else could she be suggesting? Did she actually mean that she wanted to ride with me, on *my* horse?

Normally, I wouldn't even consider that. Having a passenger only made the ride more uncomfortable, and besides, I wanted to spend the time talking to Bran and going over the information we had about the assassination attempt. We rode separately this morning, not wanting to make it too obvious to John and Thomas that we knew each other before today, but we had already agreed that this afternoon, we would switch positions so that he and I would take the lead while the other two followed behind the princess' carriage.

But now, just the idea of having Dee's body close to mine for an extended period of time appealed to me far more than it should. The saddles we had weren't meant for a passenger, so she'd need to hold onto me, and as soon as I let myself think about it, my body started to react. Luckily my long tunic concealed the evidence of my reaction at the front of my breeches.

"Doesn't the princess need you?"

I decided to start with that question before making any assumptions about what she wanted. Besides, I had reason for concern. The princess had nearly choked on her own lunch, leaving me with the impression that she could use some help taking care of herself.

"The motion of the carriage makes her sleepy," Dee explained, lowering her voice as she leaned closer to me, though the princess would still be able to hear her. "Which leaves me with no one to talk to and nothing to do. It would be much more interesting to be in the open air and be able to see the landscape we're passing through."

I could sympathize with that. Spending a whole afternoon in a hot, stuffy carriage with a sleeping princess hardly sounded like my idea of a good time either.

Whereas the idea of talking to Dee as we rode tempted me nearly as much as the thought of her holding onto me.

I still didn't have a firm grip on her expectations though.

"Do you have any experience of riding?" I asked next. No matter what my own feelings on the matter were, if she couldn't keep herself on the horse properly, it would slow us down. We wanted to be at our destination for the night before it got dark and the road became more dangerous.

Dee's lips tightened as if I'd offended her. "I am perfectly capable of handling a horse, Sean. It's not like those are wild stallions you're riding. I bet I could outride you, in my own style."

I couldn't help laughing. She couldn't honestly believe that, could she? I had never met a woman who could come close to keeping up with me on a horse, let alone outride me.

My laughter only made her frown deepen, which, for some strange reason, I found incredibly endearing. "You don't believe me?" she demanded.

"No, I don't," I told her honestly, still chuckling to myself. "If you assure me that you're a capable passenger, I might believe that, but let's not get carried away."

"Let's not," she said, but the tone of her voice made it clear that she didn't mean it as an agreement. "There's no reason to argue about it when I can prove it. What do you say to a wager?"

"A wager?" I repeated, my interest fully piqued now. "What kind of wager?"

"A race," she clarified. "You against me. The first one back gets to use your horse this afternoon."

She wanted to use *my* horse? On her own? "And where am I meant to go if you take my horse?"

"You can ride with the carriage driver," she suggested, pointing to the driver's bench at the front of the carriage.

It could be done, I supposed, though the prospect hardly pleased me. The driver was a rather large man, and the two of us on that bench would be a lot cozier than I wanted to be with anyone on this trip except perhaps Dee herself.

We should be getting back on the road any minute now, but I could hardly back down from the kind of challenge she had proposed, especially when I knew I had no chance of losing.

"If we're going to wager, let's make it interesting," I counter-offered. "The winner gets the horse for the afternoon, as you said, but the loser also has to feed and water all the horses when we arrive at the inn tonight."

Most ladies would consider that kind of work, the work of stableboys, far beneath their station. I could imagine the princess might actually faint if I suggested it to her.

Dee, however, replied completely differently. "You're on," she agreed readily, her earlier frown replaced by a satisfied smile.

Her confidence charmed me. I almost felt bad that I would have to put her in her place. Perhaps I'd keep it close enough that she wouldn't feel too badly when she lost.

"Dee, can I speak to you for a moment?" The princess had been sitting there silently the whole time, but she spoke up now, her voice tight with disapproval.

"Of course, Your Highness," Dee agreed, her own tone immediately becoming more conciliatory. "Sean, please go and see to the horses. I'll join you in just a minute."

Turning away, I left them alone, still smiling to myself as I walked over to Bran and the others.

"What's going on?" he asked, taking in my smile before I had a chance to hide it.

"Lady Elodie and I are going to have a quick horse race," I told him succinctly. "It will only take a few minutes, and then we'll be ready to go."

He looked at me as if I had completely lost my mind. "A race? With a lady? Are you sure this is appropriate, *Sean?*"

He put extra emphasis on my temporary name, attempting to remind me, without revealing it in front of the other men, of my position and true identity.

"It's just a bit of fun," I told him, brushing aside his concern. "It's a long enough day, we might as well enjoy ourselves where we can. Come, get your horse ready for her to ride."

Although Bran shook his head, he gave in. He usually did unless I wanted to do something truly reckless. Even so, he made his displeasure clear. "I hope you know what you're doing," he muttered as we untied our horses and brought them back to the road.

It took another minute before Dee's head appeared from the carriage door. She caught my eye and made a beckoning motion with her hand to me.

I hadn't gotten used to being summoned like a servant yet, but I had to admit, when Dee was the one doing it, I didn't mind all that much. Handing my horse's reins to Bran, I walked back over to her.

"The princess would like to watch the race," Dee told me as I approached. "Please help her down."

"Of course." I offered my hand first to Dee, who took it while stepping down from the carriage nimbly, before I extended the same courtesy to Princess Cordelia. "Your Highness, if you would like to wait here, I'll have one of the other men come over and escort you to a safe position to watch."

She nodded in agreement, though I noticed that she looked less than thrilled with the whole situation. Her sour expression matched Bran's almost exactly. Leaving her there, Dee and I walked over to the horses and I sent Bran over to wait with the princess. He bowed politely to her as I handed Dee the reins to Bran's horse.

"We have no mounting block," I pointed out to Dee as she inspected the horse's saddle, making me smile again. She was really taking this seriously.

"That's fine," she assured me. "I can use your knee."

I hadn't offered my knee, but now that she put me on the spot, I could hardly refuse it. Sinking to one knee, I offered the other to her, holding out my hand in case she wanted to use it too, but she ignored that additional courtesy. With one hand on the reins, she stepped onto my knee, grabbed the pommel of the saddle and hoisted herself up onto the horse neatly and confidently. I barely had time to blink before she sat securely on the horse, across the saddle. The horse never moved a muscle.

That was impressive, I had to admit.

Getting back to my feet, I quickly mounted my own horse and turned back the way we had come this morning. "A large oak stump sat in the middle of the road, not very far back," I told Dee, remembering the diversion we'd had to take around it. "Not much more than a mile. We'll race to it, around, and then back."

"Fine," she agreed. "But first, you need to change your position."

My position? What did that mean? I glanced down at my body astride the horse, finding nothing wrong with it.

When I looked back at Dee, she smiled at me, a mischievous twinkle in her eye. "The bet was that I could outride you *in my style*, right? You need to ride like me: sidesaddle."

Against my will, my mouth fell open in disbelief. I hadn't agreed to that.... had I?

Dee bit her lip, trying to hold back her grin, and just like it had in the carriage, that little action drew my attention straight to her mouth. A shot of pure desire ran through me, even through my annoyance over the way she'd just outplayed me.

"What'll it be, Sean?" she asked, raising her eyebrow in defiance. "Do you want to back out now, or do you still think you can win?"

~Cordelia~

Sean's face as he realized he would have to race me sidesaddle or forfeit the race easily qualified as one of the funniest things I had ever seen.

He had been so damn cocky and sure of himself that it gave me far more pleasure than it should have to bring him down a peg or two.

"I've never ridden sidesaddle before," he protested, his eyes dropping to my body as if trying to figure out how I had positioned myself on the horse. Unfortunately for him, my skirt covered the exact position of my legs, so he remained clueless.

"Surely someone who is as good a rider as you are can figure it out," I suggested innocently. "If a woman like me can do it, how hard can it be?"

Keeping my expression neutral as Sean tried to figure out how to respond to that proved a challenge, but I thought I managed it pretty well. His lips twitched, and twice he opened his mouth to speak and then closed it again. He closed his eyes for a moment and took a breath, and when he opened them again, a new look of determination had appeared. "So, I just move my leg over here…?"

He tried to move his leg across the horse in front of him without kicking the horse in the head, and his horse fidgeted nervously beneath him.

"Not like that," I told him, taking pity on him before he got thrown off. "Swing your leg behind, and then pivot your whole body."

He did as I instructed, his hands resting on the saddle's front edge as he got both legs to one side of the horse and twisted around to a sitting position.

"Is that right?" he asked, a rather adorable look of confusion on his face as he shifted side to side in the saddle.

"Face forward," I advised. "Bring your front knee up so that your body is straight."

He did his best to follow my instructions, each movement delightfully awkward.

"How am I supposed to secure myself?" he asked once he had the position right, looking at the saddle as though there might be another secret handhold he didn't know about.

"You'll need to use your muscles," I teased him. "Unless those are just for show?"

He looked up at me in surprise before a smirk spread across his face. "Have you been paying attention to my muscles, Dee?"

Immediately, that strange fluttery feeling returned to my stomach. "No more than anyone else's," I lied, taking a breath to try to get my body back under control. "Just remember to keep your thighs and abdomen tight, particularly on the corners, or you're likely to go flying right off."

The thought of his abdominal muscles sent a strange pulsing sensation through me, not just in my stomach, but lower too. I shifted my own weight, trying to alleviate the odd sensation.

"Are you ready?" I asked.

Sean glanced over to where Bran and Elodie, the carriage driver, and the other two escorts were all standing, watching us with open curiosity and amusement. One of them said something to the whole group and they all laughed.

"I guess so," he agreed, sounding far less confident than he had just a few minutes earlier. "I don't suppose you'll go easy on me for my first time?"

I simply raised my eyebrows at him in response, and he sighed, but not without a hint of amusement in his own eyes too.

"Three, two, one, go!"

I called out the start and gave my horse an encouraging nudge with my left leg. He responded immediately, and we were soon up to a gallop, though I could have gone faster if I really wanted to.

To my surprise, Sean actually kept up fairly well, although he bounced around on the saddle far more than he should have been. He would certainly be feeling that tomorrow, I thought with a satisfied smile.

"You're really fast!" he called out from behind me, sounding genuinely impressed.

"Faster than you," I shot back, turning my head to the side so he'd hear me but keeping my eyes straight ahead.

Before long, a large tree stump appeared, which must be the one he had been referring to. Tightening my grip on the reins and the pommel, I pulled the horse to one side and then quickly rounded it, coming back and passing Sean before he even reached the tree.

"Remember to hold on!" I shouted as I went by.

Unable to resist, I looked back to watch his turn, and sure enough, as the horse took the sharp corner, Sean began to slide across the saddle. He reached down to grab the pommel with both hands to get himself centred again, managing to keep his balance through sheer strength. He stayed on the horse, luckily for him, but his momentum had completely disappeared.

He had no chance of catching me now. As soon as the others were back in sight, I slowed to a trot, crossing the invisible finish line serenely as Sean came barrelling down the road behind me, desperately trying to catch me.

In the end, I only beat him by a few seconds thanks to my unnecessarily dramatic finish, but it didn't matter. Those few seconds were all I needed.

The watching men all laughed and jeered at Sean as he came up beside me, still being jostled in his saddle and out of breath now too.

"You made a good effort," I told him sincerely, though I couldn't resist throwing in a teasing jab too. "With a little practice, you might even be able to keep up with me."

I honestly hadn't even been sure that he would try to race once he realized that I'd tricked him, but he had been a good sport about it. I appreciated that trait. Not all men were so willing to do something that might make them look foolish.

"I have a new appreciation for all female riders now," he admitted. "It's harder than it looks."

"It is," I agreed. "But there is one benefit to sitting this way: it's much quicker to get off."

To prove my point, I slid down off the saddle now, dropping gracefully to the ground, and Sean quickly followed.

"Looks like you lost, Sean," the tall, red-haired man said as he walked over to join us with Elodie still beside him.

"Apparently," Sean agreed good-naturedly, seeming to accept that he would be hearing about this for a while. "Can I speak to you for just a minute, Bran?"

The two men took the horses and walked a short distance away as I turned to meet Elodie's chastising eyes.

"What's that look for?" I asked her. "I won!"

"I know, but I almost wish you hadn't." She shook her head at me in exasperation. "I'm afraid this will only make you bolder."

She had argued with me back in the carriage about doing the race in the first place. I explained to her how I needed to win in order to have a horse to ride, and what was the point of us switching places if I didn't get to have a bit of freedom along the way? When I appealed to her sympathy by reminding her of the things Sean had said about my future husband, her resistance crumbled, as it always did when it came down to my happiness.

"I promise I'll be careful," I told her now. "Let's get you back in the carriage. You'll be able to have a nice nap this afternoon and forget all about worrying about me."

"I'll only worry more because you're out of my sight," she contradicted, but she obeyed me anyway, turning to head back to the carriage. I helped her up and made sure she had everything she needed.

"I'll see you at the next stop," I assured her. "Don't worry, Lodee. I'll be perfectly well behaved."

I gave her a final little wave and closed the carriage door.

"Lodee?"

Sean's curious voice froze me in my tracks. I hadn't noticed him making his way back over to us, and I could only hope he hadn't heard anything more incriminating than that.

"It's an old childhood nickname for Her Highness," I explained quickly. "I thought we were alone."

"It's fine, Dee," he said, giving me a warm smile. "I never called Prince Cassian by his title when we were alone either."

An odd look crossed his face when he spoke of the former crown prince. It made me curious to ask him more about Cassian and what he had been like, but it would have to wait. "Are we ready to go then?"

"Yes. You'll be using Bran's horse, if you don't mind. The same one you raced on."

We hadn't agreed to that. "And he'll be using yours?" I asked, trying to understand.

"No." Sean smiled sheepishly. "He's offered to take my place on the carriage, so you'll be riding with me, if that's alright."

"What about our bet?" I asked. "Are you squelching?"

"Of course not," he protested. "I'll still take care of the horses when we arrive, since I lost, and you get to ride, as you wanted, since you won. It's just that Bran has been riding for several days already and wanted the break more than I did. I hope that will satisfy you?"

The idea of riding next to Sean all afternoon and having the chance to talk to him privately satisfied me more than I wanted to admit. Elodie wouldn't approve, but with the door closed, she hadn't heard our conversation, and she couldn't object to what she didn't know.

"That will be fine," I said, trying not to let him know how pleased I felt with the way this had worked out. "Let's get going, then."

~Cassian~

Anticipation swelled inside me as Dee and I walked back towards the horses that Bran held for us. We'd be on the road for several hours this afternoon before reaching the town where we planned to spend the night.

Several hours of having Dee beside me, talking to her and getting to know more about her.

I had never looked forward to spending time with a woman this much in my life, at least not outside of the bedroom.

When I realized she was going to win our bet, which I realized pretty much the second she took off down the road on her horse, her blonde hair flying behind her in the wind, I knew I needed a new plan. No way would I spend the afternoon stuck on that carriage bench with the dull driver, watching Dee and Bran ride side-by-side.

I needed to be the one riding with her instead.

So, when the race ended, when she'd beaten me soundly despite showing off at the end, her smile bright enough to lighten the darkest of rooms, I immediately cornered Bran.

"I need your horse," I told him bluntly.

His brow furrowed as he looked back at me. "For what?"

"To ride. Or for Dee to ride. I promised I'd let her have mine if she beat me."

He still looked confused. "And where were you going to go?"

"With the driver." I pointed back at the carriage where the man in question had just hoisted himself up into the seat. He took up more than half the bench on his own. "Trade places with me, Bran. Please."

After looking over at the driver and then back at my pleading face, he began to laugh. "No way. I love you, Cass, but not that much."

"It's Sean," I reminded him, taking a quick look around to make sure no one had overheard that slip. Luckily, we were alone. "And do I have to remind you that I am still your prince, whether anyone else knows it or not? I could make your life very difficult when we get home."

I didn't usually play the prince card, but desperate times called for dirty measures.

"Oh, come on," he protested. "I don't want to sit there with him. You're the one who made the bet and lost."

"The fault isn't entirely mine," I argued. "She tricked me."

"That sounds like your fault," he pointed out. "And I know you always honour your bets, so what's this really about?"

He had a point. I might make stupid decisions sometimes, but I always accepted the consequences of them. What made this different?

"I want to talk to her," I admitted. His eyebrows shot up, so I continued before he could say anything. "She's not like any lady I've met before and I'd like to learn more about her. Chances are, after twenty minutes of conversation, she'll prove herself to be just the same as the rest of them, and my curiosity will be satisfied. Please, Bran. It's just one afternoon. If not for your prince, then do it for your friend."

He sighed, and I knew I had him. "Alright. But you owe me. A big one."

I clapped him on the back in thanks and went in search of Dee. She stood by the open door of the carriage, speaking to the princess inside, and I caught just the last part of their conversation as I walked up.

I didn't know what they were talking about, but the dynamic between them intrigued me. The princess almost deferred to Dee, as if Dee were the one in charge. Dee called her Lodee, which I found a strange nickname for Cordelia. It must have a story behind it.

As I helped Dee back up onto her horse now and took my own place, I knew that I'd have plenty of time to ask her about that now and any other questions I could think of. I had never spent hours talking to a woman before. We would surely run out of things to talk about eventually, but for now, my mind brimmed with questions.

We led the party back out onto the road, Dee and I in front, the carriage behind us, and John and Thomas bringing up the rear.

"How long have you been with the princess?" I asked first as we settled into an easy rhythm. I had been impressed with how fast she rode during our race, but the easy, relaxed way she guided her horse now struck me as equally skilled. She had clearly spent a lot of time on horseback, unusually for a woman of her station.

"Most of my life," she replied. "My parents were courtiers and since Cordelia and I were the same age, we were often put together. My parents died when I was still quite young and the king and queen took responsibility for me. Cordelia and I have been practically like sisters ever since."

True affection shone in her eyes as she spoke of the princess, making it clear that being lady-in-waiting meant more to her than just a position. She truly liked the woman.

Maybe I hadn't given the princess enough of a chance yet. If she could inspire such devotion in a woman like Dee, maybe I had judged her too quickly.

"She's the only daughter in the family, is that right?" I vaguely remembered that from the information Bran had given me before our ill-fated visit. I realized now that I probably should have paid more attention to the things he had said.

"Yes, that's right. She has three younger brothers. For much of her childhood, she had only me for female companionship."

That was interesting, but I couldn't quite reconcile it with the impression I had of Cordelia so far. If she'd been surrounded by boys and someone as uninhibited as Dee appeared to be, how did she end up so reserved and formal? Perhaps she just naturally inclined that way.

"What do you like most about her?" I asked. Maybe Dee could help me see her good qualities, the ones which weren't immediately obvious.

Dee's eyes softened at the thought of her friend, and it made her beautiful face even more appealing. "She is the kindest person I've ever met, always thinking about other people and putting their needs before her own. She wants everyone to be happy. She's fiercely loyal and would do anything for those that she loves. If I had to put my life in someone's hands, I would choose hers, without a moment's hesitation."

Those were all fine qualities, I had to admit. I'd describe Bran much the same way.

It didn't mean I wanted to marry him.

"And how would she describe you?" I asked next.

That question made Dee laugh. "She would probably say that I'm ridiculously stubborn, that I never listen to good advice, and that I go out of my way to make things difficult for myself."

I laughed right along with her. She'd just outlined, almost word-for-word, how Bran would describe me.

Logically, it made more sense to prefer the kind and loyal princess over a stubborn and difficult lady, but I couldn't help the way I felt. If I were to be given the choice between the two of them right now, if someone told me I had to marry one of them or the other, I had no doubt which one I would choose.

CHAPTER FOUR

At first, Sean's questions about 'the princess' made me slightly uncomfortable, knowing that we were actually talking about me, and I tried to stick to only passing on facts about me and my family. Before long, though, I remembered that nothing I said to Sean would make its way back to Prince Eric. He wouldn't be working for him for much longer, so what did it matter what I said?

So, when Sean asked me what I liked about the princess, I described Elodie rather than trying to give an account of my own qualities, and when he asked what Elodie thought of me, I answered that honestly too.

I expected Sean to show some disapproval over the way I described myself. No man I had ever met wanted to spend time with a stubborn and disrespectful woman. My mother had made it clear that compliance and amiability were the most desirable qualities in a wife, but to my great surprise, Sean merely smiled at my self-assessment.

"I think people might say the same of me," he admitted. "Why is it that simply standing up for the idea that you should have some say over your own life is considered stubborn?"

I hadn't expected that kind of insight from him, and I pointed that out. "Well, in my case, it's because a woman isn't expected to actually want anything for herself. I don't know what your problem is."

He laughed again, an infectious sound that made me smile whether I wanted to or not. "Men can be defined by their station just as much as women can, Dee."

"I disagree," I told him honestly. "If you don't like your employer, you are free to go and find another one. You can learn a new skill and take up an entirely different trade. You can marry whom you like or not marry at all if you prefer. It is a completely different world for you."

The muscles in his cheek tightened as he thought over what I'd said. "For most men, I suppose that's true, but there are some who are more restricted than that. Take Prince Cassian, for example: he could not simply stop being a prince, nor could he choose whom he married."

He had a point. The prince would have been more restricted than most people, hampered by many of the same traditions that confined me. Once again, his insight took me by surprise. "It's kind of you to consider things from his perspective. Most people only see the privileges that royalty have and not the limitations that come with them."

Sean nodded in agreement. "It does come with great advantages, but there are downsides too. Cassian knew that better than most."

"What was Cassian like?" Sean had asked me before, back in the carriage, what we knew of Cassian, and I had told him truthfully about the limited extent of our information. But from the things he had said, it seemed Sean *had* known him well. Although I would never meet the man myself, I still had some curiosity about the man who would have been my husband under other circumstances, especially as Sean had been close to him.

Sean smiled, looking away from me for a moment before turning his chestnut eyes back to mine. "He was a lot like me, actually. Too convinced of his own importance, too quick to judge others, and too caught up in his own world to see things taking place under his own nose."

"It sounds to me like you're being pretty hard on him, and on yourself." I definitely hadn't got that impression from Sean. "What were his good qualities?"

He smiled again but this time sadness tinged it, and guilt rushed through me. Perhaps he found it difficult talking about Cassian this way so soon after his death. I should have considered that. Elodie certainly would have.

Despite his discomfort, Sean answered me anyway. "He truly cared about his kingdom and the people there. He worked hard to make life better for them. Eric works hard to increase his own wealth and his connections, but Cassian didn't care about that. He simply wanted to help his people."

That certainly sounded noble, but my stomach sank at the reminder of Eric's temperament. Wondering what type of husband Cassian might have been did me no good, not when I had to marry Eric.

Sean shook his head, as if shaking away the memories, equally ready to move on. "Enough about the prince. Tell me more about you."

As we rode, I told him a few stories from my childhood, of the trouble that I dragged Elodie into, always taking care to ensure that in the stories, Elodie took the role of the princess while I was her companion. Sean, in turn, shared stories from Cassian's youth and the adventures they got up to.

At my request, he told me more about the court at Silatria, about the king and other players at court that Eric's new wife should be aware of. He impressed me with how remarkably well informed he seemed to be about all of it. Cassian must have really trusted him in order to share all the details with him that he told me now.

Almost before I knew it, we had exited from the woods we'd been travelling through most of the day, and a town appeared in the distance ahead of us.

"Is that where we're staying tonight?" I asked, gesturing to the collection of buildings.

Sean followed the direction of my point, looking surprised at the appearance of the town. "Yes, it must be. I thought it would take us longer to arrive."

Curiously, I looked at the position of the sun in the sky, judging it as I'd been taught. "We've been travelling nearly four hours since we stopped for lunch. How long did you think it would take?"

He laughed in surprise. "I guess about that much time. I just didn't realize it had been that long already."

It hadn't felt that long to me either. The time spent talking with him passed much more quickly than time usually did.

Soon enough, we arrived at the inn on the edge of town. Bran went inside to make arrangements for our rooms while Sean and I dismounted, and I noticed him wincing as he got down from his horse.

"Are you sore from riding sidesaddle?" I asked. "I'm sorry about that."

"No, you're not," he said with a laugh, and I had to smile again, especially since he had me pegged completely. I had no regrets about it. "And you shouldn't be. You beat me fair and square. Come, I'll help you and the princess inside, and then I need to come back out and take care of the horses."

I almost offered to help before remembering that it wouldn't be appropriate and Elodie would not approve. Instead, I followed Sean to the carriage where he helped Elodie out of the carriage and escorted us to our room.

"Someone will bring you supper shortly, Your Highness," he said, speaking to Elodie rather than me. "Everything else you should need is already in your room, but if there's anything that's been overlooked, please let us know."

Elodie nodded at him, and I gave him a grateful smile. "Thank you, Sean. Have a good evening."

"And you, Dee." His eyes were warm but I thought I could see a hint of something else in them too, almost as though he didn't want our time together to end.

Or maybe I simply saw the reflection of my own feelings in them.

I had never talked to a man that way before, so freely, so easily, laughing and joking and teasing. Was this how it felt to be a regular woman, without the pressures of my position, free to speak to whomever I chose?

"Did you behave yourself as you promised, Dee?" Elodie asked me as soon as the door closed behind us.

"Of course," I told her. I had been the picture of propriety.

For the most part.

Perhaps I shouldn't have told Sean about the time I convinced Elodie to help me put moths in my vain youngest brother's travelling case when he travelled abroad with my father, so that when they arrived at their destination, all his clothes were full of holes.

But what did it matter? Sean wouldn't tell anyone, and after we arrived in Silatria, we'd probably never seen him again.

I tried to ignore the twinge of disappointment that accompanied that thought.

After eating our supper, Elodie and I changed into our sleeping gowns and climbed into the one bed in the room. She told me one of her stories as we both lay there, a story about a princess who went out in disguise and beat all the kingdom's best horsemen in a race, until my eyes grew heavy and sleep overtook me.

When I woke up, darkness still filled most of the room. The sun's earliest rays were brightening the sky outside and Elodie's soft snores still filled the room, even though I knew she had slept most of the afternoon in the carriage. After using our private privy, I threw a cloak over my night dress and went down to the kitchen.

The busy room already bustled with activity and it took a moment for me to get anyone's attention to ask where I could get some water for the princess to wash with.

"The river's just outside," a large, red-faced woman told me, clearly unimpressed with the interruption. "Buckets are at the back. Go help yourself."

Although I knew I should ask one of our escorts to do it rather than going out alone, I had seen the river the night before when we arrived. It flowed just behind the inn, not more than a couple of minutes' walk. It would be quicker for me to go on my own than to go track down one of the others and wait for them to get up and do it.

Grabbing one of the wooden buckets from beside the back door, I headed through the trees and down the sloped hill towards the water. The sky continued to brighten but full daylight would still be some time away. Just as I reached the water's edge, the trees gave way and the full river came into view.

Including the very naked man with his back to me, standing in the middle of it.

~Cassian~

After taking care of the horses, I came back to find that Bran had already taken Princess Cordelia and Dee their supper, and an irrational annoyance shot through me that I hadn't been the one to do it instead. Just one more glimpse of Dee's enchanting blue eyes would have made the whole evening better for reasons I couldn't entirely explain.

As Bran and I sat down to our own meal, tucking ourselves away in a small corner table in the inn's dining area, he gave me an appraising look that instantly had my back up. I knew that look. Whatever he wanted to say to me, I wouldn't like it.

"I think I should handle looking after the princess and her lady from now on," he started, quickly confirming my suspicions. "You've had your distraction for the day, but let's not forget that there's still someone out there trying to kill you. You need to focus."

He did have a point. The assassination attempt hadn't really crossed my mind again from the first moment I laid eyes on Dee.

"And besides," he continued, "how are you going to explain this to them both once we arrive and they find out who you are? I talked to the princess while you and Lady Elodie were having your race. In the few things she said, it couldn't have been clearer how much they care about each other. They probably tell each other everything, so if you were even considering some kind of dalliance and hoping it wouldn't get back to the princess..."

"Stop, please." I put up my hands to protect myself from the barrage of words. The last thing I needed right now was another lecture from my best friend. "I know you're right. It's impossible for there to be anything between me and Dee."

He looked at me suspiciously, as if it couldn't be that easy to get me to agree. "So, you'll stay away from her?"

"I didn't say that."

Bran groaned. "I knew there would be a catch. Tell me: what is the point of spending time with her if nothing can come of it?"

I could only shrug. I barely knew how to explain it to myself, let alone to him. "I just feel different when I'm talking to her, like she understands the things I'm not saying as well as the things I am. I've never had this kind of connection with a woman before."

"But what do you hope to achieve?" he pressed, still not satisfied with my response.

"Nothing more than enjoying her company," I promised. "I know full well it's only for this week. But can't I just let myself have that, Bran? You know I always put my duty first, but this week, nobody knows what my actual duty is other than the two of us. And besides, Dee and I talked a lot about the princess. I feel like I know her much better already than I did before."

In Dee's admiration for her friend, I could see a glimmer of hope. Maybe I'd never be madly in love with my bride, but she seemed to be a genuinely decent person. That made me feel a little better.

"Talking to the princess directly might be more efficient," Bran pointed out drily.

"She's barely said two words to me," I countered. "She looks at me like I'm nothing but trouble."

He guffawed with laughter. "Sounds like she's got you sized up pretty well then."

My eyes narrowed in mock offense. "Maybe she does. But when the time comes for me to explain myself to them, I can say that I chose not to spend time with the princess herself because it felt dishonest to try to get her to open up to me while I concealed my true self."

He grudgingly agreed that I might be able to spin something from that, and I took the opportunity to move on to talking about other things.

When the time came to retire for the night, the four escorts and the driver were all sharing one room. The carriage driver snored loudly half the night as I tossed and turned, trying to get Dee's tempting smile and the sparkle in her eyes out of my mind.

I still lay awake when the first light of dawn started to break, and I rose from my bed, leaving the others still asleep. I needed fresh air and a wash, something to clear my head before beginning the day's journey. A river flowed just behind the inn, so I made my way down there now and, as I'd hoped, no one else had ventured out yet.

Stripping off my loose nightshirt and trousers, I waded into the shallow river until I found the deepest part, which still only came to the middle of my thighs. Cold but not freezing, the water made a good distraction from the warmer thoughts that had kept me awake most of the night. But as soon as that thought crossed my mind, so did the very images I had been trying to avoid: Dee's cheeky smile as she told me a story of mischief from her youth, her blonde hair blowing lightly in the wind, and her hand wrapped around the pommel of the saddle, just the way it would look wrapped around my...

I groaned in frustration as my arousal started again, the blood rushing to my cock completely against my will, the complete opposite of what I had been trying to achieve. I came out here trying to cool off, not to get more turned on.

"Sean?"

The voice came out of nowhere. I had been so lost in my own thoughts, I'd completely lost track of my surroundings. Before I could even think about my actions, I spun around and there she stood, straight out of my dreams, her blonde hair hanging completely free, wearing nothing but a loose gown and an open cloak.

Even though she had said my name, Dee looked just as surprised to see me as I was to see her, and as her eyes darted downwards, her cheeks began to colour.

I glanced down too and quickly saw exactly what had caused her blush.

I was fully erect and completely exposed.

For a moment, my body seemed to forget how to move. I wanted to cover myself, but when I tried to, nothing happened. Agonizing seconds passed as I tried to force my body into submission.

After what felt like an eternity, I dropped down to my knees on the riverbed, the water covering me to my waist.

"What... uh, what are you doing out here, Dee? On your own?" I tried to make the question sound normal and not as though it came from someone still completely naked and hard because of her.

In fact, the sight of her standing there, watching me, made me even harder. Her flushed cheeks made her more beautiful than ever, and instead of averting her eyes or running away, as many ladies would have done, she appeared to be fighting back a smile.

Did it please her to have caught me in such a compromising position? Or did she like what she'd seen?

I couldn't begin to guess if she had any experience of men. Many ladies did, trusting their family connections to secure them an appropriate marriage regardless of their state of purity, but many others didn't, preferring or perhaps being forced to remain chaste until they were properly wed.

Which category did Dee fall into? I really couldn't tell.

"I need some water for the princess' toilette," she told me, holding up a bucket in her hands that I hadn't even noticed until now. "I didn't realize we could just come and bathe in the river."

I laughed in surprise as she teased me. I should have known she wouldn't scare so easily.

"It's by invitation only," I replied, matching her tone. "And it's quite full right now, as you can see."

I spread my arms to encompass the completely empty waterway around me.

Her lips twitched in amusement, getting the joke completely. "Another time, then."

Bending down, she ran the bucket through the water. The neck of her gown gaped as she leaned over, affording me the briefest glimpse of her ivory skin beneath it before she stood back up and turned back to the inn.

"Wait," I said. "You really shouldn't be out here on your own, Dee. Let me walk you back."

She raised her eyebrows in amusement. "I hardly think you're a respectable chaperone in your present condition."

I bit back my own grin, her easygoing manner lifting my spirits even further. "Hand me my shirt and I can make myself presentable."

I pointed to my discarded clothing just a few yards from where she currently stood. Dee set her bucket down and picked up my nightshirt, which would be long enough to give me a reasonable amount of modesty.

I waded toward her on my knees, getting as close as I could without exposing myself to her again, while Dee stood at the water's edge, stretching her arm out to me.

We couldn't get quite close enough.

"Hang on," she suggested, quickly slipping off her soft shoes and removing her cloak. Now, she wore only the white linen nightgown, and as the sun began to peek above the horizon, the sunlight seemed to pass straight through her dress, showing me the full silhouette of her body beneath the gown.

Somehow, I had never seen anything sexier, and I couldn't actually see any of her.

Lifting the bottom of her gown with one hand to keep it dry, Dee stepped gingerly into the water, my shirt still in her other hand.

"Be careful," I warned. "There are some slippery rocks."

"I'm fine," she assured me. She stretched out her arm again, reaching towards me with the shirt.

As I reached for it, our fingers brushed against each other, sending warmth through my whole body. She must have felt something too because she pulled her hand back quickly. *Too* quickly, it turned out, as the sudden motion made her lose her footing.

The next thing I knew, she stumbled towards me, into my arms, and we both fell backward into the water together.

~Cordelia~

The cold water stole my breath away as I found my whole body submerged in the chilly river. It must have only been a second or two before strong arms pulled me up again, but I gasped for air as if I had been under for minutes instead of seconds.

"Dee, are you okay?" Concern filled Sean's voice, and I opened my eyes, looking up to find his face inches from mine.

His chestnut-brown eyes were so close that I could almost see myself reflected in them. Our noses were almost touching and his breath warmed my skin. Somehow, my hands were laid flat on his bare chest, my fingers resting against the damp hair there, just as wet as the rest of us. I could feel the beating of his heart beneath my hand, strong and fast. His arms were around me, holding me upright, somehow firm and gentle at the same time.

Everywhere we were touching felt warm and tingly. I had never been so aware of every inch of my body in my whole life.

"Dee?" He repeated my name, reminding me that I hadn't answered him yet.

"I'm fine," I said quickly, the words tumbling out of my mouth as I attempted to laugh off the whole situation. "It just took me by surprise and now I'm wet and cold. But I'm fine."

Fine might have been an exaggeration. My body had never felt this way before, leaving me to conclude that there must be something wrong with me.

Ever since the moment I saw him this morning, I had felt strange. Once I got over the surprise of seeing a naked pair of buttocks in front of me, I quickly realized they must belong to Sean. Not only from the lean, toned shape of his body, although that had been a good clue, but also from the bruises across the back of his thighs. Those must be from his sidesaddle riding the day before.

I hadn't wanted to startle or embarrass him, so I simply called out his name to alert him to my presence, but when he turned around, the rest of the world seemed to fade away.

I had seen the male anatomy before. I grew up with three brothers who weren't shy about whipping theirs out whenever nature called.

I could remember one hunting trip when I was twelve or thirteen, watching the three of them having a contest to see who could spray the farthest.

I understood the basics of it.

But Sean's bore little resemblance to the ones I had seen before. He was a full-grown man, for one thing, so of course it would be bigger. That made sense, but I hadn't known it would be quite *that* big.

He simply stood there for a moment, not seeming to care about his nudity, and I couldn't tear my eyes away even as my cheeks flamed from all the thoughts going through my head.

Clearly, he was aroused, though I couldn't begin to guess at the reason for his arousal. I knew from listening to my ladies talk, the ones who happily went to bed with men like Prince Eric, what happened to a man when something turned him on. I thought I knew as much as I needed to know, but seeing the full effect in the flesh, as it were, exceeded all my expectations.

And since that moment, there had been this odd almost rhythmic pulsing feeling inside of me, as though an additional heartbeat had taken up residence somewhere between my legs.

I tried to act as though nothing had changed, to tease him and talk to him the same way I had yesterday, and I had mostly succeeded too.

Until I found myself in his arms, his naked body pressed against me as the cool water ran around us. Now, the pulsing feeling had grown even stronger than before, and something new had joined it, an aching, empty sort of feeling, deep inside.

As soon as I mentioned being cold, his arms tightened around me as though he could transfer his own body heat to me. My soaked nightgown hardly provided any insulation, or any protection from the feel of his body against mine. My nipples were hard; probably from the cold, I figured. As I shifted against him, trying to balance myself better on my knees, my hands went to his arms and my chest pressed against his, the stiff peaks rubbing against him in a way that sent a shockwave of pleasure straight through me, like nothing I had felt before.

"We should get back inside and dry off." Sean whispered the words as if it pained him to speak, or if the words were secret, meant for our ears only. I couldn't tell the difference.

Or perhaps I imagined his tone entirely. His words were sensible. Going inside was exactly what we should do.

And yet, neither of us moved.

"Dee." He whispered my name, his eyes still fixed on mine. It sounded like a request, like he wanted my permission for something.

"Sean?" My reply came out breathy and light, the word floating away into the air.

Though I couldn't say exactly what was happening, I knew I didn't want it to stop. I wanted to be closer to him, even though I was already so close that I could nearly drown in the warmth of his gaze.

Completely involuntarily, my lips parted, letting out a quiet sigh of contentment, and Sean's grip tightened even further, pulling my hips flush against his for the first time. If I had thought his cock looked big from a distance, nothing compared to the feel of it, hard and firm, pressed up against my stomach.

His face stayed next to mine, looking into my eyes as he waited for me to order him to release me.

I should do that. The prince hadn't even wanted me talking to or eating with other men on this trip. He definitely did not want me embracing a naked one in the river while soaking wet myself.

And yet, I couldn't summon the words. My mouth refused to speak them.

Because I didn't want him to let me go.

"What exactly is going on here?"

The loud voice made both Sean and I jump and he quickly pulled back from me, leaving just one strong hand on my arm to keep me steady.

On the riverbank stood one of the other escorts, the one Sean called Bran, staring at us both with an expression that reminded me very strongly of the disapproving look that Elodie gave me when she caught me doing something she thought I shouldn't.

Sean quickly moved in front of me, shielding me from view, and only then did I realize that my white linen dress had turned almost completely sheer in the water.

"We had an accident," Sean answered, his voice sounding calm and cool and completely at odds with the way I felt. While my heart raced a mile a minute, he sounded utterly in control. "Can you grab Lady Elodie's cloak, please, to cover her up as she gets out?"

Pursing his lips, Bran did as Sean asked, picking up my discarded cloak and holding it up while averting his eyes to give me some privacy. Taking my arm, Sean helped me to my feet and held onto me while I stepped out of the water and into the waiting cloak, wrapping it around myself to cover as much as possible.

When I turned back, Sean had put on his dry trousers, but the shirt I had tried to give him had naturally been soaked during our fall. He left it off, and I couldn't help but stare at the firm muscles of his chest while my fingers twitched at my sides, remembering the way his skin felt beneath them.

"Can you offer Lady Elodie your arm to help her back to the inn?" Sean asked. "I'll bring her bucket."

I had almost forgotten the bucket of water, the whole reason I had come out here in the first place.

"Of course," Bran agreed, and soon we were walking arm-in-arm as Sean followed behind. When we reached the door to my room, I held my arms out to take the bucket from him.

"I need to help the princess get ready now," I told them both. "When are we leaving?"

"Not for another two hours," Bran answered. "I will bring you some breakfast shortly, and then collect you when we're ready to leave."

I nodded in agreement. "Thank you."

My eyes moved to Sean, waiting for some kind of sign from him, something to tell me what he might be thinking or that what had just happened between us meant something to him too, but his face had returned to its usual half-smiling expression.

"My lady," he said formally, bowing before turning and walking away down the hall, his naked back the last thing I saw before heading back into my own room.

CHAPTER FIVE

As soon as we were out of sight of the princess' room, Bran grabbed my arm and pulled me into an empty room at the end of the hall.

"What the hell were you doing?" he demanded in a furious whisper, his face inches from mine. "Last night, you told me that nothing was going to happen!"

"I didn't plan for anything to happen," I protested, his stern tone making me feel like a child who'd just been caught sneaking sugar from the castle kitchen. I hadn't been scolded this way in a long time. "I went to the river to get washed up, Dee came to get water for the princess, and she fell in. Like I said: an accident."

"And she conveniently fell right into your arms?" Bran guessed sarcastically. "While you were completely naked."

It sounded implausible at best, but I could only shrug. "Pretty much."

He obviously had his doubts, and I couldn't really blame him, but I really hadn't meant for it to happen. And now, I wanted her even more than I had before.

My first thoughts as I pulled Dee up out of the water centred around her safety, naturally, but as soon as I knew she hadn't been injured, all I could do was stare at her. The water droplets clinging to her eyelashes and her lips somehow made her even more beautiful than ever. Or perhaps I had just never been quite that close to her. Those beautiful blue eyes looked straight back at me with no pretense and no agenda;

the whole situation took her by surprise just as much as it did for me, and she lost herself in the moment just as much too.

All the women I had been with before – and truth be told, their numbers were relatively small – had all been aware of my position in life from the very beginning. They could tell me they liked me for my company, or my wit, or even my body, but my crown always played a part too, somewhere in the back of their mind. A part of them always wondered exactly what a relationship with me could bring them. I'd be naive to expect otherwise.

Dee knew nothing about any of that, though. She saw me simply as Sean, a soon-to-be-unemployed prince's aide. The lady-in-waiting to the future Queen of Silatria shouldn't even deign to look at a man like that.

She did more than look. Her fingers pressed against my chest and her body melted against mine until all I could think about was possessing her, at least momentarily. And when I really went too far, pulling her against me and letting her feel my desire for her, she didn't slap me or pull away or do any of the things that a lady should.

Instead, I could see an answering desire on her face. She felt something for me too, I could tell, but uncertainty hovered there too, and that look stopped me from kissing her hard right then and there.

Her feelings confused her, and innocence had to be the source of her confusion. She was either a virgin or a very good actress, and nothing about any of my interactions with her so far suggested she had been acting.

So, even if I could get past the fact of her being my future bride's best friend, I had to consider her prospects too. If she hadn't been intimate with a man before, there must be a reason, and I had no right to ruin things for her.

My brother wouldn't have hesitated. He never worried about questions of morals or honour, but to me, the situation presented itself clearly.

Her innocence wasn't mine to take.

Therefore, I would have to actually listen to Bran's advice and stay as far away from her as possible for the next six days. Those were my orders anyway. How difficult could it be?

By the time I had changed into my dry uniform for the day and tended to the horses, we were almost ready to go. Bran took the princess and Dee their breakfast and went to collect them as I talked over the day's route with John and Thomas. The carriage driver kept to himself, as he had most of the previous day. He seemed to be a man of few words.

A flash of colour in the corner of my eye told me that the women had joined us, but I forced myself not to look as Bran helped them both into the carriage. I could hear Dee's voice and Bran's deeper one in reply but I couldn't make out what they were saying.

Once he'd closed the carriage door behind them, Bran walked over to me, his lips pressed tightly together. "Lady Elodie asked if she could ride again for a while today. You can make the call, but I'm not giving up my horse this time."

I couldn't argue with that. Yesterday couldn't have been comfortable for him, and no matter how much I had enjoyed Dee's company, I wouldn't purposefully put Bran through that again. "She can have mine this afternoon. I'm bruised from yesterday, so by the time we stop for lunch, I'll probably be ready for a change of position."

"And you'll be okay with her riding with me, or one of the others?" Bran asked.

The question was obviously a test. He wanted to know if I felt possessive over her attentions in any way.

I forced a casual smile, at odds with the tightness in my chest. "Doesn't make any difference to me."

Whether he bought my nonchalance or not, he seemed pleased that I'd made an effort. "Alright. You and I can ride together this morning so we can talk. After lunch, you can have the carriage seat."

With that settled, we all mounted our horses and set back out along the road to Silatria.

The road ahead of us today wound mostly through the forest again, but after that, the route would become more challenging. A series of hills sat between Lassaria and Silatria, and traversing them would take us at least three days before we hit the more open space of the Silatrian plains.

John and Thomas took the lead this morning, the princess' carriage behind them, with Bran and I bringing up the rear.

It meant that if I looked forward, I couldn't avoid looking at the carriage and thinking about Dee and what she might be doing inside of it.

Desperate for a distraction, I turned to look at Bran instead. "You said in your letter that you'd started making a list of possible suspects. People who you think would benefit from my death?"

"Right." Bran looked relieved that I wanted to talk business. "The first one is Eric. With you gone, along with being next in line for the throne, he also takes your titles, your lands, your accounts, and your bride."

He gestured towards the carriage, bringing my thoughts back to Dee again. I forced myself to concentrate.

"I don't think Eric is involved," I countered. "My father's always been more than fair to him. He's got his own titles and lands already. Besides, Eric has always been more interested in making money for himself than running the kingdom anyway. Diplomatic meetings bore him. And a wife? He'd much rather spend his time in the local brothel. He's probably more upset than anyone that I'm gone."

Bran pursed his lips, a sure sign that he disagreed with me. "Then what reason did he have for being in Lassaria when we were attacked? Why did he turn up at King Alfred's castle at all?"

I had no good answer for that, but I still felt certain my brother didn't actually want me dead. "Let's put him aside for now as a maybe," I suggested, wanting to move on to other, more likely suspects.

The morning passed quickly as Bran and I ran through all the possibilities, all the people I had ever offended or who might prefer Eric to be king instead of me. I had a few rivals and a few enemies, as anyone in my position would, but nobody jumped out to either of us as any more obvious or likely than the others.

"It could be someone completely unknown," Bran suggested as we reached a clearing in the forest that made a good stopping place for a rest and some food.

John and Thomas turned their horses off the road and the carriage followed, the wheels bumping roughly over the uneven terrain. I winced as I imagined Dee getting tossed around inside it.

"It could be another kingdom entirely," he continued, unaware of my wandering thoughts. "Or even someone in Lassaria itself."

"So, we've talked all morning and we've narrowed it down to someone in the world?" I summarized wryly.

Although he shot me a dirty look, he couldn't disagree. We had nothing concrete to show for our discussion.

"Maybe it's worth talking to the princess," Bran suggested. "She might have some insight into the internal workings of the Lassarian nobility."

"We're not supposed to talk to her," I reminded him, and he raised his eyebrows back at me.

"Because you've been sticking to the rules so well up until now?"

I sighed as I dismounted my horse, wincing again at the bruises on my legs. "Alright, fine. Lady Elodie wanted my horse this afternoon anyway, right? She can have it, and I'll come up with an excuse to ride in the carriage with the princess. Who knows? Maybe I'll even fall in love."

~Cordelia~

Elodie sat on the edge of the bed, wide awake, when I walked into our room at the inn with the bucket of water from the river. I had hoped to get in and get changed before she could see the state of me, but apparently, fate had other plans.

Her mouth fell open as she took in my damp hair and the puddle of water collecting beneath my feet from my dripping-wet nightdress. "Dee! What happened? Did you get caught in the rain?"

She turned to the window where the sun had started to stream in brightly, and then looked back at me with a look of such genuine confusion and concern for me that, if I weren't soaking wet, I would have rushed over and given her a hug.

Obviously, the weather offered no excuse, so I would have to give her the real explanation, or something very close to it. "I went to get water for washing," I explained succinctly, setting the bucket down on the small table in the room and flexing out my hand to alleviate the strain in it. "I slipped and fell in the river."

Elodie gasped in horror, her hands flying to cover her mouth. "Are you alright? Did you hurt yourself?"

In an instant, she moved to my side, pulling my cloak off, also wet now from the contact with my drenched dress, and then, before I could protest, she had my dress off, checking over every inch of me for scrapes or bruises.

"I'm fine, Lodee," I promised. "I'm simply cold, and even colder now that you've taken all my clothes away."

She ignored that remark, continuing to check me over until she had satisfied herself that no harm had come to me. Only then did she move to the small chest of travelling clothes that Bran had brought up for us the night before and pulled out a dress and undergarments for me, turning me to face the small mirror in the room.

"What were you doing down at the river by yourself?" she demanded as she tied up the laces of my chemise, tighter than strictly necessary. "Someone from the inn or one of our escorts should have brought the water."

"I asked in the kitchen, but they were busy. Besides, I met one of the escorts at the river," I admitted. "He helped me when I fell in."

Her eyes opened even wider than they had before. "Someone saw you in that wet dress? Dee, it was nearly transparent!"

"He didn't look," I assured her, telling a partial truth. Sean had been much too close to me to look at my dress.

As I thought of the way he held me and the way his body felt against mine, my body began to warm up considerably and Elodie noticed the flush in my cheeks with alarm. "You're going to catch a fever! You're burning up now. Maybe we should stay here until you feel better."

"I feel perfectly fine," I tried to tell her, but she ignored me. Her hand went to my forehead and I could tell that in a moment, she would be ready to pull my clothes back off to put me back to bed.

I had no choice but to tell her the truth.

"It's not a fever, Lodee, but if I'm being honest, I do feel strange."

"Strange? In what way?" The concern in her eyes as she looked at me in the mirror melted my heart. She truly only wanted the best for me.

I struggled to find the words to explain it. We had never really talked about men before, not in a strictly physical way. We talked about the type of men we would like, or if we considered someone handsome or not, but Elodie had always had far more interest in those kinds of conversations than I did.

Until now, anyway.

"Have you ever felt warmer when you think of a certain person?" I asked tentatively. "Almost as if your blood is running faster through your body?"

To certain parts of my body in particular, in actuality, but I had no intention of telling her that right now. It might give her a heart attack.

She pursed her lips as she answered me as honestly as she could. "When your mother yells at me, I feel like all the blood goes and hides in my toes. Is that what you mean?"

She couldn't be any gentler and sweeter if she tried. "No, not like that. I mean when you think of a man."

I couldn't say what I expected her reaction to be, but I certainly didn't anticipate the blush that crept into her own cheeks now.

"Lodee!" I exclaimed, genuinely shocked as I whirled around to look at her face-to-face. "Who is he?"

"It's silly," was all she said, trying to brush me off. "We're talking about you, anyway. What man is making you feel strange, Dee? Certainly not that awful prince."

"No, not him," I agreed with a sigh. I would prefer to forget his existence. For a moment, I hesitated over whether to tell her the full truth, but I had already gone this far. I might as well tell her everything. "It's one of his men, one of our escorts."

"Which one?" Once again, her reaction caught me off guard. I expected her to be angry with me, but instead she sounded almost nervous.

"The one who came into our carriage," I told her. "The one I raced against. His name is Sean."

Immediately her face cleared into a rather relieved expression. "Oh. Well, I suppose he is handsome, in a way."

In a way? In pretty much every way, in my opinion, and as it came back into my mind, the memory of the sight of his naked body in the river made my body heat up even more.

Elodie picked up my outer dress and helped me into it, tying it up as I turned back to the mirror.

"You're not encouraging him, are you, Dee?" Her concern came back in full force as she thought over what I'd said. "Remember that as soon as we arrive, everyone will know who you are and anything you did on this trip could be reported to your new husband. I already dread to think what the prince will say if he hears about that horse race."

"I'm not encouraging anyone," I promised. I hadn't intentionally fallen into his arms. "I just felt it for the first time this morning, and I'm only curious because it's something new. It will pass."

At least, I hoped it would, although part of me also hoped it wouldn't. The whole situation felt exciting and just a touch dangerous, rather like Sean himself.

When we'd finished getting ready and had eaten and packed all our clothes away, Bran came to escort Elodie and I back to the carriage. Disappointment stabbed at me that Sean hadn't been the one to come, even as I tried to push it down, and when I tried to catch Sean's eye out in the stable yard, he didn't seem to notice me.

That might be for the best, I tried to tell myself. Thinking of him in any capacity other than as our escort could only lead to trouble. I shouldn't seek him out, so if he paid me no attention, that would make things easier.

I asked Bran if I might ride again this afternoon and he promised to speak to the other men for me to see if anyone would be willing to give up their horse. Once he had closed the door behind us, I settled in for the morning ride with Elodie.

"Will you tell me a story, Lodee?" I asked, leaning back in my seat. My early start to the day and the warm air in the carriage were catching up with me and sleep pulled at my eyelids. Perhaps Elodie and I would both have a nap this morning.

"Of course," she agreed, always eager to please. She launched into one of her tales and the next thing I knew, I startled awake as the carriage bounced around us.

Less than a minute later, we came to a stop as Elodie rubbed her eyes. We must have both slept the whole morning away. The men were outside getting off their horses and pulling out things for lunch, just as they had the day before.

This time, I waited until one of the men came over to help us down, and once again, Bran came to assist rather than Sean. It certainly felt like Sean was avoiding me, and though I had just decided that would be a good thing, it troubled me too. Perhaps he felt embarrassed about me seeing him this morning? He certainly hadn't seemed shy about it at the time, but I had no other explanation for the sudden change in him.

After taking advantage of the opportunity to stretch our legs for a while, Elodie and I returned to the carriage and ate our lunch alone. I began to worry that Bran had forgotten about my request to ride this afternoon, but just when I started to give up hope, a knock sounded at the carriage door.

"Yes?" I called out, and the door swung open, revealing both Bran and Sean on the other side. Sean leant against his colleague, holding his foot off the ground.

My chest tightened the thought of him being injured, though it had nothing to do with me, and I quickly took Bran's hand and descended the carriage steps to stand in front of them. "What happened?"

"It's an old injury that bothers him from time to time," Bran explained. "But it does make it difficult for him to ride. If you were still interested in taking one of the horses this afternoon, it would actually be helpful for us."

"Yes, of course," I quickly agreed, though another pang of disappointment hit me at the realization that I would not get to ride next to Sean again.

Bran gave me a polite nod. "That's very helpful, my lady, thank you. And if it wouldn't be too much trouble, I would like to put Sean in the carriage. He needs some space to stretch out his leg and the driver's bench doesn't have it."

Though it made sense, his request still went against all the instructions we'd been given. I tried to remember what Elodie had said about how I needed to act more like her in my new role and I put on my best impression of her.

"The princess cannot spend time alone with any man." They should be well aware of that.

"I wouldn't ask if there were another option, my lady." Sean hadn't spoken to me since this morning, and as I met his chestnut eyes, I could see the restraint in them, suggesting he was holding himself back from saying what he really wanted to say. "I promise I will not bother Her Highness at all. She won't even know I'm there."

Indecision gnawed at me. Elodie would not be pleased to have to spend the afternoon with him, but if he genuinely kept to himself, what harm could it do? She would likely doze for most of the trip, and even if she didn't, Sean wouldn't do anything forward. He had me in a much more compromising position this morning and he had been more restrained than many other men would have been. He must be aware of the repercussions of taking any kind of liberties with the prince's fiancée and he didn't strike me as foolish enough to take that kind of risk.

As if he were aboard my train of thought, Sean gave me his charming half-smile. "You trust me, don't you, Dee?"

God help me, I did, though I couldn't for the life of me say why.

"Alright," I acquiesced. "Just for an hour or two. Once you're feeling better, we can switch back."

"Thank you." His eyes seemed to pierce into me as he said it, and I almost took a step towards him, completely unintentionally, until Bran brought me back to the moment.

"That's all settled then. Sean, let's get you in, and Lady Elodie, I'll help you onto your horse."

Limping a little, Sean climbed the steps into the carriage and, after a few words, Bran shut the door behind him. I apologized silently to Elodie in my mind, hoping she wouldn't be too upset with this new development, before following Bran back to the horses.

~Cassian~

Princess Cordelia's eyes went wide as I climbed up into the carriage and settled into the seat across from her. I offered her a smile of reassurance, but instead of returning it, her eyes went frantically to the door where Bran still stood.

"Where is Lady Elodie?" she asked, her voice squeaking in panic, and I tried not to wince at the high-pitched sound. It couldn't begin to compare to Dee's sultry voice and her teasing, confident tone.

"We apologize for the inconvenience, Your Highness." In addressing her, Bran's voice adopted a formal yet soothing tone that I had never heard come out of his mouth before. I couldn't help raising my eyebrows at him in surprise, but he paid no attention to me, focused entirely on the princess. "Sean has aggravated an old injury and needs to rest just for a short while. Lady Elodie has offered to ride his horse while he recovers. I promise that he is a gentleman and will defer to your wishes at all times. You have my word."

He bowed to her, looking rather like an obedient lapdog, and I had to stifle a laugh. He never behaved so politely and formally with me, or even with my father. Who knew that he had it in him to be so chivalrous?

Cordelia's look of panic receded as she listened to him, but when she glanced back at me, her eyes were still wary. She replied to Bran as if I weren't there. "I suppose it will be alright for just a short time, but I would like my lady back as soon as possible."

"Of course, Your Highness," he readily agreed. Shooting me a look that clearly meant 'behave', he closed the door behind him.

The princess quickly pulled open the curtain on the opposite window so that she could look outside rather than looking at me, and I also stayed silent for a few minutes, trying to put her more at ease as I decided how to begin.

Once we started moving again, I tried some small talk. "How are you finding the journey so far, Your Highness?"

Her eyes darted to me nervously, like I had asked her something intensely personal rather than the most mundane question I could think of.

"It's fine." She clasped her hands together tightly in her lap before turning back to the window.

"Have you travelled often?" I asked next. In the stories Dee had told me yesterday from their childhood, they were almost always at home, but perhaps she travelled on her own.

"No."

Perhaps I should try a different topic. "Are you looking forward to seeing your new home?"

She pursed her lips as though the question had offended her in some way before offering me another one-word answer: "Yes."

This felt like pulling teeth. She seemed determined to give me nothing to work with, so perhaps I needed to open up first to set her at ease. "I have travelled quite a lot myself, but even so, I think Silatria is one of the most beautiful places I have ever seen. I'm certain you will enjoy it."

I smiled at her again, but a stone wall would have given me more of a reaction. Cordelia said nothing in reply, still looking out the window though I knew she could see me in her peripheral vision. She simply pretended she couldn't.

Not ready to give up yet, I tried another avenue instead. "What are your favourite things about Lassaria? Is there anything you will miss?"

She swallowed, appearing to think it over this time before answering just as shortly as before: "No."

With a great effort, I forced myself not to roll my eyes. Did she feel that a conversation with me was beneath her, or did she always speak like this? I couldn't really believe that, not when Dee seemed to think so highly of her. They must have proper conversations, which left me with the conclusion that it must just be me.

In which case, I didn't see any way I could get her to open up about people in the Lassarian court as I'd been hoping to. I would have better luck just asking Dee about it. She probably knew more about court intrigues than the princess did anyway. I should have just started with her.

Except that I should be staying away from her. A sigh of frustration crossed my lips before I remembered that I still had company. Thankfully, the princess pretended not to notice.

What should I do now? I still had a couple of hours before we stopped again and I would really prefer not to sit here in silence the whole time.

However, as I remembered how fondly Dee had spoken of the princess, a new thought came to me: perhaps the princess would be more willing to engage with me on the topic of their friendship, just as Dee herself had been eager to speak of her.

"I enjoyed riding with Lady Elodie yesterday." Immediately, the princess' attention focused on me. An encouraging sign, at last. "She is a very capable horsewoman, and a pleasure to speak with."

New interest sparked in Cordelia's eyes as she looked at me, but I could see caution too. "My lady has many fine qualities," she agreed. "I am very grateful for her company."

That felt like a slight directed at me. She might as well say she'd prefer Dee's company to mine, but I couldn't really blame her when I felt the same way.

"She spoke very fondly of your friendship," I told her honestly. "I know how rare such a true friend is, especially to someone in your position."

Perhaps I spoke too boldly, but if the princess wondered how I would know anything about being in a position like hers, she didn't mention it. She just continued to give me a curious, almost wary look.

"I want the best for her, always, even if she fights me on it sometimes."

That made me smile as I remembered how Dee had told me yesterday that the princess would describe her as stubborn. It appeared she hadn't been exaggerating.

"I hope you won't judge her too harshly if she is sometimes inappropriate," the princess continued, speaking far more words together than I had ever heard from her at one time before. "She wants to make the most of this trip before we arrive and settle down into our new life, so please forgive her if she is too forward."

I could understand that, certainly, even if it also confused me. The princess would be settling down when they arrived, but what did Dee have to settle into?

Before I could figure out how to ask the question, Cordelia answered it for me. "I don't know if she mentioned to you that she will be getting married upon our arrival?"

For just a moment, it felt like the world had stopped moving. Dee was engaged? She definitely hadn't mentioned that. And to someone in Silatria? Who would it be? My mind raced through all the eligible noblemen I could think of, friends of Eric that he might want to marry her off to when she arrived with her mistress.

The thought of Dee standing next to any of those men at the altar, or worse, lying next to them in bed, made me want to jump out of the carriage right now and turn her back the way we'd come.

Suddenly, the confusion in her eyes this morning in the river took on a whole new meaning. If she *did* feel an attraction to me, and I would have sworn in that moment that she did, she lacked the freedom to act on it. As did I, I reminded myself, sitting across from the woman I was meant to be marrying.

"It will be a happy occasion for both of you, then, when we arrive." I tried to smile again, but a bitter taste had filled my mouth and it probably came out closer to a grimace instead. "Is it a love match?"

Would it make me feel better or worse to know that Dee actually cared for the man she would marry? I couldn't say.

Despite it being none of my business, and I half expected the princess to tell me so, sympathy appeared in her eyes as she replied. "No, but we all must do our duty."

Truer words had never been spoken, and my duty had only become clearer through this conversation: I had to stay far away from Dee, for both our sakes.

CHAPTER SIX

On the way to the horses, Bran stopped at a trunk attached to the back of the carriage and pulled out a bow and a quiver of arrows, which immediately piqued my interest. Sean hadn't been armed yesterday as we rode, so why did Bran need weapons now? Curiosity got the better of me and I couldn't stop myself from asking about it.

"What are those for?"

Bran glanced towards the carriage door, double checking that we wouldn't be overheard. Even though it remained tightly closed, he leaned closer to me and lowered his voice anyway. "There have been some reports of bandits in the woods ahead. Hopefully it's nothing, but it's better to be prepared."

A thrill of excitement ran through me at the idea of actually running into real-life bandits. What an adventure that would be. "Shouldn't I carry a bow as well, then?"

He raised his eyebrows at me in surprise. "To do what?"

Of course, he would assume that I wouldn't know how to use it, so I quickly set him straight. "I'm very good with a bow and arrow. If we really might run into danger, it's better if we're both armed. And if nothing else, the sight of a lady aiming at them might surprise them so much that they turn tail and run anyway."

Bran's eyes widened in a startled look and, for a moment, we simply stared at each other. Did he not recognize my words as a joke? Sean would have thought it funny, I would bet. Just as I was about to give in and assure him I hadn't meant it seriously, Bran laughed, slightly nervously.

"I'm beginning to see why you and Sean got along so well yesterday," he said with a shake of his head. "And if you're certain that you can handle it, I suppose it wouldn't do any harm for you to have one. Just don't aim it at me."

I bit back the retort on the tip of my tongue, which would be to tell him that my aim was probably truer than his. Since he had given me what I wanted, it would be wiser not to antagonize him. Lodee would be proud of my self-control.

Bran handed me a small riding bow and a quiver of arrows matching his own. I slung the quiver strap across my chest and once I had mounted the horse, I attached the bow to the saddle, using a slip knot that I could undo quickly if it became necessary.

My riding companion watched me with a grudging kind of respect. "I must say, Lady Elodie, you are full of surprises."

"You have no idea," I told him with my most innocent smile.

The carriage began to move and Bran and I led our horses out together after it.

We chatted about the journey, making perfectly pleasant and meaningless conversation for several minutes before I tried to steer the conversation, as I had yesterday, towards my future husband. "Have you worked for Prince Eric for a long time?"

Bran grimaced before he could stop himself, just for a second, but long enough that I caught it. "No, not for long. I had previously been in the service of his brother, Prince Cassian."

How strange. Sean had told me the same thing. Why would Eric send a bunch of people who used to work for his brother to escort me? Did he have no men of his own?

In any case, I had already heard a fair bit about Cassian from Sean yesterday, so I had no interest in hearing about him again. I would much rather know about Eric.

"You must have spent some time with Prince Eric even then though," I suggested. "I am simply asking on behalf of Her Highness. She is curious about the man she is meant to marry."

As I mentioned the princess, Bran's eyes moved to the carriage and his expression softened. "It's difficult to imagine someone like her being married to the prince."

Personally, I found it difficult to imagine *anyone* being married to the prince, but I kept that comment to myself. "We have heard some rumours about him. I'm sure you can appreciate that she has some concerns."

He nodded, weighing his reply carefully. "Yes, I can imagine she would, but please, could you tell her not to worry too much about Prince Eric? Things may not be exactly as they appear."

What on earth did that mean? Before I could ask him, the sound of galloping horses caught our attention and I swivelled in my saddle to look behind us. Two masked men on horseback were approaching at great speed.

"Damn it." Bran swore under his breath, calling out orders as he pulled his bow off his back. "John! Thomas! To the rear, protect the carriage!"

Just as quickly, I undid the knot holding my bow, pulling an arrow from my quiver at nearly the same time Bran did.

"My lady, you should hide yourself," he instructed. "I can take care of two of them."

"Why give me the bow if not to use it?" I asked, refusing to budge. "And besides, you're not counting the other two."

"What other..." he started to say, but an arrow flying past us cut him off. It came from the trees as the two additional men I had already spotted came out from their hiding spot.

Clearly, they had set this up as a trap.

Taking aim at the men on horseback first, I sent an arrow straight into the first man's bicep on his shooting arm. That would stop him from shooting back at us.

"Duck!" Bran called out. I obeyed immediately and felt the wind of the arrow as it passed by my head from the side. A spike of adrenaline rushed through me at the close call as the horse whinnied nervously beneath me. Despite the danger, I had an overwhelming urge to grin. I couldn't remember the last time I felt so alive.

Reloading my bow, I quickly returned fire at the man on foot who had shot at me while Bran took care of the second man on horseback, sending him tumbling off his horse with an impressive hit.

"Nice shot," I complimented him, taking my own shot and hitting my target in the leg, leaving just one man left.

I had my bow loaded and ready to aim again when a hand suddenly reached out and yanked me down from my horse. I stumbled onto the ground and into a set of strong, steady arms.

"What on earth are you doing, Dee? Get inside the carriage where it's safe."

Sean's incredulous expression and commanding tone nearly distracted me, but I kept my attention on the man in the trees. Bran had shot at him twice but missed both times, and now the man's bow aimed squarely at Sean's back.

"Get behind me," I instructed, taking hold of him and twisting us both around so that I stood in front of him. Taking aim, I released my arrow at the same time the other man did, catching his arrow in mid-air and throwing it off course. Before he had a chance to pull his next arrow, I had already reloaded. My shot scored a direct hit on his hand which held his bow, and he dropped it with a cry of pain.

"That's all of them," Bran shouted to the others. "Track them down and round up their weapons so they can't do the same to the next group that comes through."

He, John and Thomas all dismounted and headed after the downed bandits on foot. Only when I lowered my bow did I realize that Sean's arms were still around my waist, my back nearly resting against his chest.

"Dee, you were amazing." He sounded genuinely impressed. "Where did you learn to shoot like that?"

"I learned alongside the Lassarian princes," I told him truthfully. "They were kind enough to let me train with them."

He blinked in surprise. "Does the princess also shoot?"

How could I explain why I had learned and she hadn't? I couldn't blame it on our positions, so I settled on our temperaments. "No, she preferred to stay indoors, but she and her family let me pursue my own interests from time to time."

It sounded suspicious even to me, but thankfully, Sean asked no further questions. Neither did he make any move to release me, and I found I didn't really want him to. His warm arms and the solid strength of his body behind me comforted me in a way I couldn't entirely describe.

Still, as much as I enjoyed his presence, I had promised Elodie that I wouldn't encourage him. Reluctantly, I cleared my throat and shifted my weight away, which seemed to wake him up to the inappropriateness of our close contact, and he quickly dropped his arms.

"I should check on the princess." I handed my bow and arrows to him. "You seem recovered enough to ride this afternoon anyway, it seems. Your limp seems to have vanished."

He blushed at my observation, which seemed suspicious. Why would he be embarrassed about that? Unless he had been faking the injury in the first place? To what end? It made no sense to me, but I really should check on Elodie and make sure the attack hadn't shaken her up too much, so I let it go.

"Dee." Sean's voice sounded tight as he said my name, and it stopped me in my tracks as quickly as if he had reached for me.

When I turned back to him, the tense, unhappy look on his face took me completely by surprise. "Who are you marrying?"

Why would he think I was marrying anyone? Had Elodie said something to him? I would have to check with her to find out exactly what she had said and make sure we had our stories straight, so for now, I did my best to brush him off.

"That's a long story, and I think I hear Her Highness calling for me. Please, excuse me, Sean."

I hurried back to the carriage before he could ask me anything else.

~Cassian~

Turmoil hardly began to cover how I felt as Dee walked away from me.

Ever since the princess had told me that Dee had a fiancé, I had been trying to convince myself that it didn't affect me. What did it really matter since I had also been promised to someone else?

But when the carriage stopped suddenly and I heard Bran's call, I jumped out of the carriage to offer my help in fighting off the attackers. No sooner had I stepped outside than I saw Dee sitting on her horse with her bow and arrow, looking like some kind of ancient goddess of the hunt. Her arm brushed her blonde hair back from her face as she drew the bow, an expression of pure concentration and determination on her face.

She had never looked more beautiful.

An arrow flew back towards her, reminding me of her exposed and dangerous position, which had to take precedence over her beauty for the moment. I ran to her, pulling her down from the horse, completely forgetting my surroundings and the fact that I had no weapon of my own.

But Dee never lost sight of it. She saw me in danger, threw herself in front of me and took out the incoming arrow with a precision shot which rivalled anything I had seen from my kingdom's best archers.

And when the danger had passed, thanks to Dee's quick thinking, and I felt her warm, soft body against mine again, I couldn't deny it anymore. I was falling for this woman, hard and fast.

She was my dream woman come to life. I hadn't known that women like her actually existed, and I couldn't turn off the way I felt any more than I could cut out my own heart.

That explained why I'd blurted out the question asking her for the name of her fiancé, though I couldn't say what I intended to do with that information once I had it. Banish that person from the kingdom? Throw him in my prison cells once I took back my position as crown prince? Even if I couldn't do anything, I had to ask anyway.

No one I could think of would be worthy of her and I included myself in that statement, but damn it all if I didn't want her anyway.

To my frustration, Dee brushed me off. She claimed we didn't have time to get into it, which only made my curiosity burn stronger, so I cornered Bran about it as soon as we were back on our horses and out on the road.

"Do you know who Lady Elodie is marrying when we arrive?"

He gave me an unimpressed look. "I didn't know she was marrying anyone, but it's not really your concern, Cass."

Since we were alone, I let his slip of my real name go. "The princess told me that Dee is engaged."

Bran's eyebrows raised even higher. "You spent your time with the princess talking about Lady Elodie? You were supposed to be finding out about people in Lassaria who might want you dead."

"I couldn't get the princess to tell me anything about Lassaria. Only when we talked about Dee did she tell me anything at all."

"You're too harsh with Princess Cordelia," Bran scolded me. "She's a gentle soul, anyone can see that. You can't talk to her the same way you talk to someone like Lady Elodie."

He had that right. "I don't think I behaved harshly at all, and since when are you so interested in how I talk to my fiancée?"

Bran looked like he had swallowed something sour when I used the word 'fiancée'. "Just be considerate of her, please. She thinks she's going to marry Eric. That wouldn't put me in a very good mood either."

I had to laugh at that, and the tension that had been building between us dissipated. "Well, if you don't know about Dee's engagement, then I'm going to ask her myself. When we arrive at the town tonight, can you stay with the princess for a while so I can speak to Dee alone?"

"Is that really a good idea?" I knew once again that Bran had my best interests at heart, so I took no offense to either his tone or the question.

"Probably not," I answered honestly. "But I'm going to do it anyway."

The afternoon had grown late by the time we arrived at the town we'd be staying in that night, the last town before the hills that we'd be travelling over for the next few days, and therefore the last night I'd be sleeping in a bed for a while. We would be staying at farmhouses the next few nights where Princess Cordelia and Dee would be given a room, but the men would sleep wherever they could find room for us. I would need to enjoy the comfort tonight while I had it.

Even so, I had no great desire to get to my bed anytime soon, not when I still needed to speak to Dee.

When supper had been prepared for Dee and the princess, I took it to their room myself. As I expected, Dee answered the door, greeting me with a bemused smile.

"Oh, hello. I thought you had given up on looking after us. I figured we weren't interesting enough for you."

Her gently teasing tone drew me in as always, drawing the smile to my face that never seemed far away around her. "On the contrary, I assumed you must be tired of me, my lady. But if you're not, perhaps you'd like to join me for a short ride this evening after you've finished eating. There's a very nice lake less than half an hour from here. Probably less with the way you ride."

She smiled at the compliment, but before answering me, she looked behind her into the room. "I would like to, but I'm afraid I can't leave the princess alone. She's still upset about this afternoon."

If the events of this afternoon had shaken anyone, it should have been Dee, but luckily, I had anticipated this. "I thought that might be the case, so Bran has offered to keep the princess company if she would like."

"I don't think that..." Dee started to say, but a murmur from inside the room cut her off. She ducked behind the door momentarily and returned a few seconds later with a rather amused look on her face. "Apparently, that is acceptable."

"Wonderful. I'll be back in around half an hour then."

I left them to have their meal while I went and resaddled two of the horses and collected Bran.

"You're sure the princess agreed to this?" he asked me suspiciously as we walked back to their room. "I don't want to impose myself on her."

"She agreed," I assured him. "In fact, Dee almost refused but the princess intervened to accept."

To my surprise, his neck turned slightly redder in response to that information, closer to the colour of his hair. Before I could discover the reason why, we arrived at their door, and Bran quickly knocked on it.

Dee swung the door open wide and gave us both a warm smile. "Good evening. Bran, the princess intends to spend the evening doing some embroidery by the fire. I trust that won't be too boring for you?"

That sounded like my idea of a nightmare, but Bran seemed to disagree.

"Of course not, my lady," Bran said, bowing politely. He had never bowed to Dee before, so I could only assume he did it now because the princess could see him. When I glanced over at Dee, I could see her holding back a smile, which only made it harder to keep mine in.

"I will be back soon, Your Highness," Dee said to the princess.

Cordelia nodded at her rather sternly. "Remember what we discussed, Elodie."

"Of course. See you soon."

She all but pushed me out into the hallway, closing the door behind her.

"Quick," she urged with a conspiratorial grin. "Let's get out of here before they change their minds."

~Cordelia~

Sean didn't offer me his arm as we walked out to the inn's stable, but he walked close enough that our arms brushed against each other once or twice, and my whole body tingled every time it happened.

I had no idea what he hoped to achieve by the two of us going for a ride tonight, but I couldn't pass up the opportunity. Chances to ride anywhere aside from our own lands at home came about so rarely, and I always loved to explore new places. Without the carriage to slow us down, we could ride properly, and the prospect of a real gallop in the evening air enticed me on its own.

Then there was Sean himself. Despite my very best efforts, ever since that moment we had shared in the river this morning, I'd been unable to get him out of my mind. The way he had held me again after the bandit attack had only made things worse.

As soon as I got back into the carriage with Elodie, I asked her about what Sean had said to me. "Did you tell Sean that I'm getting married?"

Elodie's eyes were wide with disbelief. "You just got shot at by bandits and you want to talk about *Sean?* What were you thinking, Dee? You can't put yourself in danger like that."

"I wasn't in any real danger," I said, brushing her off. "Those men were terrible shots."

A weary hand went to her forehead as Elodie closed her eyes and leaned back in her seat. "You're going to be the death of me, I swear. You could have been killed! And what if they come back? Why didn't the prince send more men to travel with us?"

"I'm fine," I assured her. "You're fine, we're all fine. We're well protected here, and a larger party would have attracted more attention. Bran is an excellent shot too, so if we get attacked again, I'm sure he can defend us."

That same little flush of colour that filled her cheeks this morning came back as I mentioned Bran's name, and I gasped as I connected the dots.

"Lodee! Do you like Bran?"

Instantly, her eyes shot open and she looked at me with an expression of near-terror. "What? No! Why would you say that?"

"Because it's obviously true," I pointed out, hardly able to keep the glee out of my voice. "And it's wonderful! He works for the prince. If you really like him, maybe Eric can arrange for you to be married. I can certainly ask him. Oh, Lodee, just imagine if you got to marry someone you really cared for. Maybe something good might come out of this whole awful wedding."

"Dee, please don't interfere," she begged, her face turning more and more pink by the second. "I do feel... something... when he's around, but I don't think he feels the same. And remember, he thinks I'm the princess. He thinks I'm you. So even if he did feel anything, he certainly wouldn't act on it. He would never do anything so dishonourable."

Her certainty of Bran's principles after such limited interaction with him made me smile, but I understood it, since I felt equally certain of Sean's character after our limited time together. "I'm certain he finds you enchanting, Lodee. Who wouldn't? And just imagine how pleased he will be when he finds out that you are not the princess!"

And imagine how disappointed Sean would be when he realizes who I am, I added in my head. Which brought me back to the first question I asked her, which she hadn't answered yet.

"This conversation about Bran is definitely not over, but if you really want to change the subject right now, you can tell me what you said to Sean about my marriage."

Elodie sighed, relieved that I had let her off the hook for now, though she clearly didn't want to talk about Sean either. "You said you weren't encouraging him, but it's obvious that he is interested in you. I gently let him know that you are already promised to someone else. That way, he won't get his heart broken."

The idea of Sean's heart breaking over me caused both a stab of pain in my own chest and a rather inappropriate rush of pleasure. "Well, he asked me who I'm marrying. What am I supposed to say to that? Did you give him a name?"

She had the good grace to look apologetic. "No, I didn't really think that far ahead. I guess you could just say it's one of Prince Eric's men?"

"Because it would be natural for the princess's lady-in-waiting to marry one of the prince's men, right?" I couldn't resist the chance to tease her and watch her blush again.

We moved on to talking about other things, with Elodie twisting my arm yet again to make me promise that I wouldn't do anything to lead Sean on, but even so, Sean hadn't left my mind the whole time. And now that we were here together, alone, the world felt full of possibilities in a way it never had been for me before. Even though none of my constraints had been removed, next to him, I somehow felt freer anyway.

"You can set the pace," Sean offered when we were both mounted on our horses. "I'll try to keep up."

His acknowledgement of how I had beat him in our race made me smile, and he grinned back at me with an easy charm that set my heart racing again.

Why did it seem that he had become even more handsome since I had decided that I should stay away from him?

I set off at a canter that Sean easily matched now that he rode his horse astride as usual, heading down another path into the forest that Sean pointed out to me. We didn't speak to each other, not wanting to shout over the sound of the horses' hooves, but I glanced over at him from time to time, noticing the skillful way he handled his horse and the way his thigh muscles tightened in response to the horse's movements. More than once, I looked over to find him looking back at me, and we both quickly looked away.

When we arrived at the end of the trail we'd been following, Sean pulled up his horse before jumping off to the ground. "We can tie them up here. It's just a short way further on foot."

I dismounted, following his lead, and he took the reins from me to secure the horses to a nearby tree, making sure they had access to some fresh grass and a small puddle of water too. Sean set out into the trees down a much smaller trail where we had to walk single-file. The walk didn't take long though, as he had promised, and soon, we emerged from the trail at the side of a large lake, surrounded by trees. The setting sun cast beams of light over the water, shimmering on its surface like pools of gold.

"It's beautiful," I breathed, looking out over the quiet, peaceful scene with a sense of calmness I hadn't felt in quite a while. "It feels like there's no one else in the world."

"Exactly," he agreed, and I turned to find his eyes fixed on me, and not on the lake at all. "Dee, I need to talk to you."

He *needed* to? That seemed dramatic. "I'm not going anywhere," I assured him. "Should we have a seat?"

Some large rocks further down the shoreline would work well enough, so we settled ourselves there as I waited to find out what Sean *needed* to talk to me about.

"Who are you supposed to be marrying?" he asked once we were both seated. "You said it was a long story. We have time now."

I had expected that question to come up again and I had prepared for it. "I might have exaggerated the length of the story. It's actually quite simple. As part of the marriage contract between the prince and princess, he arranged for me to marry one of his men. I think he meant it as a gift for Her Highness, to ensure I would be provided for. I haven't actually met him yet and don't even know his name."

The lie came quite easily from my lips. I could almost believe it myself.

"I don't remember that being part of the contract," Sean mumbled, his brow furrowing as he appeared to search his memory.

"You've seen the contract?" I hadn't counted on that. Would he know I had lied?

His own eyes widened in return. "Uh, I... I had a quick look at it when I worked for Prince Cassian. When it pertained to him."

That made sense, and it gave me an easy way out of getting caught in the lie. "Perhaps it is something Prince Eric had added in later."

"Yes, perhaps," he agreed, his face turning serious again. "Do you want to go through with this marriage, Dee?"

"It doesn't matter whether I want to or not," I told him truthfully, speaking now not of my fictional engagement, but the real one. "My feelings are not part of the equation."

"What if they could be?" The earnestness in his eyes seemed to steal the breath from my body. "I have some influence at the Silatrian court. If you really want to get out of this, I could arrange it."

He could? How much influence could he possibly have? And why would he expend it on my behalf?

I decided the last question interested me most of all. "Why would you do that?"

"Because I..."

He trailed off, looking out to the lake for a second as though the words he wanted might be hidden in the water.

"I don't want you to be stuck in a loveless marriage. I don't want you to be like me."

My heart sank with his words as I struggled once more to breathe. "You're married?"

That certainly hadn't come up before. And why should it matter to me? I couldn't be with him anyway, so why did the idea make me feel as though I had swallowed something pointy and heavy and hard?

"Not yet," he corrected me. "But I'm also engaged."

"Oh." I couldn't think of anything else to say without betraying my unreasonable disappointment. For a moment, we both sat in silence, our combined engagements creating a gulf between us that seemed impossible to bridge.

"Dee." Sean's face twisted into a grimace as he struggled over the next words to come out of his mouth. "I don't want you to think I say this lightly or that I don't respect the bonds of marriage. It can be a wonderful thing when it is based on love, but you and I both know that too often it isn't. Too often, it's simply a contract and nothing more."

Of course I knew that. It certainly applied in my own case, but I had no idea why he brought it up now.

"I have met my intended bride," he continued, grimacing again as he said it. "There is nothing wrong with her, but I don't love her, and I don't know if I ever will."

"Sometimes love takes time," I suggested gently, even though the idea of Sean falling in love with someone else made my stomach ache. "It isn't always an instant moment of realization."

"But sometimes it is," he countered, looking at me with such intensity that I knew he felt the same ache inside him. Although he didn't say the words, I knew right then that the moment we'd shared in the river this morning had meant something to him too. I hadn't imagined it after all.

He turned away, as if it hurt too much to keep looking at me, and another long moment of silence passed between us, both of us unsure how to move forward.

When he turned back, the intensity had gone but a depth of emotion remained in his chestnut eyes that spoke to the very heart of me. "I never thought I would feel anything like love, Dee. I never expected it at all. So, although I wouldn't say my engagement pleased me, I had resigned myself to it. But now, it all feels wrong. It feels like there's a whole other world out there that I never even knew existed, and I don't know how I can go back to living as I did before."

I knew exactly what he meant. Every moment spent in Sean's presence made the idea of spending the rest of my life with Eric even more unbearable than it had been before. Just knowing that a man like Sean existed, someone who could take a joke, who could make me laugh, who appreciated me for the things about myself that everyone else told me I had to hide, I couldn't help imagining what it would be like if I could be free to choose to be with him instead.

As soon as we arrived in Silatria, that door would be closed to me forever, but right here, right now, on the shore of this lake with no one else around, maybe it didn't have to be impossible.

Maybe, just for a little while, we could both pretend.

CHAPTER SEVEN

~**Cassian**~

I couldn't begin to anticipate how Dee would react to my words. Although I hadn't out-and-out said that she was the one who had changed my outlook on love, I didn't think I had to. She must know it, especially since I recognized the look on her face when I told her about my own engagement. It formed a mirror image of the way I felt when I thought about her with someone else.

The idea that she might feel for me even a fraction of what I felt for her made me feel so much better and so much worse at the same time. Because I *wanted* her to want me, even though I couldn't have her. It might be selfish, but I couldn't help it.

And no matter what I thought she might say in response, I never would have imagined the words that came out of her mouth next.

"I assume you don't have to get married until we get to Silatria?" she asked, her bright blue eyes watching me closely. I could almost see the gears turning in her head, but the point of her question eluded me.

"That's right. We're not stopping at any chapels on the way."

She rewarded me for that particular joke with a dirty look. "Well, I'm not getting married until we get there either. How much harm would it do to allow ourselves a small indulgence along the way?"

My heart rate instantly switched from a steady beat to an erratic staccato. What exactly did she have in mind?

"Indulge ourselves in what way?" I tried not to let my imagination run away from me before I knew what she meant.

"Well, Lodee and I… I mean, Princess Cordelia and I… we once switched places for a few days. She pretended to be me and I pretended to be her."

"That sounds complicated," I observed, not entirely sure what that had to do with our own situation. "You never slipped up?"

She gave me a sheepish smile. "Once or twice, but not too badly. My point is that it gave us a chance to experience life differently, just for a short time. We could pretend that the constraints of our respective positions no longer applied."

I could see the appeal of that. It actually had a lot in common with my current situation, posing as Sean instead of Cassian, but it surprised me that the princess had gone along with it. I had to assume it had been Dee's idea.

She continued her explanation almost nervously. "So, what if, just for the next few days, you and I switch things around too. We could pretend that I'm actually the one that you're going to marry, and I'm supposed to marry you. Just to see what it would be like."

The devil himself could not have given me a more tempting proposition.

But how could I possibly agree to it? When we arrived in Silatria, Dee would learn my true identity, she would tell the princess everything that had happened, and they would both hate me for it, and not without reason.

But how could I say no either, when Dee looked at me with those beautiful blue eyes, full of hope?

"That sounds wonderful," I told her slowly, trying to figure out the best way to phrase my response. "I'm only worried that it's not fair to my fiancée. I don't want to hurt her. As I said, she's a nice woman, she's just not someone I'm passionate about."

Dee gave me a soft smile that I hadn't seen from her before. "That's very noble of you to be concerned about her, but you wouldn't actually be doing anything wrong. It would just be pretend."

Apparently, I had overshot with my idea of what pretending to be engaged would consist of. I knew very well how I would like to pretend that Dee was my fiancée, but that didn't seem to be what she had in mind.

"And I won't tell anyone," she promised. "It would only be for times like now, when we're completely alone. In front of everyone else, we'll act just the same as we have been."

Though I still harboured some confusion over what she wanted to do when we were alone, I had to push her first on the other point, the one where she said she wouldn't tell anyone. "What if the woman I had to marry ended up being someone you knew? You wouldn't tell her then?"

The question took Dee by surprise, and she took a moment to really think about it, which I appreciated. I wanted her to be taking this seriously, because if we actually came to an agreement we could both be comfortable with, I intended to make the most of it.

"I trust you when you say you don't want to hurt her," she said after thinking it through, looking me straight in the eye. "And I trust that when you set out on this journey, you weren't looking for this. Neither did I. But it's happened, whether we were looking for it or not. And though it has to end, I would still rather know, just for a short while, what it would be like to be engaged to you. So no, I wouldn't tell your fiancé, even if you end up marrying my own mother."

Her irreverence made me smile as always, but a memory surfaced from our conversation the day before that pulled the corners of my mouth down again. "I thought your parents were dead?"

Dee's eyes widened in surprise. "Yes, that's right," she quickly agreed. "They are. I just meant theoretically, I wouldn't tell my mother, not that I wouldn't tell my actual mother."

Her uncharacteristically nervous rambling confused me, but I ignored it, not wanting to waste time on 'what if's any more. If we were going ahead with this, and it seemed we were, then I had far more important things on my mind.

"In that case: if we were engaged, Dee, what would we be doing right now?"

Her whole face lit up with delight, her eyes sparkling as she realized I had agreed to her game.

"Well, I think in a place like this, we might walk arm-in-arm as you tell me about all the wonderful plans you have for when we're married."

Her complete lack of guile charmed me utterly and frustrated me completely. I would have all kinds of plans for her if we were to be married, but I knew her thoughts right now were far purer. Pushing down my own urges, I put on my best smile and stood up, offering my arm to her. "Let's go for a walk, then."

Dee grinned as she laced her arm through mine and we set off further down the shoreline, following a narrow trail that circled the lake. The trail grew so narrow that we had to walk closer than could be considered proper, even for a courting couple, but I certainly didn't mind and Dee made no complaint either.

"So, Sean Moran," she began, surprising me by remembering the fake surname I had given myself. "Tell me about your house. How shall we live when I'm your wife?"

What kind of house would a man like 'Sean' have? I had no idea since I had always lived in a castle. But I *had* been with Bran to visit his parents once, so I tried to describe their house instead.

"It's not very fancy," I warned her. She had grown up in a castle too, as the princess' companion. Maybe she knew as little of how other people lived as I did. "Just a small house in town, not far from the castle so that I can be with the prince as needed. There are two bedrooms upstairs and the kitchen and sitting room downstairs. In the back is a small garden for vegetables and herbs."

"It sounds lovely," Dee assured me, a soft smile on her face. "But will two bedrooms be enough? What about the children?"

"Children?" I repeated, my voice slightly higher than usual as my mind immediately jumped to the process involved in creating children with Dee. "How many are you anticipating?"

"About eight," she replied airily, sending a rush of blood to my cock which made walking in a straight line more difficult. "But don't worry, I won't be like the ladies in the castle who take to their bed in the fourth month. I want to be working and taking care of the house until the day I need to be delivered."

I never knew what might come out of her mouth next, and I had no doubt that she would do it, too. God help her husband if he tried to confine her before she declared herself ready.

The thought of Dee's actual future husband soured my mood, and Dee noticed immediately, tuned into me in a way no one else ever had been. "What's wrong?"

"It's nothing." I didn't want to spoil her game by bringing reality back into it.

"Sean," she admonished me. "If we're to have a successful engagement, you need to tell me when things are bothering you. I want a marriage that's an equal partnership."

I wanted that too, even though I hadn't realized it until now, until meeting her. Still not wanting to tell her what had ruined my mood, I decided to try a different angle instead.

"I was just thinking about how if I had my fiancée in a beautiful, secluded location like this, I wouldn't only want to talk to her about houses and children."

"Oh?" Dee's eyebrows raised curiously. "What would you do?"

I stopped walking and turned to her, taking in the pretty flush of her cheeks, the softness of her lips, and the brightness of her eyes. "I would tell her how beautiful she is. How I have never seen another woman who's her equal."

"And what if she told you that she thought you were lying?" Dee teased, smiling back at me. But despite her confident question, I could see the way her pupils dilated as she looked up into my eyes, the way her breathing grew deeper, making her chest rise more than normal.

She felt the connection between us just as much as I did. It affected her just as much as it did me, no matter how much she tried to cover it up.

I whispered my reply. "If she doubted my words, I would show her that I meant it."

Before I could second guess myself, I leaned down and kissed her right on the lips.

~**Cordelia**~

When Sean started talking about how he would praise his fiancée for her beauty, I couldn't tell if he was being serious. Did he really find me beautiful, or did he say it as part of the act? We had only just begun, and already, I found it hard to tell the difference between the truth and the game.

Up until that point, I had been enjoying our conversation about his house and our future family. It reminded me of Lodee making up her stories for me, except this time, a handsome man had taken her place. I could pretend we were going to get married, but he was no more real than the men that Lodee made up for the heroine to fall in love with. The whole thing made for a pleasant daydream and nothing more.

But when he stopped and looked at me, when I saw the look in his eyes, I realized just how different this could be from pretending with Lodee.

This felt dangerous and exciting and scary and inviting all at once. I wanted to get closer to him, even though I knew I shouldn't. If I had any self-preservation, I would walk away and put an end to this right now, but my feet made the decision for me, staying planted firmly where they were.

And then he kissed me.

His lips were softer than I expected as they pressed gently against mine, and his beard tickled my skin as it brushed against my face.

He paused for a couple of seconds, giving me the chance to change my mind, to push him away or to run away as I had just been considering a second ago. Logically, I should do exactly that. Red flags waved at me behind my closed eyelids, telling me I had gone too far.

My mind raced through a million thoughts in that single moment as I tried to decide what to do.

I trusted Sean when he said he wouldn't tell anyone about anything that happened between us, so the idea of being found out didn't trouble me. And I couldn't make myself feel badly about kissing someone when I knew that Eric did far more and far more often.

However, what if, as Sean had suggested, I got to know his future wife once we arrived in Silatria? How would I feel every time I looked at her, knowing that I had kissed her husband?

On the other hand, they weren't married yet. In this moment, in our game of make-believe, he was engaged to me, and engaged people, ones who actually wanted to be engaged to each other, did kiss each other.

Or so I'd heard.

I had never actually kissed anyone before. The princess of Lassaria would never do such a thing. No man would have dared to try to kiss me, except perhaps Prince Eric himself if I had given him the slightest encouragement the night of my engagement feast.

But Sean didn't know any of that. He knew me only as a lady, not a princess, and he had no reason to think that I hadn't kissed men before. For all he knew, I could be like one of the ladies who had invited Eric into their beds during his stay with us, another Arabella Eastam who had no trouble doing whatever she pleased.

Did he need to know otherwise? Since I was already pretending, what could it hurt to pretend a little more?

I reached that conclusion in the split second that Sean's lips rested hesitantly against mine.

As a result, I neither pulled back nor ran away. Instead, I put my hands on his shoulders and pulled him closer to me, giving him all the encouragement he needed.

Strong arms circled my body, pulling me tightly against him, just like they had in the river this morning. And just like then, I could feel the evidence of his arousal against me, though at least this time, a few additional layers of clothing sat between us too.

Sean's mouth moved against mine harder now, the softness of the initial kiss giving way to a firmer, more insistent request. My lower lip caught in his teeth as he ran his tongue across it, and my knees suddenly felt weak as all the feeling in my body concentrated in one spot, that pulsing spot in my lower abdomen, close to where his hard cock pressed against me.

Everything about this was completely new to me, and yet it felt entirely right too. Since Sean obviously knew what to do better than I did, I tried to mimic his actions, pulling his lip into my mouth just as he had. It seemed to be effective since he groaned, shifting his body just enough that his cock lodged even more firmly against me. I hadn't imagined that something that could be so flexible could also become so rigid, like the strongest steel.

Feeling him against me and knowing that his state had everything to do with me made me moan involuntarily. My cheeks flushed with embarrassment, but as soon as my lips were open, Sean's tongue entered my mouth, taking full advantage of the window of opportunity. Another shot of desire ran through me as our tongues collided, joining the already intense throbbing feeling between my legs.

No wonder people liked kissing so much. This felt incredible, connecting me to my body like never before, making me aware of every little touch and every place we were in contact.

Just as the thought crossed my mind that I never wanted it to end, Sean suddenly pulled back, taking all my breath with him and leaving me panting as I tried to replace the air he'd stolen from me.

He turned away from me and put his hands to his face in what looked like frustration, or possibly guilt. Or perhaps, regret.

"Sean?" I asked tentatively once I had caught my breath. "Are you okay?"

A storm raged in his eyes as he looked back at me, conflicted and unsettled. "Was that your first kiss, Dee?"

Colour rose in my cheeks against my will. Had it been that obvious? I thought I had done okay. It felt good to me.

I could lie to him and claim otherwise, but if we were really engaged, I wouldn't lie to him when he asked me a direct question like that. If we were going to play this game, I might as well do it properly.

"Yes," I admitted. "Was it that bad?"

His eyes widened as he let out a disbelieving laugh. "You really have no idea, do you?"

"No idea about what?" The desire I'd been feeling quickly began to fade at the idea that I had disappointed him. "Maybe I just need more practice."

He groaned again, and this time I could have sworn it sounded like frustration. "Let's head back to the horses," he said, avoiding my question as he offered me his arm. "It's starting to get dark, and we don't want to be out once the sun is down."

Remembering the bandits from earlier, I suddenly realized just how exposed we were here on our own. Sean had a small dagger on him, but it wouldn't be much use against archers. I had no weapon at all.

I took his arm and we walked in silence for a moment before Sean asked me a new question, one that seemed to come completely out of the blue. "What does the princess expect from her marriage? Does she hope the prince will be faithful to her?"

I didn't see what that had to do with anything that had just happened between us, but maybe he simply wanted to change the subject. I answered as honestly as I could, from my own perspective. "I believe she's realistic. She knows their marriage is not based on love, so if he chooses to bed other women, she will be resigned to it. She simply hopes that he will be discreet about it, and try not to produce any children outside the marriage if he can help it."

I knew from experience the problems that royal bastards could cause. My own father had a son before he married my mother, making that son technically my father's oldest child. That boy's extended family had milked the association for everything they could, and there were even those who claimed that, should anything happen to my brothers, my elder half-brother should be my father's successor.

If possible, I would very much prefer to avoid any scheming like that against my own children.

"That's a very practical viewpoint," Sean replied, sounding surprised. "I have to be honest: she doesn't strike me as that sensible of a woman."

Immediately, my back went up. What did he mean by that? It sounded like an insult to Elodie, though I couldn't say how, especially since, if I were being fair, he had it exactly right. Elodie herself would be devastated if her future husband sought comfort outside their marital bed. The practical one between us had always been me.

"You don't know her very well," was all I said.

"I suppose I don't," he agreed, his face still showing traces of his earlier frustration.

"Do you intend to be faithful to your wife, Sean?" I asked him bluntly, since we were already on the topic. I wanted to satisfy my curiosity about his views on the matter since he had already admitted they weren't a love match.

"I did," he said tightly. "But perhaps it depends on circumstances more than I realized. If she feels the same way I do, perhaps we can reach an agreement that is mutually acceptable."

His eyes met mine once again with that same startling intensity in them that he'd had earlier when he talked about love, and I didn't ask any follow up questions.

I didn't want to know what circumstances he might be referring to.

I was afraid I already knew.

CHAPTER EIGHT

The whole way back to the inn, an internal battle took place inside me. My body wanted Dee right now, my heart wanted her for a lot longer than that, and my mind spun furiously, formulating various ways to make both of those things happen.

Unfortunately, my conscience and my honour were refusing to yield. No matter how much I wanted her, in any and every way, I kept coming back to the same sticking point: her best friend. I had seen for myself the softness in Dee's eyes when she spoke of the princess, the tenderness that she had for her, and no matter what justifications I made, twisting the answers Dee had given me to suit my own purpose, I couldn't make the pieces fit.

I couldn't see a way that I could have Dee and have her respect too, and I didn't want one without the other.

The kiss we shared shook me like no kiss ever had before. What she lacked in experience, she more than made up for in natural ability. How could it feel so good, so perfect, the very first time?

Every other woman I had been with, kissing always felt rather awkward. It certainly never got me so excited all on its own.

My first time with a woman had been a prostitute that my father sent to my room on the night of my 18th birthday. He decided the time had come for me to become a man, and he sent a pretty young woman, just a year or two older than me, to make sure it happened.

Getting me hard proved no challenge. I was a young man and just as susceptible to a pretty face as anyone else, not to mention the other parts of her body, but when we kissed, it felt graceless and uncoordinated. I had been very aware of the slight whistle as she breathed through her nose and the faintly sour smell of beer on her breath. Eventually, I gave up on any attempt at romance and just let her ride me to my first orgasm; well, my first one with a partner, anyway.

I found the overall experience pleasant in the moment, but easily forgotten.

The first mistress I took caught my eye at a feast my father had thrown. A beautiful widow looking for a benefactor in exchange for some recreation between the sheets, it seemed a fair trade to me.

I found her attractive, and I had more experience by then, so I expected the kissing to be better, but it still just felt like a chore. She moaned and sighed and made a fuss over it, but I remained completely aware of everything at all times, going through the motions like a checklist.

The things the poets and artists talked about, of losing yourself in the pleasure of physical contact, I never felt anything to compare.

The closest thing I had found would have to be the moment of orgasm itself, but everything before and after usually felt stilted and forced at first, and routine after a while. When the routine became unsatisfying, I ended the relationship and eventually moved on to someone else and the pattern began again.

I began to think that the whole thing might be overrated. The idea of spending hours in bed with someone perplexed me. What would you do for all that time? I had never found anyone that I both wanted to have a conversation with *and* have sex with. The two things seemed to be mutually exclusive.

Until now.

That kiss with Dee finally showed me exactly what I had been missing. Suddenly, the poems and the songs made sense. As her hands held onto me, our mouths moving together, our bodies pressing against each other, somehow I felt more aware of my body than ever before and yet completely untethered from it too. All I knew in the world could be summed up in her kiss. Everything else completely faded away.

I asked her straight out if she had kissed anyone before because I needed to know: did she have some kind of special technique, honed through practice, that I had never come across before? Or did she make it so special by simply being herself?

And now that I knew what it could be like, how could I ever be satisfied with awkward and boring again?

My brain immediately tried to find a solution, which explained why I started asking how the princess might react if her husband had another lover. And even though Dee's answer gave me as much leeway as I could hope for, the more I thought about it, the more problems I began to see. Even if the princess could live with it, what would Dee think? The way she asked me if I intended to be faithful suggested that she put more stock in the concept of fidelity than the princess did.

Even more than that, I knew already that visiting Dee's room at night for half an hour, like I usually did with my mistresses, would never be enough. I wanted hers to be the face I saw when I woke up, the one I laughed with over a meal. I wanted to go out riding with her like this and to talk to her about things that were happening in the court.

Those were things I never did with a mistress and hadn't expected to do with my wife either. And if Dee couldn't be either, where could she fit into my life?

I simply couldn't see a place for her, and it felt like a great pit of emptiness had opened inside me at the thought that I wouldn't be able to spend any time with her again after this week.

Dee seemed equally subdued as we rode back to the inn. I had no idea what she might be thinking, and had no opportunity to ask her. Dusk had fallen by the time we arrived, and I quickly led her inside to the safety of the inn where I could collect Bran to help me tend to the horses and prepare for the night.

Just before we reached the door, Dee turned to me. "Everything is back to normal again, right?"

I heard in her query both the question she had asked and her unspoken question: she wanted to confirm that things were okay between us after our kiss.

I did my best to smile at her the same as I always had before. "Of course. We are back to being simply the lady-in-waiting and her escort."

With a quick nod of acknowledgement, Dee turned and walked into the room without knocking, making both Bran and Princess Cordelia jump in their seats. They sat by the fire, just as Dee had said they would, the princess with an embroidery hoop in her lap.

"Lady Elodie," the princess greeted her happily enough before turning to me with a less pleased expression. "Sean. Did you enjoy your ride?"

Dee and I both glanced at each other for just a second before looking away. "We saw some beautiful scenery," Dee replied vaguely before turning the question back on her. "How was your evening?"

The princess and Bran also exchanged looks before she answered. "Uneventful. Thank you for your company, Bran."

"It's been my honour, Your Highness," he replied in that overly formal way he had of speaking to her. He got to his feet and bowed to both women before walking over to join me at the door. "Have a pleasant night. We'll see you in the morning."

I'd noticed a couple of things between them before, but watching the soft smile the princess gave Bran and his answering blush, it seemed my suspicions were confirmed.

I stepped out into the hall first with Bran just behind me. We walked far enough away that I could be sure our voices wouldn't carry before I turned back to him. "What's going on?"

He gave me a startled look, like a deer surprised by a hunter. "What do you mean?"

"What do I mean?" I scoffed before attempting an impression of the way he behaved with Cordelia. "It's been an honour, Your Highness."

I imitated his bow for extra effect.

His lips pursed and his cheeks reddened. "I'm only showing her the respect she deserves."

"I have the same rank and you don't show me that kind of respect," I pointed out. "You like her, don't you? What did the two of you do in there all evening?"

Bran's mouth fell open in outrage even as his face paled. "What are you implying? I would never... she would never..."

He fell into sputtering, looking offended and embarrassed and guilty all at the same time.

"Bran, calm down. I'm not upset and I didn't mean to imply that you were doing anything improper. I honestly just wondered what you did. Weren't you bored?"

"Bored?" He repeated the word in disbelief. "Not at all. It's so... peaceful... being with her. She's so calm and kind. And she told me a story. Cass, it felt so real, like I could see it in front of me. She's just as good as any of the storytellers your father hires."

She told him a story? How did he pull that off when she barely put five words together at a time for me?

And how ironic that Bran, whom I had never seen blush before over anyone, should fall for the woman contracted to marry me? If it were at all possible, I would happily step aside and let him have her, but unfortunately, that power rested with my father, not with me.

"Listen, Cass." Bran lowered his voice as he leaned closer to me. "I think you should come clean with her. Tell her who you really are. I hate the idea that she thinks she's going to have to marry Eric, and we need information, right? Once she knows who you are, she'll tell you what you need to know, I'm sure of it."

He did have a point: the kinds of things I wanted to know about the Lassarian court, she would never share with an escort. And as soon as we arrived, I'd have to tell her the truth anyway.

But if I did, that meant my game of make-believe with Dee would be at an end. We had left it in an awkward place tonight, but I felt that tomorrow, after a good night's sleep, she would happily pick it up again.

"I'll think about it," was as much as I could say to Bran now as we headed back outside to get everything settled for the night.

This whole trip was supposed to be simple: a way to get home while figuring out what to do about the attempt on my life. How on earth had it all become so complicated?

~Cordelia~

Settling down into the seat by the fire that Bran had just vacated, I waited patiently for Elodie to start speaking. She picked up her sewing again, pretending not to notice my scrutiny, but I didn't let that stop me. I knew she would give in, and eventually she did, squirming beneath my silent gaze.

"Please stop that, Dee!" she begged. "You know I can't take it when you look at me like that."

"Just tell me what I want to know," I suggested, folding my arms across my chest as I smiled innocently at her. "Did something happen between you and Bran? I saw the way you looked at each other, Lodee. He obviously has feelings for you too."

Maybe because my own emotions were heightened after everything that had happened with Sean, I could read that quick, exchanged glance between Bran and Lodee as easily as if they had spelled it out with large letters. Some mutual attraction existed between them.

"Of course nothing happened!" She sounded scandalized at the idea. "He thinks I'm the princess. He behaved very politely and respectfully the whole time."

How disappointing. "But you talked?" I prompted. "Got to know each other better?"

"We talked, yes," she agreed hesitantly. "And I told him a story."

My eyes widened in surprise. Elodie always shared her stories with me freely, but as far as I knew, she had never told one to anyone else before. For her, telling him a story would be nearly as intimate as kissing Sean had been to me.

"But that's all that happened," she added quickly, trying to gloss over it. "Now, what about you? Did you straighten everything out?"

I had been surprised when Elodie told me to go ahead and go out riding with Sean this evening and that she would agree to stay behind with Bran. However, she told me she would agree only because it provided a good opportunity for me to clear the air with Sean, to confirm my engagement and let him know there couldn't be anything between us.

My evening hadn't gone exactly like that.

But I couldn't tell Elodie what we had actually talked about, and I certainly couldn't tell her about our kiss. Our amazing, unforgettable kiss. I told Sean I wouldn't tell anyone, even my own mother, and I meant it. What had happened would remain strictly between us, so my lips were sealed, even though I had never kept a secret this big from Elodie before.

"We reached an agreement," I answered instead, keeping things as vague as I could while still telling the truth. "He understands the situation as well as I do."

"Good." She looked relieved, but also sad for me. "Dee, I know you like him, and I wish things could be different. But it's better that you don't do anything foolish and get your heart broken."

Letting Sean lay claim to my heart would be foolish indeed.

But I had never claimed to be a genius.

The next day, we got an early start to the day's travelling. It would be slower going today as there were some difficult climbing sections on the road, heading up into the high hills that separated the land we had been travelling through from the kingdom of Silatria.

The border lay only a couple of days away now. Each step took us closer to our destination, closer to the prince and the life that awaited me there, and I couldn't help wishing that the carriage axle might break and delay the journey, or that bad weather might come and prevent us from moving on.

Anything to give me a little more time.

I spent the morning in the carriage with Elodie, not wanting to do anything that might tip her off to what had really happened the night before. We talked a while, not about anything important, and then she had a short nap, as usual. However, when we stopped for lunch, I asked her if she would mind if I tried to trade places with Bran once again.

"For what purpose, Dee?" she asked suspiciously. "You said you reached an agreement with Sean."

"I did," I agreed. "But just because I'm an engaged woman, it doesn't mean I can't speak to him. We'll simply be riding beside each other and talking. There's nothing improper about it."

"What do you talk about?" she asked, curiosity seeping into her tone alongside the suspicion.

I shrugged, not quite sure how to explain it. "Nothing in particular. Just whatever crosses my mind, but it's nice."

Elodie's expression softened even more. "That does sound nice. You always wanted a man that you could talk to."

I swallowed down the lump in my throat that her words created. "Well, Sean can't be that man, as we already know. But even so, I would like to be able to talk with him this afternoon."

She could hardly refuse me after that, and luckily, Bran made no complaint about joining her in the carriage. The prince's edict about keeping the princess separate from the escorts seemed to have been conveniently forgotten by all involved, and I certainly had no intention of bringing it up again.

Sean helped me onto my horse and we took the lead today, looking back frequently to make sure the carriage could manage up the steeper parts of the hill.

"How are you, Dee?" he asked as we set out, his tone and his body language both stiffer than usual.

They were the first words he'd spoken to me today. We had acknowledged each other this morning with a smile and a nod of the head, but no words had been exchanged.

"Is that how you greet your fiancée?" I teased him, and instantly his whole bearing relaxed, his face breaking into his easy half-smile.

He must have been worried that I had taken offense or perhaps regretted what had happened between us last night, but I didn't. That kiss had been all I could think about all night, but not in a bad way. The only thing I regretted was that we couldn't do more of it.

"You're right, I apologize. I meant to say: you look stunning today, my darling."

His overcompensation made me laugh. "Darling? I don't think so."

"What do you prefer, then?" His eyes sparkled as we settled into the game. "Dear one? Sweeting?"

I shook my head in disapproval. "I would prefer my name, or something chosen just for me. Not something you might say to others before or after me."

His face tightened just a tiny bit, and I cursed myself inwardly for reminding him of his upcoming marriage. Neither of us wanted that. I needed to focus.

Sean quickly shook it off though, the smile returning as quickly as it had gone. "How about something just for you, based on your name? You could be my dee-light? I could tell you that your lips look dee-licious. Or how dee-voted I am to you."

"Please, stop." I held up my hand to swat the words away as if they were flies buzzing around my head, laughing all the while. This charming, silly side of him seemed so at odds with his strong, imposing exterior, but it just made him that much more appealing to me. There were so many sides to him, so many layers to discover.

"And what would you call me, Dee?" he asked as my laughter died off. "Do you have a special name in mind for me?"

One instantly sprang to mind, and I bit my lip, debating whether to share it with him. I had come up with the name long before I met him, something I hoped I could one day say to my husband as a teasing, intimate term of endearment. Now that I knew who that husband would be, I knew that would never happen, but it *did* apply to Sean, more than to anyone I had ever known before.

Taking a deep breath, I let myself say the words.

"My heart's prince."

His lips parted in surprise and an emotion I couldn't identify flashed through his eyes. For a moment, I feared I had overstepped the game again. Could he tell how much I meant it?

It took him a moment to say anything, and when he did, his serious reply took my breath away. As he spoke the words, I could almost feel them being etched into my soul and I knew immediately that I would never forget them.

"I would rather be prince of your heart, Dee, than of any kingdom in this world."

~Cassian~

I'd never felt anything quite like how I felt as Dee called me her heart's prince. She couldn't possibly know how much that affected me, since she had no idea of my true position. And I meant what I said too, that I would rather have the title she had bestowed on me than any other one, including my real one.

The idea certainly tempted me. Everyone at home already thought me dead. No one expected my return, so what if I never went back? What if I just gave it all up and started a new life, one as a regular man with Dee by my side? It appealed to me far more than I could put into words.

Until I remembered the type of king that Eric would be.

As much as I wanted to be selfish and think only of myself and Dee, I cared too much about the people of Silatria. Their lives would be worse if I chose that path, and I didn't want to be the kind of man who would turn my back on that. I wanted to be someone Dee would be proud of once she knew the full truth.

As we rode along for the rest of the afternoon, teasing and laughing and sharing more about ourselves, I reached a decision. Bran was right, as usual: the time had come for me to tell the princess the truth, but not just about my identity, as he had suggested. I needed to tell her all of it: who I was, and what I felt.

I had to tell her I had fallen in love with Dee.

As far as I could see, there were three possible outcomes. In the first one, the princess would be outraged and refuse to hear me out, but based on everything both Dee and Bran had told me about her, that didn't seem likely. Perhaps she would be hurt, but Dee had said she would be practical about what her marriage would entail. She might appreciate me being up front with her about how I felt, and I truly believed it would still be preferable to the marriage she would have if she ended up with Eric.

The second possibility was that the princess would be okay with what I told her, but that Dee herself would refuse me once she knew the truth. That seemed much more possible, and the idea of it made my heart ache.

But the third possibility, the one where the princess understood the sincerity of my feelings for Dee, that she and Dee were both able to accept that I would prefer not to hurt either of them, and that somehow, possibly, we might come to an agreement that suited all of us. That potential outcome made my whole body sing.

The odds might be small that it would come to pass, but as I weighed up my options, it seemed worth the risk. If even a chance existed that I could be with Dee for real and not just this pretend game we were playing, I had to take it.

Which meant telling Cordelia the truth for a start.

Nearly twelve hours after we started out that morning, we came to the farmhouse where we'd be spending the night. The family who lived there had gone to a real effort for their royal visitor and we were all invited to join them for dinner. Normally, I would have been happy for the chance to share a meal with Dee, but we had to maintain our distance in front of the others, and being so close to her and not able to speak to her as I would have liked tortured me more than simply not seeing her would have.

It felt like the dinner would never end, but finally, the princess and Dee rose from the table to head to their room. I nodded my head at Bran, giving him our prearranged signal. He had promised to distract Dee for me so that I could speak to the princess alone. When I told him I would tell Cordelia the truth about my identity, it pleased him so much that he would have done pretty much anything I asked.

I kept quiet about the other thing I intended to tell her.

Bran made his move as we caught up to the women in the hall. "Lady Elodie, may I have your help outside for a moment? There is something I need to check with you about the carriage."

Dee looked surprised by his request, and she and the princess exchanged glances. "I'm afraid I can't leave Her Highness unattended," Dee demurred.

We had expected that, and I quickly stepped in. "I can escort the princess to her room and keep her company until you return."

Once again, Dee and Cordelia were caught off guard by that suggestion, but they couldn't seem to think of a reason to refuse. "I'll be as quick as I can," Dee promised the princess before shooting me a warning look. "Her Highness is tired from the long day."

I understood the warning well enough: I shouldn't speak to her unless spoken to. However, on this occasion, I would have to disobey Dee's request.

Offering Cordelia my arm, I led her up the stairs to the room prepared for her, the best room in the house but still rather meagre accommodation for a princess. I had to respect the fact that she hadn't complained about any of the lodgings on this trip so far. Maybe my initial impression of how spoiled she seemed hadn't been quite accurate.

As soon as we were inside the room, I turned to her. "Your Highness, I need to speak with you."

The princess' eyes widened in what almost looked like panic. "I... I don't think that's appropriate. We have nothing to speak about."

"That's not true," I disagreed. "There is something I need to tell you. Please, sit down."

I gestured towards the bed as the only suitable spot for sitting in the room, and her cheeks blushed bright red.

"Your Highness, you have nothing to fear from me but it would be better if you were sitting for this."

Reluctantly, she moved to the bed and sat down on the edge of it, holding herself rigid, her hands folded in her lap.

"I have a confession to make, Princess Cordelia. I am not who you think I am."

Her lips parted in surprise. "What do you mean?" she asked, her voice squeaking as her eyes moved to the door, clearly hoping to be saved by Dee's return. Unfortunately for her, Dee would not be coming back anytime soon.

"My name isn't Sean. It's Cassian, and I am the crown prince of Silatria, Eric's older brother."

Her eyes widened in utter disbelief. "You can't be! He's dead."

"Everyone believes that, yes, but it's not true. On my way to the feast to announce our engagement, bandits attacked us. That much is the truth. But through an accident, I managed to escape with everyone believing I had died."

"But... why haven't you said anything? Why are you here? It doesn't make any sense."

She clearly didn't believe me, and I had anticipated that. The whole thing sounded rather unbelievable.

From my pocket, I pulled out the small lace-trimmed favour she had sent to me with our marriage contract. One of the few things I had on my person when I went over the waterfall, it looked considerably worse for wear than the last time she would have seen it, but her initials were embroidered on it, and I could see in her eyes that she recognized it immediately.

"How do you have this?" She looked from the favour up to my face, confusion painted across all her features.

"You sent it to me to confirm our engagement," I reminded her. "It's a long story, Your Highness, but I have stayed in hiding until now because I believe the people who tried to kill me will try again once they learn that they failed the first time."

Her eyes darted back and forth between me and the favour and around the room, her mind clearly overwhelmed with this information. "You're telling the truth? You really are Cassian?"

I nodded in confirmation. "Yes. I'm sorry to have kept this from you. When we began this journey, I assumed we wouldn't be interacting very much so I didn't think it would be a problem to maintain the charade for the length of the journey, but things have turned out slightly differently than I anticipated."

That couldn't be more of an understatement.

"When we arrive in Silatria, I intend to reveal myself and retake my place, which means, Your Highness, that you will marry me, and not my brother."

"I will marry you...?"

She started to repeat my words, her eyes wide, and then, to my great surprise, she began to laugh.

A small titter at first, it grew louder and stronger with each passing second until she had nearly doubled over in laughter, her face in her hands.

I had never considered myself an insecure man, but that reaction would shake even the most confident man alive. Did she truly find the idea of marrying me *that* ridiculous?

When she finally got control of herself again, her arms holding her stomach as if it hurt from laughing so much, she looked back up at me with an expression of pure amusement. "I assume you have not told Lady Elodie about this?"

Why would she bring up Dee? Had Dee already said something to her about what had happened between us? Cordelia didn't appear angry if that were the case, but I still had no idea exactly what she found so funny.

"No, I haven't," I confirmed. "I wanted to speak with you first."

"I think you should tell her." I had never seen the princess smile so widely. "As soon as possible."

"I do intend to," I assured her. "But as I said, I wanted to talk to you about it first. In fact, I wish to speak to you about Lady Elodie herself."

Cordelia raised her eyebrows, still looking far too amused for my comfort. "What about her?"

"You told me she's engaged to marry someone when we arrive," I reminded her, trying to review the words in my head before I spoke them so they caused no offense. "And she told me her marriage formed part of the contract of marriage between you and I. I had no idea such a stipulation existed, and I would certainly never want to force her to marry anyone against her will."

"I don't think you have to worry about that," the princess told me, fighting a smile. "Just talk to her."

"But I still wanted to talk to you about..."

"Your Highness," she cut me off, taking me by surprise once again. I hadn't expected her to be so forceful. "Listen to me. It is no use speaking to me about this. Talk to my lady. She will be able to answer any concerns that you have."

That hadn't been my plan. I had wanted to confess to Cordelia first how I felt about Dee before I revealed my identity to Dee, but the princess seemed to have made up her mind. Before I could argue any further, Dee herself burst through the door with Bran trailing behind her.

Cordelia quickly set her face back to a neutral expression. "Lady Elodie, we were just speaking about you. I believe that Sean would like to take another ride this evening if you would like to go."

Dee looked between the two of us in surprise, and my face must have looked much the same. I had said nothing about a ride, but clearly, the princess wanted to give us a chance to talk. But why would she be so insistent that I revealed myself to Dee straight away? I must be missing something.

"Are you sure?" Dee asked the princess. "You don't mind me leaving you?"

"I can stay with Her Highness," Bran offered, and Cordelia quickly agreed.

"Yes, that's fine with me. You should go quickly, before it gets dark."

Despite sharing in my confusion, Dee turned to me with a shrug and her usual, inviting smile. "Well, it appears we're not wanted here. Shall we?"

CHAPTER NINE

I had no idea what I'd missed. Sean hadn't mentioned anything to me earlier about wanting to go for a ride tonight and he also seemed surprised when Elodie suggested it. But if it hadn't been his idea, why would Elodie be pushing us together? She had been the one telling me to keep my distance from him in the first place and not to get my heart broken.

Something definitely seemed off.

Despite my suspicions, I had no intention of passing up the opportunity to spend some more time alone with Sean, so I made no complaint as we headed back outside. The sky, which had been clear all day, had started to cloud over, and when I looked up, Sean did too, following my gaze.

"Do you think it will rain tomorrow?" Maybe my wish for bad weather to delay us would actually be granted.

"It's hard to say," he replied. "Weather moves quickly through these hills. It's probably going to be completely clear again in an hour."

I'd hoped for a different answer, but it sounded like Sean had some knowledge of the subject. I asked him about it as he helped me up onto my horse. "Have you spent much time in this area?"

"A fair bit, actually. I used to come here to train on hunting and riding as a young man. The terrain can be difficult, so it's good for training."

"Is that a challenge?" I asked, giving him a wink, and he laughed.

"Not tonight. You've already proven you can ride, and having seen you with a bow and arrow, I'm sure you can hunt too. Right now, I'd like to go somewhere we can talk."

It sounded like he had something specific he wanted to talk about, and I had no idea what it could be. We had talked most of the afternoon, so he could have told me anything he wanted to then. What could have suddenly come up since then that would be so important?

"Do you have somewhere in mind?" If he knew these hills as well as he claimed, he might have a specific destination.

"I do, actually. It shouldn't take us too long to get there, but it is a steep climb. Will you be okay on the horse?" I raised my eyebrows at the question, and he laughed again. "Alright, message received. Follow me, then."

We rode single-file up a narrow trail from the farmhouse higher into the hills, and I soon learned Sean hadn't been kidding about the path. My horse's hooves scrambled to gain purchase several times on the steep, rocky terrain. Riding sidesaddle at this kind of angle also proved a challenge and I had to adjust the angle of my body quite a lot to stay on the horse. After nearly twenty minutes of uphill climb, although I would never admit it to him, I secretly breathed a sigh of relief when the ground levelled out.

We had arrived at a small plateau in the hills. The trail continued on up until the hills above us, but it got even steeper and less defined, so my relief grew stronger when Sean dismounted. It looked like we had arrived.

I slid off my horse before he could come over to help me and he shook his head. "You can never let me be a gentleman and help you, can you, Dee?"

"When I need your help, I'll ask for it," I teased him back.

Although he smiled, I could see something else lurking in his eyes tonight. When we spoke last night, he had been conflicted at times, but this felt like something else. He almost looked nervous, a look I hadn't seen from him before.

Sean's big, warm hand brushed against mine as he took the reins from me and proceeded to tie both horses to the base of a nearby bush. He had to get down on the ground to reach the sturdy stem, and I couldn't stop myself from looking over his body as he strained to reach between the branches. The memories of the day before flooded back, both our kiss in the evening and our embrace in the river, and I could almost feel his arms around me, his firm muscles beneath my fingers and his hard arousal pressed against me. Swallowing hard, I quickly looked away. My whole body had started to thrum again, aching for his touch, and those kinds of feelings were dangerous at any time but especially when we were alone.

Thankfully unaware of my thoughts, he stood back up and brushed the dirt from his breeches. "Are you able to climb a little more on foot? There's a great spot further up where you can see all the way back to Lassaria."

A surprising pang of longing hit me at the mention of my home. I had hardly given it a thought since we left, since I had been so distracted by everything that had happened on our trip so far, but the thought of the familiar rooms of the castle, my brothers and my parents suddenly reinforced the uncertainty of everything that lay ahead of me.

Seeming to read every thought that crossed my mind, Sean reached out his hand, stroking my cheek gently with his thumb. "I'm sorry. I didn't mean to upset you."

His touch successfully drove any homesickness from my mind. "No, it's fine. I would like to see the view. Lead the way."

Almost reluctantly, his hand dropped, and he turned away to climb up the narrow trail I had noticed earlier. We went slowly so as not to slip, and it took another fifteen minutes before we reached another open, even space. The hills still continued above us and a number of small caves were carved into the rocks ahead. It felt as though we were the only two people in the world.

"Are those natural or man-made?" I asked curiously, pointing to the openings dotted around the hillside.

Sean looked over at them. "Man-made. Hundreds, or maybe even thousands of years ago. This would have been an excellent defensive position for the people of the time. You can see for miles, so you'd have ample warning of any attack, and it would be difficult for attackers to get up here with any kind of weapons."

Having finished his explanation, he placed his hands on my shoulders, turning me around slowly, and I gasped as the world opened up beneath us.

He hadn't lied: the view really was spectacular. We could see the town we had stayed in the night before, nestled at the base of the hills that we had spent the day climbing. The forest we had travelled through previously spread out like a thick blanket covering the ground, and in the far distance, I could just make out a large river which must be the one that flowed past my father's castle.

Reading my thoughts yet again, Sean pointed in that direction. "The princess' castle is just there, though you can't make it out. If it were less cloudy, you might be able to see the sunlight reflecting off the bronze roof of the towers."

My eyes darted up to the sky again as he mentioned the clouds. They were even thicker now than they had been when we set out, and growing darker. Once again, I silently hoped for a rainy day tomorrow that would delay our journey. If the steep paths became muddy, surely we wouldn't risk travelling further with the carriage until it dried out.

After we had looked out over the view for a few minutes longer with Sean pointing out a few more places that he knew, he looked down at me with that same anxious expression on his face that he'd had earlier.

"While we have some time, Dee, there's something I want to talk to you about."

I took a deep breath, trying to guess what it might be that would have him looking so worried. I already knew about his engagement, and I couldn't imagine what he'd have to tell me that would upset me more than that. "I'm all ears."

"I already talked to the princess about this after dinner. It's important to me that you also know the truth, and she thought I should be the one to tell you."

Did that explain why Elodie insisted we go out together now? What could he have talked to her about that she thought he should tell me rather than just telling me herself?

Just as I opened my mouth to ask him, a loud clap of thunder sounded in the distance, and Sean immediately looked away from me, his lips tightening as he surveyed the sky.

"That's not good," he muttered. "Maybe we should head back if a storm is coming..."

No sooner were the words out of his mouth than a fat raindrop fell straight onto my head, followed quickly by another one, and then dozens more.

"I think we're too late," I laughed, trying to cover my own anxiety now. It wouldn't take much rain for the path we had just come up to get muddy and difficult to maneuver, for both us and the horses.

Sean took a quick look around before making up his mind. "The caves," he suggested, pointing at the closest one. "They'll keep us dry."

He held out his hand to me and I took it as we both ran towards the nearest shelter. The rain came harder by the second, like someone had suddenly tipped over a bucket directly above us. My soft shoes began to slide on the damp grass, and I nearly slipped. Sean's arm immediately snaked around me, steadying me until I regained my balance.

By the time we reached the nearest cave, not even two minutes later, we were both drenched. Maybe not quite as wet as we had been after falling into the river, but near enough. My dress felt heavy, weighted down with water, and I shivered as we moved into the blackness of the opening in the rock.

Instantly, Sean's arms were around me again, his hands moving against my back to try to warm me. "I'm sorry, Dee. This is my fault, I should have been paying closer attention to the weather."

"You can't control the rain," I pointed out. I may not know as much about the area as he seemed to but it hadn't looked that close to storming to me either.

A flash of lightning lit up the cave entrance, followed by another long roll of thunder. The sound of the rain lashing the hillside made me shiver, even though we were now out of its path.

Or maybe Sean's arms around me had something to do with the shivering.

"We might be here for a while," he murmured, his voice coming from just above my head as he held me close to his chest. "We'll need to stay warm, stay as close to each other as possible."

I shivered again, and this time I had no doubt what caused it.

We were completely alone and isolated. No one would come looking for us or stumble across us here. For the time being, we truly might as well be the only two people in the world. And he wanted us to be as close to each other as possible.

Sean leaned back from me as I shivered, his face lined with concern. "Your dress is soaking wet, Dee."

"Your uniform isn't any better," I pointed out, trying to keep things light, even though my voice trembled as I said it. My thoughts were still stuck on the idea of us being here together, alone, with no interruptions and no escape.

"You're right," he agreed, looking down at his own damp clothing. "It's only going to get colder if we keep them on. I think it would be better if we took it all off."

~Cassian~

Dee shivered again as I suggested removing our wet clothes, which only made me more eager to get her dry and warm again. If she got sick because of my foolishness, I'd never forgive myself.

All I had to do was take her somewhere private and tell her the truth, but instead, I insisted on trying to make it romantic, hoping that if I overwhelmed her with talk of how I felt and the beautiful view, she would forgive me for lying to her and forgive me for who I was.

And forgive me for what I still wanted from her, even though I knew everything wrong with it.

Thanks to the summer's heat, the air outside remained fairly warm. It felt slightly cooler in the cave, but even so, we would be okay here for the night if we had to be. The real problem was how wet we had gotten in the rain. If we kept our wet, heavy clothes on, we'd only get colder, so removing our outer layers and laying them out somewhere to dry seemed like the best course of action.

"Turn around," I instructed Dee. "I'll untie you."

Dee took a step back, shivering once more before turning her back to me.

I had never actually undressed a woman before, at least not from a dress like this. My mistresses had maids of their own who would help them get ready for bed, ready for my visit. By the time I arrived, they wore only their night shift, so I didn't entirely know what to do now as my fingers fumbled with the laces holding the dress in place.

Or perhaps, my fingers were simply trembling from the idea of getting Dee out of her dress.

I shouldn't be thinking about that, I reminded myself firmly. I needed to talk to her and tell her what I had been trying to say before the rain interrupted us. If something happened after we had talked, that would be more than welcome, but for now, I had to focus.

When I finally got the laces untied, I gently eased the dress over her shoulders, down her arms and then down to the ground as she stepped out of it. I tried not to look at Dee in her white linen chemise as I found a place to lay the dress out on the ground, out of the rain but still within the airflow that came in from outside the cave. That would help dry it faster.

With my back still to her, I removed my own shirt and tunic and my outer hose, leaving me with just my linen breeches which left hardly anything to the imagination. But then, Dee had already seen me naked in the river yesterday anyway. I didn't have much to hide.

Once all my clothes were laid out, I turned back, bracing myself to only look at her face and not her body, ready to have the conversation I had been dreading. But when I turned around, Dee stood right behind me, far closer than I expected her to be, and before I could do or say anything, she reached for me, her hands wrapping around the back of my neck as she pulled my head down to her, my lips to hers.

Her kiss tasted of rain and innocence and the sweetest longing.

My body reacted to her immediately as her hands left my neck, trailing over my shoulders and down my back, the feel of her hands on my naked skin sending waves of desire through me. My cock began to harden, blood rushing there from every other part of my body, and I tried to hold myself back so Dee wouldn't feel it. But once again, she took the lead, pressing her body firmly against mine, her stiff nipples rubbing against my chest through the fabric of her chemise, and I couldn't help it: my hands went around her waist, gripped her lower back and pulled her hips into line with mine.

She couldn't have any doubt how much I wanted her, just as I knew she wanted me.

Which made it all the more difficult for me to pull away, but I had to. Before things went any farther, we needed to talk.

"Dee." Her name came out as a moan from my lips, a sound of yearning I had never made before. "I need to tell you something."

Her breath danced against my face as she looked up at me, her beautiful blue eyes full of desire. "If you tell me what you have to tell me, will it mean that I have to stop kissing you?"

I groaned this time rather than moaning, her words providing even more evidence, if I needed it, that she didn't want to stop. Still, I had to be truthful with her. "Possibly."

"Then don't tell me," she whispered, leaning close to me again, her hands still running gently across my skin. "Not yet. For now, let's just pretend."

"I can't pretend about this, Dee." My voice sounded foreign to me, so heavy with need. "This isn't a game. I want you, all of you. You know that."

"I know," she stated, not sounding hesitant at all. "And I want you too, Sean. I want you to show me what we would do if we were really engaged and stuck together in this cave for the night."

Was she *trying* to kill me? I could think of no other explanation for why she'd be saying these things to me.

"Dee..." I began, but she cut me off before I could say anything else.

"You have lain with a woman before, I assume?"

Another wave of longing rushed through me, stronger every time. Could she possibly be suggesting we do that?

Her question sounded full of curiosity but no judgement and, once again, I had to answer it honestly. "Yes."

"Then you know how," she concluded, as if that had ever been the issue.

"A lack of knowledge isn't what's holding me back, Dee," I replied, my voice tight with repressed desire.

Her eyebrows raised in curiosity. "Then what is?"

"Well, for one thing, you haven't been with a man, and I expect your new husband will expect to find you in that same condition."

She nearly snorted in derision. "What he wants is of no concern to me."

That answer confused me. "How can you say that when you don't even know who he is?"

Her eyes widened ever-so-briefly before she shrugged and gave me her usual, teasing smile. "Any man who would marry a woman by contract, sight unseen, should be prepared for disappointment."

"Is that so?" That situation applied to me too, although now I had seen the princess.

"That is my concern anyway," she continued. "Leave it to me to worry about. So, if that is the only problem..."

She leaned forward to try to kiss me again, but I stepped back again, though it nearly killed me to do it.

"There is still the thing I need to tell you about."

She brought her hands down from my shoulders, down my chest, trailing down my stomach, and my cock jumped as she drew closer to it. She stopped when she reached my abdomen, looking back up at me with that confident, determined look I found so irresistible. "I already told you I don't want to know. Not yet. You can tell me afterwards."

"And what if you hate me when I tell you?" I knew just how possible that might be. "What if you hate me for allowing myself the pleasure of you before you knew it?"

"I won't hate you." Her words were firm and sure. "This is my choice, Sean. I will take full responsibility for it. I want you, here and now. No matter what comes next, it doesn't change that. Just once, before I tie myself forever to a man I don't love and never will, I want to know what it's like to be with a man who I do."

Everything she said sounded unbelievable to me, but nothing more than the last sentence.

"You love me?" I repeated, my heart pounding in my chest harder than it ever had in my whole life. Harder than the day of my first battle, harder even than when I went over that damn waterfall.

Dee's eyes were full of warmth and desire but also a hint of vulnerability I had never seen from her before. "Yes. And I want to make love to you, Sean. Right now."

~Cordelia~

When I told Sean exactly what I wanted, stating it as plainly as I could, I almost felt the rush of heat through his body, mirroring my own.

Complete clarity on the subject had hit me as I watched him undress, watched his firm, muscled body being slowly revealed to me: I would never get another chance like this. We were completely alone with no chance of being discovered. We were already half-naked, and no reason existed why anyone else ever needed to know what happened.

His wife would never know the difference. And Eric... well, maybe he would be able to tell I had lost my virginity, but what could he possibly do about it? Our marriage contract was worth too much for him to kick up much of a fuss publicly.

If he punished me for it privately, I would accept that. The trade-off would be worth it.

And whatever Sean had to tell me, I decided I would rather not know, at least until we could no longer change our minds.

Even if I never saw him again after this trip, for the rest of my life I would know that for this one night, he had been mine.

"Are you absolutely certain?" he asked, his voice thicker and deeper than usual. His eyes pierced into mine, looking for any hint of a lie or trace of uncertainty. I returned his gaze as confidently as I could even though my knees were nearly weak from the deep, aching need for him that built up stronger inside me with each passing second.

I had never been more certain of anything in my life.

"Yes," I answered as firmly as I could. "Tonight, I'm yours."

With a low, growling sort of groan, Sean wrapped his arms around me and brought his mouth back to mine. Immediately, I found myself drowning in his kiss, just like before. His usual slightly spicy smell mixed with the rain and something earthier too, making the scent almost intoxicating on its own. His kiss only made me feel drunker.

His lips had lost all their softness. This time, he kissed me firmly and possessively, his tongue pushing against my lips until I yielded and let him in, which I did willingly enough. It felt like he wanted to devour me, and I had no complaints. I wanted him to.

At the same time, Sean's hands moved from my back to my hips and up my sides, dipping into the curve of my waist before reaching the sides of my breasts, and I couldn't help arching my back to lean further into him, pressing the stiff peaks of my nipples against his hard chest. The friction felt almost unbearably good, and when his hands moved again, cupping my breasts as his thumbs ran over the nipples, I moaned in surprise and pleasure.

Although he concentrated his touch on my upper half right now, the aching between my legs grew even stronger, demanding attention that I didn't quite know how to give it.

Almost as an afterthought, I realized that he was doing all the work here. Surely, if it felt this good when he touched me, he would like me to touch him too?

Mimicking his actions, I slid my hands up his chest and ran my thumbs across his nipples. They were small but firm, and he moaned into my mouth as I did it, which seemed a good sign that he did like it too. His hips thrust against me, almost involuntarily, drawing my attention once again to the hard shaft I could feel pressed against me there.

The image of him standing in the river, his cock standing proud and strong, filled my thoughts, and I couldn't wait any longer. I needed to touch it, to see not just what it looked like, but what it felt like too.

Running my hands down his hard, defined stomach, I pulled on the string of his breeches, loosening them enough to pull them down. Rather, I thought I had, but they got caught on his cock, which seemed to expand even more as soon as it was released.

Reaching into the breeches, I grabbed hold of him with one hand while I pulled the breeches gently off with the other.

Sean turned away from the kiss, exhaling loudly as my hand made contact, and for a moment I feared I had hurt him. When he turned back to me, his eyes were dark and hooded and full of the strongest longing I had ever seen.

"I don't know how we're doing this," he said, his breath sounding short and laboured. I ran my thumb across the hard ridge at the top of his cock, feeling it curiously, and he inhaled sharply before managing to say a few more words. "You can't lie on the dirty ground."

I hadn't really thought that far ahead. "I have seen men and women against a wall," I suggested. At the feasts my father threw, when beer flowed freely, people often lost their inhibitions. I had seen people in intimate situations more than once, though only for a moment before looking away.

Sean groaned once again. "I'm not taking you against a wall, Dee. That would be even harder and just as dirty."

"I don't know what the other options are," I admitted. "You must know some others."

"None that are appropriate for your first time," he argued, frustration clear in his voice.

"I don't care about that," I argued right back. "I just want to feel you. It hurts, Sean. I want you so badly it hurts."

"God damn it," he swore, running a hand over his face and taking a step back from me, pulling his cock out of my grip. Glancing down, I could see just how hard and ready he was. It appeared even bigger now than it had in the river.

He looked around the cave as though a bed might suddenly appear, growing more frustrated by the second. Just as I was about to tell him I would lie on the ground after all if we had no other option, he seemed to make up his mind. Taking my hand, he led me further inside where a large boulder had lodged up against the cave wall.

"Bend over here," he instructed. "Put your hands on the stone."

I did as he told me, my hands resting on the cold, smooth surface of the rock. My back flat and my bottom facing the cave entrance, the aching only got worse as I realized what he must intend to do. How much more could I want him? Every time I thought my need had reached its peak, it got stronger again.

Sean stepped back until he stood behind me, gently lifting the bottom of my chemise and exposing the bare skin beneath it both to him and to the cool air. I shivered again, but this time lust alone fuelled my reaction.

I needed him to make this aching stop, no matter what it took.

His hands caressed my exposed skin, running across the roundness of my bottom a few times until his fingers brushed against the soft folds between my legs and I moaned in anticipation and frustration.

Acting purely out of instinct, I spread my legs wider apart and Sean swore under his breath again. "You're so beautiful, Dee," he muttered, and I whimpered in reply as his fingers gently spread my folds apart, finding the entrance hidden beneath them.

Agonizingly slowly, his finger pressed into me. A sharp, tearing pain ran through me, but I ignored it to focus on the feel of him. His finger helped to relieve the pressure, but not enough.

"More," I begged him now, turning my head so he could hear me. "Please."

With another groan, he did as I requested, pressing in deeper. A moment later, his thumb brushed against another spot that nearly made my knees buckle.

"Sean," I moaned, no longer caring how desperate I sounded.

He paused for just a moment, his finger still inside me. "Dee, would you call me Cass?"

I would have called him God right now, so long as he kept going. "If that's what you want."

As reward for my agreement, his thumb brushed again against that perfect spot, followed by his finger pressing in even deeper until his knuckles pressed against me and I groaned in frustration. I still wanted more.

"This will hurt a little," Sean told me as I felt a new pressure against my aching core. "Tell me if you need me to stop."

I was ready to scream if he didn't at least *start,* but luckily, he wasted no more time on warnings. From the size and strength of it as he began to push into me, I knew that this must be his cock. I opened my legs even wider, remembering its size, and Sean's satisfied moan filled the cave air.

He reached the same spot, the spot where it felt he couldn't go any further, but this time, he gripped my hip with one hand while the other went back to that wonderful, magical place between my legs. "I love you, Dee," he whispered as pleasure coursed through me, followed quickly by another flash of pain.

I gasped in surprise, and immediately, he stopped moving.

"Are you okay?"

He sounded so worried, it made my heart melt. "It does hurt, but I'm okay. Please, don't stop, Cass."

I had no idea why he wanted me to call him that, but he seemed pleased that I'd remembered. Still moving slowly, he continued pushing into me, deeper and deeper, stretching and filling me in a way I had never imagined possible.

When he seemed to have gone as deep as he could go, he paused, letting me catch my breath and taking a few deep ones himself.

"How does it feel?" I asked him, unable to resist the chance to tease him as I tried to adjust to the unfamiliar sensations.

"Like heaven," was his breathy reply from behind me. "Are you ready?"

I certainly didn't want to stop now. "Yes. I've been ready for the last ten minutes."

His strangled laugh made me smile, but only until he began to move again. Slowly, still holding my hip with one hand, he pulled back, the hard ridge of his cock dragging against my inner walls in the most amazing way. When he pushed back in again, I couldn't hold back my moan. It came out loud, echoing off the walls of the cave which amplified the sound until it felt like it surrounded us. Perhaps I should have been embarrassed, but I couldn't bring myself to care. All I wanted was for him to keep going.

Luckily for me, Sean had no intention of stopping. He pulled out and thrust into me again, then again, slowly at first but gradually picking up speed. Each time felt just as good, and when his other hand joined in again on my sensitive spot, my legs began to tremble.

"Oh, Cass, that's so… I feel…." I had no words to explain what I felt, but it didn't seem to matter. He didn't ask me to go into any more detail.

The aching inside me had gone, but a new feeling had taken its place, a climbing, building feeling that grew stronger and stronger just as the aching had before it. And just when I thought it couldn't possibly get any bigger, something broke away, and wave after wave of pleasure rolled through me, sending my body into convulsions of sheer delight.

Vaguely, I heard Sean moaning my name in response, but for a moment, it felt like all the world disappeared, that the cave and the hills and everything around us no longer existed. The only things left in this world were me and Sean, and his cock inside me.

When I gradually floated back into my body, Sean had pulled out of me completely. With a gentle hand on my waist, he used his other arm to pull me to standing, then turned me around and helped me sit down on the stone, pulling my chemise back down at the last second to protect my bare skin from the boulder's chilly touch.

He sat next to me, his arms around me, my head leaning against his chest. I could feel his heart racing as we both breathed heavily, letting the full realization of what had just happened wash over us.

Finally, I understood what would compel a woman to go to bed with a man like Eric. If he could bring them that same kind of pleasure, it made a little more sense. And yet, the idea of having him in my bed, now that I truly knew what pleasures Sean could give me, seemed even more unappealing than ever.

"I'm sorry, Dee," Sean whispered after a couple of minutes, and I raised my head to look at him. What could he possibly be apologizing for?

"It wasn't that bad," I teased him, and he laughed, getting my joke as he always did, but a haunted look lurked in his eyes.

"You were amazing," he told me, the sincerity in his voice leaving me with no doubt that he meant it. "But I shouldn't have done it. No matter what you said, I shouldn't have agreed. Not before I told you who I really am."

CHAPTER TEN

~Cassian~

I had never felt so many things all at once.

Having sex with Dee exceeded my wildest expectations. I wished I could say that I had made love to her, but given the circumstances, it could hardly be called that. With her bent over that way, offering herself to me, pure lust had taken over. Though I tried to be gentle with her, at times I felt more animal than man, driven on by the most fundamental, primal instinct.

And yet, when she called my name, my real name, my heart soared, and I knew that no matter the position, this meant more than just sex too. She said she loved me, and I loved her too. I made sure to tell her so, even though I knew that it might not seem completely objective to say it while buried completely inside her.

I told her it felt like heaven and it really did. It had never been this good before. I had never known it could be. It felt like we were made for each other.

Still on a high once we were finished, we sat down together and I held her still-trembling body against me, and as my euphoria began to fade, the guilt hit.

How could I have lost control like that?

I knew all the reasons I shouldn't have gone so far before I told her the truth. I had been over them all in my head a million times, and I did it anyway.

And now, she might hate me, and I really couldn't bear that. I would marry the princess if I had to, and I could reconcile myself to Dee marrying someone else too, if she made that choice. But the idea that she might hate me honestly tore me apart inside.

"You have to tell me who you really are?" Dee asked, repeating my words as she leaned back from me to look at my face. I immediately missed the warmth and comfort of her embrace. "Let me guess: your name is really Cass?"

Her teasing filled me with warmth, as usual, but she had hit the nail on the head and I had to tell her so. "Yes, it is. That's my nickname. It's short for Cassian."

Her mouth twitched in uncertainty as her eyes searched mine, trying to determine if I was joking with her too.

"Cassian?" she repeated. "Like the prince you served? You shared the same name?"

She didn't get it. Not that I blamed her; no one would make that leap on their own.

"No, Dee." I forced myself to continue to meet her gaze despite my fear about what her reaction might be. "Not like him. I *am* Prince Cassian. Everyone believes I'm dead, but, as you can see, I'm not."

I expected to see shock or maybe even horror in her eyes, but neither of those looked back at me. Instead, I could only see confusion. "Why would you say that to me?"

The question confused me in return, but I answered it as sincerely as I could anyway.

"Because it's true. I wanted to tell you the truth. I know I should have told you sooner, but I never planned on any of this. I never anticipated meeting you or the way I would feel about you. I never could have expected that."

"And why do you think I would want you to be a prince?" Suspicion crept into her eyes, confusing me in turn, but I understood one thing: she didn't believe me.

Before I could respond, she kept asking questions.

"Did Elodie tell you? How long have you known?" She grew more agitated as she pulled further away from me, her absence leaving me even colder. "Was this all some kind of an act? What do you think will happen if you convince me that you're the prince?"

What on earth did she mean by that? I didn't understand a word coming out of her mouth. She asked if Elodie had told me something, but *she* was Elodie. And the only thing that would happen if she believed me would be that she would realize exactly why we couldn't be together, and how I had betrayed the princess by being with her.

Dee's anger about *that* would be understandable, but she seemed angry with me for a completely different reason instead, one that made no sense to me.

"Dee, I don't know what you're talking about. Nobody told me anything, and the way I feel about you is definitely not an act. I didn't want this to happen. I didn't want to fall in love with a woman I can't have, especially when I'm supposed to be marrying her best friend."

"Best friend?" Her growing anger paused for a moment, confusion coming back to take its place, and I seized the opportunity to explain myself better.

"Yes. Once we get to Silatria, I intend to reclaim my title, which means I will be the crown prince again. Princess Cordelia is going to be marrying me, as originally planned, and not Eric. I have to marry the princess, Dee. I don't have a choice. And I know she's your friend, I know how close you are. That's why I wanted to tell you before we... did what we just did. I know you said it wouldn't matter if I was marrying your own mother, but I knew otherwise. Deep in my heart, I knew the truth, and I kept it from you. I'm so sorry."

The anger in her expression dissipated entirely, and I watched as a range of new emotions played out across her face. A touch of confusion still lingered, but amazement joined it and something that looked a whole lot like happiness. Maybe even joy.

"You're telling the truth?" she asked, just as Cordelia had done when I confessed to her, needing to hear the words again. "You really are the prince?"

I nodded, bracing myself for her true reaction, now that she appeared to believe me. "Yes. And once again, I'm sorry, Dee. I didn't want to hurt you or Cordelia. I never planned for any of this. But you came along, out of nowhere, and you blew me away, just like that storm out there."

I pointed to the opening of the cave, where the rain continued to fall, to illustrate my point.

"I got swept up in you, Dee, falling just like we fell into that river, and now I'm in deep. I'm so deep in love with you, that I'm afraid if I fall any further, I may just drown. I know you might not feel the same now that you know the truth, but I need you to know that I never meant..."

Before I had a chance to finish my thought, Dee's lips were on mine, her arms flung around me and pulling me tightly towards her.

Once again, her reaction was the complete opposite of what I expected. Were my words really that good? I'd never considered myself capable of inspiring romance before, but I felt such relief that she didn't hate me, and so much joy in the passion of her kiss, that I didn't argue. I kissed her back just as eagerly, letting her sweet taste overwhelm me as it always did. When she pulled away, I felt nearly drunk with happiness.

Maybe we actually had a chance. Maybe she would agree to some kind of relationship with me even now that she knew the truth. I could scarcely believe it.

Dee also seemed nearly giddy as she pulled back. A bright smile lit up her face, her eyes full of happiness and hope.

"Cassian." She whispered my name, making it sound like the sweetest music I'd ever heard. "I can't believe it."

I couldn't be more thrilled about her excitement, but I still felt completely off balance. None of this had gone the way I had expected at all.

"I have to tell you something too," she said, her smile so wide I couldn't help staring at her mouth, at those delicious, inviting lips that beckoned me. "I'm not who you think I am either."

That drew my attention back to her eyes. "What do you mean?"

"My name is Dee, as I told you, but it's not short for Elodie. It's short for Cordelia."

Cordelia? So, she and the princess had the same name? Is that why she asked if I had shared the same name as the prince?

My initial jumbled thoughts made my brow furrow until I looked at her exuberant expression again and started to piece it together.

"No," I whispered in disbelief. This couldn't be real. It couldn't be true. Life never worked out this perfectly.

"Yes." She giggled, her grin only growing wider. "I'm Princess Cordelia. Lodee, the woman you know as the princess, she's Elodie Auclair, my lady-in-waiting. We traded places."

They traded places? She told me last night that she and the princess had traded places once, but I could never have guessed she meant right now. Why would I have?

If her words were true, if she really was Cordelia, then that meant... "We're going to be married." I said the words out loud as soon as they entered my head, and hearing them spoken only made them sound more unbelievable.

Dee placed a hand on my cheek, her fingers scratching through my beard, sending fresh waves of desire through me as I looked down on her beautiful face. "Yes. Your contract is with me, Cass."

The contract. She had been the one waiting for me that night, the princess I had been dragging my heels to avoid.

Suddenly, the ridiculousness of the whole situation hit me all at once, and I started to laugh, just as Elodie had done earlier. Finally, that made sense to me too. Dee joined in, the sound of her laughter feeding my own until we were both nearly collapsing, holding onto each other for support.

Her hands gripped my arms before slowly moving across my chest, and almost immediately, my cock began to harden again.

I had never had sex with a woman twice in one night. Usually, once the act ended, my need met and nothing further to be said, I left and went back to my own room, alone.

But Dee was no regular woman and we weren't in a bed anyway, not that I intended to let the lack of a bed stop me from kissing her and touching her all over again. This time, I pulled her chemise entirely off so we were both naked as we let our hands roam across each other's bodies. Although the sky had darkened outside with the nightfall, making it harder to see each other by the minute, it didn't matter. My hands served as my eyes as I explored her beautiful, rounded breasts with their taut peaks before slipping my fingers lower into the warm wetness between her legs.

Eventually, I leaned back on the stone, guiding Dee as she lowered herself down on top of me. It might not be the most comfortable position, but at this point, I had far more pressing concerns than comfort. When she took me inside her, when her perfect heat surrounded my cock, nothing else mattered. I wanted her, I needed her, and, through some miracle, I had her.

We were going to be married. She really was meant for me.

~Cordelia~

I still couldn't believe it.

Sitting on the stone after putting my chemise back on, I watched as Sean - or Cass, I supposed - tried to arrange things as well as he could to make a comfortable place for us to sleep for the night. After we finished making love a second time, he put his under-breeches back on, but the rest of our clothes were still too wet to wear. The rain had begun to taper off outside and the thunder and lightning had stopped, but it remained far too damp to try to make our way back down the hill. We would have to stay here for now and hope that the morning dawned clear and dry. I felt bad for Elodie, knowing how worried she would be when we failed to return, but I could do nothing about it for the time being.

Besides, the joy in my heart made it impossible for anything to bring down my mood for very long.

When Cass first claimed to be Prince Cassian, I didn't see how it could possibly be true. I'd never heard anything so far-fetched. Not only did he somehow escape death, but the man who fulfilled every criterion I ever had for my ideal man miraculously turned out to be the very man contracted to marry me? I liked Elodie's stories well enough, but I knew how to separate reality from fiction.

I figured he must have discovered my true identity somehow, and he thought by pretending to be the man originally intended for me, I might agree to break my contract with Eric and be with him instead. Or, if not that specifically, some equally unlikely scenario must exist in his head for how this might play out.

No matter how flattered I might be that he wanted to be with me that much, it surprised and hurt me that he would try to manipulate me that way. For a brief moment, I almost regretted what we had just done.

But as he continued talking, as I heard the genuine remorse in his voice and saw the conflicted look on his face as he spoke about having to marry the princess, who he believed to be my best friend, I realized that he honestly had no idea. He didn't tell me this because he thought it would make me want to be with him. On the contrary, he had been afraid to tell me because he thought it meant I wouldn't.

And when I revealed my true identity, when I saw the disbelief on his face gradually morph into genuine happiness as he realized that I was the woman intended for him, I felt like the luckiest woman in the world. Perhaps I should have been insulted that he had been willing to cheat on the princess - on me, in effect - but I couldn't really hold it against him when I had fully intended to cheat on my future husband as well. He lied to me about his identity, but I lied to him too. We were both equally to blame, and he certainly hadn't made me do anything I didn't want to.

With a sigh, he came over and held out his hand to me. "It's not ideal, but I think it's the best we're going to get."

I placed my hand in his, revelling once again in the idea that I could do this whenever I wanted in the future: spending time with him, touching him, being just as familiar with each other as we had been in the last few days when we had both been pretending to be someone else.

In public, we would still have to be formal with each other, in a manner befitting a prince and princess, but in private, I knew in my heart that we would always be Sean and Dee, and I couldn't be more grateful for that. Filled to the brim with gratitude for this amazing twist of fate that let us get to know each other as people first without all the trappings of our positions.

Cass had cleared all the rocks from a small patch of ground on the cave floor and folded up his tunic, the driest of the clothes we weren't wearing, to serve as a pillow.

"Next time, we'll try to do this in a bed, okay?" He lowered himself to the ground before helping me down, so that he lay on his back and I rested almost entirely on top of him.

The idea of a next time filled my heart with contentment as I cuddled up against him as best as I could, his warm arm wrapping around me and making me feel safe and secure despite the precariousness of our situation.

"What would our first night together have been like if we had waited until the wedding?" I asked curiously, certain that it would be a complete contrast to our current surroundings.

Cass laughed, clearly finding the comparison amusing too. "Well, we wouldn't have had much time together before the wedding, so, although I would have thought you were beautiful, I wouldn't have wanted you nearly as much as I did tonight."

"You *would have* thought me beautiful?" I repeated, teasing him as usual. "Does that mean you don't now?"

He nearly growled at me. "You know damn well I do. What I mean is that I would have known nothing else about you. Right now, I think you're beautiful, but that's not all I think. I also know you're clever and witty and fearless, and so much more than I could have ever imagined if I simply saw you walking into the church in your wedding gown. Is that better?"

A million times better. "I'm sorry for interrupting. Go on."

"After our wedding feast, you would go to your room with your ladies who would get you ready for the night," Cass continued as his hand trailed lightly down my arm. "Then I would come to your room with my two witnesses."

"Witnesses?" I gasped. I had heard of such things, but we didn't practice such traditions in Lassaria. I hadn't realized they still did in Silatria.

Cass chuckled softly. "I'm afraid so. We would draw the curtains around the bed so they wouldn't see us, but they would stay in the room to listen to ensure that the marriage had been properly consummated."

I wrinkled my nose in distaste. "Just the first time, I hope?"

He laughed louder. "Yes. Trust me, no one wants to listen to it more than once. And after the consummation, I probably would have gone back to my room for the night."

I shifted against the hard ground, trying to see his face better in the dark shadows of the cave. "You wouldn't have stayed with me?"

His eyes glinted in the dim light as they looked down into mine. "I've never slept beside a woman all night. I've never wanted to."

"Well, you're stuck here now. I need your warmth if I'm going to get any sleep."

His arm tightened around me. "Trust me, Dee, I'm not going anywhere."

We lay there in silence for a moment before he spoke again.

"What would you have thought of me, Dee? If you had met me as the prince?"

I tried to imagine it objectively, to picture him walking into our engagement feast as he'd been expected to all those weeks ago, and what I might have thought. "Well, I had prepared myself not to like you," I admitted. "I would have thought you were handsome, because you are. I'm not blind."

He chuckled again, his beard scratching my skin as he nuzzled against my neck.

"But I probably would have found fault with things you did. I would have been looking for signs of trouble, and if you were as formal and reserved as I imagine you might have been in that scenario, I probably would have taken it to mean that you weren't interested in getting to know me as a woman. That you saw me as nothing more than an ornament, as I would be to Eric."

At the mention of his brother, Cass sighed. "I'm sorry about him, and I'm very sorry that you thought you were going to have to marry him. I can't imagine what you were feeling. He certainly doesn't deserve you, Dee."

"And you do?" I teased.

"Not at all," he murmured into my skin. "But that doesn't mean I'm letting you go."

We talked a few minutes longer about wedding traditions in Silatria until my eyelids began to feel heavy, and the next thing I knew, the morning sun streamed in over us.

Or at least it did until a large figure appeared at the cave entrance, blocking the sun's rays.

"What on earth is going on here?"

~Cassian~

The loud, unhappy voice woke me from a surprisingly deep sleep. It shouldn't have been comfortable at all, lying on the cold, hard ground of the cave floor, but with Dee draped across me, her warm, soft body nestled against me so perfectly it felt like she'd been specially made to fit there, it ranked as perhaps the most satisfying sleep I'd ever had.

I couldn't wait to get her into my bed at home. I might never want to leave it.

But for now, I needed to focus on the voice. Squinting, I opened my eyes to try to see where it had come from, but with the sun streaming in from behind him, all I could make out was a dark silhouette in the cave entrance.

"Bran?" It seemed like the right height and shape for him.

"You're lucky it's just me," he hissed at us. "But I'm not alone. Hurry up and put some clothes on, for the love of God."

Dee's hands immediately flew across her body. She still wore her chemise, but it certainly wouldn't be proper for anyone to see her that way, especially not now that I knew her true station.

And I wore even less.

"We got caught in the rain," I tried to explain as I stood up, my limbs protesting painfully as I stretched them all out before pulling Dee to her feet after me. "Our clothes were wet."

"That seems to happen quite a lot with the two of you," Bran replied sarcastically. His reference to our fall into the river made it clear he didn't buy it for a second that the rain fully accounted for our missing clothes.

Anger underpinned every word from his mouth. Lady Elodie must not have shared the secret with him last night, so he must be upset with me for cheating on the princess. Which, to be fair, I thought I had, until Dee told me the truth.

"No one over here!" a voice cried out from the distance.

"These are all empty!" came a reply from the other direction.

"They're searching the caves for you," Bran explained as Dee and I hurried to put our still-damp but no longer soaking wet clothes back on. "John, Thomas, and a few of the farmhands came with me and we found your horses further down. What the hell were you doing up here?"

"Do I need to remind you there's a lady present?" His language surprised me when he had always been so proper and polite around the woman he considered the princess.

Bran's eyebrows raised at the word 'lady,' making it clear his opinion of Dee had taken a dip after finding her here with me, half-naked. How would he react to the news I still had to tell him?

"Let me help you," I offered to her, giving her a private smile while Bran's back was turned before clumsily retying the laces of her dress. I hadn't undressed a woman before last night, and I'd certainly never dressed one before either. It showed, but it should keep the dress on her until we got back to the farm.

"They're over here," Bran called out to the others once we were nearly dressed. "Head back down, I'll bring them down."

We could hear the shouted confirmation as the others abandoned their search, and Bran turned back to us.

"Let's get going. We're already behind schedule, we were supposed to have left an hour ago."

It surprised me that the road would still be passable after the rain last night, but I had other concerns first. I wanted to tell Bran about last night's revelations while we had some privacy, but he gave me no chance. As soon as he finished issuing his instructions, he strode away, heading back towards the narrow path we had come up the night before.

Dee and I both squinted as we came out of the cave, the sunshine far brighter out here than inside. Not a cloud remained in the pale blue sky, all traces of last night's storm completely blown away, except for Dee's hand in mine. That proved that the whole thing really had happened after all.

I went first down the trail, going almost backwards so I could hold on to Dee and make sure she didn't slip in her shoes that were far less suitable for this type of climbing than my boots were. It must have been difficult for her last night too. I wondered why she hadn't said anything until I realized she probably hadn't wanted to back down from a challenge. I loved that about her, but I would have to keep it in mind to make sure she didn't put herself in harm's way.

Finally, we arrived back at the horses who were still tied to the bush where we'd left them. They were probably hungry and thirsty, but otherwise unharmed from their night out in the rain. The trip back to the farmhouse gave me no opportunity to talk to either Dee or Bran, and once there, Bran ordered Thomas to take Dee back to the princess' room while he and I took the horses to be fed and watered.

As soon as we were alone, he rounded on me furiously. "How could you do that, Cass? You slept with her, didn't you?"

"Yes," I admitted freely, taking a little too much enjoyment out of the shade of red that his face turned. "More than once."

"You're not even ashamed?" he sputtered at me, waving his arms in the air like he wanted to punch something; perhaps me. "While the poor princess sat at her window, worried sick about the both of you, you were out there..."

"Sticking it to her lady?" I suggested crudely, hardly able to hold back my laugh as he somehow turned even redder.

"You sound just like your brother," he exclaimed, his face furrowed in disgust. "If I wanted to serve someone like that, I'd have stayed with him."

This time I couldn't stop my laughter. "Calm down, Bran, you're going to give yourself a heart attack. I didn't do anything wrong."

"How can you..." he started, but I cut him off before he could get started again.

"I fully *intended* to do something wrong, but in the end, no one got betrayed because Dee is not the princess' lady-in-waiting."

That stopped his ranting, temporarily. "What the hell is that supposed to mean?"

"It means, my friend, that the two women we're travelling with have been playing us the whole time. Dee is actually the princess, and the woman we've been calling Your Highness is her lady-in-waiting, Lady Elodie."

Deep furrows formed on his brow as he tried to decipher my words. "How do you know that? Dee told you?"

"Eventually," I explained. "After supper last night, when I went back to the room with the 'princess', I confessed to her who I really am, just as I said I would, and she laughed in my face."

Shock crossed Bran's face. "She laughed? Why? What did you do?"

"I had no idea why or what to do, but she told me that I needed to repeat my confession to Dee. That's why she insisted that Dee and I go out last night."

"The princess was in a very good mood after you left last night," Bran said, mulling things over. "Until the storm started and we realized you were caught out in it."

I clapped him on the shoulder now that he had calmed down. "First, she's not the princess. And second, her good mood came from the fact that she realized that Dee, or Princess Cordelia, as she's properly known, is actually the one who's supposed to be my wife. So yes, I slept with her last night, but seeing as I'm going to be marrying her anyway in just a few days, I think I could probably be forgiven."

At length, the full absurdity of it seemed to hit Bran, just as it had hit me and Dee the night before, and he began to smile. "Dee is going to be your wife," he repeated, just to be sure he had it right.

"Yes," I confirmed. "And you should probably get used to calling her Your Highness."

"And the princess... or the woman we have been calling the princess..."

"Is Lady Elodie, who is completely single and unattached."

Bran's cheeks turned red again, but this time anger had nothing to do with it. "This is unbelievable."

"I know. It took a little while for Dee and I to believe it too."

"I'm so happy for you, Cass." All his anger had completely washed away, and he looked sheepish now. "I'm sorry for yelling at you."

"No, you're not," I countered with a laugh. "You were right, anyway. I fully intended to cheat on the princess, but luckily for me, I won't ever have to. Now, if we could just figure out exactly who tried to kill me in the first place, everything would be perfect."

A loud clanging sound from inside the house followed my pronouncement, making us both jump and reminding me that, although we had some privacy, we weren't completely alone. Sound could carry farther than I realized in the open air.

"We probably shouldn't be talking out in the open like this," Bran muttered, mirroring my thoughts exactly. "I'm sorry I got carried away."

"You were looking out for the princess," I pointed out. "Or rather, Lady Elodie, and that's admirable. But right now, I'm going to go get some dry clothes on so we can head out once the ladies are ready. You can decide if you're riding with me today, or if you'd like to give up your horse to Dee and go in the carriage with Elodie instead."

With a grin, I turned away, but not before I saw Bran's cheeks go bright red yet again.

CHAPTER ELEVEN

With a deep breath, I tried to brace myself before walking into the room where Elodie awaited me upon our return to the farmhouse. I expected to encounter a whirlwind of emotion, and she did not disappoint.

"Dee!" she shrieked as soon as the door closed behind me. Almost before I even saw her move, she threw her arms around me and began squeezing all the air out of me. "I thought you'd been washed down the mountain or struck by lightning or eaten by a bear or carried off by bandits or kidnapped by fairies or..."

With an imagination like hers, if I didn't step in soon, we would be here all day as she laid out all the possible catastrophes that might have befallen me.

"Lodee, I'm okay," I gasped. "But I'm going to suffocate if you don't let go of me."

Instantly, her grip relaxed and she took a step back, casting a confused eye over me from head to toe. "I'm so glad you're okay, but what happened to your dress?"

"How did we jump from you being glad I'm not dead to being worried about my dress?" I teased before giving her a partial answer. "It got wet in the rain. Can you help me change into something else?"

She already began moving towards our travelling box before I finished the sentence. "I understand why it's damp, but why is it tied so loosely?"

"Well, I had to take it off to let it dry," I told her honestly. "It got very wet."

Elodie's eyes widened and a moment later, she gasped, her hands flying to her mouth as she dropped the dress she'd just picked out of the box. "Oh my goodness! I was so worried about you, I almost forgot. Did you talk to Sean?"

"You mean Cassian?" I corrected, knowing exactly what she wanted to know, and her face immediately lit up.

I had intended to play it cool and tease her a while longer, but as I took in her expression of pure delight, I couldn't keep up the pretense. The thought of Cass and being with him when we got to Silatria made me far too happy, and I beamed back at her as she squealed in delight, grabbing my hands and pulling me to sit down on the bed next to her, the dress completely forgotten.

"I didn't believe him at first. I thought it must be some kind of joke, but when he showed me your favour, I figured it must be true. How else could he have it?"

"My favour?" I repeated curiously. He hadn't shown me anything, and I had no idea what she meant.

"The one you had to send him when your parents agreed to the contract." When I still gave no reaction, she sighed and explained further. "The one you made me sew for him because you thought it a waste of your time to embroider your initials on it."

Oh, *that* favour. I had forgotten all about that. Luckily, he hadn't tried to use that to prove his identity to me, since I wouldn't have recognized it at all.

"I doubted him initially too," I admitted. "I only came around because he seemed so upset about having to tell me."

"Why would he be upset?" she asked in confusion.

I couldn't help tittering in anticipation of Elodie's reaction. "Because he thought that if he married you, I wouldn't ever consider being his mistress."

Once again, Elodie met my expectations, gasping dramatically, her eyes wide with disbelief. "Dee! He didn't ask you to be his mistress?"

"No, not exactly. He implied it instead."

"Implied how?" Her brows knitted together in the most adorable look of confusion.

"Well, he implied it when he kissed me," I told her, trying to hold back my smile as Elodie's mouth opened wider. "And when he... did other things to me."

Her stunned reaction proved all I could have hoped for. Her eyes blinked and her mouth opened and closed, but no sounds came out. I found it funny at first, but as the seconds ticked by, I started to worry I'd actually broken her.

"Lodee? Are you still there?" I snapped my fingers in front of her face. "Say something."

At last, she closed her eyes and swallowed hard. When she opened them again, her expression had morphed to despair. "Don't tell me you actually lay with him, Dee."

I simply shrugged. "Okay. I won't tell you."

With a groan, she flopped back on the bed, her hands covering her face. "I can't believe this. Your mother is going to kill me! I'm supposed to be your chaperone, and what did I do? I sent you out into the night with him and he took advantage of you!"

"Lodee, just breathe." I laid my hands on her stomach to make sure she followed my instruction. "First of all, my mother isn't here. You don't have to answer to her anymore. And second, and most importantly, nobody took advantage of me. All that happened is that I spent the night with the man I'm going to be marrying in a few days. I'll be spending every night with him soon enough. It's hardly the end of the world."

Tentatively, she peeked at me through the fingers of her hands. "I suppose that's true."

"It is true," I said, keeping my tone soft and soothing. "Now, come on, they're all waiting for us, and I'm still in this wet dress."

I held out my hand to help her stand back up, and soon she had the damp dress off of me and the chemise too, and fresh, dry clothes put on. I had never cared much about my appearance before, but today, knowing that Cass would be seeing me soon, I couldn't help smoothing the yellow dress across my stomach and pinching my cheeks to give them some colour when I could be certain Elodie wouldn't see me.

"So, what was it like?" she asked me hesitantly as she brushed out my hair. "Being with a man? Did it hurt?"

Elodie and I had discussed it before, speculating about what the act of love would actually be like. We had both heard enough stories from the other ladies to understand how it worked, but I had never anticipated exactly how it would feel.

"It hurt a little," I told her honestly. Actually, I felt rather sore today, but I had tried not to let it show. I hadn't wanted to give myself away to anyone, and I would bet it paled in comparison to the soreness Cass had sustained from his sidesaddle adventure anyway.

"And you didn't find it strange to see him naked? You weren't embarrassed to have him look at you?"

I had a feeling we were no longer talking about me. She must be trying to anticipate how she might feel in the same situation.

I answered her just as honestly as before. "Nothing about it seemed strange. It felt natural and right, because of Cass. If it had been anyone else, like Eric, it would have been quite different, I'm sure."

She gasped once again. "Dee! You don't have to marry Eric!"

This time, I laughed. "No. I think it would be frowned upon if I tried to marry both of them."

She swatted my shoulder. "I just hadn't thought about it yet. There are so many things to consider, so much has changed."

"Including the fact that I'm sure that Cass will tell Bran the truth," I pointed out. "Which means he'll know that you aren't actually the princess now too."

As I expected, Elodie's cheeks turned bright pink as she tried to pretend that change didn't interest her most of all. Once we were ready and made our way downstairs, the escorts already awaited us, and Bran and John went back up to the room to collect our things for loading onto the carriage.

Cass stood next to the driver, and he gave me a smile and nodded politely to Elodie, but he stayed put. Perhaps he thought it might look inappropriate in front of the others. To my surprise, when I glanced over at Thomas, the other escort, I found him looking right at me. He'd never paid me any attention before, and the calculating look he gave me now sent a shiver down my spine. Did he suspect something about what had happened between Cass and I in the cave last night?

Whatever the look meant, maintaining eye contact with him wouldn't be proper, so I looked away and moved with Elodie towards the carriage. At that point, Cass broke away to come over to us.

"Good morning, Lady Elodie," he greeted me formally before turning to Elodie. "Your Highness."

I gave him a curious look as he continued to use our false names, but when his eyes shifted over in Thomas' direction, I immediately understood. Changing our story now might arouse suspicion among the others, and I suddenly realized that I had no idea why Cass hid his true identity in the first place. Why had he been travelling incognito at all? We had talked about a lot of things last night, but we hadn't talked about that at all.

Just as I wondered how I might get a chance to ask him, he turned to me. "Bran has asked if he might trouble you to take his horse today, Lady Elodie. That is, if the princess doesn't mind his company with her in the carriage?"

I smiled over at Elodie, who somehow managed to look both pale and flushed simultaneously. "I think that sounds perfect," I agreed. "It's about time we all got moving."

~Cassian~

Mid-morning had already passed by the time we left the farmhouse behind. Between the late start and the rather precarious state of the road, it would be late by the time we arrived at our resting place that evening, another farm just over the Silatrian border.

Bran and Elodie were settled in together in the carriage, much to their mutual satisfaction, it seemed. I made a comment to Dee once we mounted our horses that I felt certain Bran wouldn't mind giving up his horse for the whole day, and she laughed and told me Elodie would be equally agreeable. It didn't take us both long to figure out that a mutual attraction existed between them, just as between the two of us. Dee seemed delighted to hear it.

It really felt like things couldn't be working out more perfectly than they were. Except for the fact that someone wanted me dead, a fact I had to face again when Dee asked me about why I had been posing as Sean at all.

Once she had ensured no one could hear us, she requested an explanation. "You were attacked on your way to our engagement feast and everyone thought you were dead. I understand that, but why haven't you come forward before now? Why are you pretending to be someone else?"

"It doesn't seem to have been a random attack," I explained, telling her about what I had overheard the next morning at the tavern. "Whoever sent the men to attack us wanted proof that they had succeeded in killing me."

"Do you have any idea who it might be?" she asked before leaning towards me conspiratorially. "Do you have a lot of enemies?"

Her enthusiasm over that idea made me smile once again. Most women I knew would have been terrified at the thought of someone trying to hunt down their lover, but Dee seemed to find it a bit of an adventure. Much like I did, I had to admit.

I ran her quickly through the list of likely suspects that Bran and I had already discussed. When I got to Eric, her lips pursed, a look that I had already begun to recognize as meaning that something had occurred to her. I asked her to tell me what she was thinking.

"You know him much better than I do," she demurred. "But he did say something unusual to me at the engagement feast that he attended instead of you."

I could imagine any number of things he might have said to her. Eric could hardly be accused of being discreet. "What did he say?"

She grimaced as she answered. "Well, he flirted with me rather shamelessly, to begin with."

No surprise there. "Go on."

"I reminded him that I would be marrying his brother, and he made a comment about how things could always change. I haven't thought about that again until just now, but maybe it means something? Maybe it means he already knew that something had happened to you."

An uneasy feeling settled in my stomach as her words sunk in. I really hadn't wanted to believe that Eric could be involved, but I had to agree with Dee that his comment seemed both unusual and very suspicious. "Did he speak with anyone during his visit? Anyone high-ranking who might be interested in your marriage arrangements?"

Dee gave me an apologetic shrug. "I really don't know, I'm afraid. I tried to stay as far away from him as possible."

I could certainly understand that, knowing the way he had probably behaved.

"Do you think someone from Lassaria could be involved?" she continued, picking up immediately on the reason for my question.

"It seems likely. Whoever attacked us had to know the area well. They knew just where to wait for us, and the men who were looking for me the next day, they knew where to go to find people willing to do the work for them. I can't think of any Silatrians who would have that kind of local knowledge."

Dee nodded thoughtfully, looking off into the distance as she mulled it over. "Well, the person who stands to gain the most from my marriage is my brother Edward, since he'll be the one profiting off the land that your father is giving my father. But he's only sixteen, and I've never seen him take any interest in court intrigues. It could be someone acting on his behalf, but that seems unlikely too."

We both lapsed into silence for a few minutes as she continued to think. Then, suddenly, she gasped so loudly that my horse nearly bolted out from under me.

"This had better be good," I teased her as I got my horse settled again.

"I'm sorry," she apologized, but her eyes were bright with excitement. "I just remembered that Eric spent time in the beds of several of my ladies while he visited."

I snorted in reply. "That's not really news. I could have guessed that."

She wrinkled her nose at me. "Let me finish. One of them is a woman named Arabella who is the daughter of one of our highest-ranking noblemen. However, more than that, she is half-sister to my half-brother."

My own brow wrinkled as I tried to make sense of what she'd just said. Eventually, I had to give up. "Explain that to me, please."

"My father had a son before he married my mother. That son's mother is the wife of the Duke of Eastam, one of the oldest and most powerful families in the kingdom."

"That sounds like trouble," I couldn't help observing, and Dee nodded in agreement.

"It has been. The entire family has schemed on behalf of Westley almost since the day of his birth. When my mother had me, as my father's eldest legitimate child, they were delighted, thinking that if he only had girls, a chance still remained for Westley to be named as heir."

"But then your three brothers were born," I filled in. "Surely they must have realized then it became a lost cause."

"They should have. Unfortunately, they have continued to try to manipulate things in his favour. He is currently the head of my father's home guards, though it's certainly not on his own merits. His family essentially blackmailed my father into giving him the position."

"And how does Arabella fit in?" I asked, keen to understand the bigger picture.

"She is his younger sister, born of the same mother but her father is the duke. She gained a place in my household at her family's request, and I know for certain that Eric went to her room the night he arrived. I saw them together."

I followed all of that, but I still didn't see the connection. "So, you think this family might be involved in wanting to get rid of me? How would it benefit them?"

Once again, she pursed her lips, thinking it over. "I can't see how it would benefit them directly, but maybe Eric promised them something? He might have promised that if he became king of Silatria, he would support Westley's claim to my father's throne?"

That *did* make a lot of sense, but it meant accepting that my brother really wanted me dead.

As if she'd read my mind, Dee gave me a sympathetic look. "Were the two of you close growing up?"

I had no straightforward answer to that question. "There's always been a natural rivalry between us and he always seemed to be the one to start it. I didn't necessarily want to compete with him, it just ended up happening a lot of the time."

"Friendly rivalry?" Dee asked. "Or the I-want-to-kill-you kind?"

As usual, she made me smile, no matter how serious the situation, but my smile faded as I tried to accept what seemed to be true. "Honestly, I never imagined he would do anything like this. I knew we had our differences, but I never thought he hated me that much. Maybe I should have paid more attention."

"Some people are better than others at hiding who they really are," she said with that teasing smile of hers, before her expression turned serious again. "But if it is true, what are you going to do? What's your plan for when we arrive?"

"I don't have any proof," I pointed out. "So, I'm not sure what I can do other than go to my father with my suspicions. He'll demand an explanation from Eric, but if he has a valid alibi..."

I trailed off, knowing my options were quite limited, and Dee frowned. "Then you'll still be in danger."

"But I don't really have a choice," I countered. "You're meant to marry Eric the day after you arrive, so if I don't reveal myself..."

This time she cut me off, shuddering at the thought. "Please, don't even say it."

The rest of the day passed quickly as Dee and I talked more about our future and our pasts, talking openly about everything now that we had nothing to hide from each other. And when we arrived at the farmhouse for the night, although we had already talked for hours, I still didn't want to be away from her. Unfortunately, I had no choice in the matter. Once again, the house had only one guest room where the women would be staying, while I and the other escorts would be sleeping out in the barn.

Saying goodnight to Dee, knowing I wouldn't see her again until the morning, could nearly count as a form of torture.

John took Dee and Elodie up to their room to get settled while Bran and I took care of the horses. I asked him how things had gone with Elodie in the carriage, but he stayed tight-lipped, only saying that they had enjoyed each other's company. He'd never been the kind to kiss and tell, though I honestly couldn't guess if there had been kissing or not. I also couldn't help thinking that if I had Dee alone in the carriage, we would have enjoyed each other in more ways than one. A moment later, I almost groaned in frustration.

How much of an idiot could I be? A perfect opportunity to be alone with her all day had been right there and I had completely missed it.

Determined not to make the same mistake again tomorrow, I made my intention clear. "Bran, we're switching places tomorrow. You and Elodie can ride while Dee and I take the carriage."

Bran looked confused. "I thought the princess wanted to take the horse. I'm not sure if Lady Elodie likes to ride."

"Well, you're just going to have to convince her that she does," I told him firmly. "Because tomorrow, that carriage is ours."

~Cordelia~

Lying in bed that night, I went over everything Cass had told me about the attempt on his life, over and over again, trying to figure out what our next move should be.

When Elodie and I got back to our room, I briefly flirted with the idea of telling her about the whole situation, but quickly decided against it. It would only upset her as she imagined all the terrible things that might happen. For now, it would be better if she believed that our happy ending had already arrived.

Instead, I asked her what she and Bran had done in the carriage all day. She turned bright pink, as she always seemed to do when I mentioned his name, but she claimed that they had simply talked. She told him another story, and then she slept for a while, as usual. Upon further questioning, I got her to admit that Bran had let her sleep upon his shoulder.

It definitely didn't qualify as the explosive revelation my news from the previous night had been, but for Elodie, it represented a significant step. I could tell that she was falling hard for him and I couldn't be more pleased for her, especially since Cass had all but confessed to me that Bran felt exactly the same.

After one of her bedtime stories, Elodie drifted off to sleep, but I lay awake, reviewing the options that Cass and I had before us. As far as I was concerned, we were in this together now. An attack on him constituted an attack on me too, making me equally responsible for finding a way to expose those behind it and ensure that Cass would be safe once we got to Silatria.

The more I mulled things over, the more I concluded that my connections were the only real asset that I had which might be useful. In particular, my brother, Arthur, seemed well placed to try to help us. Well aware of Westley's family's maneuverings, he had people loyal to him who would probably be able to bribe or cajole information out of the right people.

But how could I get in touch with Arthur, and especially in time to get any information that would be useful to us? We were obviously moving at a slower pace because of the carriage, but even at a messenger's pace, the ride back to Lassaria would take a full day, plus the time to get back to Silatria, and my wedding to Eric was scheduled for just three days from now. It didn't give us a lot of time to play with. Still, without any better ideas, I resolved to talk to Cass about it first thing in the morning, and after reaching that decision, I finally fell asleep.

However, when Elodie and I came downstairs in the morning, I could immediately tell that something must have happened.

Cass and Bran spoke to each other quietly next to the carriage, their tense body language and serious expressions making it clear their conversation was not a happy one. They both looked over as we approached and attempted to put on a smile, but they weren't fooling anyone.

"What's going on?" I asked, keeping my voice low so none of the other people milling around the farmyard could hear.

"Thomas has disappeared," Cass replied, his lips pulled tightly into a frown. "He took off during the night. His horse is gone too."

"Why would he leave?"

"That's what we're trying to figure out," Bran explained. "He didn't say anything to anyone. He must have slipped away in the middle of the night."

"He could already be halfway across the kingdom by now travelling at full speed," Cass muttered.

Not only did that seem to be cause for concern on its own, it also made my own plans even more difficult. When I frowned, Cass quickly guessed that I had something on my mind.

"What is it, Dee?"

"I had been hoping we could spare one of the men to carry a message back to Lassaria, to my brother Arthur. He might be able to get some information that would be useful for you, but now that we're already a man short, it will be even more difficult."

Bran and Cass exchanged glances, appearing to have a conversation with just their eyes. Elodie and I often did the same thing.

Apparently coming to an agreement, Cass turned back to me with a nod. "We'll ask John to go. If you think the information will be good, we have to try."

"But that only leaves the two of you to defend us," I pointed out. "Not that I don't think you're both strong fighters, but..."

"It should be fine." Cass cut me off with a smile. "For one thing, we're in Silatrian territory now, so bandits are less of a threat. And for another, we've got you as our backup sharpshooter in case we need you."

I knew he meant it partly as a joke, but he clearly recognized and appreciated my skill with the bow and arrow too. I had never thought I would get to marry a man who saw it as an asset.

"Have you got a message ready to send?" he asked me next, and I pulled out the short note I'd written this morning. It used a shorthand that Arthur and I had developed when we were younger so we could pass notes to each other during our lessons and our tutors wouldn't be able to decipher them. Should the message be intercepted by anyone, it would appear to be nonsense.

Cass took it from me and went to speak to John while Bran turned to Elodie with a nervous smile. "Your Highness," he began, still using my title for Elodie as we'd agreed. "It's a beautiful day and I wondered if you might like to ride with me this morning."

His request took Elodie completely by surprise. She had never known the slightest interest in riding, and I had my mouth open to protest that I could take the horse again when Bran acknowledged me with a nod.

"Sean has asked if you would join him in the carriage, Lady Elodie, so you can continue your discussion from yesterday."

So, this request came from Cass. It seemed to me we could have our conversation while riding, but he must have his own reasons. Maybe he wanted to make some notes or review some documents.

"It's not really appropriate for the princess to ride," I pointed out. If we were going to keep up the charade, we needed to take that into consideration.

Bran looked chagrined that he hadn't thought of it, but a moment later, he gave me a wry smile. "Well, if Thomas has gone and John is going, who are we really keeping up pretenses for?"

I couldn't help laughing. He made a very good point, and Elodie beamed at me, pleased that Bran had made me laugh.

"Well, Lodee, I guess it's up to you then," I said, also dropping the act. "I know you don't love to ride."

"I don't, but I could manage it for a while if His Highness needs to speak with you."

We agreed that we would switch back as soon as Elodie tired of it, and Bran helped me up into the carriage to wait for Cass to join me.

A few minutes passed before the door opened and my fiancé pulled himself up, his solid frame filling the space inside the carriage and making me immediately aware of how close we were, and how completely alone. Suddenly, his request made a lot more sense to me, and I couldn't help cocking a suspicious eyebrow at him as he settled into the seat across from me. He had brought a couple of bows and a quiver of arrows with him and he hooked these onto the carriage wall before turning to me with an expression of pure mischief.

"Why do I have the feeling you didn't ask me in here to talk?" I asked.

Cass grinned back at me, his chestnut eyes shining with amusement and something darker too, something that looked an awful lot like desire. "Is that a problem, Your Highness?"

"Oh, you're going to start being formal with me now, are you?" I teased. "It's a little late for that, don't you think?"

His smile only got wider. The carriage jolted beneath us as we began to move forward on today's journey and Cass slid off his seat, onto his knees in the space between us, his head just below mine so that he had to look up at me.

"I do need to talk to you, but not yet." I could only feel relief that he didn't expect me to think right now. The closeness of his body and his scent had sent my senses spinning. "First, I need to do something else."

With his hands on my lap, he began pulling up the skirts of my dress, bunching the fabric together in his hands as my legs were slowly revealed.

"What are you doing?" I had simply thought he planned to kiss me, but obviously he had something else in mind, and I found myself caught half-way between nervousness and excitement as I tried to guess what it might be.

He did kiss me after I asked the question, leaning in to capture my lips against his in a hungry, almost desperate way, and I met his eagerness with equal passion. I had been thinking about kissing him again all day yesterday but we hadn't had a second alone from the moment Bran woke us up in the cave.

Echoing my thoughts, Cass pulled away with a shaky breath. "It just about killed me not being able to do that yesterday," he murmured, his hands still pulling my skirt higher, pushing it up past my waist until he had completely exposed me. "And I realized last night that with the darkness of that cave, I still haven't seen what you look like when you come apart. I'm dying to see it, Dee."

What exactly did he intend to do? We were alone, yes, but laying together in the small space we had seemed impossible.

Again, he seemed to read my mind, chuckling at the look on my face. "There are ways I can bring you pleasure even without being inside you. Will you let me show you now?"

Though I still didn't know exactly what he meant, I remembered how he had put his finger inside me the other night. It felt good, though not quite as good as when he completely filled me. Would he do that again?

There seemed to be an easy way to find out. "Show me, Cass," I requested. "I want to know it all."

His eyes darkened as he took another deep breath. "Of course you do. I love your curiosity, and I want you to know it all too, Dee. I want to discover new things with you. But for now, we'll start here."

With his hands between my thighs, he spread my legs apart and hooked one of my knees over his shoulder, pulling my hips closer to him.

My heart pounded as I watched him, trying to figure out exactly what he would do next. Dampness already pooled between my legs simply from the anticipation, and then, to my great surprise, he leaned down and kissed me there, right where I ached for him the most.

I gasped as his tongue explored the folds of my skin and then dipped inside, making my whole body throb with need. "Cass," I whispered, hardly able to believe what he was doing or how good it felt. My ladies had never talked about this when they discussed the men they had entertained.

He just hummed in response, his mouth pressing harder against my skin as his tongue continued to move inside me before sliding out to circle around that incredibly sensitive spot that he had found the other night. When I thought I couldn't take any more, he plunged his tongue back inside me again.

I covered my mouth with my hand to stop the moans and sighs trying to escape. If the driver heard me, he might assume something had happened and stop the carriage. I hardly wanted that, not with Cass' face buried between my legs, and not when he was making me feel so good that I could barely think straight.

More than once, he brought me to the edge of release, the pressure building inside me, only to pull away at the last minute, placing soft kisses on my inner thighs while I panted in frustration. Finally, I groaned and pleaded with him. "Cass, please, I need…"

I didn't have the words to explain what I needed, but they weren't necessary anyway. He knew exactly what I wanted.

This time, his mouth clamped down hard on that amazing spot, sucking it into his mouth as his tongue swirled over it, and the whole world exploded around me once again. My bones seemed to melt away until nothing held me upright except his hands and his tongue, lapping up all the evidence of what we'd just done.

"So, what do you think?" Cass asked, grinning up at me as he licked his lips, a gesture that made my heart sing.

"It felt amazing," I told him honestly. "Did you like it too?"

He laughed as he pulled my skirt back down and settled onto the seat next to me. "Seeing you happy is all I need. But honestly, you taste amazing too."

Once again, I couldn't be sure how seriously he meant it, but in the next second, he leaned down and kissed me again, this time with a lingering taste on his tongue, slightly salty and tangy. Knowing where his tongue had just been made me moan again, a sound that Cass returned appreciatively.

"Do you taste the same?" I asked curiously as he pulled away, and he laughed again.

"I can't say I know for sure," he teased me, brushing back a few loose strands of hair from my face which had pulled loose from Elodie's styling. "But you can certainly try for yourself and let me know."

My gaze dropped to his breeches as I tried to figure out exactly how I could taste him, but before I could ask, the carriage stopped suddenly, nearly throwing us both off the seat.

A frown crossed Cass' face. "We shouldn't be stopping yet," he muttered under his breath as he reached across me to draw back the curtain on the carriage window a couple of inches. My eyes widened as I caught sight of the armed men on horseback who had stopped next to us. Bran had already made his way over to them.

"Bandits?" I asked Cass in a whisper. They weren't attacking, but maybe they were offering us a chance to surrender our goods first without a fight.

Cass' grim face didn't make me feel any better, nor did his answer. "No. This is much worse."

Worse than bandits? Who could they be? Once again, he answered the question before I had a chance to ask it.

"Those are Silatrian soldiers. They're my brother's men."

CHAPTER TWELVE

My heart rate had already been elevated at the thought of Dee getting her mouth on me, but now it raced for a whole different reason as she and I watched Bran lead his horse over to the Silatrian men who had just arrived.

With all the events of the past day, the situation now seemed clear enough to me: Thomas must have overheard something we didn't mean him to and he'd gone to pass that information on to Eric or someone loyal to him. Perhaps, his intentions were honourable. Maybe they had simply come to escort us the rest of the way. However, if Eric really did want me dead, as appeared more and more possible with each passing moment, this could be a trap. I could conveniently wind up dead before we ever arrived back at my father's castle.

I couldn't see any aggression in the way they were speaking to Bran, but I also couldn't hear what they were saying. The lead man, who I recognized as one of my brother's most trusted men, glanced over at the carriage, and I quickly pulled the curtain fully closed again.

"What do we do?" Dee whispered, a look of concern on her face that didn't suit her at all. I much preferred to see her laughing and teasing me. "We can't let them take you."

I tended to agree. Going along quietly seemed too risky, but even if I could get away, how could I leave Dee to go on without me? If anything happened and I couldn't get to her in time, she could still end up married to Eric and that thought frightened me nearly as much as the prospect of death.

Reading my mind in that canny way of hers, she shook her head at me. "Don't worry about me, I can take care of myself. Let's get you safe first."

Stealthily, she moved to the door on the other side of the carriage, away from the mounted men, and opened it slowly.

"Lodee!" she whispered, sticking her head out the door and waving her arm to get her lady's attention.

I peeked out the door in time to see Lady Elodie moving towards us, still on her horse, her eyes fixed to the conversation on the other side of the carriage.

"Get off the horse and hold it there," Dee instructed her, still in a loud whisper. Elodie nodded and Dee ducked her head back into the carriage, turning to me with a look of determination. "Get undressed."

"Excuse me?" Normally, that would be an order from her I wouldn't have to think about, but the timing hardly seemed ideal.

With a sigh, she rolled her eyes at me. "Quickly. Untie me first."

She turned her back to me and I did as she said, loosening the laces of her dress even though I had no idea what she had in mind. I didn't see how the soldiers finding us in a state of undress would help anything, but I also trusted Dee enough to do as she asked without requiring an explanation.

As soon as she could, she shed her dress while I removed my outer layers. She picked up my tunic as I discarded it and slipped it over her own head.

My confusion grew even stronger. "What are you doing?"

"We're trading places," she explained simply. "Put my dress on."

"What?"

That hadn't even crossed my mind and I looked at the pale, yellow fabric in confusion.

"Hurry, Cass," she urged, moving to pull my breeches on. "I'll tie you up. Just get it on."

I still had no idea what she intended, but once again, I did as she said, pulling the dress on while feeling rather ridiculous. I had never worn a dress in my life, and I couldn't say I particularly thought it suited me.

When I had my arms in, Dee turned me around and quickly tied the laces in place. "My cloak," she instructed next, pulling down the hooded garment hanging on the carriage wall next to me.

Belatedly, her plan began to make sense to me. "You want me to run?"

"They won't chase after you if they think you're me," she stated, sounding more certain of that fact than I felt. "They already think they have the princess, and they'll think they have you too. What's one lady-in-waiting, more or less, compared to those prizes?"

She tied the cloak around my neck, pulled the hood over my head, then looked me over with a frown.

"You can still see your chest hair, but hopefully if you're fast enough, they won't get a good enough look. There are coins sewn into the hem of the dress if you get into trouble and need them."

"This is insane," I couldn't help pointing out, and for the first time since she'd taken charge, Dee smiled up at me.

"I never claimed to be entirely reasonable. Now go, quickly."

"What about you?" I asked, still loath to leave her undefended.

She grabbed a wide hat from the carriage shelf, tucking her blonde hair up beneath it, then grabbed one of the bows I had brought with me off the carriage wall, handing me the other one. She took a few arrows from the quiver for herself before handing over the rest of them to me.

"I'll create a distraction. As soon as I fire the first arrow, get on the horse and go. Don't look back."

"Dee…"

The idea of leaving her behind had started to feel real, and it made my stomach twist uncomfortably.

"I'll be fine," she repeated firmly. "They won't harm me, not unless they want war with Lassaria. The most important thing for now is that you're safe. Do you have some way of communicating with Bran?"

I nodded. On that point, I could be certain.

"Good." With that, she all but pushed me out the carriage door.

Elodie's eyes went wide with disbelief as she got a look at me in Dee's dress, and she handed me the reins without a word, too stunned to say anything.

"Wait for the first arrow," Dee reminded me. "And I'll see you soon."

Her words were more than hopeful. She sounded completely certain.

I had no chance of being able to mount the horse sidesaddle, so I lifted my skirts as I waited for her signal. In just a few more seconds, I heard the whistle of an arrow through the air followed by the shouts of the men, and I quickly mounted the horse and took off up the dirt road back the way we had come, back up into the hills.

More shouts echoed out behind me, but as Dee had instructed, I didn't look back, not wanting to give any of them a glimpse of my bearded face beneath the hood. Soon enough, the noises faded into the air and I found myself on my own. When I dared to look back, no one seemed to be following me.

It seemed I would be safe, at least for the moment, but now what? Although I had some means of defense, I had no other clothing. Dee's coins would be helpful, so perhaps I could return to the farmhouse where we'd spent the previous night and buy some different clothes. It would be a start.

With no other plan, I headed back in that direction, my chest growing tighter with each step that took me further from Dee. After no more than twenty minutes, another travelling party, formed of two carriages and a mounted escort, appeared on the road in front of me. I thought briefly about trying to avoid them by going off into the woods, but they'd already seen me. It would look more suspicious now if I tried to hide. Cursing my poor fortune, I pulled the hood further over my head and hoped I could simply pass by without being stopped.

No such luck. As soon as I got within shouting distance of the lead horses, one of the men called out to me. "Do you need some help, my lady? Why are you out on your own?"

My heart beating fast, I tried to put on a high-pitched voice in my best imitation of a lady. "No, thank you. I'm just returning home, it's only a few minutes away."

At my reply, the man held out his hand and the entire party stopped moving. Apparently, it sounded as fake to him as it had to me. I swore under my breath as I kept my horse moving forward, still hoping they may let me pass, but when the sound of a sword being drawn rang out, I kicked the horse beneath me. Outrunning them seemed the best choice right now.

However, before I even had a chance to get up to speed, more men came from behind the carriage to cut me off, leaving me with no way to get past them without going into the dense trees on either side of the road, where they would probably be able to pin me down anyway. Gritting my teeth, I pulled up on the reins, stopping just before I reached the second line of men.

The man who had spoken to me before came up behind me. "Remove your hood."

"I'm not looking to cause you any harm," I replied in my regular voice. "Just let me pass and you can continue on your way."

"Remove your hood," he repeated firmly, ignoring everything I'd just said.

With no other choice, I reached up and pulled back the cloak, revealing my face. The man with the sword stared at me grimly, but I could hear a few titters among the other men gathered. I could only imagine what I looked like in Dee's yellow dress, sitting astride my horse.

These men weren't familiar to me and it didn't seem they recognized me either. That might be one piece of good luck, but I had no idea what excuse I could give to get out of this mess. Before I had a chance to even try, the door of the first carriage opened and a young woman's head appeared. The man with the sword quickly bowed to her as she looked over at me.

"What do we have here?" Her voice sounded cool as she looked between me and the other man.

"I don't know yet, my lady," he replied. "I haven't had a chance to question him yet."

She waved her hand dismissively. "There's no time for that. We need to keep moving. He can ride in the carriage with me and I'll get the whole story. I could use some distraction anyway."

The man's jaw dropped. "I don't think that's appropriate, my lady. Your brother..."

"...isn't here," she finished, her voice turning even colder. "Right now, you answer to me. Do as I say."

Clearly, I had no choice in the matter, no more than the man in charge did. The other men pulled me off my horse, relieved me of my bow and arrows, and shoved me unceremoniously towards the open carriage door.

As I pulled myself inside, I could see the lady had two other women with her, both of whom looked slightly terrified at my appearance, in contrast to their mistress.

"So," she said to me, her eyes calculating and hard. "This ought to be good. How did you come to be out here on your own and wearing the princess of Lassaria's dress?"

How had she recognized Dee's dress? My heart beat faster again, trying to make sense of any of this. This whole day had taken a completely unwelcome turn. "Might I ask your name, my lady?"

She smiled again, her smile nothing like Dee's warm, inviting one. "My name is Arabella Eastam. And I thought that you were supposed to be dead, Prince Cassian."

~Cordelia~

The first arrow flew straight through the gap between the men on horseback. That shot held some risk: if any of them had suddenly moved, I might have hit someone, but by shooting straight through the group, I couldn't fail to get their attention, so I took the chance.

Sure enough, they all scrambled for their own weapons at the same time that Cass took off on his horse.

"Hey!" the man in charge called out after him. "You there! Stop!"

He turned his horse as if he intended to follow Cass, so I shot another arrow, drawing everyone's attention back to me and the carriage.

"Stand down!" the man shouted at me. "Prince Cassian, we're not here to harm you. Stop shooting!"

So, they *did* know about Cass being here, just as we'd suspected. And while it sounded well and good for them to say they weren't here to harm him, I had no proof of that. I needed to give him more time to get away so I shot once more, over their heads this time as the man who had been speaking dismounted his horse and walked towards the carriage, his sword drawn.

"Your Highness," he pleaded, thinking he was addressing Cass. "There's no need for this. Please, let me explain."

His body blocked my shot as he got closer, and since I had no intention of actually hitting him, I put the bow down before pulling the hat off my head and letting my long hair fall over my shoulders. "I think you have me mistaken for someone else, Sir."

The man recoiled in surprise as he took in my appearance. "Who are you? Where's the prince?"

"There's no prince here," I told them truthfully enough. "But you *have* managed to frighten off one of my ladies. I hope you have a good explanation for this."

His brow knitted in confusion as he looked down the road where Cass had gone, over to Elodie, and then to me. "You're the Lassarian princess?"

"Yes," I replied, reclaiming my title in the hopes I could use any influence I had to protect Cass. "And I'd like you to answer my question: who sent you here and why?"

Bran had also dismounted and he joined us just as I finished speaking. "I told you, Steven, you were misinformed. Cassian is dead, and there's no one here but me, the princess and her ladies."

Bran looked over at me with appreciation in his eyes, understanding exactly what Cass and I had just done, but I forced myself not to acknowledge it or do anything that might give the game away.

Steven, meanwhile, huffed in frustration. "You're alone in there?" he asked, trying to see past me into the carriage.

I threw the door open wide to show him that no one had been hidden. He looked inside anyway, looking up and down as if Cass might be concealed beneath the seat or on the ceiling somehow.

"Why did your lady run?" he asked as he looked once again down the road. The 'lady' in the yellow dress had long since vanished. "And why are you dressed like that?"

I had already come up with answers for both those questions and I answered him in the imperious and accusatory tone I'd heard my mother use many times before. "You terrified my poor lady. We've already been attacked by bandits on this trip, our escorts have gone missing, and now you show up with armed men? How much more could she take?"

To his credit, embarrassment crossed Steven's face. "We didn't intend to frighten any of you, Your Highness. And your clothing?"

"I prefer to dress this way when travelling."

I stated it as though it were a perfectly normal thing to say and, despite his obvious confusion, he didn't contradict me. "Well, we are here to escort you now. We'll take you into the next town where Prince Eric is waiting for you."

My heart beat faster at that news, and not in a good way. "I thought he would meet me at the castle when I arrived."

Steven inclined his head in agreement. "That was his original plan, but when he heard rumours that his brother might be alive, he had to investigate. He will be very disappointed to learn they were not true."

I felt less certain about that, but I kept my doubts to myself.

"Well, let's move on then," I suggested. "My lady Elodie can join me back in the carriage."

"What about your other lady?" he asked, glancing once more down the road. "Should I send some of my men to retrieve her?"

I shook my head. "It's not necessary. I never cared for her much anyway."

His eyes widened in surprise, but he knew better than to argue with his master's fiancée. "As you wish, Your Highness."

He left to explain the situation to the others while Bran helped Elodie into the carriage with me. "That was quick thinking," he whispered to me. "And don't worry, Cass will be fine. He's a survivor."

I certainly hoped so. Now that the immediate danger had passed and the adrenaline had started to wear off, anxiety began to replace it in the pit of my stomach. Would he be okay on his own? Had we made the right call?

Elodie still had a number of questions about what had just happened, and I did my best to explain it all to her as the carriage continued down the last of the hills to the Silatrian plain and the town waiting at the bottom.

Almost four hours after Cass left us, we arrived at an inn in the town. Steven told me to go and get changed while he reported to Eric, who would then come to my room to speak with me. My so-called fiancé was about the last person I wanted to see right now, but I needed to be smart about this. If I could play dumb, perhaps I could get some information out of him, information that would help Cass once he returned.

No sooner had Elodie finished helping me into a new dress than someone knocked on the door, and I took a deep breath to brace myself. "You can admit him and leave us," I told Elodie.

Her brow furrowed in worry. "Are you sure? I can insist on staying."

"It's fine," I promised. "He might be more forthcoming if it's just me. I don't think romance will be on his mind right now."

Her lips pursed in disapproval, but she did as I asked, opening the door to reveal Silatria's second prince. He wore a version of the same riding uniform as his men, one not so different from the one Cass himself had been wearing the last few days. I hadn't seen Eric since he left Lassaria a month earlier, and he looked me over with that same too-familiar stare that made me want to shudder. Elodie left the room and closed the door behind her as I did my best to smile at Cass' brother.

"Prince Eric, I am surprised to see you," I began politely. "I didn't expect you to come to greet me."

"I'm not here for you," he said bluntly, surprising me with his honesty. "I need you to be honest with me, Princess. Have you seen my brother? Is he alive?"

I answered him with a technical truth, if not the full one. "I have never seen Cassian before this trip, so if I saw him now, I would have no way of recognizing him."

Eric had clearly wanted a different answer. He took a few steps into the room before turning around and walking back to the door, pacing nervously.

"I know you don't like me or trust me, but I need you to tell the truth," he said, still being brutally blunt. "If he's still alive, then he's in danger. I need to know where he is so I can help him."

I hadn't expected those words to come out of his mouth and they threw me off-balance as I tried to guess if they were true or a bluff.

"Who would he be in danger from?" I asked, watching him closely to try to gauge the truthfulness of his reply.

"The same people who tried to kill him the first time." He ran a hand through his hair as he continued to pace. "I had no idea that's what they intended. They never told me that part of the plan."

That got my attention even more than everything he'd said to this point. "What plan?"

He grimaced, seeming to realize he'd said too much. "Princess Cordelia, please just tell me: is he alive or not? Have you seen him?"

It seemed I would have to give something in return before he would open up to me. "I will tell you if you answer my question first. Who tried to have him killed?"

His lips tightened for a moment in resistance, but seeming to realize he wouldn't secure my cooperation any other way, he gave in.

"It was the Eastams, Westley and Arabella. And if we don't find Cass first, they'll try to do it again."

~Cassian~

My stomach dropped as the woman's words sank in. She'd just introduced herself as Arabella Eastam, the woman Dee had told me about the day before, the one she suspected might be involved in the plot to kill me. To make matters worse, she recognized me even with my slightly altered appearance and wearing this ridiculous dress, even though I could swear we had never been properly introduced before.

All in all, it seemed unlikely to add up to anything good for me.

"I think you've got me mistaken for someone else," I tried first, keeping my tone light and even. "I can see why you might think me a princess, dressed this way, but I'm definitely not a prince."

As I spoke, I sized her up, trying to gather as much information as I could to decide how to play this. She would be considered pretty, but not in a natural way like Dee. She obviously spent a lot of time on her appearance, making me think she considered it her most important asset. I could try flattering her, although her shrewd, calculating expression made me think she might not fall for that either. I would have to proceed very carefully.

"Oh, I am still very curious about your dress," Arabella replied, giving me an almost amused look. "But I do know who you are. I've seen you many times before, Prince Cassian."

She had? Why? How? Where? I hardly knew which question to start with.

Before I could decide, she offered up a little more information on her own. "My father used to be the Lassarian king's envoy to Silatria until just a few years ago. We spent a great deal of time in your court."

In that case, she certainly would know me, so trying to keep up my false identity seemed useless. I still didn't recognize her, but that was hardly unusual. I'd never had much time for the women at court. Although, perhaps she had met Eric there. Dee said he had gone straight to her room the night of the feast. Maybe they had known each other before that night.

"And then you returned to Lassaria as Princess Cordelia's lady," I guessed. "Which is how you recognize her dress."

She nodded in acknowledgement. "It's hard to forget such a terrible colour on her. It actually looks better on you, I think."

Despite myself, I had to laugh. Could this whole situation get any more ridiculous?

She smiled too, but the hardness remained in her eyes, telling me this woman definitely had her own agenda. Her expression couldn't be more of a contrast to Dee's frank openness.

"So, tell me how it is that you came to be out here on your own, wearing the princess' dress, when you're supposed to be dead," she asked again, though the request sounded a lot like an order, reminding me that, although I had the higher rank, she held the power here.

Until I could figure out exactly what was going on, I would have to play along. "I didn't die, obviously. Some men attacked and injured me, and I've only just recovered well enough to return home."

Her pursed lips told me that she still had doubts. "You're going the wrong way if you were really heading home, and that still doesn't explain the dress."

"Where are you heading, my lady?" I asked, trying to take the focus off me. "You have business in Silatria?"

Her eyes narrowed in calculation, clearly not fooled by my attempt at distraction, but she answered me anyway. "I'm attending Prince Eric's wedding. Or I thought I would be, but it seems like that wedding might not be happening if he's not the crown prince after all."

"And you're travelling on your own?" I asked, trying to keep the focus on her. "Without your father or brother?"

"Do you know my brother, Your Highness?" At last, something I said seemed to surprise her.

"Only by reputation."

She nodded, still in that same calculating way. "He has gone on ahead. He had some additional business to carry out, though that may also change once he learns that you are still alive. He will be very interested in meeting you. I must insist that you allow me the honour of accompanying you the rest of the way."

That could hardly sound more ominous. "That's very kind of you, Lady Arabella, but as I'm sure you can understand, I am anxious to get home and let my family know that I'm safe. If you could simply leave me in the next town where I can buy some proper clothes, and return my horse to me, I will be able to move quicker on my own. I would be delighted to entertain you and your brother when you both arrive at my father's castle."

I would be delighted to ask them a few questions while they were both under guard in my prison, actually, but I could hardly say that to her now.

"Of course," she agreed, giving me that same insincere smile. "But again, Your Highness, I am curious about your current attire and the fact that you were heading in the opposite direction when we found you. You simply can't leave my curiosity so unsatisfied."

She simply refused to be dissuaded from this topic of conversation, so I racked my brain for an explanation that sounded the least bit plausible.

"Bandits attacked me," I stated, settling on a story that had a basis in truth. "They stole all my clothes, everything that I had with me. On my way to the farmhouse you've just passed, I came upon the princess' entourage, not far ahead of you. Obviously, I didn't want to reveal myself to her in my current condition, so I simply asked her escorts if they could lend me some clothes, and they seemed to find me in this dress amusing."

I gestured down at my unlikely garments once more.

"I accepted, thinking it better than nothing until I could reach the farm, but I hadn't anticipated running into anyone else on the way. I can only apologize for startling you all so much. It certainly wasn't my intention."

I couldn't tell from her expression if she believed me or not. Arabella simply looked me over, top to bottom before asking her next question.

"You didn't speak to the princess? Have you ever met her?"

What did it matter to her whether or not I'd spoken to Dee? Something about the way she asked about her made the hairs on the back of my neck stand up.

"No," I lied. "We were supposed to meet the night of my attack, but that never happened."

That answer seemed to satisfy her, though she continued to watch me carefully. "You seem to have a lot of bad luck, don't you?"

"I have been a bit unlucky lately," I agreed, though thinking back on the time I'd just spent with my face between Dee's legs this morning, I knew I had been very lucky too.

"Well, perhaps your luck's about to change," she said rather cryptically before leaning forward and tapping on the roof of the carriage. Immediately, we came to a stop.

My heart beat faster again as she called over the man I'd spoken to earlier. He helped her out of the carriage, and they went a short distance away, speaking to each other quietly where I couldn't possibly overhear anything. I watched as he spoke to one of the other escorts in turn, who quickly set off ahead of us at a much quicker pace.

"What was all that about?" I asked when Arabella reentered the carriage, trying to sound unconcerned, like I was asking to be polite and nothing more.

She turned those cold eyes of hers on me once more. "Just making sure that everything you need is ready for you when we arrive. We'll make sure you have the reception you deserve, Your Highness."

~Cordelia~

"Westley wants Cassian dead," I repeated, watching Eric's reaction closely. He grimaced at the suspicion in my tone but eventually nodded in agreement.

It didn't completely shock me. I had named him as a suspect myself, but I definitely wanted to know more about the role Eric had played in the whole thing and the details of this plan he had mentioned.

"But you would prefer Cassian alive?" I asked next, trying to figure out Eric's motivation for being involved at all if not to take Cass' place.

Eric frowned at me, and in that expression, I could see a similarity in that expression with Cass' own serious look, forcing me to suppress a shudder. It made sense that they shared a few features in common as brothers, but I would rather not be thinking of Eric at all when I thought of Cass.

"Of course I want him to be alive," he answered, sounding annoyed that I'd think otherwise. "He's my brother. And honestly, being king is the last thing I want. Do you have any idea how much work is involved?"

I had to refrain from rolling my eyes. Was this self-absorption part of the act or for real?

"If he really is alive, it would make things so much easier for me. I never wanted the throne or any of the pressures that come with it."

Now that I looked at him more closely, he did look significantly more stressed than he had the last time I saw him. Dark circles under his eyes indicated he probably hadn't been sleeping well and his cheeks were drawn.

I decided to get straight to the point and ask the question I most wanted answered: "When you came to my home and I reminded you about my upcoming marriage to your brother, you told me that things could always change. What did you mean by that?"

Again, Eric winced under the weight of the accusation in my question. "I'll admit, that sounds bad, especially when we found out the next day he had been attacked."

"It does," I agreed, raising my eyebrows at him in a challenge. "So, what did you mean by it if you weren't planning on taking his place?"

He swallowed, looking away from me as he debated how to answer. All that confident swagger he'd had at my father's castle had vanished. Right now, he looked like a chastened boy who had just been caught stealing pies from the larder.

"Prince Eric," I pushed when he didn't immediately reply. "I will help you if I can, but only if you're honest with me. If I don't believe you're telling me the truth, then I have no reason to be truthful with you."

That seemed to spur him on. "I'll tell you everything, but only after you answer me. Is he alive? Have you seen him?"

I wasn't about to fall for that. "Surely, you can see my dilemma. If I tell you he is alive and you send your men after him, and you do actually want him dead, then I had just helped to deliver a man to his death. Whether I know him or not, that's not something I want on my conscience."

Eric almost growled in frustration. "Fine! We're wasting time here, so let's drop the pretense, Princess, all of it."

"That's fine with me," I agreed, raising my eyebrows once again and crossing my arms for good measure. "You first."

He glared at me a moment longer before exhaling loudly. "I met Arabella when her father served at my father's court years ago. We spent some time together, mostly in the bedroom."

I tried my best not to wince. Even though I knew she had entertained Eric last month, during her time at the Silatrian court, she wouldn't have been much more than sixteen. Had her family encouraged her to court him, or had he coerced her? Either way, I felt an unwelcome twinge of sympathy for her.

Eric continued talking, not seeming to notice my discomfort. "When our fathers started to negotiate the wedding contract between you and Cass, she got back in touch with me. She suggested that her brother Westley could influence your father the king to make some amendments to the contract which would be mutually advantageous to both me and her."

"What kind of amendments?" I could understand what Westley had to gain, but what would Eric or Arabella get out of it, especially if Eric, as he claimed, had no interest in becoming king?

He made a pained face before answering. "That she would marry Cass, and I would marry you."

Pure shock ran through me as I processed his words. Why on earth would Eric have cared about marrying me? And how could he have thought it would happen anyway? My father would never have agreed to that. He had no interest in helping Arabella and would have taken it as an insult for his only daughter to have married anyone other than the crown prince.

Before I could ask, Eric continued his explanation. "All I had to do was give them information on our finances and Cass' movements. I didn't really see a downside. Cass had no interest in getting married anyway, so it made no difference to him *who* he married."

"Why did it matter to you?" I interrupted, wanting to get one of my many questions answered. "You'd never met me before. Why would you want to marry me?"

He stared straight at me with that same predatory look he'd given me the night of the feast, the one that made me want to shudder. "We'd never met, but I had seen you before, Cordelia."

He had? The thought took me by surprise so much that I let it slide that he used my given name without my title. "When? Where?"

"At a fair in Lassaria last year. You didn't even notice me. Do you know how rare that is? Even without my position, women notice me, Cordelia, but you looked right through me. It intrigued me."

I bit my tongue so hard I could nearly taste blood. Could he really be that full of himself? I certainly had no memory of seeing him at any fair, and because I hadn't paid him any attention, he took it as some kind of challenge? That he could force me to take notice?

"And I knew Arabella. I knew that if Cass got her and I got you, everyone would know I got the better deal. The idea of outdoing my perfect older brother appealed to me, what can I say?"

So a rivalry definitely existed between them, even if he hadn't actually wanted Cass dead. "Go on," I invited, wanting him to get to the point. "Obviously, things didn't work out that way, so what happened next?"

Eric sighed, running a hand over his face. "Arabella invited me to the engagement feast, telling me that everything would be announced then. But when I got there, Cass hadn't arrived. It surprised me just as much as everyone else. I knew nothing about the attack, I swear to you. But when I got back home, Westley came to see me."

His face darkened as he recounted the rest.

"He told me that your father hadn't agreed to the changes, so he'd had to take matters into his own hands. He said if Arabella couldn't be queen of Silatria, then I would have to be king so I could help him the same way that she would have. He also claimed that I bore equal responsibility for Cass' death since I'd told them when he'd be travelling."

I digested all of that, trying to make sure I fully understood. "He's been blackmailing you?"

Eric nodded. "And it will only get worse if I actually become king. Please, Princess Cordelia, I'm begging you: please tell me it's true and my brother really is alive."

I took a deep breath as I thought over everything he'd said. My gut told me he was telling the truth. He didn't look like a man pleased with the way things had turned out, and I had my doubts he would have been clever enough to pull off this kind of plot all on his own. It seemed much more likely that this vain, self-important, spoiled prince had been taken advantage of by my scheming half-brother and his sister.

"He's alive," I admitted, and Eric's face relaxed in pure relief. "But I don't know where he is. He thinks you want him dead so he'll be avoiding you and your men."

Again, Eric grimaced. "I understand. I'll send some of my men out looking, out of uniform. In the meantime, I'll have to return to my father's castle. Westley's there already, and if I'm gone too long, he might get suspicious. I'll see you when you arrive tomorrow."

"Eric," I called out as he turned to go, and he stopped in his tracks. "If you're lying to me, you will regret it."

My words took him by surprise, but a ghost of a smile crossed his face. "I believe that I would. It's a good thing for us both that I'm not. Until tomorrow, Princess Cordelia."

"Goodbye, Your Highness."

With that, he headed out the door and I dropped down onto the bed with a loud sigh, trying to decide what on earth to do next.

CHAPTER THIRTEEN

The rest of the carriage ride with Arabella continued on just as uncomfortably as the first part, although thankfully, she stopped questioning me about my attire. She turned instead to asking me about myself and my plans for when I returned to my father. I kept my answers as vague as possible, trying to steer the conversation back towards her whenever possible, even though I had no interest in her life other than what it might reveal about her brother's plans for me. Unfortunately, she proved herself quite skilled at double talk, answering my questions without actually telling me anything, just the same as I did for her.

Finally, the town at the bottom of the hill came into view and I breathed a sigh of relief.

Hopefully, I could get some new clothes and get away without any further delay. Under no circumstances did I intend to remain with her a second longer than I had to.

We were almost at the town when the carriage stopped again. From my seat, I couldn't see what was going on, but I could hear men talking. Arabella clearly wanted to hear it too as she shushed her ladies and opened the carriage window, letting the sound carry over to us.

"We've been travelling along this road all day," Arabella's man said, the same one who had spoken to me earlier. "We haven't seen anyone."

Instantly, my nerves were on edge. Was someone looking for me? If so, why would the man lie to them?

They spoke a few moments longer, confirming where the travelling party had set out from this morning, whether they had seen anything suspicious, and who travelled inside the carriages. Arabella's man confirmed only Lady Arabella and her ladies were inside. He seemed to be covering for me, but why?

When the man doing the questioning seemed satisfied, he and his colleagues continued on back up into the hills and our entourage began moving forward again. I could see the men on horseback as they went by, four men in plain clothes. Although they didn't wear the uniform of the men we had seen earlier, I could swear that at least one of them worked for my brother.

It seemed Eric hadn't given up. Did he know I had escaped from his men earlier? Had he somehow made Dee talk? My heart constricted at the idea that she might be in any danger or had been injured in any way. I wished more than anything that I could be with her now.

My wish seemed to be answered when we pulled into the courtyard of the inn where Arabella's party would rest for the night, and I peered out the window and caught sight of Dee's carriage. They were staying at the same inn, which meant things seemed to be going my way again.

I glanced over at Arabella to see if I could spot any hint of recognition on her face, but none appeared. The carriage Dee had been using was plain and unadorned as they hadn't wanted to draw any attention to the fact that a princess travelled inside. It paled in comparison to the bigger and fancier carriage Arabella used or even her companion one.

Satisfied that Arabella didn't suspect anything, I tried to decide what to do next. As much as I wanted to rejoin Dee's travelling party, it might put them all in danger now that people were discovering my death had been exaggerated. But if I could see Dee and speak to her before I headed for home, I could find out what happened with Eric's men and it would make me feel a hundred times better to see her safe.

At last, the carriage door opened and the man who had spoken to me earlier appeared. After bowing to Arabella, he turned to me. "Once the ladies are inside, some of my men will take you in so you can change into something more... comfortable."

I ignored his mocking tone and turned back to my host, attempting to say my goodbyes. "Thank you, my lady Arabella. I appreciate the ride and your company, and I will look forward to seeing you at my father's castle in the next few days."

"Oh, you can't possibly leave tonight," she exclaimed, putting on a look of dismay that couldn't have felt more forced. "It's far too late to be travelling alone. If you must travel ahead of us, I insist that you stay tonight and get an early start in the morning. I've already arranged a room for you."

Could that be the message she'd sent on ahead earlier? I had imagined something more sinister.

Again, I quickly weighed my options in my head. Travelling alone at night could be dangerous, both because of the usual night dangers and because my brother's men might still be looking for me. Speaking with Dee might be easier once everyone else had gone to sleep. I could find a way to evade her guards in the darkness of night. Overall, staying the night might be my best option, so long as I got away early before anything else could go wrong.

"That's very kind," I gave in. "Thank you."

The fake look of dismay faded, replaced by her more typical cool smile. "Wonderful. I'll come and see you once you've had a chance to change."

I tried to protest that it wouldn't be necessary, but she had already stepped out the door, followed by her ladies. When they had gone, I made my own way clumsily out of the carriage, trying not to trip over Dee's dress. If nothing else, I couldn't wait to get some proper clothes on again.

The men escorted me to a small room with a single bed where a change of clothes had already been laid out for me. Only when they left me alone did I realize that I had no one to help untie the laces of the dress, so it took a good five minutes of struggling and contortion before I managed to grab hold of one of the ends and pull it enough to loosen it. The yellow dress fell away as I sighed in relief and quickly put on the new clothes, looking for all the world like one of the Eastams' men in their gold and green livery colours.

Once presentable, I opened the door to the hall slowly, trying to get my bearings to see how I could figure out where Dee's room might be. However, two of Arabella's men stood outside my door and immediately blocked my path.

"Is there something you need, Your Highness?" one of them asked.

So, Arabella had revealed my identity to them. Were these men here to protect me, or to keep me in?

"I'm looking for Lady Arabella," I tried, wondering if they would allow me to pass with that intention.

"She will be with you very soon," the man assured me. "Please wait inside."

He all but shoved me back inside and closed the door behind me, answering my question: I wouldn't be free to simply walk away.

My room had a window so I headed there next, throwing open the shutters. Only one floor from the ground, I should be able to lower myself slowly before letting go, making the drop fairly inconsequential. I was half tempted to try it right now when the door opened again and Arabella appeared.

Wearing a new dress designed to draw attention to her chest, her eyes moved from me to the open window and back again, a hint of accusation in them, as if she knew exactly what I had been thinking. She said nothing about it though, choosing to examine my new attire instead. "You're looking more like yourself, except for the beard and the longer hair. I can't really say it suits you."

My eyebrows raised of their own accord. I couldn't care less about her opinion of how I chose to wear my hair.

"I have some news," she continued, undeterred by my reaction. "Would you believe that Princess Cordelia's party has also stopped here for the night?"

Instantly, my heart leapt into my throat. How did she know that? I would have sworn she hadn't recognized the carriage, so had she actually seen Dee? Was Eric here? Once again, my mind raced with a hundred different questions.

In my reply, I did my best to sound unconcerned. "That's not surprising. There aren't that many inns between here and my father's castle."

"I suppose," she acknowledged with a tight smile. "But I thought perhaps you would like to meet her, since your marriage contract is likely to be enforced once people realize you're alive."

She planned to introduce me to Dee? That could be interesting, and I struggled to hold back my smile. How would Dee react? I could almost see the amused look in her sparkling blue eyes.

"That's very kind of you, Lady Arabella. I'd be honoured. Have you already spoken to her?"

"Yes. We can meet her down in the dining room."

That surprised me. The whole trip, Dee and Elodie had eaten in their room, but I had no idea what had happened since I'd left them earlier today. If they were in the dining room, there must be a reason for it.

"Lead the way," I invited, following her out the door and past the two men who stood on either side of it. They followed behind us as we walked down the wooden steps back to the common rooms of the inn.

As we entered the dining room, my eyes swept the room, looking for Dee's familiar blonde hair, but I couldn't see her. A few small groups sat at separate tables, mostly men. The women who were all older and clearly of a lower social class.

Confused, I turned to Arabella, who watched intently, as though this might be some kind of test. Did she want to know if I'd been lying to her about not having met the princess?

"Is she here?" I asked as politely as I could.

Arabella's lips twisted upwards. "Do you see anyone who looks like a princess?"

I had no patience for games right now, but I forced my face to remain neutral. "Then where is she? You said you would introduce me."

Arabella clapped her hands, and instantly, her men entered from behind us and roughly escorted all the diners out of the room as they protested in vain. In less than a minute, we were completely alone.

"Bring her in," Arabella called out to a back door and a moment later, another man entered, his hand gripping a young woman's arm as he pushed her in front of him less than gently.

As had happened far too many times already today, the sight of her left me feeling completely off balance once again. This woman wasn't

Dee, but she bore a strong resemblance to her. Richly dressed with silky blonde hair, she could be considered attractive, but the vacant look in her eyes told me immediately there was something not quite right with her.

No sooner had I thought so than she laughed, loudly and without reason, her shouts of laughter echoing through the room before she abruptly stopped, as quickly and without warning as she had begun.

The woman was clearly mad.

"What is this?" I asked Arabella, growing more frustrated by the second. I had no idea what she hoped to sell me, but I had no interest in buying it. "I haven't met the princess but I know plenty of people who have. No one ever described her like this."

"That's because the woman they met is not the princess." Arabella leaned towards me conspiratorially. "Another woman has been posing as Cordelia for the past few years to conceal the truth until the king and queen could marry her off. They will present the other woman as the princess, let her marry the prince, which would be you, and then once you are wed, they intend to switch her out and leave you with the real princess."

She pointed at the woman who played with her hair now, holding it out in front of her and staring at it as the candlelight reflected off the golden tresses. Where did this woman come from? There couldn't be any truth in what Arabella said... could there?

I would rather not entertain the idea that Dee had lied to me for even a second, but thinking about it rationally, I had to remember that she had in fact lied to me from almost the moment we met. The only real proof I had of Dee's identity as Princess Cordelia was her word.

"How do you know this?" I asked, trying to put the pieces together in my mind. "And why is she here?"

Whoever this woman might be, she hadn't been travelling with Dee. I knew that for certain.

"My family is very close with the royal family," Arabella said, her voice still lowered to give an illusion of confidentiality. "My mother was the king's lover for many years and he still confides in her. And as for why she's here, it's because of the wedding. She is following behind the 'official' princess' entourage, the one containing the imposter."

"Where did they find the imposter?" I asked, wondering what story she would give me to explain Dee.

"She's an orphan that someone brought to the castle," Arabella told me. "She grew up nearly wild, hunting and playing with the boys, until someone noticed that she bore a rather striking resemblance to the real princess, and that's when they decided to switch them."

There were enough details in what she said to give me pause. Dee had told me about how her parents had died and she had come to live with the princess, but I had assumed afterwards that it had all been part of her act. What if it had actually been true after all? Growing up among the boys in the castle would help to explain why Dee could ride and hunt the way she could, the way I had never seen any other princess do.

"And how do they intend to switch the women?" I asked, curious to see how detailed Arabella could be about this plot, real or not.

"It will be after the wedding," she explained, not missing a beat. "They will take the fake princess to her chamber to get ready for your visit, and then will put the real princess in your bed. There is a drink they plan to give you to dull your senses so that you aren't able to tell the difference until after the marriage is consummated."

If she had constructed this entire tale, Arabella had certainly put some thought into it, I had to give her that much credit.

"And they don't think I would object the next day when I find a completely different woman in her place?"

Arabella shrugged. "By then, it would be too late. You'd already be married and have consummated the marriage in front of witnesses. There wouldn't be any recourse."

As fantastical as it sounded, it wouldn't be entirely impossible. I had heard stories of such plots before, carried out by desperate families. True or not, though, I still didn't see what Arabella had to gain by telling me any of this, so I decided to ask her directly: "What do you suggest I do then, my lady?"

She smiled at me with that chillingly cold smile of hers. "I think the logical solution is to ensure that they can't make you marry the princess at all."

"My father won't dishonour the contract," I pointed out. I had argued about it with him enough times to know that for certain. "Unless you can prove everything you've said, and even then..."

"You don't need to worry about the contract," she interrupted. "Not if there is another reason you couldn't get married."

She obviously meant something specific, but I couldn't guess yet what she had in mind. "And what would that reason be?"

Her eyes met mine confidently, without a hint of warmth. "If you were already married."

~Cordelia~

By the time I had explained my conversation with Eric to Elodie, she had grown so upset that I had to help her lay down on the bed in our room, where she promptly curled up on her side into her ball.

"It will be okay, Lodee," I tried to soothe her, rubbing her back as I spoke, but she would have none of it.

"Don't even say it, Dee," she moaned with her head in her hands. "This is too much! We've lost the prince, the other prince is being blackmailed and I just know that Arabella won't be satisfied she's got her claws into one of them or the other. I wish we had known all of this before we left home! Your mother would have dealt with Arabella properly then."

I couldn't argue with that. If my mother had any whiff of what Arabella and Westley were up to, she would have had the whole family declared traitors, no matter what Westley's parentage might be. Maybe we could look forward to that when this all had been sorted out, but we had a lot to do before we got to that stage.

"Just breathe, Lodee," I urged. "I'm going to run down to the kitchen and get you something warm to drink to help calm your nerves."

She must have really been distressed because she didn't even protest at me leaving the room on my own. Even so, I preferred not to leave her alone, so I found Bran's room and explained the situation to him. He promised to go and wait with Elodie until I got back.

As I got downstairs, a large group of people were standing around in the main hall, complaining angrily about something. It seemed wiser not to get involved so I snuck past them all instead, heading towards the kitchen. Supper had already finished for the evening so the cooks had left and the only people remaining were the two washers, cleaning up after the evening meal.

Neither of them paid me any attention as I walked into the room, so I headed straight to the two large pots bubbling away over the fire. One contained some kind of stew that I assumed would be tomorrow's meal, but the other had a clear broth in it which would serve my purpose.

As I looked around the room for a cup to use, a familiar-sounding voice caught my attention. It came from the adjoining room, and the door between the two rooms stood open just enough that a few snippets of conversation could be heard.

My curiosity aroused, I snuck closer until I could hear better. I definitely hadn't been hearing things. The voice belonged to Arabella Eastam, my former lady-in-waiting and just about the last person I wanted to run into right now besides her brother, Westley. What on earth was she doing here?

And when a man's voice replied to her, my stomach dropped to the floor. Cass? My heart beat faster at the familiar sound, filling me with relief over his safety, desire to be near him and fear on his behalf. I could hardly believe how much I'd missed him in the few hours we'd been apart.

But how did he get here, and with Arabella, no less? After what Eric told me, I knew that any reason for the two of them to be together had to be bad news. My feet itched to rush in and separate them, but I forced myself to stay put, trying to hear what they were talking about.

Having come in partway through the conversation, I couldn't quite figure out what they were discussing but it sounded like it had something to do with Cass' wedding and switching places. Had he told her what happened on our trip? I couldn't think of any reason he would have, but nothing else made sense to me in the context.

Although I couldn't entirely follow the conversation, I could read their tones well enough. Cass' voice sounded tight, betraying his unhappiness about whatever was being discussed, while Arabella had that smug, self-satisfied tone that told me she thought she was about to get her way.

Then Cass asked her what she thought he should do to avoid marrying the princess, and a pang of hurt shot through me. I must have missed something. I hoped I had. Why would he want to get out of marrying me, and why would he be asking Arabella for advice?

She replied that he should ensure he already had a bride before going home, and my throat seemed to close up as I waited for his response. He couldn't really be considering this, could he? He wouldn't have lied to me about how he felt? He had been so happy that we were going to be together, the things he said to me when we were alone and naked together still burned into my mind and heart. They couldn't be a lie. My heart ached at even the idea that he didn't feel the same way I did.

My mind spiraled as I held my breath, my face pressed against the cool wood of the door, waiting for him to say something, each second of waiting feeling like an eternity.

Finally, he began to laugh.

A low chuckle at first, it gradually got stronger until Arabella spoke again, sounding rather annoyed.

"This is hardly a laughing matter, Your Highness. I don't think you understand..."

"Oh, I'm pretty sure I understand completely," Cass cut her off, his voice conveying a mix of amusement and anger. "I'm guessing that you are very selflessly offering to marry me yourself to save me from this terrible fate?"

"Well, yes," she admitted, sounding uncharacteristically flustered. "I would like to help you, Prince Cassian. I believe that we could help each other."

"I'm sure you do believe that, and I have to hand it to you, Lady Arabella. You almost had me going there until you overplayed your hand."

That sounded like my cue. Without wasting another second, I pushed open the door connecting the kitchen to the dining room and walked in.

Cass and Arabella both turned to look at me, a look of delight crossing his face while dismay clouded hers. My attention, however, immediately went to the woman standing in front of another door, being held in place by a man dressed nearly identically to Cass. I had never seen this woman before, but she wore one of my old dresses and she looked remarkably like me other than the unfocused look in her eyes.

Who on earth could she be? I hardly knew what to think, but I forced myself to focus back on what I'd come in to do.

"Lady Arabella." I addressed my former lady using the icy tone I had learned from my mother that I reserved for very rare occasions. Cass' eyebrows raised at the sound of it since he'd never heard me speak this way before. "It sounded like you, but I thought I must be mistaken. What would bring you to Silatria, right on my heels?"

Her face puckered as though she had swallowed something sour, but she managed to reply to me politely enough. "Good evening, Your Highness. I didn't know that you were here."

Clearly. Cass looked between the two of us in fake surprise. "Your Highness? I don't believe I've had the pleasure of meeting this enchanting woman before. Would you care to introduce me, Lady Arabella?"

Her lips pressed tightly together as she tried to suppress her displeasure at this turn of events. "It would be my pleasure, Prince Cassian. May I present Princess Cordelia of Lassaria."

His expression formed such a perfect picture of astonishment, it took all the self-control I had not to laugh. "Princess Cordelia? But I thought you said..."

"We can discuss it later," she interrupted, her face having turned nearly puce with repressed anger. "Please, excuse me, Your Highnesses." She directed the other man and woman in the room to leave, and quickly followed behind them out of the room.

"Cass," I whispered, taking a step towards him as soon as we were alone, but he quickly shook his head.

"Not here," he answered in an equally low voice. "Outside."

We returned back through the kitchen and out the back door of the inn, finding ourselves in a quiet street beneath the darkened sky. Cass looked around each corner, making sure we were completely alone before he pulled me towards him.

His kiss was hard and bruising, full of pent-up need and emotion and it made my heart soar, healing every second that we'd been apart. I kissed him back just as greedily, inhaling his scent as his tongue invaded my mouth. It hardly seemed possible that I had seen him this morning and touched him in the carriage. It felt like a lifetime ago. Time seemed to lose all meaning without him beside me.

When he pulled away, we were both panting, short of breath. My heart raced within my chest and I would have bet anything that his did too.

"I'm sorry," he whispered, his words taking me by surprise far more than the force of his kiss had.

"For what?"

"For doubting you for even a second."

I had no idea what he meant, but it seemed important to him, so I kissed him again and his arms tightened around me. All too quickly, he drew away again.

"I can't stay here," he whispered next, his chestnut eyes piercing into mine through the hazy darkness. "But I can't leave you either. I'm still in danger and now I'm afraid that you are too."

I knew immediately that there must be a threat from Arabella, though I didn't know exactly what she'd said. But based on what Eric had told me, Cass' life was indeed still in danger, and rejecting Arabella's ridiculous offer of marriage probably hadn't improved his odds at all.

I had a million questions, but I trusted Cass enough to wait until later to ask them. As long as I had him beside me, we could figure the rest out together.

"Then we'll run," I told him. "Both of us, right now. Wherever you go, Cass, I'm going too."

CHAPTER FOURTEEN

Although I knew we had no time to spare, I hugged Dee tightly to me again. I couldn't seem to stop touching her, needing her skin against mine to convince myself she was really here and safe. When she walked through the door into the dining room, the most incredible feeling of lightness and happiness filled me. There weren't words to do it justice, but I knew what it meant.

I loved this woman completely and I trusted her completely too. Those small doubts that Arabella had managed to plant in my mind completely washed away as I watched Dee take charge of the room, putting Arabella in her place with no effort at all. She might not be a typical princess, but she was *my* princess, now and forever.

And now she wanted to run away with me, not even asking if I had a plan, not bothered at all about what dangers might lie ahead. And though I knew somewhere in the back of my mind that I should protest, that I should try to keep her safe and away from me, the truth remained that I couldn't stand to be away from her again for any real length of time. I needed her beside me, and in all honesty, she could probably take care of me just as well as I could take care of her.

"We'll need a horse," I heard myself saying. "And a few supplies."

"What kind of supplies?" Dee asked, immediately focusing on the task at hand.

I listed them off. "Food, drink and ideally some blankets. We'll need to find somewhere safe to spend the night, and then if we ride full-out tomorrow, we can be at my father's castle by afternoon."

Dee nodded. "I'll see what I can find. And you'll get a horse?"

"I'll try my best," I agreed. "Come and meet me out at the stables as soon as you can. And be careful, Dee."

She nodded again, but I noticed the way she bit her lip as she looked up at the inn above us.

"What's wrong?" In such a short period of time, I had learned so much about her little gestures and what they meant.

"Lodee will be so worried when I don't come back," she explained, and my heart melted at the obvious love and concern she had for her friend.

"I'll get a message to Bran somehow," I offered, though I didn't know yet just how I would do that. "It's too dangerous for you to go back upstairs. Arabella's men could be waiting for you."

"You don't think Lodee and Bran will be in danger, do you?" Although I could hardly see her face in the darkness, the worry etched on it showed clearly.

"I don't know," I replied honestly. "But Bran will protect Elodie with his life if he has to."

That may not have completely reassured her, but she nodded one more time. "I'll meet you at the stables then."

Dee ducked back into the door we had come out of, looking carefully to either side before heading in, while I made my way cautiously around the side of the inn. A few men had gathered outside the front of the inn while the stables lay a short distance away, across the courtyard. If I went out into the courtyard, they'd be sure to see me, but I couldn't tell from where I stood if they were Arabella's men or simply other travellers.

As I tried to figure out how to create some kind of diversion, the door to the inn opened and all the men turned to look. Grabbing my opportunity, I ran as quickly and quietly as I could across the open courtyard into the shadows of the stable.

From this angle, I could see the door better, and I could see that some of Arabella's men had just come out. They spoke to the men who had been standing at the door before, and though I couldn't hear what they were saying, Arabella's men gestured around the area and the other men turned to look all around. Pressing myself back against the dark wall as much as I could, I tried not to even breathe and, to my relief, no one seemed to see me there.

They went back to their conversation and I headed as quietly as possible towards the carriage that Bran and Elodie would be taking in the morning. It seemed the best place to leave a message that Bran would be sure to see.

Picking up a stone from the ground, I quickly carved a couple of symbols into the door of the carriage. It would look like random lines to most people, but I knew Bran would understand, and he should see it when he opened the door for Elodie in the morning. Hopefully they wouldn't worry too much about us in the meantime.

With no time to be picky about a horse, I simply went to the nearest one and began to untie it, throwing the occasional glance back over my shoulder. The men were still all standing by the inn entrance, which would make it difficult for Dee to get over to me without being seen.

With the horse free and saddled, I pulled myself up, my eyes still trained on the inn door and the back street that I had come from. Dee could be coming from either direction and I wanted to be prepared either way.

At last, I saw her emerge from behind the inn at the same spot I had, a blanket across her arm and a basket in her other hand, and a deep appreciation for her filled me from head to toe. She was a wonder, getting all of that together so quickly. So many women in her place would be panicking, but Dee remained level-headed and resourceful and so damn perfect I could hardly believe it.

She paused when she saw the men, just as I had, and her eyes moved to the stable. I couldn't tell if she could see me in the shadows. She gave no indication that she could.

Once again, I turned my mind toward creating a distraction, but before I could do anything, Dee stepped confidently out into the court-yard, striding toward me as if she didn't have a care in the world.

Blood rushed through my ears as the men saw her and immediately called out to her. "My lady, stop there."

Dee turned to them with an unimpressed look. "It is Your Highness to you and I do not answer to you."

So, she planned to play the princess card. Would that work? I held my breath as I watched from the darkness. The men moved towards her but Dee did not back down, taking a few more steps towards the stable.

"It's not safe for you to be out here alone after dark, Your Highness," one of the men said, his words solicitous but his tone far less friendly. "Please, allow me to escort you back inside."

Dee would not be put off. "I need something from my carriage and my escort is unavailable. I trust that you will stand watch here and keep me safe. Now, let me pass."

Her quick thinking impressed me, but even so, success seemed un-likely. If she came to the carriage, they would be watching her and could well see me too. It looked like bolder action would be required.

Giving the horse a nudge, I made my way out of the stable. The sound of the hooves on the stones immediately caught everyone's attention and they all turned to look at me.

"Do you need a ride, Your Highness?" I called to Dee.

Her face broke into a grin, immediately understanding my meaning, and she switched the things she carried to one arm, leaving her other arm free.

"That's him!" the man yelled, starting towards me, but I simply gave the horse a kick, heading straight at the group that had gathered.

Everyone jumped out of the way, everyone except Dee who extended her arm to me. Reaching down, I grabbed her across her body as she grabbed hold of me, and I lifted her onto the horse in front of me so smoothly, anyone would think we'd done it a million times before.

"Wait! Stop!" The men behind us shouted uselessly as Dee and I took off down the back road and through the streets of the quiet, dark town.

"That was amazing!" Dee laughed as she rearranged the blanket and basket on her lap, shifting her weight to get her balance right.

"*You're* amazing," I told her, closing my eyes for a moment as I inhaled the sweet scent of her. Her body pressed right up against me, her hip against my pelvis, sent a shot of desire through me.

Finally, we were together again and alone, and although I should have been focused on everything we needed to do to ensure we both stayed safe, at the moment, my body and my mind refused to cooperate. I could only think of one thing.

When I spoke again, my voice had grown heavy with need. "Let's get out of town, and then we'll find a place to spend the night."

~**Cordelia**~

Cass' tone of voice and the growing hardness I could feel against my thigh set my pulse racing. What he had in mind couldn't be more obvious, and I tried to shift my weight, worried that he might be uncomfortable. A low groan sounded in his throat.

"Please stay as still as you can, Dee," he requested, his voice thicker than usual. "At least until we get somewhere private."

"Sorry," I quickly apologized. I had been trying to make things better, not worse, and Cass seemed to recognize that, leaning down to kiss my temple.

"It's not your fault," he assured me. "You can't help what you do to me. Let's talk about something else for now to take my mind off of it."

We had a lot to talk about. Once we got out of town, the road grew quiet, all sensible travellers already out of sight for the night, so I took the opportunity to tell him everything that Eric had said, watching his face beneath the moonlight as I revealed to him the plot that his brother had agreed to.

His jaw clenched as I reached the end of my explanation. "I suppose I should be happy that he doesn't want me dead, but it doesn't excuse what he tried to do or the stupidity of getting involved with the Eastams in the first place."

"The good news is that he's on your side now," I pointed out. "And maybe if he can convince Westley that he's still in league with him, we can use that to our advantage."

"Make Eric a double agent?" Cass asked, mulling it over. "I'm not sure I'd trust him, but it's worth considering."

"Your turn now," I requested. "How on earth did you end up with Arabella?"

I listened in surprise and then in outrage as Cass outlined the sequence of events that led up to me surprising them in the dining room. Had Arabella honestly thought her plan would work, that Cass would agree to marry her just like that?

"Do you have any idea where she found that other woman?" he asked once he'd told me everything. "She did look quite a lot like you."

I had noticed that too. "I've never seen her before, but we'll get to the bottom of it. Once we expose Westley, Arabella will follow and we can find out everything from her then."

Cass frowned. "The one thing I really don't understand is how that woman ended up here. Arabella must have had her in reserve, so to speak, but for what? What is she planning to do with her?"

"And why is Arabella going to the wedding at all?" I wondered.

"I don't know," Cass admitted. "We'll have to figure it all out tomorrow. For now, we should try to get some rest."

I had been so caught up in our conversation that I hadn't been paying any attention to our location. We had arrived at a small copse of trees, just large enough to provide us some cover so we wouldn't be seen from the road by anyone passing by. Cass led the horse off the road into the trees until we could no longer see the road behind us and then he stopped, dismounting first before taking the basket and blanket from me and helping me down. He tied the horse to one of the nearby trees while I looked around, trying to determine the most comfortable spot for sleeping before laying out the large blanket on the ground.

Cass grimaced as he joined me at the spot I chose. "It's better than the cave, I suppose. We've got grass on the ground and the blanket, but it's still not much."

"It's fine," I assured him. "And it's only for tonight. Tomorrow, we'll be at your castle and you'll be back in your own bed."

His hands went to my waist, pulling me close to him. "I can't wait to have you in my bed, Dee. Tomorrow and every night after."

I laughed, though it came out shakily because of how difficult I found it to breathe, pressed up so close to him, my body going haywire. "I don't think we're supposed to spend the night before the wedding together. People might talk."

"Let them talk," he declared before kissing me hard, just like he had behind the inn, but somehow with even more urgency.

Instantly, my body hummed with longing for him, wanting him even closer to me even though not even an inch of space existed between us. My tongue pressed against his lips, wanting to taste him and he moaned in appreciation of my eagerness as he opened his mouth to me. Hands travelled across both of our bodies, each of us wanting to get beneath the clothes we were wearing but not wanting to break the kiss long enough to take them off.

As if he read my thoughts, Cass pulled back from me. "I think you should keep your dress on, Dee," he whispered. "As much as I want to touch all of you, it will be too cool in the night air without it. I don't want you to catch a chill."

I hardly thought that likely with the heat currently coursing through me, but I knew he did have a point. The brief break from kissing him helped to clear my head and gave me a chance to remember what had happened this morning in the carriage, and what had been about to happen when we were interrupted by the arrival of Eric's men.

I offered my own proposal. "I'll agree to that if you show me how I can taste you instead." Cass exhaled in what almost sounded like pain, and I immediately looked at him in alarm. "Are you alright?"

He gave a tight, short laugh. "I will be, if you stop trying to kill me, Dee. Are you sure that's what you want?"

I nodded in the moonlight, my hand straying to the straining fabric at the front of his breeches. His cock felt hard and warm even through his clothes and he groaned again as I pressed my hand against it.

"Let's get more comfortable," he suggested, taking my hand and leading me onto the blanket before sitting down and pulling me down with him.

Again, he kissed me, our bodies drawn together by some invisible string, a pull we couldn't resist. His tongue ran across my lips, my teeth, my own tongue, exploring every inch of my mouth until no part of it remained that he hadn't claimed as his.

His body leaned into mine, pushing me back until it felt like I might fall, but his arms were there to soften my landing as my back hit the ground and he lay on top of me, his arms supporting some of his weight even as his hard cock pressed against me, right against my aching core. I wanted him there so badly that I almost second-guessed my request to taste him, but my curiosity won out.

Taking him by surprise, I pushed him over so that we rolled together until he lay on his back with me on top of him.

"You have to tell me what to do," I whispered against his lips. "Tell me how to make you feel good."

He looked up at me with disbelief in his eyes. "You don't need any help from me, Dee. I have never felt so good."

"You know what I mean."

I reached down again to run my hand firmly down his hard shaft, still hidden in his breeches, and he inhaled sharply. "Okay, but you can change your mind whenever you want to."

I had no plans to, not if I could make him feel as good as he had made me feel back in the carriage.

"Open my breeches," he instructed and I climbed off him to do just that, kneeling beside him.

"Where should I go?" Would a particular position or angle be best to give him the most pleasure? For now, I undid the laces holding him in and his big, thick cock sprang loose, like a caged animal just waiting to be set free.

"Just beside me, just like you are." His voice sounded nearly hoarse with restraint. "On your hands and knees, but bring your feet towards me."

I followed his instructions until I knelt beside him facing his feet, my own feet near his head.

"Now, just touch me, Dee," he continued. "Use your hands, your mouth, whatever you want. I promise, whatever you do is going to feel good. I'll tell you if it doesn't."

Once again, I did as he said, trailing my fingers gently up and down his long shaft, exploring the feel of it, the hard ridges and the softer head. Cass' breathing sped up the harder I touched him, and as my fingers flicked across the underside of it, his cock jumped, making my own body clench in response. Just touching him this way gave me pleasure too, and I knew now that he hadn't been lying to me before when he told me he had got pleasure from what he did to me.

Still curious about the taste of him, I bent over further and tentatively ran my tongue along the hard ridge beneath the tip of his cock. Cass groaned as my tongue made contact, and his groan made my own throbbing worse.

Emboldened, I licked him again, this time running my tongue all the way down to the base and the dark, curly hair there. My fingers went instinctively to that hair, running through it as I licked my way up again, circling his tip with my tongue.

"Dee." His soft moan came from behind me, feather light in the night air. "That's perfect."

His praise made my body clench again and the next thing I knew, my skirts were being lifted and Cass' hand ran up my thigh beneath my dress.

"What are you doing?" I asked in surprise.

"Don't mind me," he said, not sounding innocent at all. "Keep doing what you're doing."

Still suspicious but equally curious, I returned my attention to his cock which seemed to grow bigger every time I looked at it. Taking it in my hand, I lifted it so it stood straight up and brought the tip to my lips.

Cass sighed, a sound of pure joy, as I parted my lips and took him into my mouth, sucking on him to satisfy my curiosity before pulling back again. He tasted a lot like he smelled, masculine and spicy and earthy. I wanted more.

"That's good," he encouraged me as his hand stroked my leg. "You can use your hand, up and down, to mimic how it feels when I'm inside you."

I tried again, lowering my mouth onto him as far as I could while my hand stroked the rest of him, and Cass groaned in approval.

As I sucked to the tip again before going back down, Cass' fingers moved between my legs, making my body jolt in surprise. "Open your legs for me," he requested. Though I didn't know exactly what he had planned, I could guess it would be good, and I hurried to comply.

The next time I sucked him in, his finger pressed into me at the same time, making me moan against his hard shaft, and he groaned in response.

"Don't stop," he begged.

I had no intention of stopping. I went faster instead and he matched my pace, adding another finger to my aching core while his cock filled my mouth.

He swore beneath his breath as we both drew closer to our release, the whole world fading away once more until the world consisted of only the two of us on this blanket beneath the moon and the pleasure we were giving each other. Nothing else mattered.

The sensations built until I couldn't take it anymore and I reached my peak, waves of pleasure washing over me as my legs trembled beneath me. As my body clenched around his fingers, Cass let go too, his hot seed filling my mouth. I swallowed it with his cock still in my mouth, sucking once more before gently releasing him.

Completely sated, I collapsed back on the blanket next to him as he kissed my forehead. We were both quiet for a moment until he turned to me with a curious look. "So, how do I taste?"

Just as he had done with me in the carriage, I leaned up and kissed him, letting him see for himself.

With one last groan, he pulled away, laying his head back on the blanket. "You never fail to amaze me, Dee."

"I'm amazed by you too." Lying there with him beneath the stars and the moon, it felt like a dream I could have never imagined coming true.

He kissed my forehead once more, pulling me snugly against him so we could share our warmth. "We should try to sleep now. We've got a busy day ahead of us tomorrow."

Today had been one big adventure, but tomorrow promised to be just as eventful. Hopefully, by the end of it, we would both be exactly where we belonged.

~Cassian~

With Dee at my side, I fell into the deepest, most satisfying sleep I could remember. It didn't seem to matter where we spent the night: as long as we were together, I couldn't imagine anything better.

At least until I woke up with a sword at my throat.

"What do we have here?" an amused voice asked and my eyes flew open even as I tried not to move against the sharp metal pressed against my skin. My arm went to pull Dee closer to me, but I could feel only empty space beside me.

Rage and panic flowed through me, and before I even fully thought it through, I had pushed the sword away with my arm, got to my feet and had the man who had been standing above me down on his knees, his sword arm secured behind his back as his weapon fell to the ground. "Where is she?" I shouted.

"I'm here, Cass, it's okay." Dee's sweet voice in my ears instantly calmed my panic and I spun around to see her standing behind me, her arm held by another man with a sword. There were seven or eight of them altogether, most of them with their swords now aimed directly at me.

Realizing we were outnumbered and not wanting to put Dee in any more danger, I dropped the arm of the man in front of me. "Who are you?" I demanded. We were now in my kingdom and everyone in it technically answered to me. "What do you want?"

"Calm down," the man who had woken me up said with a scowl, shaking his arm out before picking up the sword he had dropped. "We won't hurt you or the woman either. We just need money. You're one of Eastam's men, right? He'll pay a good ransom for your return."

My eyes dropped to the clothes I still wore, the ones Arabella had given me. I couldn't deny I looked like one of her family's men, but I really didn't have time for this.

"I'll give you money," I offered. "Follow me to the king's castle and I'll give you whatever you ask for. We can't be delayed."

The man laughed. "Follow you to the king's castle where you'll have me arrested? Not likely. I'm not that stupid."

I grimaced as I thought it through from his point of view. It certainly sounded like a trap, and I couldn't convince him otherwise without revealing my actual title to him, which would be a bad idea. Surely, the ransom on my own head would be bigger than if one of the Eastams' men. Keeping my identity secret seemed like the smarter choice.

"Dee, have you got any money with you?" I remembered that the dress she had given me to wear yesterday had some coins sewn into it.

"A little, but probably not as much as they're looking for."

"The lady understands us," the man in front of me said, giving Dee a grin, and my fists clenched at my side. If he kept looking at her like that, he would answer for it, no matter how many more of them there were than me.

"How about we play for it?" Dee suggested, and everyone immediately turned to her. "We can make it a challenge."

"What kind of challenge?" the man asked, clearly intrigued. His eyes registered a new level of interest that made me want to punch him even more.

"An archery competition," Dee explained, pointing to the bow and arrows slung across the man's back. "Your best archer against me. If you win, we'll go with you willingly. If I win, you let us go for the money I have with me."

All the men laughed at her proposal and I could see Dee's cheeks start to colour in indignation. I gave her a small smile and shook my head at her gently, urging her not to react. It would be better if they underestimated her. Overconfidence would only hurt them.

"Why not?" the first man said, still chuckling. "I could use some entertainment this morning."

All the men laughed again and the man holding Dee let her go as they decided amongst themselves who would take the shot. She strode quickly over to me and I pulled her into my arms, grateful once again for her quick thinking and level head.

"Are you alright? Do you know who they are?" I couldn't be sure how much I missed before I woke up.

"I don't think so," she whispered back. "And I'm fine. I think he's telling the truth. I don't think they want to harm us, they just want money."

So, they were bandits, but not violent ones. It could be worse, but there shouldn't be bandits in Silatrian territory at all. Why weren't these men properly employed?

The men came to an agreement about which of them would challenge Dee, and the leader called over to us. "The target is that tree there, the one with the white trunk." Dee and I both turned to look at the tree, at least a hundred yards away through a maze of other trees. "Closest one wins."

"Fine," Dee agreed without hesitation.

"Are you sure?" I asked her under my breath. That would be an incredibly difficult shot. I certainly couldn't make it.

"Are you doubting me, Cass?" she teased, giving me a wink, and instantly, all my worry evaporated.

"Of course not. I can't wait to see you blow them all away."

"Ladies first," the man offered as Dee walked over to him, handing her a bow and a single arrow.

"I'd rather you show me how it's done," she demurred, gesturing for the group's archer to take his shot. "Please, go ahead."

The man stepped forward with a smirk, taking aim at the distant target. He adjusted the angle of his bow a few times, one eye closed as he scanned the terrain. When satisfied, he released and the arrow flew forward forcefully, flying through the trees before hitting a tree just before the target.

While not perfect, the shot was far better than I could have done. His friends all cheered and congratulated him.

Dee also gave him a nod of acknowledgement. "Not bad," she said, drawing a chorus of derision from the gathered men.

Stepping up to the same spot the man had fired from, Dee drew her own bow back, the arrow resting against her face for stability. I could almost see the calculations going on in her head as she surveyed the other trees, the wind, and all the other factors which might affect her arrow's trajectory. With a confident stroke, the arrow released.

I held my breath as it raced through the trees, straight and true, past the tree the other man had hit, and landed dead centre in the middle of the white trunk.

"What the devil?" the man who had shot the other arrow grumbled while all the other men looked at each other and over at Dee in shock.

Dee tossed me a wink before turning back to the men, offering their bow back to them. "I believe that I've won, gentlemen."

The man who had first threatened me this morning took the bow from her with a grudging look of respect. "Impressive, my lady. We could use someone of your skill. I don't suppose you're looking to join a gang of ne'er-do-wells, down on their luck?"

Dee laughed at that, but I stepped in to question him before she answered. "How is it that men like you are reduced to this? If you have no lord, the king's army needs good fighters and would pay you a decent wage. There's no need to harass travellers this way."

The man's face hardened as he turned from Dee to me. "A decent wage? Where have you been? Since Prince Eric took over the army a year ago, all wages have been cut. There are men who haven't been paid in months, families that are starving."

Dee gave me a worried look as I tried to hide my own concern. Eric might be selfish, but he wasn't maliciously cruel enough to do something like that. I could only guess that he had passed off responsibility to someone else and didn't know the full situation.

"Come to the castle in a few days," I proposed to the man in front of me. "Ask to speak to Prince Cassian and tell him that Sean sent you. He'll sort all of this out."

"Prince Cassian is dead," the man replied, giving me a funny look. "Haven't you heard?"

"Just trust me on this," I requested, unable to say anything more right now. "Now, we can give you your payment and we'll move on. If you'll allow me, I can use your sword to cut the coins out of the lady's dress."

The man looked over at Dee and down at her dress. "Forget about it. The lady won fair and square and I wouldn't want to destroy her dress. You seem like decent people, though why you're working for an ass like Eastam, I can't imagine."

They seemed like decent people too. I really needed to get to the bottom of this and figure out what had gone wrong in my father's army.

Bidding them goodbye, Dee and I grabbed our basket and blanket and untied the horse, heading back to the main road. Now that we had the sun's light, we were able to move much quicker, and I kept one arm around her as the other held the reins. Dee fed me breakfast from the provisions she'd taken from the inn as we talked over what had just happened and what still lay ahead of us today.

It seemed like there were more than a few things about my brother I hadn't paid close enough attention to, but that would end today. Starting now, Prince Cassian was back.

CHAPTER FIFTEEN

When the turrets and high stone walls of the Silatrian king's castle appeared in the distance, I breathed a sigh of relief. The journey to get here had been more eventful than I could have ever imagined, but with a much happier ending too. I wouldn't have changed a moment of it so long as it meant that I got to be here with Cass right now.

He pressed on at a gallop, the same as we'd been riding all day, only slowing the horse's pace as we entered the small town surrounding the castle. The large stone structure looming ahead of us was bigger than my father's castle and better fortified. A deep ditch surrounded it while armed archers patrolled the top of the walls. Even in peacetime, it sent a message that Silatria should not be underestimated.

Despite that security, no one in the town paid us much attention as we went by, likely assuming from Cass' clothing that we were here on behalf of the Eastams. No one seemed to recognize Cass as their lost prince.

The drawbridge lay open, and when we got to the castle gate, the guard there only glanced up at us for a moment. "Your business here?" he asked.

"Philip," Cass replied, sounding amused. "It's me."

The man looked up again, his brow furrowed as he looked at Cass more closely, and then his whole face brightened in excitement and disbelief. "Prince Cassian? But you... they said... how..."

Cass laughed as the man struggled to form a complete sentence. "It's a long story. I need to see my father, is he here?"

"Y-yes," the man stuttered, still in shock. "He should be in the Great Hall."

"Thank you. I'll see you later."

Leaving the guard to recover from his shock, Cass led the horse into the castle courtyard which hummed with activity. For a moment, I felt a pang of longing for my home, wishing I could see my brothers come around the corner or hear my father's laugh, but it quickly passed as excitement took its place, excitement to get to know this place and claim it as my own, along with the wonderful man beside me.

Cass stopped outside a large door with a small set of steps leading up to it, and a stable boy quickly ran over to us to take the reins from him. Cass dismounted first before helping me down, leaving the blanket and basket with the boy before taking my hand and leading me inside.

Despite the heat of the day outside, the stone walls kept the inside air cooler. Our eyes slowly adjusting to the darker interior, we headed through the entrance foyer where people milled around talking to each other, and towards another large set of doors on the opposite side of the hall. Two men dressed in the Silatrian red and black colours stood on either side of the door, each armed with a sword.

One of them held out a hand to stop us as we approached the threshold. "The king is conducting private business. Entrance is by invitation only."

Cass sighed. "I really need to change out of these clothes," he muttered to me before turning back to the man. "Anthony, let me through. I need to see my father."

The man's mouth dropped open and his eyes widened as he examined Cass' face. "Your Highness? Forgive me, I..."

"It's fine," Cass said, clearly not wanting to waste any more time. "I'll explain later."

The man stepped aside, and as we entered the Great Hall, I couldn't suppress my gasp of surprise. Twice the size of my father's hall, it had four fireplaces, two on either side, and beautiful tapestries covering the walls between. An oak hammerbeam ceiling soared above us and beneath our feet, wood slats covered the dirt floor. I had heard of such innovations, but I'd never seen them for myself before. My father had the money to pay for luxuries like these but generally considered them a waste when the current methods worked well enough. He claimed he hadn't gotten rich by spending money unnecessarily.

I didn't have time to fully take it in as Cass pulled me along, marching straight to the end of the room where an older man sat on a wooden throne on a raised dais. My attention moved to him as we approached, and despite the fuller beard and greying strands of hair, I could see a family resemblance between the king and both Cass and Eric. Cass was by far the most handsome of the three, in my opinion.

Speaking of Eric, he stood there too, standing at his father's side and his face lit up as we approached, looking genuinely pleased to see us.

"Father," Cass greeted the king as we got to the foot of the dais, bowing deeply. "Please excuse my late arrival."

A gasp and murmurs of surprise circled among the gathered crowd but the king himself must have had some advance warning, because he leapt to his feet with surprising agility and hurried down the steps to his son.

"Cass," he chortled happily, pulling him into a warm embrace that made me smile. It heartened me to know they had a good relationship, no matter what the situation with Eric might be.

Eric also came down the steps towards us, much more hesitantly. "I'm so relieved to see you," he said to his brother, and the warm smile Cass had worn for his father swiftly fell away.

"I understand why you're relieved," Cass told him coolly. "Princess Cordelia has told me everything."

The king turned to me with an expression of both delight and confusion. "Cordelia? We weren't expecting you until later. How did you come to be with my son?"

Cass and I both smiled as we exchanged glances. I bowed my head before answering the king. "That is quite a long story, Your Majesty."

"I'm sure," he agreed good-naturedly. "Come, let's speak in private. I'm sure we have a lot to catch up on."

He clapped Cass on the shoulder before turning and leading us through a much smaller door to the rear of the throne. It led into a small receiving room, much less formal but still richly decorated. Two more guards stood in here, but otherwise, we were alone, just the king, his two sons, and me.

"Eric told me that he heard you were alive," the king explained to Cass as we all took a seat. "I'm delighted that you've managed to stay that way."

"Thanks to Cordelia," Cass acknowledged, sending a warm smile my way. "She saved me more than once."

"Why are you wearing the Eastam colours?" Eric cut in, his voice laced with confusion.

Cass grimaced. "That's also a long story, but the most urgent thing right now is that we detain Westley Eastam. Do you know where he is?"

Eric looked away guiltily, and immediately my heart sank. Whatever he had to tell us, it wouldn't be good news.

"I tried to speak to him when I got back yesterday, but he had his suspicions about where I had been. He must have received some other information because when I went to find him this morning, he had gone. No one knows where he went, or if they do know, they're not telling me."

"Arabella," I whispered under my breath to Cass and he nodded. She must have gotten a message to her brother somehow and warned him that we were on our way.

"I've ordered the palace guard to arrest him on sight," the king told Cass. "Eric has explained to me exactly what he agreed to."

So, Eric had come clean with his father. I couldn't help wondering how that conversation had gone.

The king continued as if he'd heard my unspoken question. "Eric's penance is still being determined, but for now, Eastam is our focus. If he attempts anything else, we'll know about it."

"Add Arabella Eastam to that blacklist too," Cass stated firmly. "I don't want her anywhere near the castle or near Dee."

"Dee?" the king repeated curiously.

Cass almost blushed, looking rather adorable as he glanced quickly over at me. "Princess Cordelia, that is."

The king raised his eyebrows as he looked between the two of us, a smile twinkling in his eyes that reminded me of Cass' own playful side. "It appears the two of you have gotten quite well acquainted."

I had to push down my own blush too, remembering the things we had done to each other last night. "We have spent some time together," I admitted, ignoring Cass' cheeky smirk at my vague response.

To my relief, Cass stepped in to change the subject. "The princess' lady should be arriving later today. In the meantime, are her chambers ready? I am sure she would like to rest and freshen up after the journey."

"What will you be doing?" I asked, not particularly pleased about the prospect of being pushed to the side.

"I will fill my father and brother in on everything that's happened, and we'll decide what to do next. Don't worry, I'll tell you anything important that comes up later on."

Since I believed that he would, I acquiesced. The king called for some of my new staff who led me to the rooms that would be mine, the rooms set aside for the crown prince's wife. I had an entire suite consisting of a bedroom, a small privy, and a sitting room to sit with my ladies during the day. As they helped me to bathe and change into some fresh clothes, I couldn't stop my eyes from wandering to the small door in the corner, the one which I instinctively knew led to Cass' own rooms. He would come through that door tomorrow night to consummate our marriage when we were officially bound to each other.

I really couldn't wait.

When they had nearly finished dressing me, the door to my bedroom opened and I turned in anticipation, expecting to see Cass. Instead, Elodie flew at me, taking all the ladies in the room by surprise.

"Dee!" she almost sobbed in relief. "You had me so worried."

My heart went out to my dear friend as I told the other ladies in the room to leave us for a moment. "I'm so sorry, Lodee," I whispered to her when we were alone. "I wish I could have told you, but we had to leave. Staying there would have been too dangerous."

"I understand," she sniffed, tears in her eyes as she pulled back from me. "Bran went looking for you when you didn't come back and he ran into the men looking for you. He didn't know who they were, but he figured that if they were looking for you, it must mean they hadn't found you, so he thought you must have gotten away. This morning, we saw your message."

I took her hands in mine. "Arabella's men were the ones who questioned you. She's the one looking for me, and for Cass too."

Elodie's eyes hardened in a very uncharacteristic look for her. "If I get my hands on that woman, I'm going to..."

"No, you're not," I cut her off with a laugh. "You couldn't hurt a fly, Lodee. But don't worry: Cass has ensured she can't get anywhere near us. He'll find her and Westley too, and they'll both answer for their scheming."

"I hope so." She sighed as she looked around my new room. "It's all over now, right? We've made it?"

As I followed her gaze around my new home and thought of my soon-to-be husband and our wedding tomorrow, I had to agree. Everything looked pretty perfect right now. "We've made it," I told her firmly. "Welcome home, Lodee."

~Cassian~

More time than I'd hoped had passed by the time I found myself standing in front of Dee's door. It had taken a while to fill my father and brother in on everything that had happened and for Eric to tell me everything about Westley.

I asked him what on earth gave him the right to interfere with my marriage, and he just shrugged apologetically. "I honestly didn't think you'd care, Cass. You never paid any attention to who you were going to be marrying, not once."

I couldn't argue with that. Before meeting Dee, I honestly thought that one woman was pretty much the same as the next. I knew now just how wrong I'd been, and I couldn't be more grateful that I would get to marry her.

My father explained that the wedding would still take place the next day since the arrangements were already made, but he insisted that I shave and get my hair cut so I looked more recognizable to the general public. He didn't want there to be any doubt about my identity; it would be easy for rumours to get started that we were trying to pass someone else off as the dead prince. It had been done before.

I had to concede that point, but I had to admit I would rather miss my new look. Hopefully, Dee wouldn't mind too much.

On my way back to my rooms, I ran into Bran in the hall, and we embraced each other happily.

"You made it." He stated the obvious with evident relief.

"I did, and Dee's fine too, she's in her rooms now. Did you and Elodie have any trouble?"

He shook his head. "There were some men looking for the princess, but I pretended we had nothing to do with her and they let us be."

Quick thinking from Bran, as always. He followed me back to my rooms where the barber met me to take care of my hair and beard and I filled Bran in on everything that had happened with Arabella, Westley and Eric.

"I'll lead some men out now," he volunteered as soon as I'd finished. "We might not catch up with Eastam himself, but if Lady Arabella is in her carriage, she should be easier to find."

He would always have my back. "I appreciate it, but it's not necessary. All the guards have been instructed not to let them into the castle grounds tomorrow, and a day or two after the wedding, I'll head out myself. You can come with me then."

"What's your plan?"

"I'll head back to Lassaria. It's the most likely place for them to go, and even if we don't find them immediately, I can explain the situation to the king there and he can take appropriate action against the family. They'll be ruined if nothing else."

Bran nodded slowly. "Alright, but are you sure you want to wait? I can leave now and get a head start."

"And miss my wedding?" I teased him. "I thought you'd be there gloating in the front row."

That made him laugh. "True. I would hate to miss the chance to say I told you so."

When the barber had finished, I left Bran to go to Dee's new rooms, the rooms that had always been reserved for my wife. They'd sat empty for a long time, but knowing that Dee occupied them now filled me with joy and anticipation.

The door opened swiftly for me when I knocked, revealing another guard. "Your Highness." He bowed to me, blinking in surprise. Word must have spread around the castle already that I had not died after all, but I would probably be getting this reaction from people for a while.

Giving him a nod, I stepped inside the sitting room that formed the entrance to Dee's rooms. Several ladies filled the space, but not Dee or Elodie.

I decided to address the room at large. "Where can I find Princess Cordelia?"

The ladies all exchanged smiles with each other. "She's in her bedroom, Your Highness, with Lady Elodie. Shall I fetch her for you?"

"No, thank you, I'll go in." A few scandalized gasps followed my statement, but after everything Dee and I had been through, propriety had dropped to the bottom of my list of worries.

Still, I knocked on the bedroom door rather than simply entering, and Elodie answered. She looked genuinely pleased to see me and gave me a polite bow as she stepped aside to let me in.

"Sorry I took so long," I apologized as Dee gave me a curious look. It took me a moment to remember the barber's work. "What do you think? My father insisted."

I ran my hand along my smooth cheek, hoping she wouldn't find me any less attractive now.

She answered me as honestly as always. "I think I prefer the beard, but it's probably because that's how you looked when I fell in love with you."

I had never known what it meant for a person's heart to melt before I met her. "He wanted me looking the way people expect me to for my wedding, but I can grow it back afterwards if you like."

Walking over to me, Dee ran her fingers down my other cheek, sending little shivers through my body. "We'll see. I could get used to this too."

I pulled her towards me, but just before our lips connected, Elodie cleared her throat dramatically. "May I remind you, Your Highness, that you should not be entertaining a man in your private rooms before you are wed?"

Dee laughed, turning to her friend. "Really, Lodee? You already know that Cass and I have slept together."

She did? Perhaps I shouldn't be surprised that Dee had told her, they did seem very close.

"Yes, *I* know that, but the whole world doesn't need to, and you've already been in here quite long enough, Your Highness. Any longer and the ladies will be talking of nothing else. Now, go!"

Those were the most words I had heard Elodie put together so far, and in a far more commanding tone of voice than I expected. I looked over at Dee for her direction and she simply shrugged at me. "I've tried arguing with her before, but I usually lose."

"I'll come to you tonight then," I offered instead, but Elodie shook her head firmly.

"Several of the ladies will be here with her. It's tradition, Your Highness. *Your* tradition."

Damn it. I hadn't paid that much attention to Silatrian wedding customs before. I had never thought it would matter to me where my bride spent the night before our wedding.

"You'll be married tomorrow, and you can spend time alone together after that. Until then, shoo!" Elodie opened the door again, leaving me no choice but to go.

"Sorry," Dee whispered apologetically as I backed away towards the door. "I'll see you tomorrow though."

"See you tomorrow," I whispered back before nodding at Elodie with a slightly bemused expression. Bran would have his hands full with her if he thought her as meek and mild as I previously had.

From the moment I woke up the next day, I didn't have a moment to myself. There were guests to greet and diplomatic meetings to be held with visiting dignitaries. Everyone wanted to hear the story of my survival, and by the fifth retelling, I had started to bore myself. By the time I actually made it to the church for the wedding, I was exhausted and desperate for even a glimpse of my beautiful bride.

When she appeared, my heart nearly stopped. Dee always looked beautiful, but the stunned whispers circulating the stone cathedral made it clear just how stunning she appeared today. Her golden gown glittered with jewels, sparkling in the light that drifted in through the church windows. Her blonde hair had been braided elaborately in roped patterns, her cheeks and lips looked even pinker than usual and her blue eyes looked more vibrant than ever against the gold of her dress. She looked like an angel as she came to stand beside me, someone I hardly recognized, but when she gave me a private wink, it proved my unpredictable Dee was still there.

The ceremony passed in a blur. All I could really remember afterwards, besides kissing her, was the enormous relief of knowing that we had, against all odds, managed to end up married to each other. A feast followed, and again, well-wishers and other people eager for a moment to address their own concerns monopolized all my time. I hardly had a chance to look at Dee, let alone talk to her.

My heart leapt when Dee stood to make her exit, followed by her ladies, to prepare for her wedding night, but following tradition, I stayed a while longer. The men of the court would place bets on how long the groom could last before following his wife from the room, and if I didn't hold out at least a short while to prove my own stamina, I would never hear the end of it.

The minutes passed agonizingly slowly as I imagined Dee being undressed and eventually, I couldn't take it any longer. I returned to my own rooms along with Bran and the two men from the church who had been appointed as witnesses to follow me to Dee's room. I hadn't been joking when I'd told her about this custom, but hopefully once they had evidence that we'd completed the consummation, they would leave us alone and I could have my wife to myself for the rest of the night.

My wife. Smiling to myself, I could hardly believe those words referred to Dee. I couldn't wait to spend not just the night but the rest of my life with her.

Bran helped me out of my elaborate wedding clothes and into the simple nightshirt I would wear for the ceremonial walk to Dee's rooms. Just as we were about to leave, someone knocked on my door. I gave Bran a curious look and he shrugged back at me. Nobody should be disturbing me now.

He spoke to the person on the other side before coming back to me with a cup and a folded piece of paper.

"What is that?" I asked, looking at myself in the mirror one more time to make sure I looked my best for Dee.

"They said it's from the princess," Bran told me, sounding uncertain. "I think there's a note."

He handed me the piece of paper and I quickly scanned the contents.

Dear Cassian,

My ladies have prepared this special drink for you, they say it will help to enhance the evening's activities. I'm not sure what that means, but I'm looking forward to finding out. Please drink it and come to me as soon as you can.

Yours, Cordelia

An uneasy feeling settled over me as Arabella's words came back to me. Back at the inn, when she'd tried to convince me Dee was an imposter, she mentioned I would be given a drink that would cloud my senses, so I would mistake the other woman for the princess instead. Did this have something to do with that?

The note sounded suspicious too. Dee never called me Cassian or referred to herself as Cordelia, at least not to me.

Something must be wrong. I dropped the note and ran out into the hall with Bran and the witnesses trailing after me.

"Cass, what's going on?" Bran called from behind me, but I didn't stop, racing past the servants and other onlookers who had gathered to watch the traditional walk to the bride's chambers. They would be shocked by me running by them like this, but they could think what they liked. I had to see Dee.

Bursting into her room, I startled all the ladies in the sitting room, but again, I didn't spare them a glance before heading straight to Dee's bedroom, letting myself in without knocking.

"Your Highness!" One of the ladies inside squeaked in alarm at my sudden appearance.

"Where is she?" I demanded, looking for my bride. I couldn't see her or Elodie either.

"She... she's waiting for you in bed," the lady stammered, pointing a shaking hand towards the curtained bed.

My heart pounded against my chest as I walked over and pulled the curtain back, desperately hoping that I had overreacted and it would, in fact, be Dee waiting for me within.

But as the light shone into the curtained interior, my stomach dropped and my knees nearly gave way.

She looked like Dee, maybe even more now than she had the first time I saw her, but the vacant eyes looking at me from the woman in the bed were not my wife's.

What had they done with Dee?

~**Cordelia**~

When I left my home a week ago, I could have never imagined my wedding day being such a happy occasion. Knowing that by the end of the day I would be married to Cass and sharing a bed with him properly put a smile on my face from the moment I woke up.

I hoped that he would come to see me in the morning, but when I asked the ladies who had been assigned to serve me, they told me Silatrian tradition dictated that we wouldn't see each other until the wedding. When I asked about any other traditions I should be prepared for, they explained how I would leave the wedding feast before Cass. When ready, he would come to my room not through the private passageway but through the main halls, along with his witnesses. People would line the halls, all checking to make sure that he did, in fact, visit my room.

As Cass had already warned me, the witnesses would stay in the room to listen to us and make sure we did actually consummate the marriage, after which Cass would leave with them, back through the halls.

Only I and Elodie knew that he had promised to return to me afterwards using the private passageway. I really couldn't wait for *that* part of the day.

It took all of the morning and half the afternoon to get me ready. Thank goodness for Elodie who kept me entertained while the ladies scrubbed and perfumed my skin, practically sewed my clothes onto me and did my hair in a way that looked like it would take just as long to undo as it did to do it. By the time they were finished, my patience had reached its end, but when I got a look at myself in the mirror, I had to admire the overall effect.

Every second spent proved worthwhile when I saw the way Cass' face softened at the sight of me, that small smile on his lips just for me. Dressed in his finest clothes, his hair cut short and his face clean shaven, he bore little outward resemblance to the Sean I had first met and fallen in love with, but his smile felt just the same. I winked at him as I approached the altar and he grinned back, making my heart leap happily as we were declared husband and wife.

Even at the feast, though we were seated together, we had no time to talk. I waited for one of my ladies to give me the signal that I could take my leave, and when it finally came, all my ladies followed me out, Elodie first among them.

"You really did it!" she squealed happily as we got back to my room. "You've married your prince."

I could really call him *my* prince now. I could hardly believe it myself.

It took another small army of women to remove my wedding gown and untie my hair, but at last, they brushed it out and brought me a simple but luxurious nightdress for me to wear to await my husband's official visit.

Most of the ladies drifted back to the sitting room just outside my bedroom while Elodie and a couple of others remained with me in case I needed anything while I waited for Cass to arrive.

I went and sat on the bed while Elodie sat beside me to tell me a story to pass the time. Although I tried to pay attention to her, I kept getting distracted by one of the ladies standing by the window as she kept raising her hand in an odd way.

"Why are you doing that?" I asked her curiously.

She simply looked back at me with a rather insincere smile. "You'll see, Your Highness."

Elodie and I exchanged glances. "That was strange, right?" I asked her under my breath.

Elodie nodded. "Shall I remove her?"

As my primary lady-in-waiting, Elodie outranked all the other women here. She could assign roles to the different ladies as she saw fit.

Still, I hesitated. It seemed reckless to offend anyone for no good reason. My new ladies were all daughters of Silatrian nobility, and I didn't know all the details yet of whose good side I needed to stay on.

I decided to let it go for now. "Keep going with your story, Lodee."

A few minutes later, I heard a knock and, for a moment, my heart leapt again, hoping Cass had arrived at last. But a second later, I realized the knock had come from the private passageway rather than the main door.

The lady who had been by the window went straight to the door and opened it, and Elodie and I both scrambled to our feet in alarm as four armed men entered, their swords drawn.

"What is the meaning of this?" I demanded while Elodie gripped my arm nervously. "Explain yourselves immediately."

"I don't think you're in any position to ask questions, Princess," one of the men sneered, stepping towards Elodie. I immediately put myself between him and her.

"Go for help!" I instructed the other ladies in the room, but they both stood there, stock still, and my stomach sank. They didn't meet my eye, nor did they look surprised. They must have known about this in advance.

But what *was* this? What did these men want?

When another person stepped into the room through the private passage, things became clearer, though I still had a lot of questions.

"Arabella." My jaw clenched as I took in her smug smile. These men were obviously with her. "What are you doing here?"

She couldn't resist gloating. "I would love to explain, but we have to get you out of here before the prince arrives."

"I'm not going anywhere with you," I told her firmly. "Cass and I are already married and there's nothing you can do about that."

"I always have a back-up plan," she told me, her eyes glinting coldly. "And it's your choice, Cordelia: either you go with these men, or they slaughter your precious Elodie in front of you."

That seemed to be some kind of prearranged signal, as the men suddenly all moved at once. Two of them grabbed hold of me while the other two took Elodie, one of them holding his sword to her neck. She stared back at me in terror, her face pale and her eyes wide, and my own eyes pricked with tears to see her in such distress.

Would Arabella really go so far as to kill her? I couldn't take the risk to find out. I had to give in. "Fine. I'll go, but Elodie stays here."

Arabella shook her head, tutting at me. "And lose my only collateral over you? I don't think so. She'll go with you, with that sword at her neck the whole time. You make the slightest wrong move and she will pay for it."

I had no argument to combat that and Arabella knew it. She smirked at me as she continued talking.

"I've watched you, Cordelia. Studied you. I know how your mother always threatened Elodie to get you to cooperate. You can thank her for teaching me your weak point."

Maddeningly, she had it absolutely right. My mother had always done it because she knew it would work, and I couldn't fight against it now any more than I had then.

"What do you want, Arabella? What do you hope to gain out of this? Cass will never marry you. Even if he hadn't already married me, he never would."

"That's where you're wrong," she said. "He will if his only other option is being married to her."

One more man entered the room from the secret door, pushing in front of him the woman from the inn, the mad-looking woman who looked so much like me.

"Who is she?" I asked, partly to try to stall Arabella long enough that Cass could arrive and partly because my curiosity required it. Where had she found this woman who looked so much like me?

"You really don't know?" she replied, shooting me a look that was almost pitying. "No one ever told you about your twin sister?"

For the second time in a matter of minutes, my stomach dropped and this time, the room swayed around me too. For only the second time in my whole life, I felt close to fainting.

"You're lying," I whispered. That couldn't be true. I didn't have a sister, and certainly not a twin.

"Am I?" She looked back and forth between the other woman and me. "I'll admit the resemblance isn't as strong as it could be if she'd had the same easy life that you did."

A stab of pain shot through me at the cruel tone in her voice. What did that mean? What kind of life had this woman had?

"The birth went badly," Arabella explained, her eyes returning to their usual coldness. "You were delivered first, but when your sister came out, she got caught, her air cut off. By the time they got her out, everyone thought she had died and the priest took her away. Your mother, the Queen, swore everyone there to secrecy. No one had known she carried twins, and she didn't want any rumours to start or any long-lost princesses to resurface years later. You know how these stories can get out of hand."

I knew all about rumours, but the rest of what she said still confused me.

"If that's true, then how do you know all this?" I demanded. "Why would you have been told and not me?"

Her heartless smile sent a chill through me. "My mother saw the whole thing. She attended the birth and she went with the priest to bury the child. Except that when they got to the church, the child began to cry. It hadn't died at all. My mother saw her opportunity and she took it."

"She stole the baby?" I whispered in horror. Elodie may have been able to make up such a fantastical story, but Arabella's imagination had never been that good.

Arabella nodded as if the whole thing made perfect sense. "She didn't know when or how she would come in useful, but she knew she would someday. Unfortunately, that time she went without breathing affected her. She's not all there, as you can see. We have had to care for her all these years, but she's finally ready to serve her purpose. When Cassian sees her in your place, he'll believe that this had been the plan all along, that you had fooled him, and he'll do whatever it takes to get out of being saddled with a mad wife for the rest of his life."

"He won't believe you," I warned her. "He'll look for me and he won't give up. He's already beaten death once."

She laughed at my confidence. "You have an awful lot of faith in him, but I have it all worked out. If he drinks the drink I send to him, he'll sleep with your sister, thinking it's you. If he doesn't, I have a plan for that too. Even if you're right and he does try to find you, it won't matter. By the time he gets to you, it will be too late."

Before I could ask any other questions, she motioned to her men, and Elodie and I were dragged out of the room, through the narrow passageway to a circular stone staircase which led to the courtyard below. More armed men awaited us there along with a carriage that Elodie and I were shoved into, followed by two of the armed men, one of whom immediately placed his sword back at Elodie's throat just as Arabella had promised.

I hoped that someone would stop us along the way, one of the soldiers or castle guards, but no one did. We proceeded unimpeded out of the castle yard, across the drawbridge and through the darkened town. Before long, we were out on the road, heading back in the direction we had arrived from just the day before. Back towards Lassaria, but I knew in my heart that my father's castle wouldn't be our destination.

Just what they had in mind for us, I didn't want to imagine.

CHAPTER SIXTEEN

My heart pounding, I spun around to the woman who had spoken to me when I entered the room. "Where is the real princess?"

She shrank back as my voice came out low and growled, but before she could answer, Bran entered, having finally caught up with me. "Cass, what's happening..." He trailed off as he got a look at the woman in the bed, his eyes squinting as he looked at her more closely. "Who is that?"

"That's what I want to know." I kept my eyes fixed on the lady as I answered him. "Where's the princess? And Lady Elodie?"

Bran's face paled as he scanned the room, taking in Elodie's absence.

"There is someone who will explain it to you," the lady replied to me in a near-whisper. "Just send everyone else away."

Bran immediately shook his head, not willing to leave, but I needed answers and I needed them now.

"Go," I said to him despite his protests. "Lock down the castle, make sure no one leaves and start a full search. Find Dee and Elodie." He nodded and began to turn away before I called out one last instruction. "And find Eric. Remind him of what happened at our siege of Rythendrium."

Surprise flashed in Bran's eyes, but he nodded again, letting me know he got the message. At Rythendrium, we managed to get access to the king's chambers through the castle's secret passages, and that must be the way any intruders had gotten into Dee's rooms now.

It would also be the best way for Bran to reenter the room once he'd taken care of the other tasks I'd given him.

The two church witnesses were standing just outside the door, having followed me here from my room, surrounded by Dee's other ladies who all tried to peer into the room and see what had caused all the commotion. As Bran left the room, I went to the door and addressed them all. "There is something I need to discuss with my new bride. I'll let you know when we're ready for you."

As soon as I closed the door, the lady ordered me to lock it, sounding more in control now that we were alone. I did as she asked, pulling the heavy beam across the door to prevent anyone from getting in, secure in the knowledge that Bran and Eric could still enter through the secret passages.

"Now, talk," I ordered.

Instead of answering me, she went over to the door in the corner, the door which led to those very passages. Having already figured out that someone must have used them, it didn't surprise me when she knocked on the door and it opened from the other side.

However, the person who walked through the door *did* shock me.

"Arabella? How the hell did you get in here?"

I moved towards her angrily, but two armed men followed in close behind her, extending their swords to block my path. I had no weapon; I literally came here wearing only my nightshirt. Following the custom for my wedding night, I didn't even have my breeches underneath.

As a result, I had no choice but to stop moving, but rage continued to build inside me as I looked at her smug expression. All the guards had orders to arrest her on sight, so how did she get past them into the castle yard? And how did she know about the passageway?

"My brother and I have a lot of influence with the castle guard," Arabella stated calmly, appearing to be unaffected by my anger. "And the army too. That's what happens when the prince assigned to oversee things delegates his authority and the funds get redirected to people willing to switch their loyalty. Your army answers to us now, for all intents and purposes."

Westley Eastam had control of our army? Immediately, I remembered the things the men Dee and I met had said about the changes in pay and the poor conditions within our forces. It sounded like it might all be

Eastam's doing. Eric must have passed off the work of running the army to someone else, someone who could be bought. I knew my brother could be lazy, but even I hadn't expected things to get quite so out of hand.

I would need to know more about that in time, but right now, only one question sat at the front of my mind. "Where is Cordelia?"

"*This* is Cordelia," Arabella insisted, pointing at the woman in the bed, currently playing with the curtains hanging around her, apparently unaware of anything else going on. "The other woman had always been a decoy, as I warned you back at the inn. You should have listened to me then, Prince Cassian, but it's not too late. You can still get out of this."

I took a step towards her, ignoring the men with the swords, and repeated my question through gritted teeth. "Where is Cordelia?"

The muscles in Arabella's cheek twitched, a sign of her frustration that I refused to take her bait. "I'm telling you the truth. This is the Lassarian princess. My own mother was present at her birth and there are other witnesses who could confirm it. She has been hidden away because of her condition, but the king always intended to present you with the other woman so you would marry her and to switch them once you had no recourse. The other woman has been taken away by the princess' family, as they always planned. Where they have taken her or what they intend to do with her, I have no idea. It's none of my business."

"I don't believe you." I had no reason to entertain her craziness for even a moment.

She took a deep breath, trying to remain calm. "That is your choice, but I would recommend that you do. Eventually, you will need to face facts, Your Highness. That other woman is gone, and the woman here is the one you are married to. But, since you don't seem to have drunk the drink they sent you and haven't consummated your marriage, there is still hope. I can still help you get out of this."

Though I had no interest in whatever insane scheme she had come up with, perhaps if I got her talking about it, I could get her to admit something about where Dee had gone. I swallowed down my anger, though sarcasm still tinged my words. "It's very kind of you to be so concerned about my wellbeing."

She heard my insincerity, but she smiled back at me with that cold, calculating smile of hers. "Your wellbeing is important to me, as your future wife."

She couldn't possibly be serious. "As you so clearly pointed out a moment ago, I am already married."

"Yes, but as it hasn't been consummated, the marriage can still be annulled. I have a priest with me who can make it all official. He can cancel your marriage, marry us instead, and witness our consummation. My brother will lead the army on your behalf to seek revenge on the Lassarian throne for daring to insult you in this way and trying to chain you to a woman like this."

She pointed once again at the woman in Dee's bed, but the thing she had just said about seeking revenge on Dee's family had caught my attention. At last, I could see their full plan in my head. "And when the Lassarian royal family is punished, your brother can take his place on the throne as the king's rightful heir."

That was the purpose of all of this. Westley wanted the Lassarian throne, and he wanted to use Silatria to help him get it. All of this - the attempted interference with the wedding contracts, Arabella's scheming and the infiltration of our army leadership - had been in support of that goal.

Arabella smiled again, looking pleased that I had caught on. "That's right. And by marrying me, you and he can join the two kingdoms together, working as one to rule over the whole area. You will be unstoppable. You don't have to love me, Cassian. You don't even have to sleep with me beyond the one time if you don't want to, though I assure you I would show you a good time. But it *is* in all of our best interests for you to marry me, now."

It all made sense in a completely twisted way. This must be the reason Westley had wanted me dead. He must have realized that Eric would be much more pliable and likely to fall for this madness than I would be. If Eric had been confronted with this woman in his bed and told he was married to her, he would have panicked and he probably would have followed along with whatever Arabella told him to do.

The fact that I hadn't died should have been the end of it, but clearly, they were already too invested so they tried to pull it off anyway. But they didn't count on one thing: they didn't count on Dee and I falling in love.

I had heard enough of this insanity. "What is in your best interests right now, Arabella, is to tell me what you've done with Cordelia, if you want that head of yours to still be attached to your body by morning."

Arabella's smile faltered for the first time. "You can't threaten me. In case you haven't noticed, I'm the one in control here."

She gestured to the men beside her who immediately moved towards me. They had only taken a couple of steps when the door behind her opened again and Bran and Eric rushed in along with half a dozen other men, all fully armed. Swords clashed as Arabella leapt out of the way and the woman in the bed began to scream, covering her ears with her hands.

Before long, my men had neutralized Arabella's backup and Bran had Arabella herself in hand, his sword held to her neck.

Hatred burned inside me as I walked over to her and looked down into her evil face. If she had done anything to harm Dee, no punishment in this world would be strong enough for her. "Let's try this one more time, Arabella, and remember that your life depends on your answer. Where is Cordelia?"

~Cordelia~

As the castle grew smaller in the distance, I tried to take stock of our situation. Four armed men on horseback accompanied the carriage that Elodie and I occupied. Inside with us were two more men, both armed with swords and each carrying a bow and a quiver of arrows on their backs. If I could get my hands on one of the bows and a few arrows, it would even out our odds, but I couldn't see an easy way that would happen.

We had nothing else on us that could be used as a weapon. Elodie still wore her dress from the wedding, while I had only my nightgown on, the one I had dressed in to wait for Cass. I didn't even have shoes on my feet.

"You don't need to keep that blade so close to her," I snapped at the man holding the sword against Elodie. Every time we hit a bump in the road, she flinched, and I'd had enough of it. "I'm not going anywhere, am I? Put it down until we stop."

The man's eyes narrowed but he did as I said, dropping his arm and shaking it out. He must have been getting tired of holding it up anyway.

"Where are you taking us?" I asked him next. He might not know, but any information he had could be useful.

He smirked at me, clearly enjoying the feeling of power his sword seemed to give him. "I don't know where you're going, but I know who we're giving you to."

I had a pretty good idea too. "It's been a while since I've seen Westley."

The man scowled at me, annoyed that I had guessed his secret. "I bet you're going to wish it had been even longer until you saw him again."

I let that go without a response. He said he didn't know where Westley planned to take us and I believed him, so it seemed I'd exhausted the information he did have. Chances were, if we were being handed over to Westley, the carriage would come to a stop at some point, and we would have to make our move then.

Now, I just had to decide what that move would be.

We needed to get out of the carriage, that much seemed clear. In this confined space, our options were too limited, whereas outdoors, far more opportunities existed to create distractions and cause confusion. In the darkness, we might be able to get away and hide, at least for a while.

How could we get the men to let us out of the carriage?

"Lodee." All eyes in the carriage moved to me as I said her name, but I ignored the two men and spoke only to my friend. "Do you remember the story of the princess who wanted to avoid the king's birthday feast?"

I knew she would. It involved a princess who pretended to be sick so that she could sneak out and practice her archery rather than attend the feast and dance being thrown at the castle. She had based it on me, obviously, as she had so many of her stories.

What I really wanted to know right now was not if she remembered it, but if she understood what I meant by bringing it up. She thought it over for a minute and then she nodded at me slowly, her eyes confirming her agreement. "Yes, I think so."

"Remind me, did the princess or the lady-in-waiting have the upset stomach?" In code, I asked her which part she wanted to play.

"I think the lady-in-waiting did."

"Shut up, both of you," the man next to Elodie growled. "We don't need to listen to your nonsense."

I glared at him for show, but I'd already gotten the information I wanted anyway.

As we carried on in silence, my thoughts strayed to Cass and a wave of worry washed over me. I couldn't imagine what he would think when he got to my rooms and didn't find me there. If our roles were reversed, I would be distraught, and my heart ached at the idea that he might be suffering because of me.

I meant what I told Arabella, though: Cass wouldn't believe her, and he would come to find me. I had no doubt of it. All I had to do was keep myself and Elodie safe until then.

~Cassian~

Arabella's eyes betrayed her fear as the flat of Bran's sword pressed against her body, the edge of it dangerously close to her neck, but her voice remained defiant. "You won't kill me. If you do, you'll never know where she went."

"If you're not going to tell me, then it makes no difference to me whether you're alive or dead, does it?" I glared down at her, not breaking eye contact for a second. She needed to know just how deadly serious I was right now. "I'm not playing games, Arabella. You have three seconds to start talking or my face is the last thing you're ever going to see."

Bran's grip tightened on her, the edge of the sword making light contact with her throat and she jumped. At last, a single word came from her lips: "Westley."

I grabbed hold of Bran's arm to stop his sword. "Westley has her?"

She clenched her jaw miserably but thankfully, she kept talking. "Not yet. My men are taking her to him."

"Where?"

"I don't know exactly," she said, and Bran's grip immediately tightened again, making her inhale sharply. "It's the truth! They were going to meet on the road to Lassaria and he would take over. I don't know what he has planned for her after that. I swear to you, Cassian, I don't know."

Her head leaned back, trying to keep her neck away from Bran's blade, as real panic filled her eyes.

I nodded to Bran. "Take them to the dungeon, all of them." I gestured to include Arabella, the woman in the bed, and the priest that Bran's men had brought in from the passage. She really had brought a priest with her; she hadn't been exaggerating. "Make sure you trust the person watching them. In fact..."

I turned to my brother.

"I'm leaving you in charge of this. If anything happens to any of them, if they're not there when I get back, you'll answer to me personally."

Eric didn't look too pleased about that, but he nodded anyway, recognizing that arguing with me right now would be a bad idea.

"Then go find a half dozen of my own men," I instructed Bran. "The fastest riders. We'll leave immediately. I'll go saddle the horses."

Bran glanced down at my body for a second. "I think you need to get dressed first, Cass."

Damn it, I had almost forgotten. "I'll meet you down in the courtyard then, no more than five minutes. Let's go!"

~Cordelia~

I had no idea how long it had been by the time the carriage came to a halt in the road, but my heart rate immediately quickened as our forward momentum stopped. This must be it. Westley must be here.

"Stay here," the man who had been speaking to me earlier instructed. The order seemed to be directed at both us and the other man guarding us. The first man opened the carriage door and climbed down, closing the door behind him.

I gave Elodie a quick nod and she immediately began to moan.

"What's wrong, Lodee?" I asked in exaggerated concern. "Are you alright?"

"I... I don't think so," she replied, clutching her stomach. "I think I'm going to be sick."

The man's face next to me wrinkled in distaste. "Let her out," I prompted him when he made no move. "If she's going to be sick, you don't want her to do it in here, not if we all need to travel in here for who knows how much longer."

He looked conflicted as he looked between Elodie's hunched-over body and the carriage door. "He said to stay here."

The other man must be his superior. "And how pleased will he be when he comes back to find chunks of vomit all over his seat?" I asked, purposefully being as colourfully descriptive as I could. It seemed to work as the man blanched in disgust.

"Just let us out the other door," I suggested, pointing to the side of the carriage opposite the way the first man had gone. "It will only take a minute. You've got your sword and we're just two weak women, one of whom is about to empty the contents of her stomach all over you."

Elodie moaned louder, gagging for good measure, and the man scrambled for the door. "Alright, but you stay right next to me, both of you, and make as little noise as possible."

That played into my plan perfectly. The man exited the carriage first before helping me down so that I could help Elodie. He didn't seem to want to be anywhere near her. I tried to ignore the stones in the road that stabbed my bare feet and the chill of the air through my nightdress. The darkness of night surrounded us, with only a dim light from the moon when it appeared through the clouds overhead. The voices of men speaking just ahead of us drifted over, and I thought I recognized Westley's voice among them, but we were too far away to hear what they said.

I wanted to get farther away anyway, so I led Elodie off the road into the field we had stopped beside. Stalks of wheat grew tall enough that we might be able to get lost in them. I certainly hoped so, anyway.

"That's far enough," the man accompanying us hissed under his breath. "If you're going to be sick, do it now."

Elodie pretended to retch, bent over the ground, and the man covered his own mouth, clearly susceptible to the power of suggestion. That left his sword held loosely in his other hand, and as Elodie let out a particularly convincing groan, I made my move.

Pretending to be equally disgusted by Elodie's illness, I stumbled back, straight into the man, and then spun around, grabbing the handle of the sword with both my hands.

"What the..." the man started to exclaim, but I had the tip of the sword at his throat before he could finish the sentence.

"Your bow and arrows, on the ground now," I ordered. When he didn't immediately move to obey me, I moved the sword closer, grazing his skin, as Elodie came to stand beside me, perfectly recovered. "I said: now."

If he hadn't been trying to deliver us to my evil half-brother, I might have almost felt sorry for the man as he looked between the two of us, completely at a loss. I glared at him instead, and to my relief, he pulled the weapons from his back and threw them to the ground.

"Elodie, pick them up," I instructed, keeping the sword trained on the man. My arms were starting to tremble, but I hoped he wouldn't notice. I had little experience with a sword and I hadn't expected it to be quite so heavy.

Elodie quickly bent down to retrieve the bow and arrow, but before she could get them to me, we heard a shout from the carriage. "Hey! They're gone!"

Elodie's startled eyes met mine in alarm and we spoke at the exact same time: "Run!"

CHAPTER SEVENTEEN

~**Cordelia**~

As the voices of the men at the carriage grew louder, I threw the sword I still held onto the ground. "Lodee, the bow!"

Understanding me immediately, she handed me the bow and arrows in her hands.

"Go that way!" I pointed to the field to our left. "They'll care more about me than you. Get out of sight and don't come out, no matter what. Not until I come for you, or someone you trust."

"What about you?" She sounded so worried that I forced myself to sound unconcerned, even as fear and adrenaline rushed through my body.

"They'll have to catch me first," I told her, giving her a wink as I pulled out an arrow from the quiver. "Go!"

The man close to us dove for his sword, so we both wasted no more time, separating and running into the field of wheat in opposite directions.

"She went that way!" I heard him yell out to the others, and as I glanced back, I could see him pointing after me. That gave me one less thing to worry about. If they only chased me, hopefully Elodie would be safe.

Each step was agony on my bare feet, but I ran as fast as I could, the crops brushing and scratching against my bare arms and legs as I pushed through, the moonlight barely lighting my way.

Despite my best efforts, the voices behind me grew nearer, and I knew that as long as I kept moving, they'd be able to hear me. Eventually, I would have to stop and hide, so taking a deep breath, I did just that, ducking down to the ground with the bow and arrow still firmly clenched in my hand and turning back to face the direction I had just come. If I heard them come close, I could stand up and get one or two arrows fired before they pinpointed my location.

My ears were trained on the space ahead of me, so much so that I didn't hear the movement behind me until it was too late.

A hand went over my mouth as another covered my hand with the bow in it, preventing me from using it.

"Shhhh," a low voice whispered in my ear. "Don't move."

I had no idea who the voice belonged to or where he had come from, but I had no intention of giving in without a fight. Rearing back with my free arm, I caught my attacker directly in the gut with my elbow.

"Damn it!" he muttered under his breath as he let go of my mouth to grab my other arm. "Stop! I'm here to help."

Help? I twisted around to try to see the person holding me, and though I couldn't see much in the moonlight, I could tell that he didn't wear the Eastam uniform, nor did he look like the men who had brought me here.

Squinting closer at his face, I gave a gasp of surprise. "You!"

He stared back at me, equally amazed. "My lady. You do have a habit of getting yourself in trouble, don't you? What does Eastam want with you now?"

Of all the people in the world, the man I had met the day before, the bandit whose men I had beaten in the challenge, stood behind me in the wheat field. How did he wind up here?

Before I could ask, the voices of Arabella's men grew louder, so I motioned with my head towards them and indicated the bow and arrow in my hands. The man immediately understood me and released my hands, drawing a dagger from a scabbard at his side.

He let out a short whistle, and immediately, half a dozen whistles answered him, scattered through the field around us, and hope rose up in me.

We had some back-up.

His hand rested lightly on my arm as we waited for the voices to come even closer, and just when my heart felt it would beat right through my chest in anticipation, he gave the order, shouted loud and clear: "Attack!"

~**Cassian**~

We had been riding at a full gallop for what felt like forever and we still hadn't seen any hint of them. With every second that passed, I grew more and more anxious. What did Westley intend to do with Dee? What if I couldn't get to her in time?

Just as my thoughts threatened to spin out of control, we caught sight of something on the road ahead: a carriage stopped at the side of the road, its doors open.

Had Dee been in that carriage? If so, where had she gone? Were we too late?

My throat began to close up in panic, but a moment later, I heard it: the sound of swords clashing, the sting of metal on metal, coming from the field to our right.

"What the hell?" Bran muttered, mirroring my own thoughts. Who would be fighting and why? I had no idea, but if even a chance existed that it involved Dee, we were going in.

"Dismount!" I shouted to the group. "Fall in!"

My men obeyed immediately, jumping off their horses and drawing their swords in a matter of seconds, and we ran into the field towards the sounds of the battle. An arrow flew past my head, dangerously close, and I squinted into the darkness ahead of me, trying to make out the various shapes ahead.

"Dee!"

I yelled out her name as loud as I could, not caring that it would draw attention to me or alert the others we were there. It must have done just that because I heard the briefest of pauses in the sounds of skirmish before the clanging of swords resumed.

Then the answering cry came, filling my heart with relief and joy and fear all at the same time.

"Cass?"

Thank God. She was here, and alive. Now, I just needed to find her.

~Cordelia~

At first, I thought I must be hearing things. I had fired a shot at the new men just arriving at the field, assuming they were more of Westley's men, and my near miss frustrated me. I didn't have many arrows left and I couldn't afford to waste any of them. The bandit beside me gave me cover, holding off any would-be attackers while I took out anyone I could with my arrows, but my ammunition supply wouldn't last forever.

A second later, Cass' voice called out, and my heart leapt in response. He came for me, just as I knew he would.

And I had nearly just shot him.

As soon as he heard my voice call out his name in response, he began running in my direction, but I stayed rooted to the spot, knowing everyone else would have heard him too. Sure enough, two of the men wearing the Eastam colours began to move towards him, looking to intercept him before he got to me.

I drew another arrow back and fired it at the man nearest to Cass. It hit the shoulder of his sword arm and he stumbled, tripping over the stalks of wheat and disappearing from view as he hit the ground.

Triumphantly, I went to grab another arrow to take out the other man, but my hand found only empty air in the quiver. That must have been my last one.

Panicked, I could do nothing but watch as the man reached Cass, swinging his sword, but thankfully, Cass saw him coming. He blocked the attack and parried back, his strong body wielding the heavy sword like it weighed nothing. They clashed again before Cass pushed the man back behind him to where more of his men were coming up. I thought I recognized Bran, or someone tall enough to be him, but the darkness made it impossible to be certain.

The fighting continued around me, but all I could see was Cass in the moonlight, and as I moved towards him, I saw the moment he saw me too. He broke into a run and so did I even though my battered feet protested with every step I took.

It didn't matter. I would have run across an ocean of nails to get to him.

It seemed an eternity before his strong arms were around me, lifting me off the ground and off my aching feet.

"You came for me," I whispered to him, my forehead pressed against his as tears of relief and happiness filled my eyes. Although I had believed he would, the realistic side of me had always known there was a chance he would never find me.

Cass' arms tightened around me as he kissed my lips gently, holding me like he never wanted to let me go. "Always, Dee. No matter what, I will always come for you."

~**Cassian**~

I had almost forgotten anyone else existed in the world as I held Dee against me, my heart full of joy and relief at having her back again.

However, Bran soon reminded me as he came up behind us and cleared his throat. "Maybe this reunion can wait until there aren't men with swords and arrows attacking us?"

Dee and I smiled at each other sheepishly in the moonlight.

"Who's fighting back?" I asked her, still not entirely sure what we'd walked into. The man who had attacked me wore the Eastam uniform, but I had no idea who fought on the other side.

"It's the men who tried to abduct us yesterday," she explained. "The bandits. They came to my aid."

Really? It seemed my instincts about them being good men were correct, and their presence here was an extraordinary piece of luck. I quickly passed on that information to my men and told them only to attack those wearing the Eastam colours. They quickly ran ahead to join the fray.

I stayed put, however. I had no plans to let Dee out of my sight, or my arms, for even a moment.

"Where's Lady Elodie?" Bran asked, surveying the scene.

"I'm not sure," Dee admitted. "Hiding somewhere out of the way. I told her not to come out until she knew she'd be safe."

Of course she did. While she shot at people and teamed up with bandits, she told Elodie to go and hide. It didn't even surprise me.

"And Eastam himself?" I asked. "Is he here?"

The dim lighting made it impossible to tell one person from another until you got close, and I had never seen Westley Eastam before.

Dee nodded. "I heard him, but I haven't seen him yet or spoken to him myself. I have no idea what he had planned to do with me."

My arms tightened around her at the reminder of just how much danger she'd been in.

"What happened when you found me gone?" she asked curiously. "Did you find Arabella?"

"I'll tell you all about it later. I think we're wrapping things up here."

My men and the bandits, having joined forces, seemed to have subdued all of Eastam's men, so I ordered them to bring the prisoners back out to the road where we could see everyone better. I started heading back that way, still carrying Dee in my arms.

"Cass, put me down," she admonished, wiggling against me as she tried to get free.

I refused point-blank. "Not until I'm sure it's safe."

I held onto her until we got back to the road where our horses were scattered along with others which must belong to Eastam. There, I set Dee down gently, but she winced even so, and only then did I realize she had nothing on her feet.

"You don't even have shoes?" I asked in disbelief. Arabella should consider herself lucky to have dozens of miles between us right now. Seeing Dee's slight grimace of pain sent rage rushing through my veins, knowing she probably felt much worse than she let on.

"We left in a bit of a hurry," she replied drily, and I shook my head, both amused by her and still furious with Arabella.

The captured men were brought to stand in front of me, each restrained by one of my men or one of the bandits. "Which of you is Eastam?" I demanded, and they all looked at each other furtively. When no one replied, I asked again. "Answer me! Where's Westley Eastam?"

"Cass." Dee spoke quietly from behind me, her voice tinged with worry. "He's not here."

"But you heard him," I reminded her.

"I did, but he must have left during the fight, like a coward."

That sounded about right, if incredibly frustrating. I would have far preferred if we could have taken care of everything tonight. Now, I'd still need to figure out a way to track him down later.

"Tie them up," I instructed the men. "Use the ropes from the carriage horses. We'll leave the carriage here and the ladies can ride with Bran and I."

At the mention of ladies, Dee turned back to the field. "Lodee!" she called out. "It's all clear! Come out now."

Bran, Dee and I all listened carefully for a reply or even just the sound of someone moving through the fields, but I couldn't hear anything.

"She must have gone out of earshot," Dee mumbled, starting to move towards the field, but I quickly grabbed her around the waist.

"You're not going anywhere on your bare feet. Bran will go and find her."

I nodded at him and called on two of the others, and the three of them immediately moved out in the direction that Dee pointed them. She stayed standing there, biting her lip nervously as she watched the men disappearing into the darkness.

Once Eastam's men were all securely tied up, I went over to the leader of the bandit group, the one we had spoken to the day before and held out my hand to him. He took it and shook it firmly.

"Thank you for your assistance. I'm in your debt."

He shrugged it off. "We happened to be in the area and saw Eastam's men stop here. It seemed like a good opportunity for us to get the ransom you denied us yesterday. Assisting the lady was merely a happy byproduct."

"Be that as it may, I would like to repay you properly. We didn't get properly introduced yesterday, but my name is Cassian. Prince Cassian."

The man's eyes widened in surprise before he gave me a wry smile. "I'd heard you were dead."

"That rumour got out of hand," I agreed. "But hopefully you can see that I'm sincere in wanting to help you. I will be reassigning control of the army tomorrow and we could use good men like you and your group to help bring it back up to its former standard. Come and see me at the castle and I will find a place for you."

The man gave a huff of amusement. "If it's all the same to you, I think I'd rather work for her." He pointed over to where Dee stood, still staring into the darkness waiting for Elodie's return.

He meant it as a joke, but as I thought it over, I could see some possibilities. "Perhaps that could be arranged. My wife could use some personal protection."

"Wife?" I had taken the man by surprise once again. "I had no idea. Congratulations."

"It just happened today. We're supposed to be having our wedding night right now."

That made him laugh. "Well then, we'll leave you to it. But we will come and see you soon, Your Highness."

"Please do."

I extended my thanks to the rest of them and they took their leave, heading back to wherever they had come from in the first place.

With all that finished, I rejoined Dee, who still stood staring out into the distance. My arm went around her shoulder as I pulled her close to me. She must be freezing in her simple dress, but she paid no attention to that now, her eyes focused on the field in front of her. We could hear the voices of Bran and the other men, shouting for Elodie, but still with no success.

"Something's wrong," Dee murmured to me as I came to stand beside her. "She wouldn't have gone that far."

It broke my heart to hear the worry in her voice, but I couldn't do much to help. The darkness made it impossible to do a proper search. If she didn't come out on her own, we wouldn't have many other options until it got light.

"Your Highness?"

One of my men spoke from behind us, and I turned to him, my arm still resting on Dee's shoulder. "Yes?"

"One of Eastam's men just told us that he saw Westley Eastam leave the fight on horseback."

We had assumed as much.

"He wasn't alone," the man continued. "Apparently, he had a woman with him."

Panic filled Dee's eyes as they met mine, and I swore under my breath before calling out to the men in the field. "Bran! Come back!"

"Cass, we need to go, now!" Dee appeared to be on the verge of tears. I'd never seen her so upset.

"I know," I assured her, trying to swallow down the lump in my throat. "We will."

I gave the other man instructions to take the prisoners back to the castle before quickly filling Bran in on what we'd learned.

"What are we waiting for?" he growled before heading to his horse.

I picked up Dee once again and helped her onto another horse before mounting behind her. We couldn't know how much of a head start Eastam had or which way he had gone, but I knew we had no other choice: even if we had to ride all night, we couldn't stop until we found him.

~Cordelia~

I had never felt as scared in my whole life as I did right now. Why would Westley have taken Elodie? What could he possibly want with her? It must be to use her to get to me, just as Arabella had done, and the idea that the most gentle, selfless person I had ever known was in danger because of me nearly killed me.

We were so close to having everything she had dreamed about and planned since we were little girls together: me and my handsome prince and her and her dashing knight, the prince's best friend, living together side by side, maybe even raising our children together as she'd always hoped. It couldn't be any more perfect.

We just had to find her.

"We have to find them," I repeated out loud to Cass for at least the tenth time since we started down the road.

And just as he had the other nine times, he tightened his grip around me and murmured back to me, "We will, Dee. Don't worry."

I appreciated his assurance, but he knew as well as I did that we had no guarantees. We were merely hoping that Westley had continued down the road to Lassaria, trying to put some distance between us, but that might not be true. He could have gone somewhere to hide, or he could have gone off the road instead, heading in a different direction. If he got away, it could be weeks or even months until we found him, and who could say what he could have done with Elodie in that time?

I didn't think I could take that. My heart already felt ready to explode as it pounded furiously in my chest.

The world around us was silent and dark as our horses raced down the empty road beneath the moonlight. The wind chilled me in my thin dress, though Cass kept one arm wrapped around me, trying his best to keep me warm and comfortable. The scratches on my arms and legs stung every time I shifted in my seat, not to mention the dull ache in my feet, but all the physical discomfort paled next to the emotional turmoil going on inside me.

Why hadn't we stuck together? I would have protected her with my life and I should have done just that. Instead, I'd sent her straight into the jaws of the monster.

As if he could feel my anxiety too, Cass placed a kiss on my temple and whispered again in my ear. "We'll find her, Dee. We won't stop until we do."

Just then, a new sound reached our ears: horses' hooves coming down the road in the opposite direction. It sounded like a lot of them.

Cass signalled to Bran and they both eased up their pace to avoid a collision, and a moment later, the approaching horses came into view. Once again, making out any details in the dim light proved a challenge, but I could see ten men or so on horseback, and as we got closer, it looked like one of the riders at the front wore a skirt.

"Lodee?" I shouted into the darkness, my breath catching in my throat. Could it really be her?

"Dee?"

Her voice came back filled with just as much concern and worry, and Cass exhaled behind me in relief. Thank God she was okay, but who on earth were the men accompanying her? What had we missed?

"This is Cassian, prince of Silatria," Cass called out to announce himself. "Identify yourselves."

The man in front, the one with Elodie on his horse, held out a hand and all the other men immediately brought their horses to a stop. He continued forward towards us on his own, and only when he got closer did I recognize the colours he wore: Lassarian colours.

"Arthur?"

My brother's smiling face appeared from behind Elodie, and I had never been happier to see him in my whole life. "Hi, Dee. Sorry I'm late. Your message arrived during a hunting trip, so I came as soon as I could. I think I picked up something that belongs to you on the way."

I dropped to the ground, ignoring Cass' protests as my bare, battered feet hit the road, and Arthur quickly dismounted to help Elodie down. I threw my arms around her as she did the same to me, my heart finally relaxing as I felt for myself that she was unharmed.

"What happened?" I asked through tears of relief and happiness.

"Westley found me," she explained, confirming what we'd already suspected. "When you all started fighting, he decided to leave. He said if you survived the fight, you'd come looking for me and he'd set a trap for you there. He said such awful things, Dee, but luckily, we ran into Arthur, and now it's all okay."

Thank God for Arthur.

"You have Eastam, then?" Cass asked from behind me, speaking to Arthur.

"We do," he confirmed, gesturing to the men behind him. "I tied him up and planned to bring him to you as a wedding present, but you've spoiled the surprise."

I let go of Elodie to give my brother a playful smack on his arm before pulling him into a hug. "Thank you," I whispered to him. "Your timing is perfect."

"Anytime, Dee," he replied genuinely before giving me a nudge back. "Now are you going to introduce me to your husband properly?"

I turned back to Cass to do that, but my eyes were immediately drawn to Elodie instead. Somehow, she had ended up in Bran's arms, and their mouths were fused together in a deep, passionate kiss.

I looked at Cass in surprise and he laughed before giving me a shrug. "Can't say I didn't see that coming."

True enough, but this kind of public display still shocked me. Maybe we'd be having a second wedding sooner than I realized. Introductions were made before we all got back on our horses, Elodie riding with Bran this time, and we made our way back to Cass' castle with Arthur and his men following behind.

By the time we arrived in the courtyard, dawn had begun to break and the castle staff were already up and about, beginning the day's preparations.

"We've missed our wedding night," I exclaimed in disappointment as Cass dismounted his horse and pulled me down into his waiting arms.

He laughed as he held me tightly against him. "I promise we'll make up for it, but right now, we need to get you taken care of."

Ignoring the curious looks of all the castle staff, Cass carried me inside and all the way up to my rooms. The guards inside jumped to attention as we appeared and two sleepy-eyed maids quickly got to their feet.

"Wake Her Highness' ladies to attend to her," Cass instructed the maids, setting me down on one of the chairs in my sitting room before kissing me gently. "I will send the doctor to take a look at your feet."

Looking down at them now in the light, I could see the torn skin and bruises, along with the deep scratches on my legs and arms. I was a mess.

"Once they've taken care of you, you need to have a rest," he instructed, and when I began to protest, he quickly cut me off with another kiss. "I will do the same. I promise I won't speak to the Eastams without you."

"You better not," I threatened, and he laughed again.

"I don't plan on doing anything without you again if I can help it," he assured me, his eyes shining with such love and admiration that my heart melted instantly.

"And what about our... official consummation?" I asked, lowering my voice so the guards didn't hear me.

"As soon as we're rested," he promised. "I want you full of energy, Dee, because once we get in that bed, I don't plan on letting you sleep again for a very long time."

CHAPTER EIGHTEEN

~**Cassian**~

As soon as I left Dee, I tracked down two of my most trusted men who hadn't been with us overnight and instructed them to stay at Dee's side until I returned to her, not to leave her alone for a second. The Eastams obviously had inside help within the castle and I wasn't taking the chance that anyone might remain loyal to them even after their capture. We were going to have to do a thorough investigation and remove anyone who had been working with them, but that would have to wait while we dealt with the more pressing matters first.

Once my men were dispatched and the doctor sent to Dee, I made my way down to the dungeons. Eric stood by the guard's table, looking dead on his feet, but he had obeyed my instructions and stayed on watch personally.

"Arabella's still here?" I asked as I walked in, making him jump.

"Yeah." He gestured down the hall to the cells. "They're all there, and Bran just brought Westley and his men in. It's a full house."

He tried to play it off but I could see the fear in his eyes. Even with Westley behind bars, Eric was still afraid of him, and I got the feeling that leaving him in charge down here might end badly.

"You can go take a break now," I told him, trying to make it sound like my motivation came out of concern for his well-being. "But leave someone you trust in charge, someone who won't fall prey to Eastam's manipulations. I'm going to rest, but Dee and I will be back later to question both of the Eastams and the others."

We still had the priest and the substitute princess to deal with too, needing to determine if they had been willing accomplices or were here against their will.

Eric nodded. "I will. I'm glad you found the princess, Cass."

I could see that he meant it, and not just because I'd hold him responsible if I hadn't. Still, no matter how sincere he might be, we had a long way to go before I could fully trust him with anything again.

With that taken care of, I made my way back to my own rooms and collapsed onto my bed. All the stress and strain of the last day washed over me and I fell asleep within minutes.

When I woke, the sun streamed into my room brightly, sitting high in the sky, telling me it must be mid-afternoon. As quickly as possible, I redressed, had something to eat, and made my way back to Dee's rooms to see if she had awoken yet.

As I approached her door, her brother Arthur came up from the other direction and we greeted each other cordially. "I was just coming to see how she's doing," he explained. "And to find out if you've spoken to the Eastams yet."

"Not yet," I told him. "Dee wanted to be there, so I'm here to collect her."

Arthur gave a nod. "Perfect timing, then. I'd like to be involved, if you don't mind. I have some news for them from my father which might influence how willing they are to cooperate with you."

I had no problem with him being involved, since his throne had been Eastam's ultimate target. "What exactly happened last night? How did you come across Eastam and Lady Elodie?"

"I'd love to claim that I planned it, but it came down to pure, dumb luck. We were coming to see you in response to Dee's message and we came across Westley going the other way. He tried to run once he realized who we were, but my men were faster, especially once they realized he had Lady Elodie with him."

Luck really had been on our side last night. I thanked him again and we both went into Dee's sitting room together.

"Is the Princess awake?" I asked the ladies who sat there with their sewing. I couldn't help smiling as I remembered how I'd always pictured my wife passing her time the same way. I couldn't have been more wrong.

One of the women got to her feet. "She woke just a short time ago. I can check how they are getting on, Your Highness."

When she knocked at the door, one of the men I had sent last night to guard Dee opened it, and a moment later, Elodie appeared at the door. "Your Highness," she greeted me politely with a small curtsey. "Prince Arthur."

"I'm delighted to see you looking so well, Lady Elodie," Arthur said with a smile.

"Thanks to you," she replied gratefully. "Princess Cordelia will be with you in just a moment..."

She didn't get to finish her sentence before Dee herself appeared, coming out of her room with a couple of ladies trailing after her, still holding onto strands of her hair.

"I'm ready now," she announced before turning to the women and shooing them away. "It looks fine as it is. Leave me."

Looking scandalized, the ladies did as she said, retreating back into her room.

Arthur turned to me with a grin. "I hope you're ready for a lifetime of that."

"I can't wait." I gave Dee a wink and her warm smile in return filled me with joy.

"Are we going to see Westley and Arabella now?" Dee asked eagerly, taking another step towards me. I noticed her wince as she did.

"Your feet?" I asked sharply. "How are they?"

Dee grimaced and raised her skirts enough that I could see them wrapped in bandages and covered only in loose slippers to accommodate the dressing.

"That's it, then," I announced, stepping over and scooping her up in my arms once again just as I had the night before. "You're not walking again until I say so."

"Cass, you can't carry me everywhere!" she protested, but not in anger. A hint of laughter lurked in her voice.

"I can and will," I argued. "Let's go and get this over with."

With Arthur following behind, we made our way back to the dungeons and into the room we used for interrogations. Dee made a face as she took in some of the more gruesome instruments lining the walls.

"I don't intend on using those today," I assured her as I placed her down in a chair. "Unless you want to give them a try."

She shook her head quickly. "No, but I meant to ask you yesterday: what did you do with the other woman, the one Arabella brought with her?"

"She's here, in one of the cells," I said, gesturing towards the hall.

Dee immediately paled. "Oh, no! Please release her immediately. I should have thought of it sooner. That poor woman has been through enough."

The strength of her reaction took me completely by surprise, and I glanced up at Arthur, who also looked taken aback.

"What do you mean?" I asked. "What has she been through?"

Dee swallowed. "I'm not entirely sure it's true, I'll need to speak to my mother to be certain, but Arabella claimed that woman is my twin sister."

"What?" Arthur obviously had no idea about any of this.

Dee could only offer him a shrug. "I'll explain later, but even if it's not true, she clearly didn't do any of this of her own accord. She doesn't deserve to be locked up."

I gave the orders to have her brought to us, and Dee stood up as she came in, giving the other woman a tentative smile.

"Hello. I'm Cordelia. What's your name?"

The woman looked around the room, obviously confused, but when she looked at Dee, something seemed to connect. "My name?" she repeated, her voice sounding rough, but not entirely unlike Dee's. "Charlotte, they say. Charlotte, stay quiet."

Clearly, she'd heard those words many times and I could see the pain on Dee's face as she took that in.

"I'm pleased to meet you, Charlotte," my wife said, doing her best to keep a smile on her face. She pointed to the guard who had brought Charlotte in. "This man is going to take you to a nice room with a bed where you can rest. I'll come and visit you later, okay?"

The woman nodded, seeming to understand the message, and the guard led her away. Dee appeared quite affected by that encounter, so I tried to focus on the task at hand, looking between her and Arthur. "Which of the Eastams should we speak to first?"

Arthur gave me a grim smile. "It's up to you, but personally, I'd bring them both in together. There's a good chance they'll turn on each other if we can play them against each other."

I assumed he knew them better than I did, so I agreed to that, giving the order to have both of the Eastams brought in. A few moments later, the guard reappeared, his face white as a sheet.

"What is it?" I asked, a feeling of unease settling in the pit of my stomach.

"I have Arabella Eastam," the man said nervously. "But the cell Westley Eastam occupied is empty. He's gone."

~Cordelia~

Cass' jaw clenched furiously as the guard told us Westley had escaped, mirroring my own outrage. He had always been slippery, and clearly his influence within the Silatrian castle went even deeper than we'd realized.

"What do you mean he's gone?" Cass shouted. "Where did he go?"

"I... I don't know, Your Highness," the guard stuttered. "The man assigned to watch him has gone too."

He must have convinced his guard to let him go somehow. What magical charm did my half-brother have that made everyone jump to do his bidding? As frustrating as the whole situation might be, we could do nothing about it right now, and at least we still had Arabella. Westley had left his sister behind, and soon, she sat in front of us, looking miserable.

"There's no defense for what you've done," Cass pointed out, his voice still full of anger over Westley's disappearance. "You lied to me, attempted to manipulate me, and put my wife in danger. Is there any reason we should spare your life?"

Arabella glanced furtively between me and Cass and Arthur, trying to decide where she would find the most sympathetic audience. She decided on Arthur. "Your Highness, surely you won't allow a foreign prince to threaten one of your father's own noble families? Any punishment I am due should come from Lassaria and not Silatria."

I hadn't expected that tactic, but Arthur appeared to be prepared for it.

"Actually, Arabella," he began, omitting her title. "I spoke to my father before I left. He told me that if Dee's suspicions were true and you and Westley really were plotting against me and my brothers, I would be authorized to strip you and your family of all your titles and lands. Since I find you here in the Silatrian dungeon with the prince accusing you, I am doing just that. You are no longer a Lady, and Lassaria no longer recognizes you. You are entirely at the mercy of the Prince and Princess of Silatria, so I suggest that you make yourself as useful to them as you can. If Westley is so bold as to return to Lassaria, he'll find the same fate waiting for him there."

Arabella's mouth fell open in disbelief and, were it not for what she had done, I could almost feel sorry for her. A few seconds passed as she recalculated, weighing her options in her head.

"I only tried to help my brother," she tried next, looking between me and Cass, trying to sound meek even though we all knew she couldn't be further from it. "But I can see now how he wronged you. I can help you to find him if you let me live."

"That's a very convenient offer when he has just escaped," I pointed out. "Did he leave you behind for that purpose? So that you would have a bargaining chip and could be his new spy, perhaps?"

Her face darkened. "He said nothing to me before he left. I didn't know he planned to."

If true, she must be livid about that, but we could hardly take her word for it.

"You will give my men all the information you have about where he might be hiding," Cass instructed. "Contacts, people he could turn to for help, everything you know. If I am satisfied with the information you provide, we *may* allow you to live."

Arabella's face tightened, but she nodded stiffly. "I understand."

"And I have a job for you in the meantime." Her eyes snapped back to me. "My sister will need someone to wait on her. As you're no longer a lady, you can't be a lady-in-waiting, but you will serve as one of her maids, under constant supervision. If you so much as think about trying to leave or cause her any kind of harm, you will be thrown back into these dungeons and locked away out of sight and out of mind."

Her obvious distaste for the assignment I had given her filled me with satisfaction. After trying to use my sister against me, I could think of nothing more fitting than having to serve her.

"I think we're finished here for now," Cass announced, and I stood back up. Before I could take a step, he had picked me up again.

"Cass, this really isn't necessary," I admonished him.

"That's for me to decide," he argued as he walked out of the room with me in his arms. "For now, I am taking you back to your room, and then I will go and collect my two witnesses for our consummation."

Really? It was not even supper time. He wanted to do that now?

"You don't need to worry about Westley?" I asked tentatively as he began climbing the steps back to my rooms, his strong arms supporting me.

Cass' lips pursed. "I will have plenty of time to worry about him. I suspect we haven't seen the last of him, but he'll also need some time to regroup. I'll let everyone know to be on the lookout for him, but if I had to bet, he's getting as far away from here as he can right now. Besides, this has been put off long enough."

He returned me to my rooms, where I quickly informed my ladies of the new plan. As they had the night before, they helped me back into my nightgown, a new one since the one from last night had been torn, and helped me into the bed to wait for Cass. As I sat back and imagined him joining me here, getting to enjoy each other in comfort and without any danger hanging over our heads, my body began to hum in anticipation. At last, I would get to sleep with my husband.

This time, the wait didn't take long. A knock sounded at the door and when my ladies opened it, Cass stood there in his nightshirt, Bran standing behind him with a slightly amused look on his face, and the two men from the church.

Bran and Elodie ushered everyone out of the room other than the two witnesses, closing the door behind them as they left, and Cass joined me in the bed, pulling the curtains closed behind him.

"This is really weird," I whispered to him as he crawled over to me. As much as I wanted to be with him, the idea of anyone listening to us put a significant damper on my mood.

"I know," he replied into my ear, keeping his voice low in reply. "But we don't have to actually do anything while they're here. They just need to think we are."

A grin spread across my face as I understood his meaning. He wanted us to play a part and give them what they came for. I could definitely do that.

"Oh, Your Highness!" I moaned loudly to start, and Cass guffawed, quickly covering his mouth with his hand to keep from being heard. His eyes shone with amusement as he looked back at me.

"That's it, Princess," he growled back loudly, making me laugh too, and I quickly grabbed a pillow to muffle the sound. "Just move that leg over here."

I made a few more moaning sounds before crying out, "No, wait! I don't think that goes there!"

Cass grabbed the pillow from me, his shoulders shaking with laughter as he tried to be quiet. "You're going to pay for that one," he warned me under his breath before responding out loud: "Trust me, Cordelia."

"Oh!" I yelled out loudly as we both dissolved into giggles again. Shuffling could be heard from the other side of the curtain, and I could only imagine what might be going through the heads of the two men on the other side.

Cass got to his knees, bouncing up and down so that the bed swayed beneath us as he grunted like some kind of animal. "That's it, Princess, almost there..."

With a loud groan, he rolled over, landing almost right on top of me.

I wrapped my arms around him before asking out loud in a curious voice, "Is that all?"

This time, we couldn't keep our laughter in. The sound of Cass laughing only set me off more and he seemed to feed on my amusement in return. By the time we finally stopped, tears streamed down my face and my stomach hurt.

When Cass drew the curtain back, the churchmen's faces were both pale, their eyes filled with confusion.

"Thank you, Princess," Cass said as he got to his feet, giving me a wink that the other men couldn't see. "Until next time."

The other men followed him to the door, still in shock. I could imagine they'd never heard a consummation quite like that one before.

As soon as they were out the door, my ladies came rushing back in. "Are you alright, Your Highness?" one of them asked, giving me a sympathetic look as if I had just been through something awful.

"Quite all right," I assured her. "But I would like to rest now."

I knew Cass would be back soon, using the private passageway, and I definitely didn't want any audience for our *real* consummation.

She nodded in agreement. "Of course. We'll just change your sheets first."

My sheets? My mind went blank for a moment as I realized what she meant. They'd be looking for blood, the sign of my lost virginity, and they wouldn't find any. Not only because we hadn't done anything just now, but because my virginity had been lost back in the cave several nights ago.

To my great relief, Elodie stepped in. "I will take care of it," she announced, pushing the other women from the room. "Her Highness is quite private about these things. You are all dismissed."

"Thank you, Lodee," I breathed gratefully as she closed the door behind them. Using her imagination as quickly as always, she found a small pouch of red wine among my belongings and splashed it over the bedsheets. When we were both satisfied that it looked believable, she bunched the sheets up to take to the launderer, and I helped her to put new ones on in anticipation of my husband's true visit.

"It didn't take very long," Elodie ventured curiously as we both sat down on the freshly-made bed. "Is it always that fast?"

I had to laugh again. "No. It only went that fast because nothing actually happened."

Her brow furrowed in confusion. "Why not? I thought you wanted to be married to him."

"I do. I just don't like the idea of an audience. But Cass is coming back so we can have some time together for real, he should be here any moment..."

The words weren't even out of my mouth before the door in the corner opened and he appeared, the amusement still clear on his own face, though he tried to hide it as he caught sight of Elodie.

"My lady," he greeted her politely.

"I was just leaving," Elodie exclaimed, jumping to her feet. "Shall I come and check on you later, Your Highness?"

I glanced over at Cass, who shook his head at me, a warm smile on his face.

"That won't be necessary. We'll call if we need anything, but otherwise we'll see you in the morning."

"Very well," she agreed before giving Cass a slightly embarrassed nod. "Have a good evening, Your Highness."

As she closed the door behind her, Cass went over and drew the beam across it, locking us in and the world out before turning back to me with a look of pure desire. "I don't know about you, Dee, but I intend to have a very good evening indeed."

CHAPTER NINETEEN

~**Cassian**~

After all this time and everything that took place on the journey to get here, I could hardly believe that Dee and I were alone in her room. No more distractions, no more interruptions, and an actual bed to use. I didn't intend to waste another second.

As soon as I'd locked the door, I pulled my nightshirt up over my head, revealing my naked body underneath and my cock nearly fully erect already. Although our 'official' consummation had been a joke, just being with Dee in the bed had been enough to start making me hard, not to mention that I found her sense of humour an incredible turn-on. Walking back to her through the passageway and imagining what awaited me at the end had only gotten my blood pumping faster.

Dee's eyes swept over my body, drinking me in without hesitation. When her eyes returned to my face, they were filled with longing. "This is the first time I've seen you in the light, other than that morning in the river."

The thought of it nearly made me laugh. Could that really be only a week ago? She had already captivated me then, even though we'd just met and I had no idea who she really was.

"Well, I *still* haven't seen you in the light," I pointed out. The only time she'd been fully naked for me, we were in the cave, which, though amazing, had not given me the view I felt so desperate for now.

Thankfully, she had no plans to deprive me of it. She reached down instead, lifting the bottom of the gown, and just as I had done, pulled it up and over her head, tossing it to the ground next to her.

She was just as beautiful as I'd imagined from the feel of her: the soft curves of her waist and hips, her perfectly rounded breasts with the deep pink nipples stiff and puckered. I couldn't wait to get them in my mouth, and so, I didn't. In one quick movement, I lifted her up and placed her on her back on the bed, crawling in afterwards and hovering over her as my head lowered to one breast.

Dee's hands ran through my hair as my tongue swirled around the stiff peak of her nipple, tasting and teasing her before I took the whole thing in my mouth and sucked hard. Dee moaned, her hips tilting up towards me instinctively, and I couldn't resist that invitation either. As I continued to suck and nibble and tease her with my mouth, my fingers strayed down between her legs and she eagerly opened them wider for me, not playing coy or holding back at all.

I moaned in appreciation against her breast as my fingers slid between her folds to find her already wet and ready for me, just as ready as I was for her. As tempting as it might be to slide my hard cock into her right now, if I did, this would be over much too quickly, and I wanted to bring her more pleasure than that first. I continued my current activity instead, switching my attention to the other breast as my fingers flicked against the sensitive spot between her legs, brushing and circling it to tease her before sinking one finger into her, slowly and deeply as I sucked hard again on her nipple.

"Oh, Cass," Dee moaned, her hips raising again to take me in further. My name on her lips made for the sexiest sound I had ever heard, and even though I wanted to hear it again, I needed to kiss her. I raised my head so our mouths connected as my fingers continued to stroke her on the inside, pushing in and out, first the one and then adding a second as Dee whimpered against my kiss.

"I want to worship you forever," I whispered to her, the words disappearing into our kiss.

"That sounds good," she murmured back, making me laugh. "But only if I get to worship you too."

I groaned as my fingers pressed into her again, my thumb pressing against her and making her gasp. Her little sounds were like music to me. Everything about her was perfect, and I told her so.

"You're so beautiful, Dee. Let me show you how much I adore you. Show me how you feel when I do, my perfect princess."

The words combined with the actions of my hand gave her the last little push she needed, and I watched in wonder as her orgasm washed over her in a beautiful release.

I had never seen anything more amazing.

At least, I hadn't until she caught her breath and opened her eyes. If I hadn't already been lying down, the look of love in them would have knocked me off my feet.

"My heart's prince," she whispered.

~Cordelia~

Even though I just had the most satisfying climax, as soon as I called Cass my heart's prince, which he had most surely proven himself, his eyes darkened with desire and immediately, my body began to ache for him again.

Would this feeling of need for him ever be fully satisfied? *Could* it? At that moment, I found myself hoping the answer would be no.

Cass shifted his weight above me, removing his fingers from my core so that he could place his hard, long cock against my entrance instead.

"Keep watching me, Dee," he said, his voice nearly a plea in its intensity. "I want to see your eyes as I fill you up."

A current of longing ran through me, both at the promise of him filling me and at the emotion behind his words. Although we had done this before, it had never been this intimate. Now, we'd made our vows to each other in front of the whole kingdom. All that remained to join us together forever was this one act.

"I love you, Cass," I whispered to him, keeping my eyes locked on his as he'd requested.

With a shuddering breath, he pushed his cock into me, slowly but steadily until I felt there couldn't be an inch left of me that he hadn't claimed. "I love you too, Dee."

As he began to move inside me, Cass never took his eyes off me. His hands stroked my face tenderly, in vivid contrast to the more forceful movements below as his pace increased.

"I never want to go another night without being inside you," he said, his words punctuated with small grunts as he thrust into me, each time feeling just as good as the last. "You're my home, Dee."

"And you're mine," I assured him, my hands trailing down his strong, firm body until they rested on his hips, feeling the muscles there contract and ripple as he pushed into me harder. "Forever."

"Forever," he agreed, his voice breaking as his own climax neared. His eyes closed and his mouth opened as his cock pumped deep inside me, and the sight of his pleasure was all I needed to find mine again too, my body gripping him tightly as it shuddered in release.

We were husband and wife now in every way, and no one could ever try and come between us again.

It could have been seconds or minutes or even hours that we lay there together, him still inside me, relishing what had just happened between us. Eventually, Cass rolled over, laying back on the bed beside me and pulling me towards him, his warm body feeling solid and safe.

"Will you go back and sleep in your own bed tonight?" I couldn't help asking, remembering how, back in the cave, he told me that would have been the way our first night together ended.

Cass chuckled. "Well, first of all, we're not finished yet, Dee. And even when we've had enough for tonight, I'm not going anywhere. My bed is wherever you are."

That sounded perfect to me, and as we talked and laughed and made love again, several more times before the morning came, I knew that no matter what troubles we might face outside of this room, as long as we had each other, we could handle anything else that came our way.

~Cassian~

It felt like I had just drifted off to sleep when Dee and I were both awoken by a loud rapping on her bedroom door.

"Your Highness?" Elodie's voice drifted through the door. "There are some men looking for Prince Cassian. I don't suppose you have seen him?"

Elodie's tone made me laugh and when I met Dee's eye, she giggled too. Obviously, Elodie knew I was still here, but she didn't want to make it obvious to the others outside that she knew.

"I guess that's my cue," I whispered to my wife, giving her a kiss I meant to be quick, but somehow, once our lips connected, it seemed almost impossible to part them again.

Finally, Dee pushed me away with a teasing smile. "You better go before they send out a search party."

"Fine," I grumbled playfully. "I'll see you down in the audience chamber as soon as you're ready, and I will be back here tonight."

"You better be," she warned me, planting one more kiss on my lips before shoving me firmly towards the secret door and throwing my nightshift after me. I could see her slip her own nightgown back on before moving to the main door to unbar it as I closed the passageway door behind me.

As I reentered my own bedroom, the bed still untouched, Bran already sat there, waiting for me. "It's about time," he complained good-naturedly. "You do still have a kingdom to help run, Cass."

"Unfortunately," I agreed. I'd much rather spend the day in bed with Dee. "Fill me in: what have I missed?"

He ran through the briefing from the castle guards as I got dressed for the day and ate the breakfast that had been brought up for me.

"Apparently, nobody saw Eastam leaving." He scowled as he got to that part of the report. "Which can only mean that someone *did* see him and isn't saying anything because they've either been bribed or blackmailed not to."

I had to agree. We'd been betrayed at every turn, and there were so few people I felt I could really trust right now. Which meant I would have to make a request of Bran that I would prefer not to, especially since I knew that things were warming up between him and Lady Elodie. Unfortunately, I trusted no one else quite as much.

"I'd like you to go back to Lassaria with Arthur. Arabella is supposed to be giving us some names to start with, people who might know where her brother is, and there may be others in the Lassarian court who know where to find him. I won't be able to fully relax until he's found, and I know this is personal for you too."

Bran's face darkened at the reminder of Westley kidnapping Elodie. "You don't need me here?" he asked, clearly torn about going, and I could only offer him an apologetic shrug.

"I would love to have your help here, but I need you there more. I wish I had ten of you, honestly."

Bran looked almost embarrassed at the praise. "Thanks, Cass. Of course I'll go if that's where you need me most."

"Thank you." I offered him my arm in thanks and he gripped it firmly. "You can liaise directly with Arthur but I believe he intends to set out this afternoon."

"I'll go see him right away then," Bran agreed. "But there are a couple of other things I need to tell you. The men from the other night, the ones who helped Princess Cordelia and Lady Elodie, have arrived to see you. They're waiting in the audience chamber. And the priest who came with Lady Ar... I mean, Arabella Eastam, he's asked to speak with you. He says he has some information that will be useful to you."

I nodded as I took that in. "Okay. Send someone to bring Dee down to meet me in my father's sitting room and we'll start there."

Bran and I parted ways and I made my way down the stairs to the small room where my father and brother were already waiting for me.

"Cassian." My father's voice sounded tight and he used my full name, never a good sign. "Eric has told me what happened with Eastam."

I glanced over at my brother who grimaced in embarrassment. "I'm working on sorting things out now but I would like your permission to take over control of the army while I complete my investigation."

That would mean taking it over from Eric, and the loss of a great deal of income for him, but to my surprise, he made no protest.

My father immediately agreed. "I will be sending Eric with Prince Arthur this afternoon. Since he got himself messed up in this plot to overthrow Arthur's father and Arthur himself, Eric will serve as his retainer until Arthur agrees the debt has been paid."

I exhaled in surprise. That would be quite a blow to my brother's pride and his position, but I couldn't argue about the reasoning behind it. Eric didn't argue either, though from the look on his face, I imagined there had been some words exchanged before I arrived.

"Hopefully, with Cordelia's help, we can smooth over any ruffled feelings with the Lassarian court," my father continued. "We need their support now, more than ever."

"What do you mean?"

He looked at Eric, who grimaced again. "Apparently, Eastam managed to siphon a great deal of money from our treasury along with all the other mischief he caused. If it weren't for Cordelia's dowry, we'd be almost broke."

Damn it. Was there any part of Silatria that man didn't have his hands in?

One of my father's guards opened the door to reveal Dee, dressed for the day in a sunny yellow dress which immediately reminded me of the one she had given me to wear, and I couldn't help smiling. No matter how bad things were, she could immediately lift my mood.

"Good morning, Your Majesty," she greeted my father politely, curt-seying to him gracefully. "Your Highness." She gave Eric a polite nod before turning to me with a wink. "Cass."

"Good morning, Dee," I replied, as though I hadn't just left her bed half an hour ago. "There are some people waiting to talk to us if you're ready."

"As you wish," she agreed, extending her arm to me. I placed mine beneath it, her hand resting gently on top of mine. "Lead the way."

~Cordelia~

Cass didn't mention who we were meeting with, so when we entered the audience chamber and the men we had encountered on our journey were presented to us, I was both surprised and delighted.

"Your Highnesses," the lead man greeted us, bowing awkwardly. It must be strange for him to see us in the castle like this after the way he had originally encountered us.

"I'm Princess Cordelia," I introduced myself, realizing I had never given my name, nor learned his either. "And you are?"

"Garrett Hastings, Your Highness," he said, bowing his head again. The other men all introduced themselves in turn.

"We came to discuss your offer," Garrett told Cass. "And to help settle a bet amongst us."

Cass raised his eyebrows curiously. "What kind of bet?"

Garrett turned back towards the others with a grin. "We want to know if Her Highness could make that shot again or if it was just a fluke."

Cass and I both laughed and the men joined in too. "I'm sure the princess will be pleased to give you all some pointers," Cass said, his amusement clear on his face. "Once you're sworn in as her guard."

My guard? Obviously, I had missed something here. When I gave Cass a curious look, he winked at me.

"Nobody is ever taking you away from me again. You'll need some kind of personal guard, and Garrett mentioned the other night that he'd be interested."

I turned my surprised look on the man in question, and he nodded to me. "We would be honoured to serve a woman of your ability and bravery, Your Highness."

"The honour would be mine," I told him sincerely.

Cass gave them instructions on who to speak to about arranging their accommodation and training, and we bid them goodbye for now as Cass led me back out of the room.

"You could have given me a warning about that!" I admonished playfully once we were alone.

He shrugged. "I like being able to surprise you now and then. And to be honest, I couldn't be entirely sure they'd turn up, but I'm very pleased they have. If I know you're safe and protected, it will be one less thing for me to worry about." That reminded me of all the other things he had to be concerned with, and he brought one of them up now. "Would you accompany me back to the dungeons now? The priest would like to speak to us."

I agreed and the next thing I knew, he had me in his arms again. "Cass, honestly!"

"I let you walk into the audience chamber by yourself," he reminded me. "But in private, I'm calling the shots."

I couldn't help laughing. "We'll see about that, Your Highness."

He smirked at me but didn't put me down until we were back in the interrogation room from the day before. The guards brought the priest in a minute later and he sat down in front of us, looking very anxious.

"I hear you have information for us," Cass said, his voice hard as he addressed Arabella's accomplice. "What is it? Do you know where Westley Eastam has gone?"

"I... I'm afraid not," the man stuttered. "But I can tell you about Princess Charlotte."

Immediately, my heart beat faster as he used the title to describe the woman who might be my sister. "What do you know about her?"

He looked at me with an apologetic expression and what almost looked like shame in his eyes. "I attended your birth, Your Highness, you and your sister. I was the one who went with Lady Eastam to bury the child, when we thought her dead."

"So, it is true?" That all matched exactly with what Arabella had told me.

"I'm afraid so," he admitted, his face twisting painfully. "I didn't want to hide it from your parents, but Lady Eastam threatened my family if I said a word to anyone. I had only just become a priest, my brothers and sisters were still children, and she threatened to have them all killed if I breathed a word of what I had seen."

"And how did you end up here?" Cass asked, his voice still firm.

"The Eastams have called on me many times over the years, whenever they needed help for one of their schemes. At first, they only threatened my family, but eventually they started to blackmail me by threatening to reveal Charlotte's existence and claim that I had stolen her away. They're such a powerful family, Your Highness, I felt I had no choice. I'm afraid this plot to marry Arabella and the prince was just one more they roped me into."

Cass questioned him further about what Arabella had intended, but my mind had wandered to my sister and the life she must have had. I could only hope that I would be able to make it up to her somehow. My mother had never been the most affectionate woman, and I knew my brothers wouldn't be interested beyond mere curiosity, so I would rather that Charlotte stayed here with me instead of returning to Lassaria.

We had only just got married, and already I needed to ask a favour of my new husband, but after he sent the priest away, he turned to me before I even had the chance to say anything. "There is a place for Charlotte here if you'd like her to stay with you."

My heart instantly melted. How did he always know just what I needed? "Thank you, Cass. I would like to get to know her and see if we can help her."

"I can see it means a lot to you, Dee, and wherever I can give you what you truly want, I always will. Now, I'm afraid I need to meet with some men about the army and it's likely to keep me busy for the rest of the day, but I will come and see you for dinner, if you like. We can eat in your rooms."

He didn't add that he would stay with me again afterwards, but he didn't need to. I knew he would. Cass carried me back to my rooms, putting me down outside my door so I could walk in with some dignity, but once inside, he kissed me gently in front of everyone. "Until I see you again, Princess."

My heart felt light as he walked away, even with all the things we still had to worry about, but as soon as I entered my bedroom, my stomach sank as I saw Elodie sitting in front of the fire, tears in her eyes.

"Lodee?" I rushed over to her, kneeling on the floor at her feet. "What's wrong?"

"Oh, Dee." She quickly wiped her eyes dry, looking embarrassed to have been caught by me. "It's nothing."

I pursed my lips in disapproval. "If it's making you cry, it's not nothing. What are you upset about? Tell me."

"It's just..." she trailed off, her lip trembling, before looking back up at me. "Bran's leaving with Arthur to try to find Westley. He doesn't know how long he'll be gone for."

"Oh, Lodee." I threw my arms around her, tears coming to my own eyes. Cass hadn't mentioned it to me, but I could guess why Bran had been chosen. It made sense, but it felt unfair to my sweet friend. "He'll come back to you as soon as he can, I know it."

She let out a shaky little laugh. "I hope so. He did say that he'd like to marry me when he gets back."

"What?!" I shrieked in excitement as Elodie blushed. "You could have mentioned that first!"

She laughed again, but her joy mixed with sadness as her lips turned downwards. "So much could happen before then, though."

"Give that imagination of yours a rest," I instructed. "I'll tell you exactly how this story is going to go: Bran is going to go and find Westley and bring him back here in less than two weeks. He'll be a hero and you'll have a huge wedding with the crown prince and princess of Silatria as your attendants, and we'll all live happily ever after."

She gave me a smile full of affection. "I really hope so, Dee."

"I know so," I told her firmly. "Trust me on this, Lodee. Our story is only just beginning."

~~THE END~~

IF YOU ENJOYED THIS...

The adventures continue in Lassaria in the next book in the series, *King in Training.* Turn the page for a sneak peek at the first chapter.

KING IN TRAINING

~Elodie~

Round, lazy raindrops fell silently to the cobbled ground of the castle courtyard as I sat by the open window of the princess' chamber. In the outside space below me, people went about their business, moving food into the castle larders, delivering messages, or arriving or departing for meetings with the king or the prince. Their steps quickened as the rain hit them, trying to get somewhere dry. High above them, I jotted down a few sentences in the book I always kept with me, whilst simultaneously keeping my ears attuned to the one sound I hoped to hear above all others: the sound of horses' hooves, bringing my fiancé, Bran, safely back home.

It had been three weeks since Bran, Arthur, and Eric left to try to track down Her Highness' scheming half-brother Westley Eastam. Three weeks, and yet no matter what else I tried to focus on, my heart remained in that moment when Bran told me he had to go.

It took place here in Princess Cordelia's rooms. If I looked up, I could almost see him as he appeared then, his large frame almost filling the door entirely. I assumed he had come on behalf of the prince, so I bowed to him politely. "I'm afraid Her Highness isn't here. She went to meet with His Majesty a short while ago."

"I know," he replied, looking around rather nervously at the other ladies in the room. "I'm actually here to speak with you, my lady."

Immediately, I understood his meaning and it made my stomach flutter. Whatever he wanted to say to me must be personal in nature.

"Please," I said simply, inviting him into the princess' small study. Her personal space to write letters and carry out whatever duties her husband the prince assigned to her, this room hadn't been put into use yet since we were so recently arrived. It seemed the most private place for us to go.

As soon as the door closed behind us, Bran dropped the air of restraint he had worn in front of the others and took me by the hands instead. My heart soared in anticipation.

Since our very first meeting, I had been drawn to this gentle giant of a man with his unusual red hair and his kind eyes. At the time, he thought I was the Lassarian princess rather than her lady-in-waiting. My mistress Dee, or Princess Cordelia as most people knew her, had insisted that we swap identities for the trip to Silatria where she would marry the crown prince. I had been unable to resist her pleading, as so often happened, and so, even as Bran and I spent more time together and my feelings for him became clearer, he still kept a respectful distance, believing me to be his employer's fiancée.

Eventually, the whole truth came out, not only about Dee being the princess, but that one of the men with Bran, a man we had known as Sean, was actually Prince Cassian, Dee's original fiancé who we had all believed to be dead. The twist of fate amazed us all, but for me, aside from being delighted that my dear friend could marry the man she had fallen for, it also meant that, if he were so inclined, Bran would be allowed to reciprocate my feelings at last.

We were the same, he and I: two people from rather humble beginnings who had a close friendship with our royal masters. With Dee and I living in the Silatrian castle now, nothing prevented Bran and I from pursuing a courtship, if we so desired.

However, he behaved so properly and respectfully at all times that I really hadn't known if he felt our connection the same way I did. I didn't know it for sure until the night before this meeting when he had helped to rescue me after Dee and I were abducted, and made his feelings far clearer than they had previously been by kissing me in front of all the soldiers, and in front of Dee and the prince too.

Although Dee's excitement knew no bounds, I tried not to get carried away. In my head, the happy-ever-after ending had already written itself, but I had to remind myself that Bran had not actually told me how he felt or what he wanted from me. So far, we had only our quiet, week-long friendship and that one unforgettable kiss.

So, when he took me by the hands and I looked up into his deep blue eyes, I couldn't help hoping that this would be the moment I had been waiting for my whole life.

"Elodie, I need to leave for a while."

For a moment, the deep rumble of his voice as he said my name distracted me so much that I completely missed what he actually said. When it finally registered, my lips parted in dismay. "Leave? When? Why? For how long?"

He answered me precisely, in the order I'd asked the questions. "Now, because the prince asked me to. I don't know how long I'll be."

His explanation left a lot unanswered, so I added one more question: "To do what?"

"Cass wants me to go with Arthur and Eric to try to track down Eastam. If we're lucky, it might only be a week or two. If we're not lucky..."

He trailed off, but I didn't need him to explain any further. I understood; if they couldn't find him, it might be months rather than weeks before he returned.

My heart ached at the idea of not seeing him for so long, but I tried to put on a brave face and look on the bright side. That had always been my nature. "The prince trusts you very much to give you such an important job."

Bran nodded in agreement. "He does, which is why I can't let him down, no matter how much I would prefer to stay."

Did he want to stay because of me? The way he looked at me seemed to suggest that might be the case, but he still hadn't actually said so.

"We are subject to the whims of our superiors, both of us," he added, giving me a gentle smile. "Whether it's pretending to be someone we are not, or going somewhere we would rather not go."

"I understand," I assured him, smiling back at him. No one understood that better than I. "I will be wishing you good fortune and praying for your safe return."

"Thank you." A sincere smile of gratitude graced his lips before his eyes slid away from me and a new, nervous expression crossed his face. "And when I get back, perhaps we could... I mean, if it's okay with the prince and the princess, and if you want to... or if you would at least agree to consider it... perhaps we could discuss..."

He had lost me in all the conditions, and I tried to move him along to the point. "We could what?"

He swallowed before forcing the words out. "We could... get married, perhaps?"

It felt like my heart stopped beating for a second. Did he really just ask me to marry him? This sweet, kind, loyal man truly wanted to be mine? Dee had suggested he might want to marry me but I thought she had only exaggerated to make me feel better, as was in *her* nature to do.

"Elodie?" He said my name again, nervously this time, and I realized I hadn't actually answered him yet.

"Yes? I mean, yes. Yes, we could. If you would like to."

"I would," he agreed. "If you would like to."

This could go on all day, I could see, unless one of us took responsibility for the decision, so I limited myself to a two-word response. "I would."

This time, a smile of relief and genuine happiness broke out across his face, but before long, sheepishness replaced it. "I know this isn't the most romantic proposal ever. It's not getting stuck in a cave in the rain together or making a moonlight escape on horseback."

I smiled as he recounted Cass and Dee's adventures. "That's okay," I promised him. "They have their love story; this is ours, and I think it's perfect."

"I think you're perfect," he whispered before pressing his lips gently to mine in only the second kiss of my life. The first one had been a shock, and this one surprised me too, so full of tenderness that it made my heart melt.

I knew being with a man as husband and wife involved more than just kissing. Dee had told me about what she and the prince did together and how she enjoyed it, but I couldn't imagine anything that felt better than this.

When he pulled back from me, both joy and sadness played in his eyes. "I didn't want to go without telling you how I feel, but now, I must leave. I'll return to you as soon as I can."

I believed that with every fibre of my being, and before he went, I gave him my favour, the small linen square embroidered with my initials that every lady in my position kept to gift her knight when he went into battle.

Bran's destination wouldn't be a battle, thank goodness, but he still needed good luck, so I gave him the cloth and my best wishes with it before he took his leave.

"No sign of them today?" Dee's cheerful voice pulled me out of my reminiscence as she walked into the room, a couple of her other attendants trailing after her. She shooed them away with her usual straightforwardness and closed the door behind them, leaving the two of us alone.

I could pretend I had another reason to sit by the window besides listening for the horses, but it seemed pointless. She could read me like a book. "Nothing yet," I told her.

I spoke too soon, though. A moment later, the clatter of horse's hooves reached our ears and we both headed to the window just in time to see two cloaked men dismounting in the wet courtyard below. They pulled their hoods back as they got under cover, and my heart sank at the sight of their dark heads. Neither one could be Bran.

"Never mind," Dee said, trying to cheer me up. "They might have news! Let's go and see."

At her insistence, we headed downstairs to the great hall where the king received petitioners. The guards caught sight of Dee as she entered and escorted her to the front of the room to take a seat next to Prince Cassian. He gave her a curious but affectionate look as she joined him, and she leaned over to whisper something in his ear. The prince's eyes moved to me and he gave me a sympathetic nod and a smile. He knew all about me and Bran.

The men we had seen approach arrived soon afterwards, saying they had a message for the king's ears only. Rising from his throne, the king, the prince and Dee all moved towards the king's private receiving room while my heart sank once again. Although Dee would tell me what they said, I had still hoped to hear it for myself if it had anything to do with Bran.

Just before the door closed, however, Dee's face reappeared and she beckoned to me, indicating I should join them. With a quick glance around, I did just that. It might not be entirely proper, but my curiosity overruled my sense of propriety.

The men were already speaking as I entered, and Dee and I stayed near the door, careful not to draw attention to ourselves.

"We have a message, Your Majesty, from Prince Arthur of Lassaria."

I'd hoped for exactly that, and my heart beat faster with the news. Had they been successful? Were they on the way home? Dee's hands gripped mine as we waited to hear the rest of what they had to say.

"He says they had almost cornered Eastam but the bastard managed to elude them again. Unfortunately, during the skirmish, one of your men went missing. They believe Eastam has taken him."

"Eric?" the king demanded in agitation, wondering if Eastam had managed to capture his own son. Cassian's younger brother had also gone to help in the search.

The messenger shook his head, and I knew deep in my heart what the next words out of his mouth were going to be before he said them. "No, he took one of the prince's men. His Highness said you would know him as Bran."

~Cordelia~

I couldn't tell who looked more upset when my brother's messengers announced that Bran had been captured: my best friend, holding onto me for dear life, or my husband who had sent him away in the first place. Guilt and worry flashed across Cass' handsome face as he pressed the men for more information.

"When did this happen?"

"Three days ago, Your Highness," the man who had delivered the news replied. "Prince Arthur's men are attempting to track him, but Prince Eric thought you would want to know right away."

That was surprisingly considerate of Eric. Perhaps the few weeks he'd been away were already starting to do him some good in terms of thinking of people other than himself. We could only hope.

Cass looked to his father, clearly torn. "I know you don't want Eric and I both gone at the same time..."

"I don't," the king quickly agreed. "You can send a small contingent of soldiers back with these men, but you need to remain here. You still have a lot of work to do."

Cass' lips tightened and I could see how much he wanted to argue, but he held his tongue. He had been working non-stop for the last few weeks, trying to clean up the mess that Westley Eastam had made of the kingdom's army and finances. The work needed to be done, but I knew that in his heart, he wanted to jump on his horse right now and go make sure his best friend was safe and sound.

"Dee?" Elodie whispered my name beside me and I quickly turned my attention to her. "What would Westley want with Bran?"

"I'm not sure." Who could say why Westley did anything he did? My father's illegitimate son had been a thorn in my family's side for as long as I could remember, but only recently did we come to realize the full extent of his scheming. He had infiltrated the Silatrian court, blackmailed the hapless Prince Eric and attempted to kill Cass, all in an attempt to place his half-sister, Arabella, on the Silatrian throne as Eric's bride, enabling him to take over my father's kingdom of Lassaria.

The whole plot felt needlessly complicated, full of treachery and fraud, and only due to the lucky accident of Cass surviving the attempt on his life and coming back to Silatria in disguise had we been able to fully uncover it. However, Westley himself had escaped capture, and continued to do so from the sounds of it.

What *would* he want with Bran? He might try to get information from him, or to hold him for ransom, perhaps. There were many scenarios I could think of and many others I probably couldn't, but sharing any of those with Elodie right now wouldn't be helpful, not when she looked pale with worry and so fragile that a light breeze might blow her over.

"What is she doing in here?" The king had, unfortunately, heard our whispering and noticed Elodie's presence in the room.

"She's with me, Your Majesty," I replied confidently, even though I knew a better reason than that would be required for anyone to be in the king's private receiving room without his permission.

"Then you both can leave," he ordered. Elodie's hands trembled in mine at the king's tone, but I didn't take it personally. His anger and frustration had much more to do with the situation than with us, frustration over the news that Westley hadn't yet been brought to heel. Cass shot me an apologetic look as I led Elodie out of the room and back up the stairs to my own chambers.

Refusing the assistance of my other ladies, Elodie and I barricaded ourselves in my bedroom, as we often did when we wanted a bit of privacy.

"Do you think he'll be okay, Dee?" she asked as we sat down on the bed together, tears pooling in the corner of her eyes. "If something happens to him..."

"Don't fire up your imagination now," I commanded firmly. "He'll be fine. Cass will send his very best men to go and find him, and Bran will be back here with us in no time."

"You don't really believe that, do you." She didn't even phrase it as a question, just a quiet statement, all the more devastating for its simplicity. Usually so optimistic, it pained me to see her lose faith. "Westley is ruthless. He tried to kill His Highness and replace you, and who knows what he would have done to us if we hadn't escaped from him. Perhaps he has already killed Bran."

Two tears spilled over, trailing down her cheeks as I quickly pulled her into a tight hug. "No, we're not thinking that. Bran has been in worse messes than this, Lodee, and he always pulls through. Cass has told me just some of the things the two of them got up to when they were growing up. If he can survive being Cass' friend, he can survive anything."

I hoped to make her laugh, but her lips trembled instead. More tears slipped down her cheeks, faster and faster until I couldn't take it anymore. Elodie was the sweetest, most selfless person I had ever met, and for the first time, she wanted something for herself. I would be damned if Westley Eastam, of all people, would take it away from her.

"Stay here," I told her, grabbing a blanket and wrapping it around her. "Climb into my bed if you want to. I'll be back as soon as I can."

"Dee? Where are you going?" Her tear-stained face broke my heart as she looked up at me.

"To fix this," I promised, jumping to my feet and leaving the room, heading back down the way we came.

The throne in the great hall sat empty, which I took to mean the king and Cass were still in the king's private room. I made my way back there, the guard opening the door for me deferentially as I approached.

They were, indeed, still inside, and alone now, which suited me even better. Both men looked over at me as I walked in, Cass' face softening the way it always did when he saw me.

"How is Lady Elodie?" Cass asked, referring to my lady-in-waiting by her proper title in front of his father.

"Distraught," I replied bluntly and honestly. "And I know that you are too."

He might not be crying about it like Elodie, but I knew how much it must be upsetting him.

His brow lined with concern and frustration. "I wish I could go, Dee. My father and I have just been discussing it, but..."

"The crown prince of Silatria cannot abandon his duties to go look for one man," the king interrupted, addressing his lecture to me as if he expected an argument. "Eric and your brother are responsible for the safety of the men under their command. Cassian must remain here."

"There are no circumstances under which you would allow him to go, even for a short time?" I wanted to be sure I understood exactly what the rules were.

"No," the king insisted. "Not for one man."

"But he came after me when Arabella's men took me," I pointed out.

"That's different. You're his wife, the crown princess. In that case, we could make an exception."

Ah-ha. I could work with that. "Very well," I conceded. "I understand, Your Majesty."

I bowed my head to my father-in-law before turning back to my husband.

"I will see you later, Your Highness."

"Dee?" He gave me a suspicious look, his eyes narrowed. "What's going on?"

He knew me too well. He suspected I had something up my sleeve and he was absolutely right, but if I told him now, it would ruin my plans.

"I will see you later," I repeated, taking my leave and returning back to my own rooms once again to where Elodie waited for me, still wrapped up in the blanket. Her eyes were dry now but still filled with that look of hopelessness. I would drive that feeling from her heart, no matter what it took.

"What happened?" she asked as I walked in, determination in every step.

"We need to pack, Lodee. You and I are taking another trip."

MORE FROM THE AUTHOR

<u>**Contemporary Romance – 18+**</u>

Callahan Series
A Matter of Time
A Piece of Land
A Change of Heart
A Work of Art

Christmas in the City Series
Mistletoe Mistake
Candy Cane Challenge
Tinsel Temptation
Gingerbread Gamble
Stocking Standoff
Eggnog Experiment

Standalones
Leading Lady
A Set of Three
Charity Case
Hired Lover

Contemporary Romance – New Adult/Clean
It Figures duet
It Figures
Figuring It Out

Historical Romance – 18+
Lady in Waiting Series
Lady in Waiting
King in Training
Princess in Hiding

Paranormal Romance – 18+
Cold Lake Pack Series
The Curse and the Prophecy
The Spell and the Legacy
The Dream and the Destiny

Mismatched Mates Series
Mismatched Mates
Misguided Motives
Mistaken Meanings

Serena's Story
The Alpha's Second Chance
The Returned Mate
The Vampire's Consort

Sacrifice Series
Blood Donor
Life Giver

Paranormal Romance – New Adult/Clean
The Alpha's Prey

KEEP IN TOUCH

Daily updates from my works-in-progress, bonus chapters and more can be found on my Ream account, Chilli & Chocolate, along with Emma Lee-Johnson:
https://reamstories.com/chilliandchocolate

You can find and follow me on Facebook at:
facebook.com/melodytyden

Join the Facebook group Melody's Romance Corner for fun games, interaction with the author and exclusive news and excerpts.

You can also sign up to my newsletter at www.melodytyden.com for all the latest news.